ILLNESS & GRACE
TERROR & TRANSFORMATION

WISING UP ANTHOLOGIES

FAMILIES: *The Frontline of Pluralism*

LOVE AFTER 70

DOUBLE LIVES, REINVENTION & THOSE WE LEAVE BEHIND

VIEW FROM THE BED: VIEW FROM THE BEDSIDE

SHIFTING BALANCE SHEETS:
Women's Stories Of Naturalized Citizenship & Cultural Attachment

COMPLEX ALLEGIANCES:
Constellations of Immigration, Citizenship, & Belonging

DARING TO REPAIR:
What Is It, Who Does It & Why?

CONNECTED:
What Remains As We All Change

CREATIVITY & CONSTRAINT

SIBLINGS: *Our First Macrocosm*

THE KINDNESS OF STRANGERS

SURPRISED BY JOY

CROSSING CLASS: *The Invisible Wall*

ILLNESS & GRACE
TERROR & TRANSFORMATION

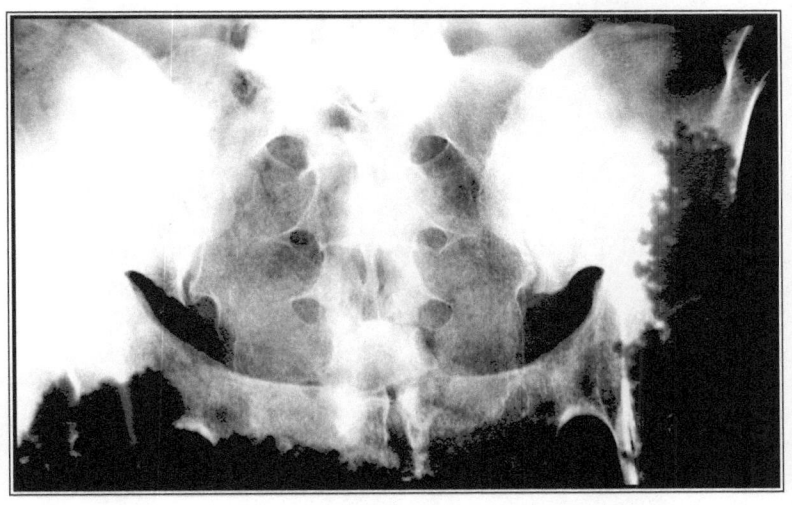

Heather Tosteson and Charles D. Brockett
Editors

Wising Up Press

Wising Up Press
P.O. Box 2122
Decatur, GA 30031-2122
www.universaltable.org

Catalogue-in-Publication data is on file with the Library of Congress.
LCCN: 2007939632

Wising Up ISBN-13: 978-0-9796552-2-7

TABLE OF CONTENTS

FOREWORD
Heather Tosteson

Slow Dancing with Mortality   2

ILLNESS AND GRACE

Pamela Z. Daum
    A Matter of Perspective   15
Jane Levin
    Complexity   22
Sunipa Basu
    Gulmohur   25
Robert C. Knox
    The Five A.M. Inquisitor   36
Darlene Montonaro
    The Crane   48
Mark Barkawitz
    Better Boobs   53
Joan Potter
    In Chemo World   61
Kimberly K. Farrar
    "Big C. . . little c. . ."   68
Darlene Montonaro
    Ultrasound   79
    Heart Music
    A Small Inheritance
Cinda Thompson
    Type I: Room 210   84
Carol V. Davis
    This Illness, This Childhood   92
    Illness
Mary V. Davidson
    The Birthmark   94
Michael Onofrey
    Rain   97

Adele Steiner
    Fever Healing   *104*
    Teleology
Merry Speece
    Sick   *108*
Lucille Lang Day
    Intensive Care   *113*
    MRI Scan
    The Hot Tub
Terry Sanville
    Blues from the Stepdown Ward   *118*
Patricia Smith Ranzoni
    Husband Cut My Hair   *123*
    Another Long: 26-29
    Another Long: 43
Marion Deutsche Cohen
    On Reading To Sick People   *128*
    March 6, 1998
    One Woman Show
    Calling a Spade a Spade
Phyllis Langton
    Mission Accomplished   *132*
Mary-Lane Kamberg
    Artist's Eye   *138*
Susan R. Norton
    Watching Mother Go   *139*
Heather Tosteson
    Once My Mother Knew My Name   *141*
    Intelligence of Loss
Susan Hodara
    After the Accident   *146*
Susi Gregg Fowler
    After the Stroke   *160*
John Holbrook
    Envision   *161*
Sara Lippmann
    The Dying Tradition   *164*
Marian Kaplun Shapiro
    Memorial Service for a Quaker   *177*

Merry Speece
Sweet Face of the Khmer Woman   *180*

TERROR AND TRANSFORMATION

Greggory Moore
Dirty, Pinkish Sky   *184*
Cathryn Cofell
Womb, Belly, Gut, Cave   *186*
Anxiety Attack
Christina Gombar
In the Company of Ghosts   *191*
Andrea Rosenhaft
Sharp Edges   *205*
Heather Tosteson
Skin Deep   *216*
Hannah Thomassen
Phone Call from My Schizophrenic Son   *220*
James H. Coffman
Main Event   *221*
Aelena Thompson
Another Attempt   *223*
You See
Ross West
Crazy Diamond Shine   *227*
Laura R. Sommers
The Momster   *238*
Claudette Mork Sigg
That Too   *241*
Lori Anderson Moseman
Beauty Secret   *242*
Denise Miller
Unfinished Ghost Story   *245*
The Thing I Improvise
Adele Steiner
Quick Kisses   *250*
Elizabeth di Grazia
Family Reunion   *252*

Rebecca Payne
    Week of the Hyacinths Blooming   *260*
Carol V. Davis
    Fear   *265*
    Fear II
Wendy Brown
    Rage   *268*
Marci Greer Jaffer
    The Wall   *271*
Victoria Elizabeth
    April 19th   *277*
    Privacy
    Secrets
Heather Tosteson
    Faith   *281*
Mary C. O'Malley
    Boy in the Water   *298*
Joel B. Peckham, Jr.
    Ruins   *300*
Kathleen M. Heideman
    The Transfiguration Box   *317*
    A Light Like Fireflies

AFTERWORD

Heather Tosteson
    Writing Ourselves Back into the Flow of Life   *322*

AUTHORS   *335*

ACKNOWLEDGEMENTS   *340*

EDITORS   *341*

FOREWORD

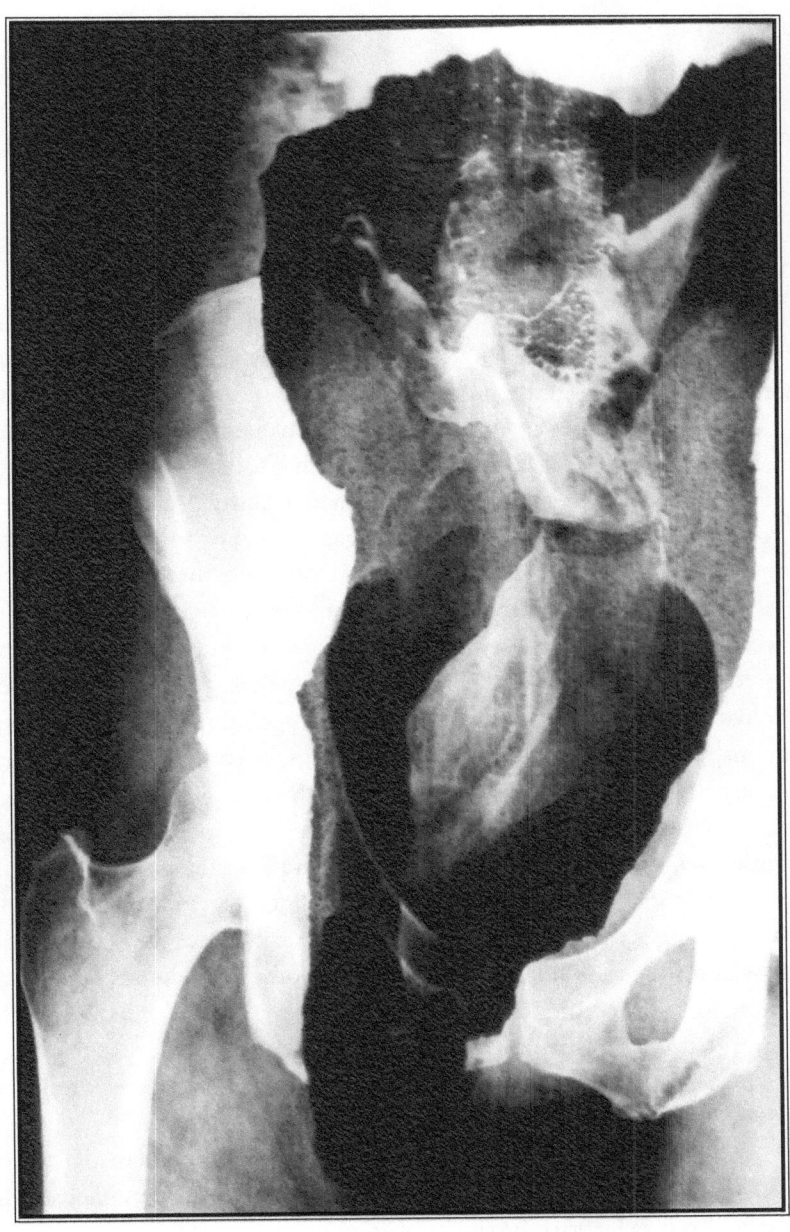

HEATHER TOSTESON

SLOW DANCING WITH MORTALITY

I wanted us to compile this anthology for several reasons. One is a lasting interest in how we understand and share with others the astonishing experience of our own mortality, which comes most often through our direct experiences of illness and trauma. By mortality I mean both our experiences of death in life and life in death. How irreconcilable and indivisible these terms are—and what, if anything, do they have to do with the sequelae of nausea, the drumming of an MRI magnet shifting fields, the barrage of voices a schizophrenic forges through, the comfortingly sheer edges of an anorexic's ribcage? What, in other words, do they have to do with our sensuousness? Literature—stories, memoirs, poetry—felt the way of knowing through which these dissonances could be most fully and naturally explored, since the focus of literature is the meaning of life as we live it: scaffolds of thought, conflagrations of sensation, floods of feeling, crazy intuitions, wild imaginings, bleak understandings, intention and happenstance and everything that lies between—the whole shebang of being human.

I was also interested in putting writers side by side, each of whom is tightly focused on the mystery of their own particulars—something that is particularly distinctive of literature about illness or trauma. I wanted to see what changes in our understanding of our experience and our art come from seeing it set shoulder to shoulder with other equally self-consuming and transformative experiences. Does the experience of uniqueness itself becomes a source of communion? I wanted art that was created as art to return home—to the experiences that elicited it, experiences that we all share and of which we each desire to make gracious, unique sense.

Finally, I was interested in the healing qualities of creative writing itself as a way to shape, explore, transform, or absorb experiences that, almost without fail, shock us out of ourselves in so many ways—our sense of physical integrity, psychological coherence, social embedding, essential wantedness.

We started with the idea of two anthologies—one focused on illness and the other on trauma and its core emotion, terror. However, they quite naturally elided into one. The line between them is somewhat arbitrary, and authors who submitted under one heading have quite often gravitated upon repeated reading into the other category. The first section, *Illness & Grace*, focuses more on physical disease. The selections in the second section, *Terror & Transformation*, include some physical diseases where the social or psychological reality of the experience is dominant.

But in both, our interest is in how, as readers, we can listen faithfully to the stories here—and by extension to the stories we tell ourselves or the stories our friends, parents, spouses and children try to tell us about what it means to them most specifically to experience that moment of mortal fear, mortal grace many of these authors try to describe in all its sometimes excruciating, sometimes tedious specificity because its meaning is permanently enfolded in these particulars.

Kimberly Farrar writes in "Big C. . . Little c":

> . . . I was afraid to mention dying. Afraid because every book and person we knew did not mention it. I watched the lights refract and shimmer. Because we had not openly discussed it, I thought about it more and more. Each time the thought of death passed into my mind, it was like trying to capture a stray cat with a pillowcase. The more I chased it, the weaker I got and the more vicious it became.
>
> Finally I blurted, "You know I could die." Jeff nodded his head and leaned against me. "I don't want to say it, but it's true. I don't want to die, but I could and I won't and. . ."
>
> "I know," he whispered. "I've thought of it too." Then he looked away from me which made talking about it easier for both of us.

And the main, the only, character in Michael Onofrey's "Rain" finds his own unique, precise way to a very similar place:

> What led him to the hospital and then to the operating table was belief, belief in statistics, numbers, and percentages—people with hernias and all the operations that corrected them. But at the same time the skin of this belief became transparent while they were

slipping that needle into his vertebra. . . No matter how much
support he had, and there was plenty, and no matter how powerful
the statistics, Jack was alone in this. This was his experience, an
experience his body would deal with in its own individual way.
Pain was evidence of this truth.

Faithful listening to illness and trauma stories, whether the stories
are written or haltingly spoken, requires returning to three basic faithful
assumptions of story telling and writing in general. The first is that life
recounted presupposes meaning. The second is that for this meaning to
hold, it needs to follow the contours of our own experience. It has to have
verisimilitude, the appearance of being real. We assess the power of a story
by testing it against what we know, personally, of life. Which means this
meaning is both very concrete and precise and also always changing as we
change. As writers, our fidelity to what we know in our own bones is what
allows our writing to ring clear and resonate with the equally precise, equally
unique truths of our reader. As readers it is the same.

Which brings us to the third presupposition of writing— communion.
We write because we need to believe that we can be understood and that we
can understand. Even a story of great isolation or alienation presupposes
in its very writing the grace of being read, heard—whatever the narrator,
the character, or even the author says to the contrary. In the act of reading
we become one with other readers and enter, as well, into relationship with
the author—even, especially, when the author is ourself. The promise of
the process completes itself in the simple act of setting words down and
returning to read them. We are, even in deepest alienation, conjoined word by
word. (But this is a subject I explore more fully in the afterword.)

Here, what I would like us to focus on is what we are listening for as
we read. If we can listen to these stories, through these stories, we may be able
to listen better to the people around us—and to ourselves—when something
similar happens most dissimilarly to us personally. It is inevitable that every
one of us is going to experience illness and most probably some form of
trauma. We are going to be shocked out of ourselves and need to find our
way back into faithful relationship with the enormity of our own category-
destroying experience and our own need, irreducible, equally enormous, for
sustaining meaning.

But let's get back to particulars: the authors we are going to meet
here in this collection. This is an open, over the transom anthology because

at Wising Up Press we want to encourage contemporary writers. Regular writers for regular readers on topics of fundamental concern—like illness and trauma. Most of the authors here have not made their writing career out of a focus on illness—but bring to the experience of illness their abilities as writers. The diseases they write about are the ones they have personally experienced directly or indirectly. We encounter as we might expect many stories on cancer, but none on cystic fibrosis. We have not tried to create an artificial spread of diseases, or to restrict the number of stories that describe encounters with a specific disease. Indeed, we have respected this normal aggregation. But the distribution is interesting to note because it focuses on the diseases that provoke us to write because they are meaning challenging, meaning changing—either because of the metaphorical properties of the disease, its fearsomeness or frequency or both, or because of the uncertainties it presents us in terms of cause or prognosis. We write because the disease or the trauma has been much written about but none of that writing seems to match our own experience in the ways that really matter, or because it has been written about so little we need to name and claim it as part of the normal range of human experience.

The question of the meaning of an illness or a trauma, how it slips and slides, is an important feature of all these writings. Writers both seek to define and to explore the ambiguity of these experiences, sometimes simultaneously. We see this in the numerous meditations on cancer, both how it changes one's basic assumptions about life and about what it means for one's future. People write about the intensified perceptions they have when undergoing MRI scans, ultrasounds, awaiting diagnosis. Or the experience of something that was once abstract, statistical, comes home in such a different form that it now means something completely different.

There are also many accounts of stroke, dementia—the aging of our parents. As our parents age and die, our own life stories shift meaning as well. Susan Hodara in her memoir of her father captures this shift well:

> Then I become almost giddy when I realize my father won't be hovering over every dish I leave unwashed in the sink, every chair I pull out from the table and don't push in when I get up, every crumb that drops from my toast to the floor. In the shower, it occurs to me that I don't have to worry about the hairs I might leave behind, but then I automatically wipe them away with the dry yellow sponge that sits on the edge of the sink,

quickly scanning the bathroom for anything else askance, not out
of habit, but in deference to my father.

This fluidity of meaning is apparent in the writings in the trauma
selections as well. Some of the most troubling of these memoirs and poems
are the ones concerning suicide or diseases that can be understood as exercises
of a perverse will, such as anorexia. In our illness narratives, our narrators,
in general, stand firmly—perhaps for the first time—on the side of life. We
like this. It can serve to simplify our inner narrative. In these other stories
and poems, though, the identifications and commitments are not always that
clear. "I spit on the dusty sidewalk and look at the wad of brownish phlegm,
disgusted by myself, disgusted by my dying, the way it's happening, the decay,
the rot, the deliberateness," Greggory Moore writes.

Andrea Rosenhaft in her beautiful, disturbingly ambivalent description
of her experience of anorexia writes:

> There is a constant battle going on inside my mind that
> is being played out with the anorexia. I want to live and I want
> to die. I am slowly but surely killing myself by starving my body
> of the nutrients that it needs to survive, yet I take myself to the
> emergency room because I am afraid I will die of a heart attack.

The main character in Marci Jaffer's story "The Wall", recovering
from an abusive marriage, finds herself in an anomalous sexual encounter
with her next door neighbor:

> We both somehow know that there's nowhere else for this
> conversation to go. It's pointless because there is something
> desperate happening between us. It's tense and electric and
> strange. When he grabs my hand I let him guide me over to his
> mattress and roughly throw me down on it because this is not
> about love or depth or meaning, it's about something more and
> it's about nothing at all.

One thing that did strike us as we read our submissions was how
often we were reading poetry and memoir rather than stories. The stories
themselves, like the poetry and the essays, focused tightly on a single
sensibility, a single point of view. This makes sense, of course. People in
intense experiences of illness or trauma have been knocked out of their

familiar sense of themselves. They are deeply insulated. Their focus is on finding a way back into their self, first.

In Sunipa Basu's story, "Gulmohur", the narrator describes the mesmerizing isolation of pain:

> Around me everything, everyone, is silly, irrelevant, impotent. But how can anyone understand, who has felt only the pain of a toothache or a headache? Women who have experienced the ferocity of a difficult labour may have an inkling of the tearing, the searing that shoots through my body. It blots everything out, even self-pity. Nothing exists in the world but me and my agony and we ascend higher and higher regions of pain till it seems I can bear no more.

She is also aware of how this intense experience now separates her from her daughter:

> As I scream and quarrel with Ratna, I am conscious that her devotion to me is exemplary, she is doing everything she can for me, she is not God. But why is she not God, why can she not rescue me from this cage of pain? Or, why can she not get me a capsule of cyanide? I roar my frustrations at her. The scarlet flowers blaze with a baleful life.

This desire to return to known understandings is intense. "I want to eat that kiwi," Kimberly Farrar begins her account of surviving cancer. "Take pleasure, Baal. . ." Mr. Reese bargains in Robert Knox's story. "Take the fatted calf. I'll get by on a few leafy greens and a spoonful of sesame seed. All I want is my simple, earth-bound, short-sighted existence back. . ."

It isn't just the experience of life as we have known it that we want to have return, but the familiar bounds of relationships. Joan Potter writes:

> He wasn't always a great husband; he could be sarcastic, critical, and remote, but he was also a reader, a music lover, a moviegoer, an appreciator of ethnic food, and a clever person whose funny observations could always make me laugh. Looking at his gaunt features, his long, bony body under the thin blue blanket, I knew then that I'd take it all if I could have my old husband back.

One could call this bargaining, but in another sense it is a belated valuing—with a very different basis of comparison. Again that kaleidoscopic, slip slide of meaning.

There is a quality in much of this writing, the exclusive focus on the individual, the intense sensory detail, the refusal to move very far from physical details to emotional responses or interpretations, that is distinctive to writing about illness and trauma. Especially at the beginning, we are still trying to understand what has happened or is happening at the most basic sensory level. We have direct sensations, often intense, contradictory, irrepressible and seemingly indescribable, which are very loosely, if at all, attached to interpretations. Sometimes we release these interpretations voluntarily, as Potter does in her essay. I would take it all, she says. The good and the bad, all those qualities I've been dividing and subdividing.

Merry Speece captures the wilderness of associations that is part of traumatic imagining in her hallucinatory montage, "Sick", as well as their arbitrariness: "I've been lying here a long time. In this bed where I have, through the years, turned adversity to my pajamas. Every morning when I wake, I ask, what will a new day bring? A newspaper. Besides *that*. No, just a newspaper."

The slow dance between experience and meaning, both with their own center of balance, is at the heart of our listening to illness stories in good faith. It means hearing when and why it is important to stay focused on the particulars as a way of grounding ourselves in a very new world. It means noting when interpretations and summations and poetic turns of phrase are used to foreclose experience. It requires at other times that we let our attention shift into soft focus so we can see the larger patterns these details make possible. So we can respond to the richer story that is coming, tired detail by tired detail, to take the place of raw experience, a story that can absorb more ambiguity.

Jane Levin captures this kind of listening in "Complexity":

> Judy wants me
> >   without hair
> >   breasts
> >   hope
>
> >   without anything to give but my gratitude
> L'Chaim

This expanded capacity for ambiguity is apparent in many of the trauma narratives, where our writers are needing to name and to react to what happened to them and also, at times, to make fine distinctions between potentialities and realities, past and present. Elizabeth di Grazia in her essay "Family Reunion" explores her need for family and her fear of the potential of repetition in family patterns of violence. Where exactly is that potential located? How can she, as parent, as sister, protect herself from it? Change it?

In many trauma narratives, the reclaiming of physical and sensory integrity is an essential first step, but so is moving beyond that to hold the story in new relationship. In some ways, these stories are more complex than stories of physical illness because the original story of the sensory experience must be deconstructed several times before an authentic, and authentically mysterious story can be told. Often we need to discard not only the perpetrator's but also the survivor's story to go on.

Sometimes the story that needs to be deconstructed is in the reader's, not the narrator's, mind. For example, Christina Gombar's experience of illness includes the social trauma of having a disease that isn't uniformly recognized as a disease: "They say that ghosts wreak havoc because the spirits don't understand that they are dead." And, more sadly but resiliently, she says elsewhere: "At times I feel that I, too, have moved on into the next world; at least in part, at least in spirit. We ghosts are the advance party, leading the way to a place others are just starting to sense is even there."

Other times, it is the narrator's deconstruction of their own story that frees, as in Rebecca Payne's "Week of the Hyacinth's Blooming":

> Here this week we each try to give up a bit of our guilt, we cry for our lost innocence. Anne strews "I love you's" around, he lets loose with unaccustomed tears, and I try to make sense of past injustices. Only mortal people dealing with mortal problems. Hyacinths will not spring from our tears. Nevertheless, this is the drama of our lives. These are the flowers we create.

Or in Denise Miller's poem, "The Thing I Improvise":

> ... and now i play
> out my father's fury i beat out my
> child story on the soft of your
> soul but i want to begin here begin

now to improvise myself out of
whiskey and bad blood into
safety and sandalwood i want to
transpose terror into tenderness meld
memory into nothingness and be
always right here in the cleft
of your throat.

This faithful hearing of trauma stories is painfully and delicately
described in Joel Peckham's memoir, "Ruins", where he and his dead wife's
parents construct and deconstruct stories of her death because "the banality
of accidents" is more than any of us can take.

He speaks of his mother-in-law's desire to blame their tour guide for
the accident:

> But I don't think she believes it. Because when you meet a good
> man in this world, you know it. And Ahkmed was simply and
> beautifully good. And if he was reckless then, he was reckless
> like a man who has discovered the reality of God and finds in
> that belief no answers, just some powerful creative presence that
> may or may not be just or kind. Whose ways are foreign to us and
> whose powers beyond our understanding. And so he dances on
> the ruins, thankful for his little life, his little death.

It is the fullness of experience that we as faithful listeners want to
encourage. When do the details—the small shiver as we reclaim our balance
on a cold floor, the eerie similarity between a moonscape and an ultrasound
image, the equal unexpectedness of a fateful knock on the door and a breath-
taking illness—contain the clarity and flow needed to create a story with room
for grace and transformation? When do the interpretations themselves ring so
strong and so clear that we need to pause together until all the reverberations
stop? Repeat the words so we can all take them in—appreciate the healing
tensions they now contain. Life in death, death in life. Again and again.

Listen to Patricia Ranzoni's stark poem:

thirteen years
running on infusions
rationed time
how she's used it
how it's used her

Or Marion Cohen:

> Just being there, the one he began with, the one he'll end with
> The one who's been too much in the middle.

Or Wendy Brown's closing to her poem "Rage":

> Each day I awake
> to the knowledge of this:
> it hurts but I live
> it never ends but I am free.

Or Carol V. Davis, in her poem "Fear II":

> But what I meant to say
>
> is that the face is
> on both sides of the window

Or Terry Sanville in "Blues from the Stepdown Ward": *"For me, singing sweet blues is the same as rejoicing—just a different way of doing it... helps me know what I'm feeling is real."*

Or Hannah Thomassen in her painfully poised poem, "Phone Call for my Schizophrenic Son":

> Oh, I said, nodding my head.
> Love, we said; we said goodbye.
> . . .
> It could have been the sun and mourning doves.
> It was Joe. It was dark-eyed juncos in the rain.

When we listen in this way, when we resonate with that ring of truth in another's experience, we experience communion. The grace of meaning unfolding, enfolding, moving on.

ILLNESS & GRACE

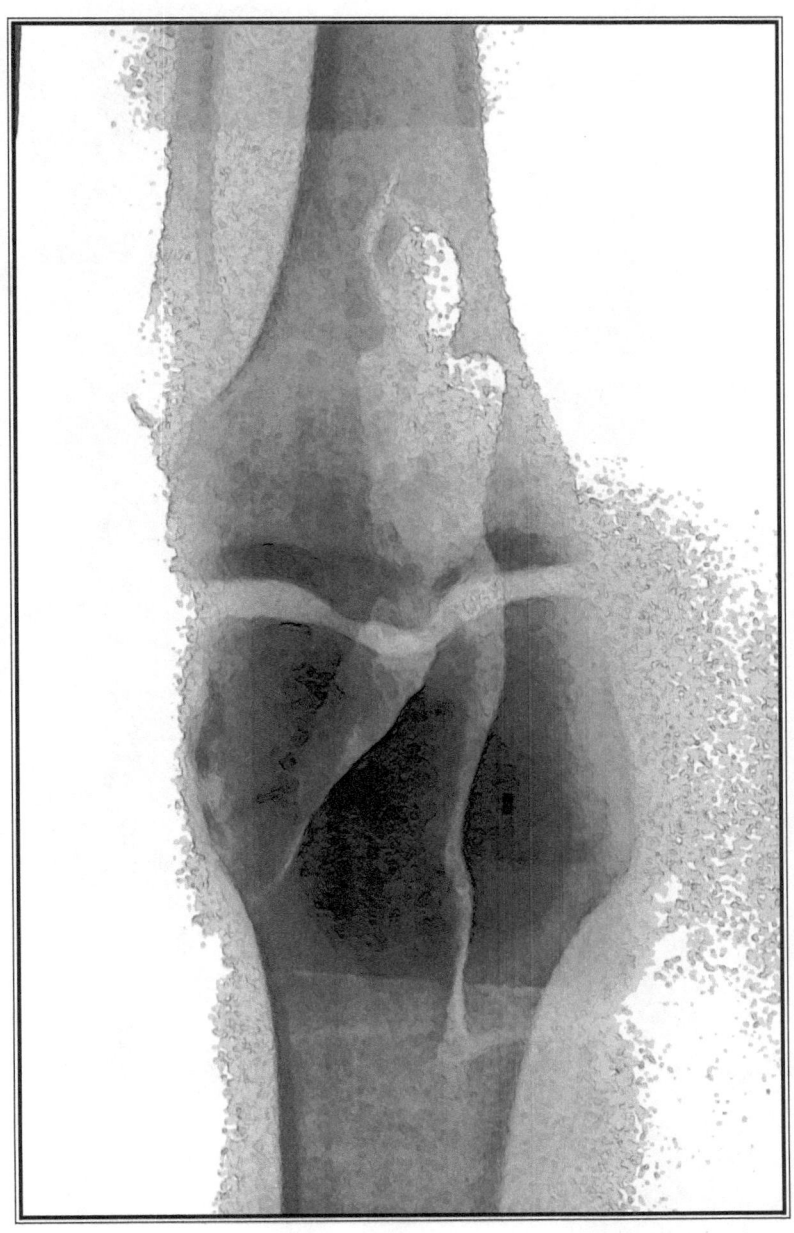

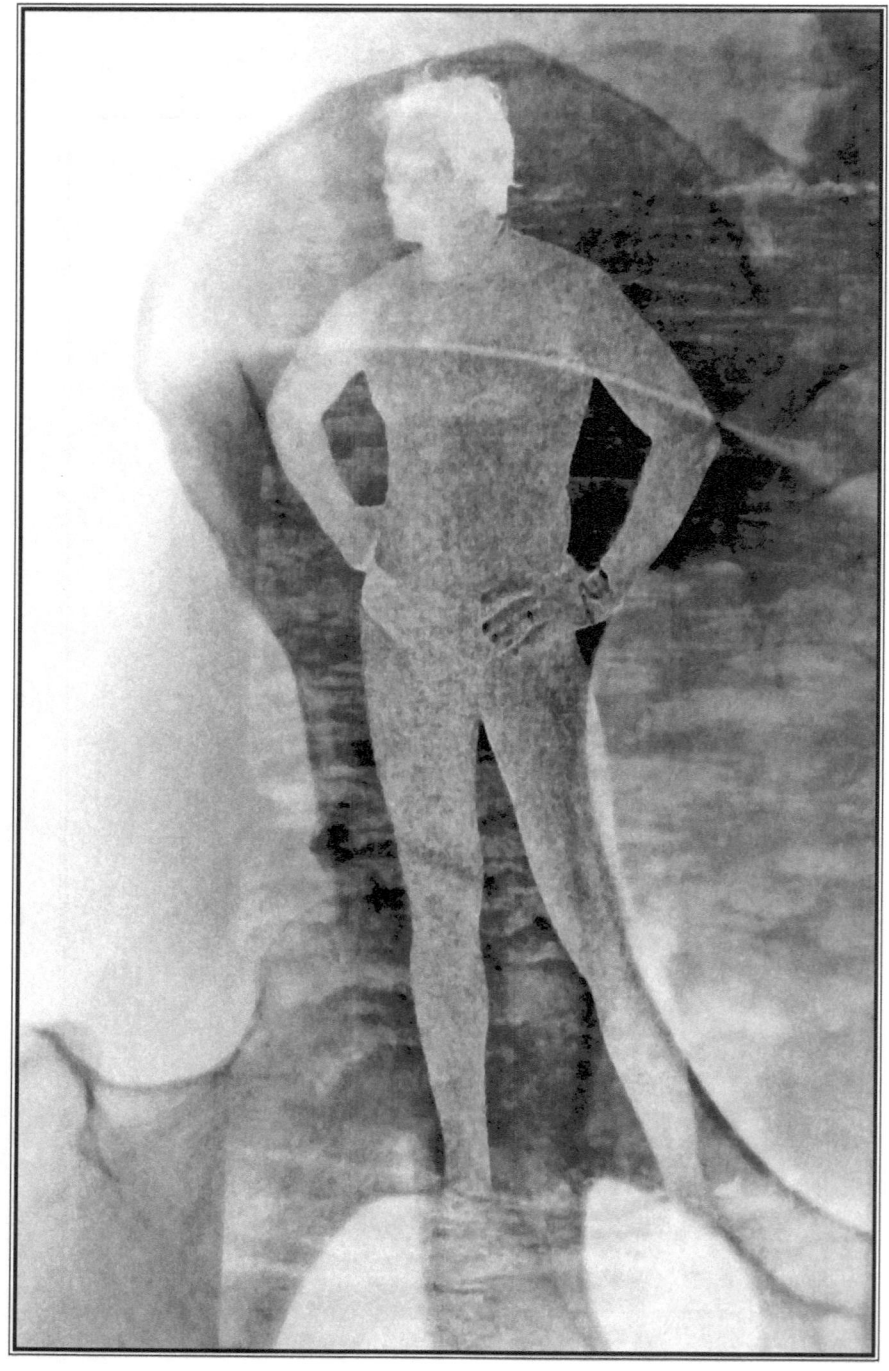

PAMELA Z. DAUM

A MATTER OF PERSPECTIVE

I am observing my world from the bottom of a goldfish bowl. The smoky room holds a sweet, yet pungent aroma. Led Zeppelin's *Kashmir* thrums within my body, but for some reason, it's only a muffled sound to my ears. If I didn't know better I'd say they are stuffed with cotton. My mouth is so dry that I might as well be spitting the same phantom cotton stuffed into my ears. I laugh at this thought. Airhead! Yes, a head filled with cotton would be light as air.

I've come off-campus to visit my boyfriend at a house he shares with five other Sig Ep fraternity brothers. It has the carefree shabbiness of college housing. The walls are shedding their faded, flocked paper like a snake throws off its skin. Even though it is only five days into fall quarter, dirty plates and empty beer cans already litter the chairs and floors. The Robin Trower *From Earth Below* album cover hides an empty condom wrapper that I swat to the floor so that I can recline back on the sagging, lumpy couch. Beside me—and slightly higher since he's not sucked into the couch valley that I'm in—sits Joe, straddling a coiled spring that's poking its metal head through the frayed fabric. His arm lightly skims over my breast as he reaches across me to flip on a black light. The psychedelic colors of his tie-dyed shirt assault my eyes. Chartreuse! Fuchsia! Lemon yellow! Orange-orange!

We are alone in the room. His pale, moon-like face comes into my view—Weeee-Wooow!—"What are you laughing at?" he says. His mouth moves but the words don't hit my ears at the proper time, leaving me with the image of a badly dubbed Japanese monster movie. I laugh again. "Here, have another brownie," he says. The sugary sweetness blooms in my mouth with a rush. Chewed, the brownie has the texture of sawdust. It hangs in the back of my throat.

"Milk," I say, nearly choking. Joe hands me a full glass that is sitting on the battered steamer trunk he has been using for a coffee table. The glass is slick with condensation, and it almost slides out of my hand. I grab it in both hands, placing its rim to my lips—actually a jelly jar, I now notice by the thickness of the rim—and gulp down the entire contents. I bang the glass down on the trunk as if I have just chugged a beer.

"Wow," he says. "Kick-ass weed, huh?"

My head is a gyroscope, and the room is swirling around too fast to latch my sight on any one object, too fast to catch my breath. My heart is racing, racing. Racing like an over-revved engine.

He is suddenly on top of me. "I...can't...breathe," I say. Panic is starting to surge through me, like a buzzy electrical current.

"Relax," he says. "Go with the flow." His brown eyes appear amber in the light and his shoulder length hair smells like strawberries as it brushes across my nose when he lowers his face to kiss me. The kiss intensifies; his tongue is in my mouth. His body writhes as if to the rhythm of the music. He is like a warm blanket encircling me and my body heats up, starting to respond to his urgency...

"Leigh, are you all right?" I awake to an intolerable pain and a gut-wrenching guilt. In the time span of a dream I've fast-forwarded twenty years. My husband, Joe, is sitting on the edge of my hospital bed, concern etched into his sun-leathered face. I need to tell him what I've done. I know I should. He's stroking my hand in his. It's a warm, light touch, just enough to feel the presence of life. His hands have calluses in strange places: one at the base of his pinky finger, one at the crease of the second digit of his middle finger, one at the cradle between his thumb and his index finger. He bears the marks of his livelihood as a touring golf pro.

"You're freezing," he says. "I'm calling the nurse." He reaches across my shoulder to the call button; the light turns red to his touch. "You were moaning in your sleep. I'll ask them to increase the morphine pump dosage, ok?"

Joe seems miles and miles away from me at the top of a deep well while I am stuck at the bottom. His voice rings in my ears. I am too weak to lift my head from the pillow. It feels like I'm wearing a lead hat, weighted down with words and worry and worship of a poison that is my only hope for survival.

There is a pain in my abdomen. I imagine being shot clean through with an arrow over and over and over. I twitch when the arrow first enters. By the time it slices through me it is a familiar jab. But then it enters me again. And again. And again. I'm sure it would be unbearable without the morphine, and yet, I don't want anymore.

My mouth opens, trying to wrap itself around a word. "No," my brain says, but the sound cannot escape my chattering lips. The word is frozen in my throat; I gag trying to dislodge it.

Joe jumps up from the bed and races out of my room. "Nurse, Nurse!" He calls down the hall to anyone that will listen. His voice is tight and piercing, and my ears intuitively react in the same manner that a dog might to the frequency of a whistle that only she can hear. My brain sends a signal to my body. *Relax. Breathe deeply. Relax.*

The nurse who reaches my room first is the sweet one, Sally. She is young, not yet hardened by the constant death she faces working in the cancer ward. When she's on the night shift, she brings me her photo album to look at. It holds snapshots of her baby daughter, Courtney, a pudgy, apple-cheeked, midget version of herself, cradled in her husband's beefy arm.

When Sally walks in now and sees me, she says, "You need a little more to ease the pain, don't you, Mrs. Halsey?" I often evaluate my own condition by the concern registered on the faces of those around me. Today I give Sally's look a 7 on a scale of 1 to 10, with ten being the most fearful look, the look I imagine I'll see near the end. It is not unusual for me to place a numerical value on life: I am a mathematician. Before my current situation I taught Mathematical Theory at the college. Even now I am trying to calculate the logic of an infinite series. Numbers pop into my brain: 10...2...1,002...5. I cannot string them into a logical sequence or consequence. This panics me more than the cancer eating through my bowel. I try to form words into a sentence to say to her, "Please. No more morphine."

She reaches up toward the digital monitor on my IV tree, punching in numbers and codes. Ah, numbers. I try to concentrate on what she is doing, but her fingers tap out lightning-fast entries, making my head swirl from the force of my attempt to focus. I'm certain that if I weren't under the influence, I'd straighten this whole thing out. If I could just lift my head off this pillow, clear my mind of this fog. But my mouth is no longer hard-wired to my brain; it has short-circuited, and I am unable to vocalize my objections.

A burning liquid hits my bloodstream, heating my veins as it courses a path to my brain. A heavy, dark blanket covers my present thoughts, pulling me back into a time and place in my mind that I had long since forgotten.

I am at a Pink Floyd concert. Joe and I have been seeing each other for a while. We have lawn seat tickets, and have laid our camp blanket in a location where we can hear the concert yet the band appears no larger than ants crawling across the stage. It doesn't matter, though. Stretched out on our backs, the blackened sky above us glitters with a million stars. A meteor shower. Stars streak across the sky at random intervals in all directions. Their splendid brilliance is magnified by the hypnotic sounds of music. When the first chords of *Comfortably Numb* sound from David Gilmore's guitar, Joe sits up. "Ah, yes," he says. He reaches into his army surplus jacket, pulling out a Zippo lighter and a joint. In one swift movement, he flips open the top of the lighter and rolls his thumb against the flint-wheel. The flame sparks and he lights the number, inhaling deeply, holding his breath in for an impossibly long time. He waves the joint in front of my face. "Um?" He is still holding his breath, so the sound he makes is from his throat and not his mouth.

"Sure," I say. Sitting up beside him, I inhale, but not so deeply as him. The acrid smoke bites into my mouth and throat. I cannot hold my breath very long. Even so, after a couple of hits, my body is whooshing. The music surges into my ears and pulsates through my entire being. I lay back down on the blanket and stars start rushing down toward me, streams of light etching tracks through the sky and highlighting my dew-glossed arms. Though my body is buzzing, the ground beneath me is a cool, solid base, connecting me to earth. I reach my hand out, palm up, as if to coax a star to land there.

Joe lies down beside me. Mesmerized, he too turns his palm up. Light flickers off our hands like embers from a sparkler. "This is amazing," he says, in awe.

My arm grows tired, and I let it fall limp to my side. Joe does the same, then reaches over to grab mine. His hand is smooth and warm. I am comforted by his touch. I relax into the moment, the music, flashing stars, and Joe.

I awake into the gauzy haze that has become my existence. Joe sits at my side, his eyes riveted on the TV set attached to my hospital room wall. The sound is off. With great effort I focus onto the screen. It is a golf tournament. The Masters. Joe had to withdraw from the Masters because of my latest hospital stay.

I must tell him now, absolve myself of this guilt.

A stabbing gut-pain forces me to moan. Joe's attention shifts to me. His look registers a 9.5 on my scale. He grasps my clammy hand in his warm one. I wonder how many more tournaments he will have to miss; how many tournaments he will choose to miss after I am gone.

"Hi, Baby," he says. His face reveals what he is trying so hard to conceal. It is a rubbery mask with a phony smile. Sweat beads on his upper lip. He stares down at my hand in his. Closing his eyes, he pulls my hand to his face, running the back of it against his cheek. My illness has turned my skin rice-paper-thin, and his coarse stubble is like sandpaper abrading it. A tear drops from his eye, landing on my hand. It is rubbed into my skin with his movements. More tears fall. He stops the rubbing, burying his face into my hand.

How long has he sat by my bed? Time to me now is a matter of perspective. Numbers are bubbling up to the surface of my consciousness.

Two: the number of times I miscarried. Once was in the restroom at Lutece in New York. We were celebrating our fifth anniversary. Joe had finished near the top of the leaderboard at the Buick Classic the day before. He had ordered a bottle of Perrier Jouet to celebrate. "I shouldn't," I said, because of my condition. He smiled. "I understand," he said.

"Well, maybe just a sip," I said, and he poured a small amount into my champagne flute—beautiful leaded crystal that sang out with a lovely *ping* as our glasses touched. "Here's to five great years," he said, smiling.

"And 55 more," I said. No sooner did the glass touch my lips then a fire in my belly unleashed, bending me in two with pain. Somehow with Joe's help, I made it to the restroom. He waited outside until the other occupants beat a hasty retreat at my owl-like screech of pain. The washroom attendant started when Joe rushed in. He nearly tore the stall door down trying to get to me. Terrified, he grabbed the attendant's shoulder and steered her to the door, saying, "Go call an ambulance." But it was already too late. A bloody blob lay at the bottom of the toilet. He cradled me as I sat there, my black lace underwear puddled around my ankles, my black satin garter belt still around my waist. The black silk stockings with the 1940's-style hem up the back that Joe found so sexy now looked trashy lolling above my knees.

The second miscarriage was less scary but no less depressing. It happened while I was watching Joe birdie—on TV because I was teaching—the fifteenth hole at the Bob Hope Desert Classic to put him in the money yet again. I didn't tell him what had happened until after he lost in the playoff.

"Oh, Baby, I'm so sorry I wasn't there for you this time." I could tell by the crackly hiccup in his voice that he meant it.

One: the number of times I was unfaithful. A truly stupid and foolish and dangerous act. A selfish act. I had just seen Joe playing at the Ryder Cup—again on TV—and the camera panned across the spectators' gallery, stopping on a beautiful woman who seemed to be saying something to my husband, and whose hand was touching his shoulder—in a familiar way?—as he headed toward the clubhouse. That night, when the graduate student who worked as my teaching assistant—Rally—flirted with me in his usual way, I didn't brush him off. Several hours and many beers later, I awoke in his bed, rumpled and sticky, the smell of sex stifling the air. I dug through the sheets, hunting for my clothes and hurriedly dressed before he woke up. I snuck out of his apartment, looking left and right as I exited the building, realizing that in my drunken entry just four hours before, I had not been so concerned as to who saw me go in with him.

Rally thought it was true love and pursued me relentlessly until he graduated the following quarter. That was the longest, most miserable four months of my life. Guilt has clung to me like a lost puppy. I've never been able to shake the sense of betrayal I've carried since that night.

Three: the number of months I've been in and out of the hospital, fighting to survive a losing battle with cancer. I know the chemo is not working, but I haven't wanted to give in. Odds are numbers. The higher the odds, the more interesting the numbers seem to me.

With all the strength I can muster, I gently tug my hand away from Joe's. He raises his face to gaze at me, tears streaming down his cheeks. I realize how much I will miss him. I imagine where I am traveling is infinite. I dread floating through infinity without him. How I could ever have been unfaithful to him, I can't fathom, but now I must tell him. The thought of this brings tears.

Closing my eyes, I can see my husband as my boyfriend in college.

I will myself to release the words forming in my mouth. It is but a whisper, but I still manage to make it heard. "Joe, remember the Pink Floyd concert?"

What on earth compelled her to recall that, he probably thinks. My question puzzles both of us. My intent had been to tell him about Rally.

His warm hand reaches over and squeezes mine. Don't leave me, it seems to say. He clears his throat, composing himself. "The meteor shower." His answer echoes in my ears from a vast distance away. "Shooting stars raining down on us. I remember you saying it was like flashlights beaming from heaven."

Numbers flash and flutter through my mind, much like the stars that were seeping from the sky so many years before. Arranged in ascending order, digits cascade into numbers squared, then cubed. They effortlessly tumble into algebraic equations, theorems, rational and irrational roots. The odds of my proving the mathematics in the Goldbach conjecture—or of even seeing another meteor shower—are now as unlikely to me as ever having thought of unburdening my guilt at my husband's expense. Sustained in the moment by Joe's gentle grasp, I feel the numbers wash over me, continuing to astonish me with their magical formulas. Looking up at Joe, I smile.

"Like heaven," I say.

This is what I want him to remember.

JANE LEVIN

COMPLEXITY

I

Like intertwining grape vines
forgetting and remembering
are rooted together
juicy fruit indistinguishable
whether from terror or joy
I wrestle the branches apart

Desperate to forget

Sterile white uniforms
speak apologies
for needles spurting astrobright chemicals
I offer up my bruised and punctured arm

A volcano of nausea builds, gathers speed
crashes into a cave of unconsciousness
I am
     three weeks
of darkness

Desperate to remember

Mosaic monarchs
needle-noses suck up sweet orange nectar
Ascend on their
     three week journey
of light

II

Two branches

we struggle to put our bodies together

Judy wants me

        without hair
        breasts
        hope

        without anything to give but my gratitude

L'Chaim

SUNIPA BASU

GULMOHUR

The red blur clears, vision returns. The scarlet *Gulmohur* blooms fling their clustered challenge at the sky. I hadn't expected to see the sky or flowers ever again, so I stare out of the window, fascinated. Is that a squirrel fluttering the leaves on the branches?

"Mother, . . . how do you feel, Ma?"

Ratna's voice, with a touching new softness, recalls me to my hospital bed. I encounter her tear-swollen eyes, pull her to my bosom and a gust of weeping shakes me as she sobs out loud. Our tears flow, and wash away every question, every memory of desperation. For a long time, we, mother and daughter, hold each other. The weeping subsides at last, but still we cling together. Later, much later, Ratna lifts her head and looks at me, we smile with our moist eyes, and the sunshine of our smiles unfurls a rainbow around us. Wordlessly each asks the other's forgiveness, each forgives the other, draws the other closer.

"Ma!"

The voice of Arun, my son-in-law, filled with concern.

"Grandma, tell me a story!" begs granddaughter Milli as she climbs on the bed exactly as if she were at home.

The *gulmohur* flowers skip in exuberant relief. My eyes mist again. Had I really taken a fistful of sleeping pills? Had I been so selfish as to want to leave these dear ones, just to avoid further suffering and illness?

"Jayanta?" I ask for him.

Ratna's face hardens a bit.

"We spoke to him, says he's very worried. He's sending some money by draft."

"But when's he coming?"

"Seems his children are having exams, he can't come just now."

"Write to him to come, anyway!" I tell Ratna.

She shrugs.

Then I am ill, very ill. Time to me is a continuum of sleep and a drugged haze. Before I can ask for it, the glass of water is at my lips, before the sunbeam lances my eyes, blinds go down on the window. Waiting upon the slightest flutter of my eyelashes, over every sigh, Ratna watches. She is pale and tremulous herself, her hands and teeth clenched, feeling guilty, poor thing, for what is no fault of hers. I know. I am her mother!

During the long months of my illness, I have often been hospitalised during bouts of acute pain. That is when I bite my lips, squeeze my eyes shut, clench my fist, tear my hair, curl myself into a foetus, spring back in recoil, arching like a bow. Around me everything, everyone, is silly, irrelevant, impotent. But how can anyone understand, who has felt only the pain of a toothache or a headache? Women who have experienced the ferocity of a difficult labour may have an inkling of the tearing, the searing that shoots through my body. It blots everything out, even self-pity. Nothing exists in the world but me and my agony and we ascend higher and higher regions of pain till it seems I can bear no more.

But there is more, oh, so much more, and in the end I have lived through that. It is only after the spasms subside and leave me weak, draining my muscles of all tension, that my lips tremble uncontrollably and tears charge down my temples and mingle with the sweat in my hair. The dread of facing another attack sends strong shudders through me. I cannot endure the agony again. How can I escape? Every time, in a day or two, the hospital sends me home in a slightly improved condition. If you can call constant pain, inability to eat, skin like poor quality toilet paper, an improved condition.

But this time, I am told that I am lucky to be alive after swallowing so many pills. My stay in hospital is prolonged. Now all acquaintances, friends and relations come to see me, some during the proper allotted time; others outside visiting hours, coaxing and bribing the watchman at the gate for the privilege. Every evening, Ratna changes my dress, combs my hair, and props me with pillows at the head of the bed, as if I were a *Mughal* potentate preparing to give audience. I am not permitted to talk much, but I can listen.

While the *gulmohur* peeps inquisitively in at the window, my visitors try to entertain me. One minimises my ailment; another derives pleasure from describing the most horrendous illnesses and repulsive deaths. A few arrive as soon as visiting hours start, and after spending a most sociable evening chatting with other visitors, are shooed out by the night nurse when she comes on her rounds. Some come merely from a sense of duty: after a desultory exchange of words, they start looking at their watches, calculating how soon they can decently leave. I am glad to see them all, for they reach to me the air of the outside world. From far cities come letters and get-well cards, and Ratna, decreeing that I am too ill to write, replies to all of them on my behalf. Sumi sends some money. "Buy some fruit for Eldest Aunt," she writes to Ratna.

My confinement in the hospital seems interminable. How long can Ratna be on leave? For me an *ayah* is engaged, and Ratna joins her duties. Doctors, nurses, injections, tests, drips, drugs. These are the rituals of my life in hospital.

In between I watch the *gulmohur* tree, my only constant companion, in whose varied moods I find a reflection of my own. My visitors argue whether the tree, *Delonix Regia*, could be called *gulmohur*, or was it merely *krishnachura*?

"*Gulmohur* has only golden yellow flowers, '*mohurs*', gold, see?" insists one student of botany, while another quotes chapter and verse to prove that scarlet is the proper colour of the blooms of *Caesalpina Pulcherima*. I don't know the right name, nor do I care. I simply love the tree, covered with fiery flowers. How bravely it blossoms when all plant life is limp and despondent with the heat, when the lushest plants fold their leaves down and hoard their moisture like misers. Hot winds blow in though the open window, but I object if anyone tries to close it. I can't bear to lose the sight of the tree for a moment, my only contact with the normal and natural world. It responds to my emotions, I swear. I watch keenly, for I have a vague feeling that the *gulmohur* is trying to tell me something important.

The ceiling fan stops as the electricity goes off; flies buzz around the steel cot. Ratna has kept a hand fan under the pillow, but lassitude paralyses my arm, and I shrink from the effort of fluttering the fan. I shake my head to dislodge the flies. The *ayah* is either asleep on the couch, or away gossiping in this ward or that. As the water jug empties, she is never around to fill it. And I am dying of thirst. If I say anything to her, she shows red eyes to me. When I complain to Ratna, she says, "Mother, you know all about servants these days. Even after spending so much money, one can't get servants to one's liking. We have to make do with whatever is available. Give me the jug, I'll fill it for you. And don't fuss, or we won't even have any *ayah*!"

So I wait patiently for Ratna to come to me after office. Later in the evening, Arun brings Milli. Milli fills my little cabin with her chatter, till at eight they all tell me to sleep well and depart. Then I lie down and stare out. I cannot see the Milky Way from my bed; the scarlet flowers fill the sky. Gently a little wind touches the tree. The *gulmohur* shivers, shorn now of all its green leaves. Here and there in the gaps in the foliage a star twinkles like a diminutive sequin on a velvet jewel case.

And at night, the pain comes on. It comes flooding; I am carried away and dashed on the rocks, pounded by oceans of pain. My flesh is aquiver, and every inch of me is raw, exposed nerve; I am crouching and growling, I want to bite my own bones, scream at any face I see.

In my days of health and strength, I had the notion that pain and suffering burn off the dross, purify and ennoble the human being. I was thrilled to discover Neitzsche's insistence that suffering improves character. But now I know that pain wrenches the soul. In extreme pain, each one stands alone with her agony and is kin to the beast. In pain she forfeits her privacy, her intelligence, her will, and even her personhood. She is an object to be stared at, examined inside and out, poked and prodded, pushed and pulled about like a sack of potatoes. Willy-nilly, she is treated, objectively, as a 'case'.

I am on tenterhooks, watching for the next bout with pain, waiting like some poor novice of a boxer sure to be pulped by the champ. Self-pity floods me; I long for a release from my painful life.

So weak I am, and so dependent, on Ratna, on the doctors, on the nurses, and even on the owl faced *ayah*, who snoozes while the desert thirst burns my insides up. After a couple of weeks my evening visitors have stopped coming. Everyone continues with his or her own life. Only Ratna, poor Ratna, cannot get back to normalcy, for her the daily duty of attendance on mother. Milli does not come every evening, now. Her exams are nearing. Ratna had asked me openly, "Is it right to bring the child every day? She can come on week-ends."

I had agreed, "Yes, that's a good thing, poor child, it is too much of a strain on her, and she has her studies."

That is why she does not come, and of course her father has to stay at home with her, so I don't get a chance to see my son-in-law these days. He sends solicitous inquiries through Ratna.

Also there have been no letters for a while.
"Why isn't Jayant here?" I ask Ratna
"Don't ask me, he doesn't even bother to reply to my letters!"
"Then ring him up again."
Ratna's face darkens in anger.

The pain is as harsh as ever. They prescribe stronger and stronger doses of pain killers, analgesics, whatever they call those things. Nothing really helps. They change drugs, tiny multicoloured pills, transparent capsules with variegated granules in them, pristine white tablets, injections, sometimes mixed into intravenous fluids. The pain comes shouting down and routs them all, triumphant. One day they try a new drug. The pain laughs loudly and turns itself into a tumult, I see a great repulsive thing, its throat slit red and wide, sitting on my chest, choking me, then violet and green faces, and great festering wounds, ringed with slopes like a volcano, up which I try to climb, sand-trapped. All with the undertow of pain. The *gulmohur* is a ball of fire, an angry sun glaring in. In the evening I tell the doctor, I like my pain plain, thanks, and will he please not garnish it with hallucinations! What right have the doctors to do this to me! They can't relieve my pain. Why not let me sink into senselessness and death, why must they force me to bear the unbearable, day after day after day, again and again? Why, why, why?

Poor Ratna comes every day, bathed in sweat, weary with travel by bus and train. I see the circles around her eyes darken, and she is losing weight. So I try to hide my petty troubles from her, my feeling of being neglected by the nurses and the *ayahs*. I keep hoping that the pain will not seize me when she is around. Yet every day I wait, when will Ratna enter through that swing door? Every day she brings fruit; peels and cuts it or squeezes the juice, feeds me. Sometimes she keeps the fruit in the little bedside cupboard, telling the *ayah* to give it to me later. The fruit remains, and when an over-ripe smell emanates from it, the *ayah* says, "How will you eat this rotten fruit, I'll take it for my grandson." She then opens the warped metal door of the cupboard which refuses to close properly, and eagerly transfers the fruit to her plastic bag.

Though it is the mango season, Ratna never brings mangoes for me. I tell her to bring me some. The next day she arrives with the same insipid grapefruit in her plastic basket. I am furious. She cannot satisfy one little desire of her old sick mother! When she tries to make me sip grapefruit juice, I push the glass from my lips and turn my face away.

"What's wrong, it isn't sour, taste it," coaxes Ratna.

"I won't take grapefruit, ever!" I say.

"Why?" Ratna scowls.

"Everyday I come rushing here after office, carrying this and that for you. And you want to make excuses and not take it. You refuse the juice now. If I leave it for you to take later, you let it all rot. What a waste! I can't even afford to give fruit to Milli, and here you say calmly, 'I won't take it'!"

As if I am snatching the food from Milli's mouth!

"Don't bring any more fruits for me!" I scream at her, "I don't want any!"

"No, why should you want it," retorts Ratna, her voice all mean and bitter, "Don't take what the doctor orders. Hanker after things you are not allowed to take. Then you can lie happily in that bed day after day and have us dancing attendance!"

As I scream and quarrel with Ratna, I am conscious that her devotion to me is exemplary, she is doing everything she can for me, she is not God. But why is she not God, why can she not rescue me from this cage of pain? Or, why can she not get me a capsule of cyanide? I roar my frustrations at her. The scarlet flowers blaze with a baleful life.

And the pain stalks. I can sense it coming, a fine tremor inside of me. A feeling of heat rises through my body, on soles of my feet, palms and lips, a fevered warmth, nostrils and ears fuming like overheated griddles, brain dizzy with the heat, intensifying unbearably till it all bursts out in an explosion of drenching sweat and agony, the agony seizes my insides, pincers in my organs, as if an enormous crab has me in its relentless grip, talons gouging my flesh. Oh, mercy, I am not *Prometheus*, I have not gifted stolen fire to mankind, I have lived for myself alone, then why this torture? I bite my lips and turn to the pillow to stifle the cries and the imprecations that tear out of me. The next instant I fling off the bedclothes, in an effort to cool my burning body, splash water from the jug on my face and shoulders, my temples. I want to leap out of my smouldering bed and my clothes. I want to flee. The flesh is weak, weak!

I want to read, to divert my thoughts. Ratna, thoughtlessly, brings me Dostoevsky. 'Scarlet Flowers', yet!

Today Ratna is late. She wearily pushes back a few strands of hair that are plastered to the temples with sweat. A procession has played havoc with traffic, she has barely managed to reach the hospital after trudging through kilometers of city streets, lugging a large jar of 'Horlicks' in her plastic bag, a bulging office bag, umbrella and a carry-bag of fruit. As soon as she arrives, she picks up the flask in which she gets me tea from the stall outside the hospital gate.

"You'll have to drink up your tea fast, Ma, I don't have time to sit today. I don't know how I'll get home. . ."

She sets out for the tea.

The grapes Ratna has bought are on the metal bedside cupboard. They have not been washed yet, but I long for the juicy, sticky sweetness, so I reach for the fruit after some hesitation. I wipe a few on my hospital gown. The first grape bursts with all its tartness upon my tongue, just then Ratna returns with the tea.

"What happened, why are you making a face?"

"These grapes are so sour; you have been cheated again!"

Suddenly Ratna seems to catch fire: "I can't carry on like this any more! All this running around and spending money, I'd be happy to do all that for you, but never can I satisfy you, always complaint upon complaint. Nothing has ever suited you but what that precious son of yours does. Why doesn't Jayant come and look after you? Tomorrow onwards I won't come any more!"

That is an empty threat. How can she not come, she is connected to me by an umbilical cord, we are doomed to be tied together, to drag each other down.

Tonight, the ultimate indignity. I collapse on the bathroom floor, in a mess of blood and shit.

"You should have asked for the bed pan," the *ayah* repeats again and again, "Am I not here to tend to you!"

"When you can't move properly on your own, you must not do some foolish things and make yourself worse," the nurse says severely as she hooks me on to a tangle of bottles and tubes. Humiliated, into oblivion I sink.

I wake alone, in the dark. Infinitely weaker than before, I lie there, and many things float up into my mind, vast complex cosmic mysteries, Milli's comic book and the *Bhagvad Gita*. Trying to sleep, I stir restlessly and my hand brushes against the lamp switch. Conjured up by the light, the *gulmohur* glows, wide awake in its nocturnal business of living and growing, and it whispers to me. A stray breeze nudges its canopy. An old flower lets go its hold upon the stem and drops out of sight, making way for the fresh flowers to blossom tonight. Wafting downwards, the flower will come to rest on the roots, mingling with the soil to nourish the awakening buds.

And we, humans, we dare not let go! As if the 'I' and its continued existence is all that matters. Greedily grabbing and consuming resources, demanding the time and the attention of the community, to keep alive the mortal body. We have lost the key to preparing the mind and spirit for the inevitable end, for passing on the baton in the relay race of life. Our ancestors practiced *vanaprastha*, leaving the householder's life and turning into ascetics when life's duties were done; we cling on to the material world to the bitter end. Why don't we learn from beings which have no ego? Why can a man not see his continued existence in the survival and development of mankind, rather than his own physical self?

To let go willingly, like the spent flower. Not in anger, nor in pique. Not in frustration or desolation. Not with the selfish motive of escaping from pain, like the last time. Rather in a mood of great optimism, of profound faith in life. Dispassionately deciding that as I have no more need to live, I must not occupy a hospital bed and divert the attention of medical and paramedical staff from cases more worthy of treatment. I must relieve Ratna of a colossal burden, remove my parasitic shadow from young Milli's life. They will live and flourish, and through them and their progeny will I live on through the ages: what need have I of preserving this decayed body? Scientists though they are, the doctors will not see reason, will not stop intervening to preserve this strained and constrained life… There should be a law!

    I am thirsty. Slowly I push myself up to sitting position. Fighting dizziness, I reach out a hand to the water jug and lift it. It is full. The sudden weight on my hand almost topples me. With an instinctive flow of strength, I mange to grab the side of the bed with my left hand and keep myself from falling out, but not before the right wrist catches painfully on the sharp metal edge of the door of the bedside cupboard. As I lie huddled, breathing heavily, a warm trickle into the hand hanging over the edge of the bed tells me I have cut my wrist. I lift my hand, bring it close to my bleary eyes. There is a deep cut, over the fleshy part of the palm and along the wrist. While I look, the blood drops freely on to the sheets; a cluster of deep red flowers instantly bloom on the bed. Help will appear at the push of that switch marked with a bell. Should I call? No, this is best, the slow ebbing away of my life-blood, while I lie on the bed, passive. I try to lie straight in the bed, letting my right hand trail down, towards the floor. I glance at the tree. The *gulmohur* stands alone in the rectangle of light from the window and weeps large red tears in farewell. Lying on my bed, at dead of night, I watch the blood flow out of my wrist till vision blurs.

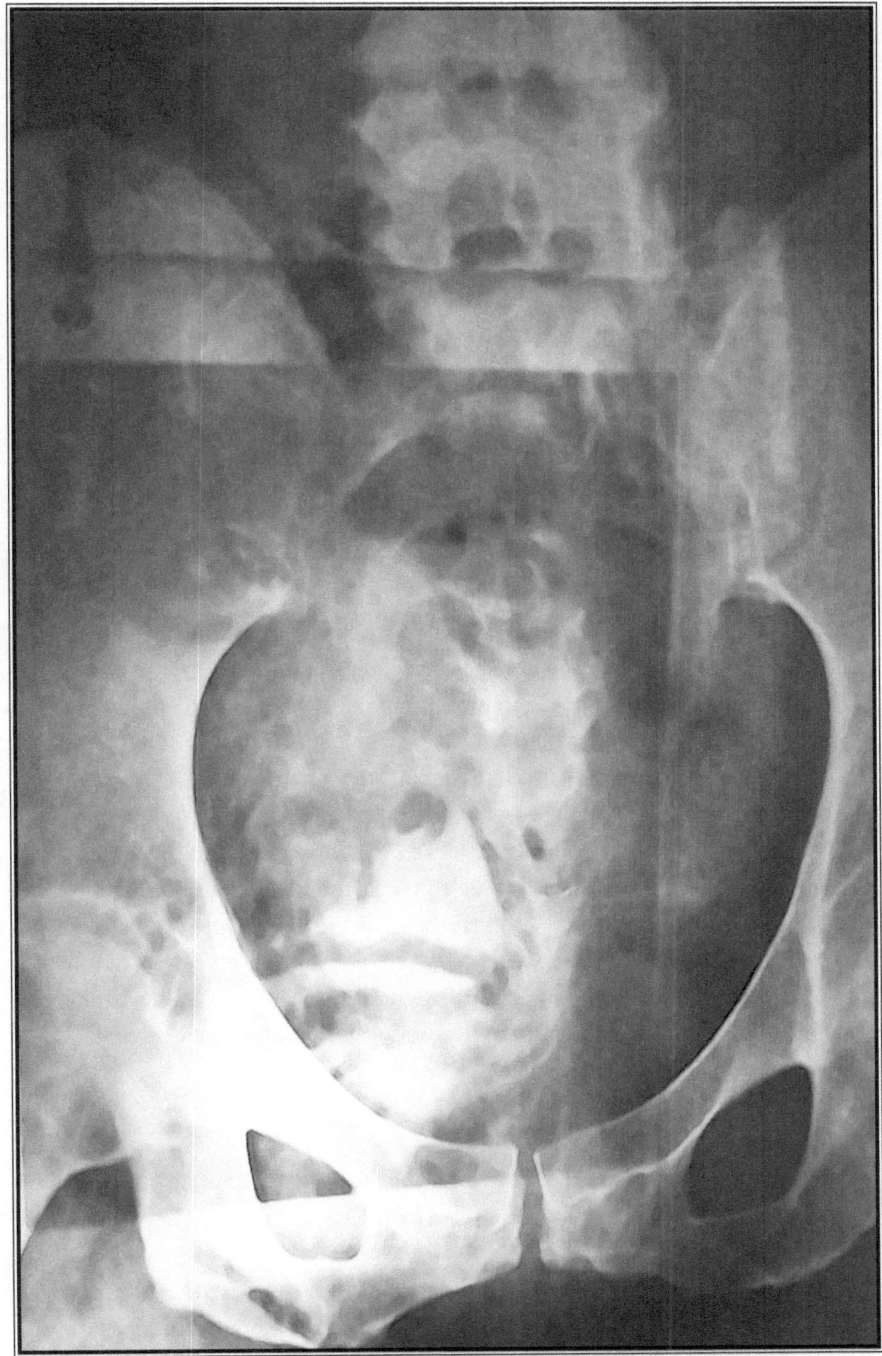

ROBERT C. KNOX

THE FIVE A.M. INQUISITOR

"Morning," he said.

But I had watched the night forever. I was out of mornings. I was out of everything.

"Morning," I echoed, doubtfully (suppressing a laugh: it would hurt), turning his greeting into a question.

"What?" he asked. "Do you have something against mornings?"

I glanced at a bedside window full of darkness.

"This is morning? It doesn't look any different from the last eight or ten hours. . ."

A brief diagnostic glance; was the patient regressing? "What do you mean?"

"I mean the watches of the night are all the same. Dark, solitary, voiceless, indistinguishable one from the next."

The gray-eyed resident considered his shoes. Had he foregone sleep himself and started his rounds at five thirty in the bleak a.m. for this?

"How are you today?" A different question; the only question.

"I hardly know."

My reply was not very helpful to medical opinion, and we began the old game of prying, trying to tease the body into giving up its secrets. Was I eating? drinking? Not enough. Hardly anything.

"What's wrong?"

"In a word? Nauseous."

"I'm not really in favor in using drugs to counter nausea," the resident confided, frankly. "We're just masking a problem. I think maybe you should try to eat through it."

Eat through it? I pondered the phrase. Like a rodent? An insect?

But how could I eat when I could barely tolerate liquids. Forcing down a few drops, a few halting sips, after a sustained, conscious effort... Is the citadel still standing? Has the shaking stopped? All right, then, take a few more sips, even though everything tastes like paint remover. *Eat through it?* Easy for you to say, I grumbled silently. It isn't your cities that will fall, your fields and villages that will lie in ruins.

I shrugged—best I could do—and my five a.m. inquisitor blinked, one gray eye developing a little fit, a little rebellion of sleeplessness all its own. He looked at the clutter of items piled beside the bed; some books, a Walkman, the headset still resting on my lap.

"Music too," he commented.

Too? Along with all my other resources? "I just listened to Brahms," I confided. "The Third."

It was a confession, but a complicated one; part challenge. "So sad," I added, in case he hadn't grasped the significance of this disclosure. "So incredibly sad."

My inquisitor smiled, as if at some admission of weakness, and delivered a mild reproof. "Maybe you should be listening to more upbeat. Something lighter. Mozart—"

"Mozart?" I could not believe my ears. "Mozart is not light."

"A concerto," he continued, ignoring me. "Something—happier."

Let me tell you, I thought, about the clarinet concerto. Yes, I added silently, continuing this satisfying rumination, there is happiness and delight—even light-heartedness—to be found in music. But do you not hear the deeper song? I opened my mouth to speak this last thought aloud, but my inquisitor had departed.

That day I took up a regime of liquids. I had ginger ale for breakfast, ginger ale for lunch, ginger ale for dinner. In the morning—the conventional daylight morning, when the sun had climbed above the neighboring building and filled my window with spattered urban light—the blue-suited food staff brought me a large tray loaded with plastic-covered comestibles. I could not look away; the tray paralyzed me, like the totem of some hostile deity. It contained oatmeal, juice, a ceramic mug of once heated water intended for tea, a small bowl of a greenish liquid that was sweating noxiously beneath its clear plastic covering—something clenched in my stomach at the smell— and several bulkier plastic-wrapped items. I could not bring myself to taste anything, and the untouched idol was still sucking the air out of the room when the resident board of examiners made its collective appearance, gathered in a circle around my bed as if for a levitation, and delivered a judgment.

"We want you to eat," said the spokesman, a red-toned fleshy man with a serious face, gentle manner and slow, Plains State style of address (one imagined solid earth, big sky). "But if it's difficult"—I nodded—"just take a few bites of something. Anything. It's a start."

I nodded without enthusiasm.

The plain-spoken leader of the pack turned his gaze on the heap of neglected offerings on the tray. "So what's with the lumberjack breakfast?" he asked.

Good question, I thought. Took the words right out of my mouth. (If only we could put some food in it.)

"I didn't ask for any of that stuff," I said. "The problem is I can't think of anything I can even imagine eating..." A weird sensation came over me. "Except maybe"—I shrugged—"a pickle."

The circle of residents looked at me as if I were deranged.

Ginger ale for breakfast; ginger ale for lunch. Here a sip, there a sip. Even the few bites of the team's recommendation exceeded my powers. The residents wanted to get me going, to launch me on the flight path to recovery. I wanted to survive. The regime wobbled; I felt it shudder. It held by a thread. I did not want to be underneath when it toppled over.

Please, I begged, no violence. I implored invisible captors with fear in my eyes. A kind of dreary, timeless stalemate ensued; like a hostage event on a cop show, with lots of commercials.

The nurses warned me: drink more liquid or we will have no choice but to bind you once more on a cross of tubes. I stared past their warnings, already bound in a land of no speaking. I attended not to well-meaning, though somewhat smirksome night nurse Naomi, transfixed by a vision (invisible to others) of the fierce and horrible belly-god Nausee. Why have you beset me? I whimpered. Why *me*? What do you want? Why do you linger, unsated by my suffering, hour after hour? I begged for relief. I begged for a spell of expulsion: get thee hence, demon.

Some time around midnight, yet another endless night, Nurse Naomi held a hypo high in her hand. Heedless of the teachings of the five a.m. inquisitor, Nurse Naomi spelled relief in her own way.

Later in that long black night of the body, the charcoal executioner appeared in his surgical garb, his head wrapped for battle, his tunic opened across the chest, his face oddly smudged as if he had been trying to start a fire by blowing on ashes. He said his name—Doctor Something—but I missed it. I had never seen this apparition before. He had a distinct, slightly bullying (exhausted, maybe; battle weary) aura; coolly intimidating. With a glance at my prone dysfunctional form, Dr. Something reached for the plastic envelope that dripped the waters of life through the I.V. and shook it, disdainfully. He muttered some figures, looked at me warningly, and shook his head. "That's not enough to sustain life," he pronounced, looking on me as if I were the unsatisfactory answer to a long and complicated equation.

"You are in the hands of an angry god," he—or perhaps his manner—said to me. "Without our benevolent intervention—without *mine*—your transitory existence will come to an end. You will dry up like a withered leaf and blow away with the first cold breeze of winter."

How do you plead? his black eyes queried.

It's bad enough, your honor (I tried to reply, though the word refused to be spoken), to be diagnosed with a life-threatening disease, but imagine the insult of waking from surgery to find yourself trapped in the colicky body of a fifty year-old infant. Give me a better body, and I'll give you a better recovery.

"—milligrams," the charcoal executioner repeated, shaking the bag. "That's about two Cokes."

"I would like to drink those Cokes, doctor," I replied, speech forming at last, "but I can't."

"Okay. I'll give you this bag, and maybe one more...But after that. . ."

After that I am attacked by terrorists. They sneak up through my dreams, climbing toward my mouth, unconcerned that sleep has been banned by constitutional decree. I try to sleep, going so far as to play the "relaxation tape" that worked so well before surgery. "Find a comfortable position," the tape begins—okay, so much for erstwhile good advice: no such thing as a comfortable position. The bed goes up and down all night, spreading the stress around the sore spots. The place that holds me together becomes the sore spot, a moving target. Many cunning shifts involving four pillows and eighteen sequentially married physical steps (lean left, grab pillow, place pillow, flex leg, lean back, scrunch rear, etc.) are carried out in strict order, lungs panting, but still the fond repose that breeds death's second self escapes me. The ratty sleeve of care remains unknitted.

What is this unlooked-for state of oblivion then that overtakes me some time in the still dark hours? I know it only by its sudden terminus when violence breaks out on the bed, and I am coughing—well, chuffing: my cough is a pitiful thing—and lurching, still pinned to my back, across the wasteland of raveled blankets, sheets and pillows to the place where the mind last remembers secreting some unemptied paper cups of detestable liquids.

For I am desperate. Unslaked, chaos in the cough-control center will tear me apart. Even in my dazed condition, I recognize the origin of the surface tickle in the deep right-hand quadrant of my throat as the place where the unseen enemy has established a beachhead. By day I have aimed elixirs at this point of irritation, but nothing seems to quell it permanently. Now its alarm has been activated by the dream's violent incursion—there is a bomb at the airport, I think, and a bacterial agent has been loosed on the city. I envision this secret killer in the midst of my flipped-tortoise struggle toward the imagined relief of the partially filled paper cup: the stuff is white and gritty, like chipped paint. It coats all surfaces inside my mouth; won't come up, can't go down. Unlikely, I think (or dream), that anyone should bother to rescue me, an old man stranded in a foreign country by the collapse of his schemes, a failed visionary, history's dust bunny; but I struggle on. I reach one of the paper cups and drink my pitiful few sips, vowing never again to slip so heedlessly, helplessly, into slumber. I breathe hard, remembering myself. Perhaps someone will hear my cry; perhaps the enemy commandos will somehow not find me here.

But as soon as I nod off once more, the foe seizes his chance to foul the works. He makes a subtle raid from the deep sewers of the watery intestines, climbing upward through the esophagus until he can lob his foul incendiary into the root cellar beneath the tongue. I start into consciousness, envisioning brilliant chemical explosions inside my mouth: golden flares and maroon coronas plume like the death of a star, a supernova. I taste the bitter coating that spreads over my mouth and tongue, covering it with tiny sticker-stars of *yechh*. I pull myself bolt upright—a hopeless business with surgically impaired stomach muscles, requiring the force of both arms and hideously

slow—a single word vibrating on my filth-encrusted tongue:
"Reflux!"

Five a.m. My inquisitor explains the facts of life. We cannot send you home, he tells me, until you are capable of eating normally and moving your bowels.

"To arrive at eating normally," he points out, "you must begin by eating *something*."

His logic, I agree, is unassailable.

"All right," he says, making his plan. "You go on regular food today. Eat something today and we'll send you home tomorrow. I'll take your stitches out myself."

It's a bridge too far, I fear. I would walk across it if I could. I tell him about the reflux. I tell him what charcoal executioner said (sort of). I tell him what Nurse Naomi did with her hypo as I groaned in the night.

I see the emotion—disappointment—fill his gray, sleep-starved eyes. "All right," he says, "just do your best."

There is sadness in his voice; I am letting him down. I watch him step quietly out of the room in his black inquisitor's shoes. Remorseful, I meditate a plan of my own.

To implement my plan I beg Nella, the personal care attendant who has a more intimate knowledge of my bodily processes than I would wish on anyone, to sneak beyond the precincts of the hospital—that vast, multi-storied, vassal-ridden, slow-grinding city of the sick—and beg real food for me from a real kitchen. I have gone too far along the path of institutional rejection to come back to hospital food, I tell her. I have swept away too many offerings of greenish liquids dripping withered smiles down the lips of the antiseptic cleanser-stinking bowls; brown concoctions of gravy and despair fogged with the peculiar odor of mass-concocted food; unidentifiable juices frosted with icy crystals and tasting of the chemical plant. I need food from a happier place.

Nella fishes my clothes from a closet and I fish out a few rumpled bills, imploring her to seek food from Rebekah's, a nearby deli where I have supped in heartier days. Nella looks into my eyes, shakes her head, then mutters, "All right, Mr. Reese, I'll go for you. But this better not get me into trouble."

In the hour after hospital lunchtime, when old food smells linger on the unsettled stomach, the girl returns, having scrounged the last baked potato from Rebekah's. Also some thinly sliced beef, a puffy roll, a stunted banana with brown spots shaped like the continents; and a huge, gnarled, knobby, toad-skinned pickle. I thank her, gratefulness overwhelming my shaky state. I press money on her, but she refuses.

I unwrap the baked potato, break off the meagerest fraction, and maneuver some of the whitish substance onto a plastic fork. (Is this act familiar? Do healthy people do it every day?) I plunge the fork into my tentative mouth, chew slowly.

Absolutely nothing inside me celebrates this gift of life. Nevertheless, potato flesh disappears down the gullet. Wrinkled potato skin lingers on the paper plate.

"Enjoy your lunch?" afternoon nurse Mel asks me later. Oh yes, I reply, exaggerating my accomplishments—a roll (some crumbs), the potato (a full quadrant), roast beef (a very thin slice), a few diameters of banana. I omit mention of the pickle (which I have wrapped in a napkin and stuck in a drawer), deciding I'm not quite ready for it yet, waiting for the hour when this strange, almost spiritual craving will explain itself.

And I am not sick. Hours pass; I am as I was. Down is down; up is up. Likewise at dinner time (the name the healthy use, so I recall, for the hour after dusk) I perform the same slow, faint disappearing act with a some portion of the cup of instant noodle soup heated for me by Mel in the staff kitchen. ("We don't normally do this.") I munch a bite of leftover roll and cold beef too, so I can add them to the victory list. Look on my deeds, ye mighty: potato, soup, bread, meat…still no pickle. The nurses shift; the hours drift away. The old man on the other side of the curtain (that other whose sufferings I politely ignore, as he ignores mine) rumbles into sleep. The sum of my day's mastications sits in my stomach. Just get through the night, I tell myself: don't blow it.

Some time during the watches of the night I am visited: a presence, leaning over my bed. Not, I realize, the five a.m. inquisitor. Nothing so well meaning. Something old, I think, smelling faintly of incense, fear, and bodily fluids; something that urges without words, refusing to depart until it gets what it wants. Something that sends me to the commode.

Baal, I think, the name appearing in my thoughts by some impulse of its own.

I whisper the name, fearfully, but the power from below doesn't loosen its grip. I feel it laugh deep inside me, and shudder.

"All right, Baal," I plead, "what do you want? Can we make a deal here?"

Baal leans in closer, drawing the room's shadows tightly around the tender flesh, impinging on the inner organs. She whispers unintelligibly in the ancient and irresistible tongue.

"I don't understand," I protest.

Baal knows how to persuade. She sends me back to the bathroom, once, twice, three times. I lose count, before I stop running. "All right, Baal," I say, panting on the bed, chilled, extra blankets pulled up tight around my neck, "what do you want? *Realistically?*"

Baal leans forward. I feel the silence of the shroud, smell the earth drawing near.

Who is more important than Baal, she whispers, Goddess of Digestion? Who deserves place before her?

"All right," I concede, gasping. "I won't forget—first place in the pantheon. What more do you want? A sacrifice?" I promise her several children I don't plan to have, offer her my share of a raft of aging relatives.

No good. Baal squeezes.

"Okay," I say, "take whatever's coming to me." I mention a quick shopping list of once beloved indulgences: red wine and chocolate, raspberries and cheese, good dark coffee. "Coffee, period," I offer, "take it forever. Take what you want. Everything fancy; everything special. Just let me keep down what's already there so I can get out of this place." (*Standing*, I add, mentally.)

Take pleasure, Baal, I bargain, silently, sure the power can read my thoughts. Take the fatted calf. I'll get by on a few leafy greens and a spoonful of sesame seed. All I want is my simple, earth-bound, short-sighted existence back, modestly munching (enough, as the dark doc put it, "to sustain existence"),masticating, swallowing, moving the load downward, acid-washing, dissolving it, breaking it down, pushing, always downward (*no coming back*), deconstructing. Eating just enough, that is, to get by.

Gotta eat, Baal. Gotta go.

A shudder: Baal's laughing.

"I admit," I acknowledge, "the second half of the equation is being pretty well taken care of right now."

Baal amuses herself by making cement factories of my intestines, clogging the works, backing up production. If she won't bargain, if she's just playing with me, then I'll have to endure. Rallying, I shuffle out of the darkened bedroom into the brightly lit corridor, passing the bathroom with a calculating glance, and once outside the door begin a measured revolution of the familiar surgery/oncology hallway, determined to walk myself back to health. I make slow, rolling sweeps down the silent, empty corridor, an old man with a donkey cart, pulling his little dog "I.V." behind him. I trod past the familiar work rooms, each with its own perfectly appalling odor: the burnt gravy of death, the chemical rage of the disinfectants—in a word, nauseating. Don't think about it, I tell myself; keep walking. One more night, one long dark night of the G.I. system, I encourage myself, before the promised day of release. Providing, that is, I can hold my cookies.

When I return to the shadowy sick room, Baal is still there, but her influence has changed somehow—farther away, less ominous, less humorously malevolent. I appreciate the breathing space, though I feel something has happened to my room. My books are still there; my music… What, then, has she taken? Will I miss it?

I rest. I try to rest. If I succeed in sleeping, will the terrorists of yech invade my throat again? Will Baal come back to harvest me in the dark? I close my eyes amid a host of self-counselings. Don't get sick, don't collapse, don't let nurse Naomi come marching to your rescue with a sharpened hypodermic; don't fall off the bed and rip your stitches open, don't wake up screaming; don't wake up coughing, gasping for air, convinced some pack of bearded terrorists has chased you over the sands of your rasping throat to settle a long-standing grudge over an oil bill. Tell me, Baal, better to wake or to sleep? Perchance to dream?

When daylight comes blasting in on me, I am astounded and confused. *Morning already? How late is it?* I am dream-stuck, caught between worlds, neither here nor there, neither my happy, wholesome self nor the paranoid old man with the oil bill nightmare. Why happened to my five o'clock inquisition? I had come to rely on it. Instead of the gray-eyed, black-shoed, disappointed resident, the white-robed circle of examiners is staring down at me.

"Morning."

I feel confounded, transfixed, speechless, in need of a time-out to count up body parts, but reasonably whole. Baal? I think, worried her ancient voodoo will queer my chances with the doctors; but I sense she's gone.

"So how did yesterday go?" asks the fleshy, red-faced posse leader in his hopeful plainsy drawl.

"Yesterday." I blink at the daylight, trying to get a handle on the question. Then this, I work out, must be today. But what is the question? Does this well-meaning young man and his panel of serious-faced playmates want to hear about the gaseous vigils, the long walks with little I.V., the race to the commode? About Baal?

"Uhm...," I say. I lift my head and shoulders, struggle to become more vertical, to stiffen to the light.

"What I mean.... That is, what we really want to know—were you able to eat anything yesterday?"

Think—think back. Before the endless night.

I am about to slobber out some confused reply, when the five a.m. inquisitor, who has snuck into the room behind the others, looking clear-eyed and rested, clears his throat. "Didn't I hear the nurse made you some soup last night?" he prompts.

Yes. It all comes back. "Ram Dass noodles," I say (something like that). "I also had some baked potato, some sliced roast beef, some roll..." I tell my tale of proud, tiny victories. I watch the team take this in, hoping they don't quiz me too closely. If I eat enough to keep a pigeon alive, I will bob and coo when I walk—so long as it's out of here. When I run out of words, I nod my gratitude to the five a.m. inquisitor, the bringer of morning, med-chat and Mozart-lite.

"All right, Mr. Reese," the feet-on-the-ground team leader replies in a conclusive tone of voice, "we're planning on cutting you loose today."

I pick through the contents of the room, throwing out newspapers and paper cups with teeny puddles of liquid in their bottoms, gathering my clothes, tapes and books into a plastic bag. I open the drawers in the nightstand—nothing; nothing I want— then come upon the oozing remains of what looks like a knobby, ritually sacrificed bullfrog. The bouquet that puts formaldehyde to shame.

> The pickle. Half-eaten.

> *Baal?* I know the other half is for me.

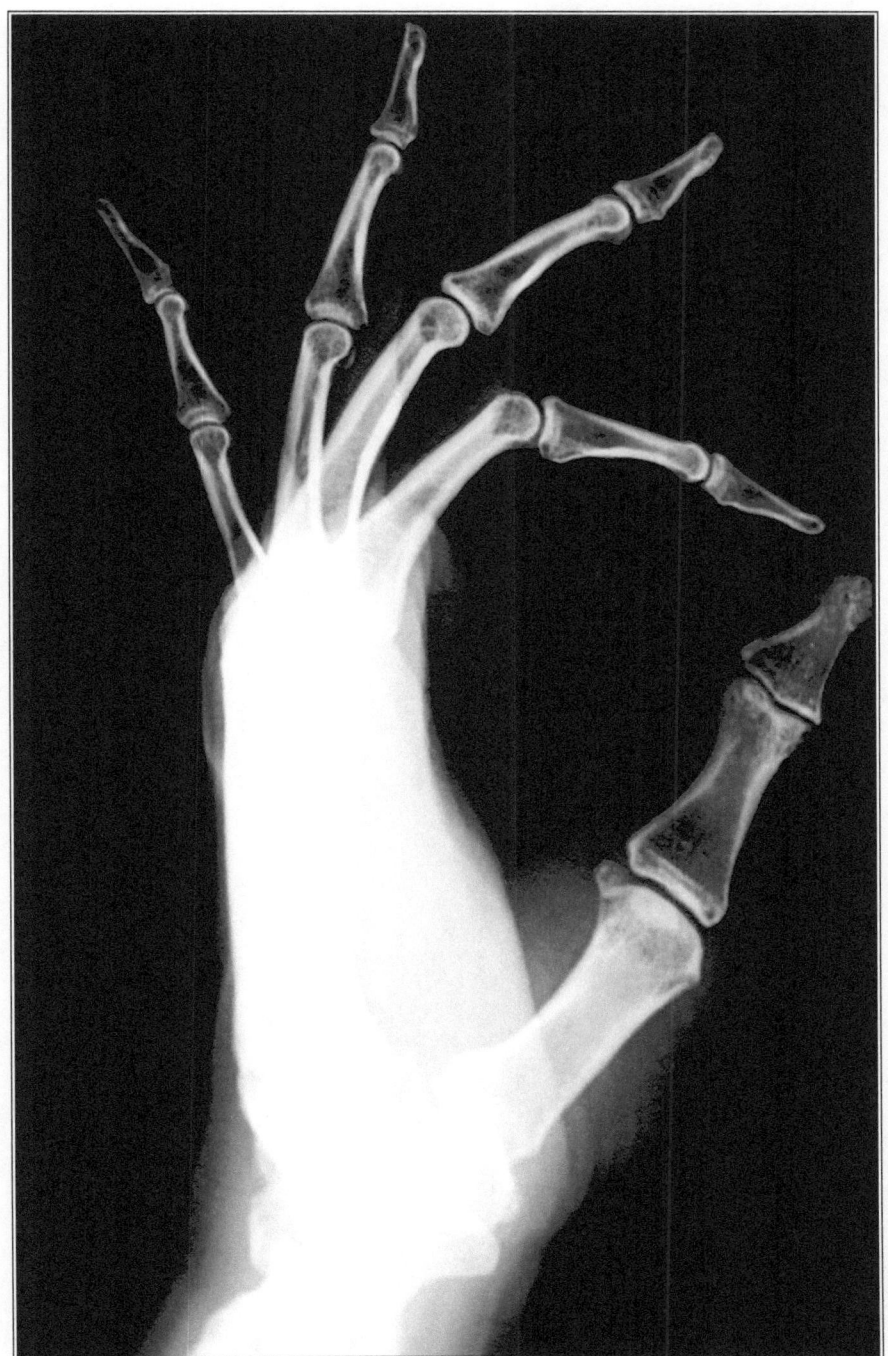

DARLENE MONTONARO

THE CRANE

1.

Begin with a square of paper
Vera spills the wrapping-paper birds
from a plastic shopping bag.
Silver wings and pink swirls,
origami cranes. Japanese ancients,
she says, believed the crane lived
a thousand years.

2.

Valley fold the side flaps to center crease
To fold a thousand cranes, Vera tells us,
brings good health and long life.
                              This information
comes too late. Had I known in time,
I would have begun right then.
Like Kakamura's cranes
released after battle
each with a prayer strip on its leg,
I would have made each fold a petition,
each bird an augury.

3.

Mountain fold side flaps
Twelve-year-old Sadako Sasaki,
dying slowly of radiation poisoning
from Hiroshima, is told the legend—
Fold a thousand cranes, her friend says,
*and receive from God
one single wish.*

          I see her small hands
folding and believing, the way Kath believed
that rosary beads passed through her fingers
make a divine chain to the heavens.
How many beads, we wonder,
will be enough?

4.
Valley fold the model in half
This is what we do, take our lives
folded down to half, then half,
then folded down again. Against my fingers
the papers slice, resist, crack.
I try again and again
to get it right.
          Sadako's brother
hangs the cranes she makes in chains
from the ceiling of her hospital room.
I make, remake Kath's bed
in the cancer ward, squash fold,
petal fold, pull the sheets tight
and smooth. Precision, I think
will bring order.

5.
Valley fold the pointed flap
Origami is a craft
of precision. Each corner
must neatly meet the next.
One slip, one lazy fold,
and the architecture is doomed.

6.

Valley fold the pointed tip,
which is to become the head
Despite what we know
the talisman becomes a sweet seduction.
Rosary beads, medals,
stones etched with 'hope'—
we hold them in our hands like charms.
Fragile as paper cranes, moving against
the hospital's recycled air.

7.

Mountain fold the model in half
There is a place on the mountain path
the seeker knows the summit
has been reached. Descent is inevitable.
To make a mountain fold, the paper—like hope—is halved,
and halved, then halved again
                          Sadako sleeps. Her hands
are idle. Childhood friends press her on and on
knowing they cannot do the work.
They push paper beneath her fingers.
Sadako sleeps.

8.

Pull head and neck into position.
Press the creases flat. Adjust the head
and press it flat
Sadako dies. She completes only 500 cranes,
one half a wish, one less petition with which the gods
must concern themselves. Her classmates
finish folding the rest. The cranes
are buried with her.

The beads
fall from Kath's fingers. In the dark,
while we sleep to the sound of oxygen,
the metronome of a Geiger counter, cancer
takes her hands, her feet, and then her speech.
Her lips can no longer form the prayers.
Who knows how many Hail Marys
she fell short? There is no legend to guide us
no way to tell, in the way of origami,
which corners we failed to match,
where our attempts proved to be unequal.
                    The beads fall. We place them,
hard wood, against the satin.

9.
Finally, the finished crane.

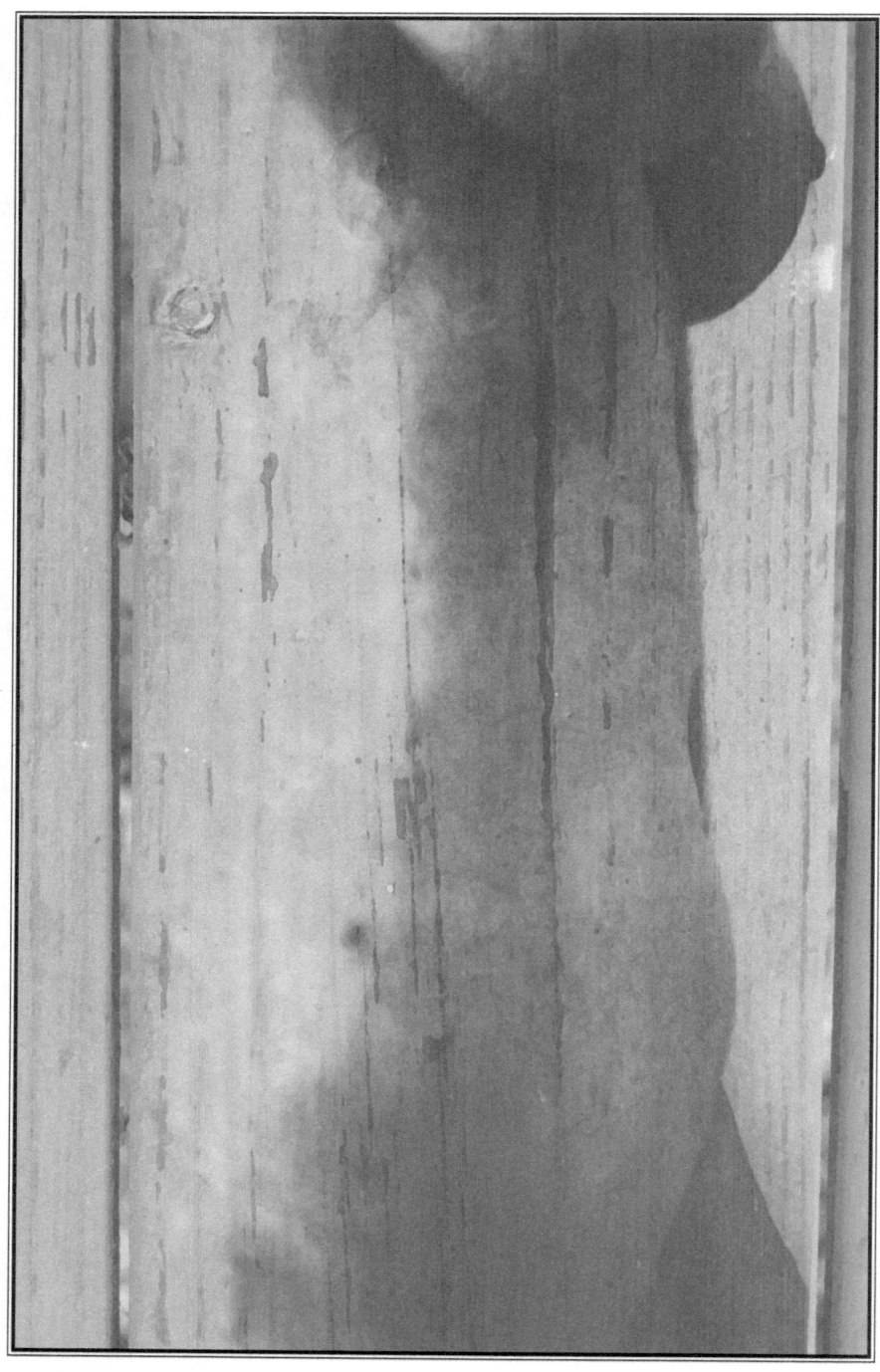

MARK BARKAWITZ

BETTER BOOBS

"How do you like my new boob, Mike?" Kelly smiled as I approached her on the front porch of her Sierra Madre cottage. She stuck her left one forward for me to inspect. It was impossible to detect any difference under her sweater and bra.

"Looks good to me." I'm a painting contractor, mostly residential, so I tend to work with a lot of women in their homes. I drink a lot of coffee and tend to talk a lot, too. Sometimes, they confide in me. Last year, just as I was putting the finishing touches on Kelly's kitchen remodel, she was diagnosed with breast cancer. Her sister had died a few years ago of the same cancer. Kelly had gone through a lot in the year since I'd seen her: mastectomy, chemo, radiation, recovery, and finally—her new boob. We hugged.

"You look good, kid."

"Thanks. I feel good." She smiled again. "Gary likes it, too." Gary was her husband.

I laughed. I do that a lot, too. We went inside. She poured me a cup of coffee. I leaned against the counter, sipped her strong, hot brew, and we gabbed for the next hour or so about everything except cancer. We finally got around to scheduling a starting date for some touch-ups around the house. I put my empty coffee cup in her sink.

"You have another job to go to today?" she asked.

"Yup. Or I'd let you feed me, too." She was a good cook. We both laughed. Kelly did that a lot, too. Probably why we got along so well.

"Next time," she said.

We hugged goodbye and I hurried out to my truck, where I'd left my cell phone on the seat. One missed call. I recognized the number; it was Waters', my next job. I called back.

"Haylo?" It was the housekeeper's voice.

"Mariela?"

"Si. Is that you, Mikey?"

"Si."

"Margo wants to know if you still coming today?" Margo Waters was the homeowner. It had been a few months since I'd last worked at the Waters' Castle, as I called it. It was an old, two-and-a-half story, twenty-eight room, concrete-walled, multi-million-dollar mansion on Pasadena's west side above the arroyo overlooking the Rose Bowl. I'd painted one room seven years ago and had worked there doing odd jobs on-and-off ever since.

"I'm on my way. Did you miss me?"

"Oh, si. You so nice. You always help Mariela."

I carried groceries up the back stairs for her, nothing any gentleman wouldn't do for a lady. No big deal.

"I have sooprise," she said.

"For me?"

"No, ees not for you. But ees sooprise."

A few minutes later, I turned into the long driveway that led back to the castle. I parked, opened the tailgate, grabbed a few hand tools I figured I'd need, and headed up the back stairway. Through the row of kitchen windows on the landing, I saw Mariela inside at the sink. I knocked on the door, but opened it myself.

"Morning."

"Hi, Mikey. Coffee ees in microwave for you." She continued to wash dishes in the sink. "Mar-rgo go to gym. Leave note for you." Without turning towards me, she indicated with a nod it was on the island.

I turned on the microwave, checked the note. I recognized Margo's handwriting:

-fix latch on cab in Butler's Pantry
-paint walls in Guest Room

"Margo's sister went home?"

"Si."

"How is she?"

Mariela shook her head. "Ees no good. Berry sick."

I nodded. Margo's sister was currently going through what Kelly had gone through last year. But her sister had been pregnant at the time the cancer was discovered, which had delayed and complicated her treatment and the cancer had spread. The oven dinged. I took out the cup, sipped the steamy coffee, went back to the list:

-replace all burnt-out light bulbs
-move potted trees from east patio to west patio
-assemble automatic cat box

"Automatic cat box?"

"Si. Mar-rgo get a new kitty."

"Really?" In all the time I'd worked in the castle, the Waters had never had a pet. From under the island, a black paw reached out for my shoelace. I put down the cup, got down on one knee and bent low. Yellow-green, almond-shaped eyes stared back at me from the jet black face of a young feline—too old to be a kitten, too young to be a cat—perched like a sphinx, ready to pounce. "Hey, there." I reached in to pet its head between ears pointed upright. "What's it's name?"

"Hair-rball."

"'Hairball?' That's funny. How you doing, Hairball?" It purred gently. Then I noticed each nail on its front paws was coated with some kind of clear, plastic sheath. I took its paw in my hand to inspect it more closely. "What the heck?"

Still at the sink, Mariela looked down. "Ees so kitty won't scratch furniture."

"You're kidding?" I ran my fingers across the floor in front of Hairball, who reached out to spoke my hand with its paw. The soft, acrylic sheaths kept its fingernails from digging into the skin on the back of my hand. I had to laugh. "What will they think of next?" Then I remembered the list—"*-assemble automatic cat box*"—and figured I'd find out soon enough.

"How's you knee?" Mariela asked.

"Not bad. Rehab took awhile, but I'm back up to five or six miles a run now." I'd hurt it last summer. Didn't know how. Just woke up one morning and out of nowhere the darn thing was swollen like a volleyball. I sipped the coffee and found the loose latch in the adjoining pantry, took the Phillips screwdriver from my back pocket and carefully tightened the guilty, loose screw heads. "How's your back?" I asked through the doorway.

"Oh, ees bueno. I'm so glad. I tell Mar-rgo ees no more heavy lifting." She had been wearing a brace because of a lower back strain, but it was hard to tell under her baggy sweatshirt if she was still wearing it. She dried her hands on the dishtowel, turned to me with a funny, conspiratorial sort of look on her face. "You remember what we talk about last time you are here?"

I thought back.

"Come on." She prodded me. "You remember." She smiled and winked.

"Oh." I did suddenly remember—breast implants. Mariela had lost thirty pounds over the last year-and-a half but had confessed to being unhappy with how the weight-loss had left her breasts, so she had consulted a plastic surgeon in the San Fernando valley. I glanced down slightly, but the loose-fitting sweatshirt hid any clear indication. So risking a faux pas, I was compelled to ask uneasily: "Did you do it?"

She pursed her lips and nodded.

"Really?" I looked again. More closely. "Obviously, you didn't opt for the Ds." Her husband's suggestion, as I remembered.

"No." She shook her head. "Ees a full C."

"Ahh. A full C."

"You want to see?"

"What?"

"Come on. I show you." She walked ahead of me farther into the house. I followed—What else could I do?—through the dining room, where from a wall-sized painting the luminous faces of Renaissance men and women stared judgmentally down at me, into a small hallway, where she closed the doors at both ends. She turned to me and pulled up the baggy sweatshirt, under which firm, twin mounds—like cantaloupe halves—were wrapped snuggly by a cotton crop top.

"Oh." I couldn't help staring. But didn't figure it rude in this instance anyway.

"Ees no bra," she stated proudly.

"No, bra? You're kidding?"

She shook her head. "No. Ees too sensitive." She covered them up again, smiled again. "Eh?"

"To quote my favorite sitcom: 'They're spectacular.' Good for you. Good for your husband, too," I kidded.

"Oh, he crazy now. He keep asking doctor: 'How soon? How soon?'"

"So you haven't tried them out yet?"

"No, no, no." She wagged her index finger like a mother playfully instructing a child. "Ees too sensitive. Doctor say ees okay for Saturday night."

"Really?" I smiled, thinking of her husband. "This Saturday?"

She nodded, wagged her finger at me again. "Doan you tell no one. Ees secret. No want Mar-rgo to know. I tell her I have back surgery. Take two weeks off. Thees morning she look over while I cook. But I no tell her."

"Yeah, she might get pissed-off now that her housekeeper has better boobs." We both laughed.

A door closed with a thud from the kitchen end of the house.

"Ees Mar-rgo. I go now." She hurried out the doorway towards the kitchen. I knew she'd clean-up my half-finished coffee cup on the way.

I went the other direction, up the stairs to the guest room, where the pillows were perfectly arranged on the bed and the bedspread was pulled snuggly across the mattress—not a wrinkle to indicate a human being had ever slept there. The blue walls didn't really need patching or painting, but Margo quite often changed colors on a whim—sometimes her own, sometimes her interior decorator's. A paint chip card was scotch-taped to the wall; the soft yellow color was named: "Morning." I took the flat-head screwdriver from my back pocket and began removing the brass faceplates, putting them all together in an empty wastebasket. A few minutes later, Margo poked her head in the room. "Hi, Mike."

"Hey, Margo. How goes it?"

"Okay." But she sounded weary, not convincing. She wore a designer work-out jacket and pants. Had recently turned forty, but was quite fit and attractive. A personal trainer at the gym and the Wonder bra under her little, white T-shirt helped.

"Sister moved back home. Huh?"

She nodded. "Yeah. She and the kids left last week." They had been staying with Margo during her sister's treatment at the USC-Norris Cancer Center.

"How is she?"

She shrugged her shoulders. "It's too early to tell." Sounding like a doctor, she educated me on the billions of cancer cells that had made up the multiple tumors that had forced the removal of both breasts, then maximum chemo and radiation treatments. Her sister's hair had fallen out. She had lost twenty-five pounds.

Trying to give Margo some hope, I told her about Kelly and her new boob.

"That's nice. But it won't save your friend if the cancer comes back."

I got more stuff from the truck, covered the furniture with plastic and the carpet with dropcloths. I'd paint the walls tomorrow. Change-out the lights and assemble the automatic cat box, too. Today, tomorrow? What the hell did it matter? I didn't see Margo or Mariela on my way out. But it was a big house. You could get lost. So in the kitchen, I wrote a note on the island to let them know I'd be back first thing tomorrow. From under the island, the black paw reached out for my pant leg, but its prophylactic nails couldn't hook me.

No one was home when I got there, so I put on my running shorts and shoes, covered my bare skin with sunscreen, pulled down the bill of my cap, and went for a run. A long run. A very long run. But the melancholy followed me like a dog on a leash—*if the cancer comes back*. By the time I got home, it was nearly dark and my wife's car was parked behind my truck in the driveway. My knee ached again, as I climbed our front porch steps. My daughter let me in. She was thirteen. And wearing a bra now. They ought to make those damn things cancer-proof. That'd be a Wonder bra.

"Hi, Dad. How was your run?"

"I don't know."

She screwed up her face. "You're so weird."

"Where's your brother?"

"At the Mall with Valerie." My son was seventeen. Valerie was his girlfriend. She drove a hot yellow, convertible Mustang, which made my wife uneasy. "Mom's in the kitchen."

But I had already smelled our dinner on the stove, where my wife was grilling a salmon steak in a black frying pan. I leaned against the door frame, watching her carefully flip the big, red piece of fish with the spatula. Truly, she was a beautiful woman.

"Smells good."

"Oh." She flinched, looked over at me. "I didn't hear you come in."

"Sorry. Didn't mean to startle you."

She turned to get something from the sink, stopped, stared back at me. "What?"

"What 'what?'"

"What are you looking at me that way for?" She eyed me suspiciously.

"Just looking." I grabbed a quart bottle of Gatorade—Cool Blue—from the refrigerator and unscrewed the top.

"Oh, Margo's housekeeper called. Something about an automatic cat box? She said you'd know what she meant."

"Yeah. I know." I took a big gulp of the cold, pale blue liquid, then remembered—*How soon? How soon?*—and I laughed again.

"What's so funny?"

"'Ees secret.'" I took another sip, then before leaving to shower, leaned against the door frame and asked my wife: "You busy Saturday night?"

She answered with a question: "Why?"

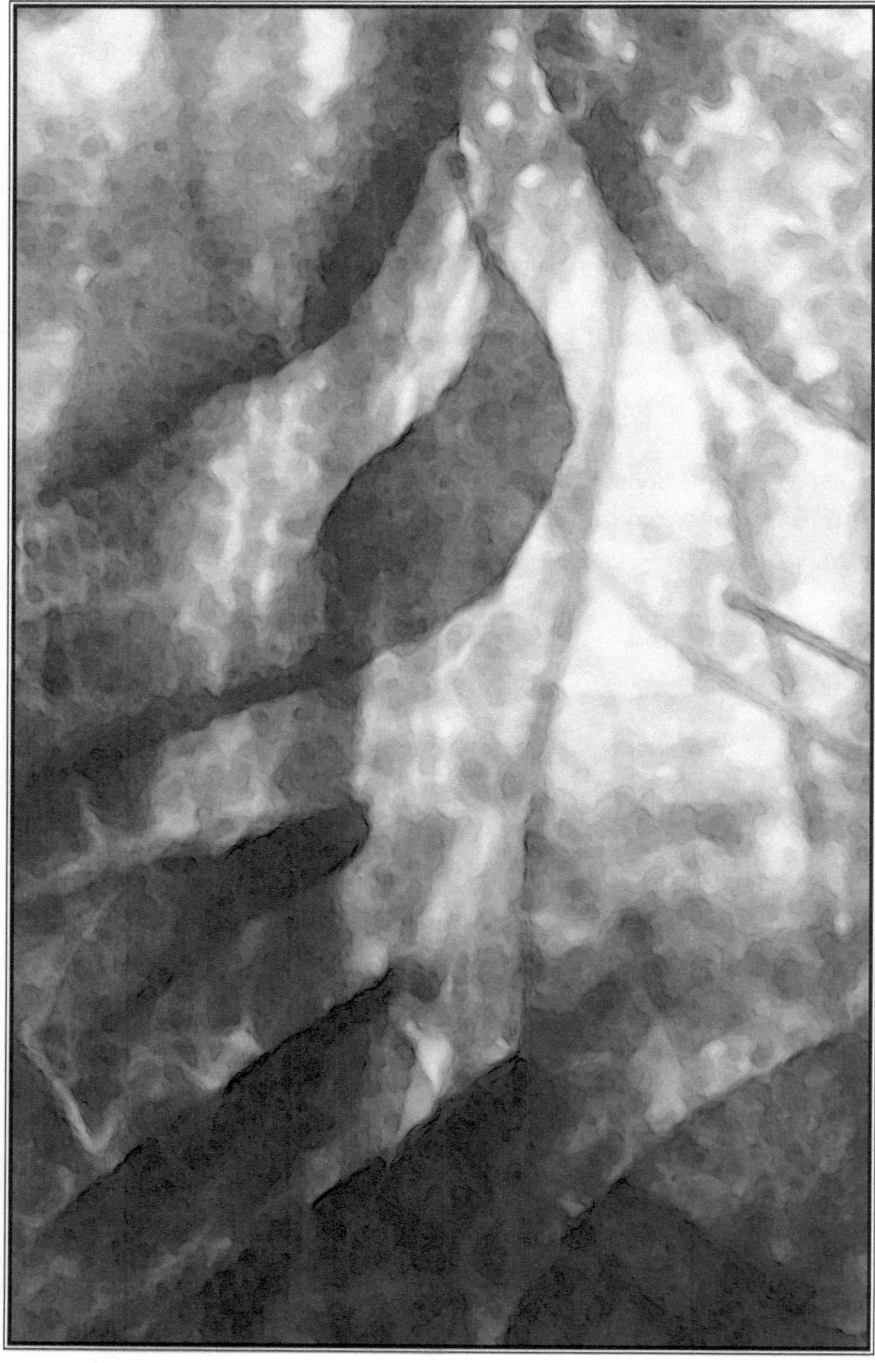

JOAN POTTER

IN CHEMO WORLD

We're all sitting in Infusion Suite II—the old lady in the grey wig snoozing under a bright yellow blanket, the hairless man wearing a baseball cap and reading the Daily News, the woman with short streaky brown hair in jeans and high-heeled boots, my lanky, bearded 77-year-old husband, Roy, and me.

I'm keeping my husband company and trying to read a magazine. Everyone is reclining on soft grey leather chairs. All have thin transparent tubes attached to their chests or the backs of their hands or the crooks of their elbows. Roy's tube pokes out between two buttons of his red plaid flannel shirt. Pinkish and colorless liquids drip into the various tubes from plastic bags hooked onto IV poles.

A heavyset blond nurse walks in from time to time and moves quietly around the room, examining the bags and tubes, adjusting some and adding to others. A TV mounted high on one wall mumbles faintly. Roy turns a page of his paperback mystery and smiles at me. This is the second once-a-week chemo treatment he's had since his colon cancer surgery. Only 50 more to go, or so we've been told.

Three months earlier, I was sitting by Roy's side in the ambulatory surgery center; he was resting up after a colonoscopy. I was happy to see that the sedative had worn off and he seemed in good spirits, looking forward to getting up and going home. The beds in the recovery room were separated by curtains, and we could hear doctors making their pronouncements to other patients: "Looks good...all clean...come back in five years."

Finally Roy's doctor appeared, dark hair slanting over his forehead, slightly crossed brown eyes, impassive expression. "So," he said, "I removed a couple of polyps that we're sending out to the lab, I saw a little diverticulitis, and, oh yes, a mass suspicious of cancer. Make an appointment with a surgeon." He scribbled something on a slip of paper and handed it to Roy. Very matter-of-fact. No hopeful or consoling words.

After he disappeared a nurse came in to get Roy ready to leave, and I moved to a chair outside the cubicle. As I waited there clutching my bag and Roy's jacket I glanced at a man sitting nearby, next to a woman I assumed was his wife. They both looked over at me with what I thought were pitying gazes.

Roy called the recommended surgeon and made an appointment for the coming week. We were strangely calm that evening, watched a movie on TV and didn't talk about the upcoming doctor visit. The next morning I woke up in a panic, my mind racing ahead into the terrifying unknown. But when Roy came to the breakfast table he seemed almost cheerful. "I'm glad I have good doctors," he said over his toast and coffee.

How did we spend the next six days? We went out to lunch, friends came for a visit, we talked about going to the movies but Roy was too tired. One sunny day I felt optimistic: it's probably not cancer, the doctor just said "suspicious of." But the next morning, the trees outside the window disappearing into a gray fog, I found myself fighting off that smothering feeling that overtakes me when life seems impossible and there's no way out.

The surgeon was a stocky, unhurried man who spoke slowly and calmly and whose eyes crinkled slightly as if he was amused by a secret joke. He told us the lesion was malignant and surgery was required. We didn't react with gasps or sobs. We asked a few questions and then went home.

Another week to get through. We had to tell our four children and a few friends. Everyone seemed to know someone who'd had the same surgery and recovered successfully. My sister e-mailed from California: her husband's brother-in-law had colon cancer surgery and a year of chemotherapy and now felt fine and looked ten years younger. "Great news!" Roy wrote back. "I can't wait to look ten years younger."

The operation was scheduled for the day after our 51st anniversary. We couldn't go out for a celebratory meal; Roy had to fast. But in the afternoon a florist he'd called delivered an azalea plant covered in pink blossoms. We weren't talking much about the surgery. I didn't know how scared he was, and I didn't want to ask.

Then once again we were together in a hospital room. Roy was being prepared for the operation. He was flat on his back in a narrow bed while various people came and went: the nurse to hook up the IV, the anesthetist to describe his procedure, the man to shave Roy's belly, which gave us a laugh, and, finally, the surgeon, still calm, still with that amused expression in his eyes. Then two men in green scrubs came and pushed the bed out the door.

When your husband is being taken away on a stretcher for an operation that you hadn't dreamed of a mere 15 days before, the focus of your life changes. Your concerns narrow and many disappear. The arguments, disappointments, and resentments that mark 51 years of marriage lose their meaning. You sit in a straight-backed chair clutching the pair of glasses and the gold wedding band the nurse has handed to you. You're struck by your husband's bravery, his humor, and his vulnerability as you watch the stretcher roll down the long corridor and vanish around a corner.

Then the waiting began. In the dreary room with the blaring television and the exhausted-looking people leafing through worn copies of old magazines; in a chair by Roy's bed in the critical care unit, where he drifted in and out of sleep, monitors beeping and nurses hovering. Later, sitting day after day next to the window in his hospital room, I wished he weren't so frail and lethargic. I wondered if he'd ever be himself again, the man who'd taken up so much of my life.

He wasn't always a great husband; he could be sarcastic, critical, and remote, but he was also a reader, a music lover, a moviegoer, an appreciator of ethnic food, and a clever person whose funny observations could always make me laugh. Looking at his gaunt features, his long, bony body under the thin blue blanket, I knew then that I'd take it all if I could have my old husband back.

After nine days in a hospital bed—his release was delayed by Labor Day weekend when much of the staff disappeared, and a quick trip to another hospital to have stents inserted in a newly discovered blocked artery—he was ready to come home. The surgeon had explained the stage of his colon cancer—somewhere in the middle of the seriousness spectrum. The oncologist, a round, balding man with a gentle voice, had said to come to his office to discuss treatments when Roy had regained his strength.

With Roy at home, my life was devoted to making him better. I delivered healthy meals to his bedside—soups and eggs, applesauce and cottage cheese—and watched with pleasure as his face lost its grey pallor, and his voice, so thin and wispy in the hospital, grew stronger. The first couple of weeks, though, too weak to leave his bed, Roy needed an aide to help with the things I couldn't handle, or didn't want to—bathing, the bedpan, getting up in the middle of the night when he called.

The aide, a competent but bossy ex-reggae musician from Jamaica named Conrad, ordered me down to Rite-Aid every few hours: get some drinking straws, some protein drink, some moisturizing lotion, more toothpaste. But as annoyed as I was by his constant chatty presence, his obsessive viewing of CNN, and the long, mysterious conversations on his cell phone, I couldn't have gotten through those weeks without him.

Conrad used our extra bedroom and I arranged sheets and blankets for myself on the living room couch, where I spent most of the night on the edge of sleep. At every sound—Roy's sigh, his cough, the ringing of a bell he kept by his bedside and the soft sound of Conrad's bare feet as he padded down the hall—my eyes flew open and I stared into the darkness, my heart pounding.

With Conrad there, I could go out and do some of the things that had filled my normal life. Along with trips to the drugstore and supermarket, I taught my weekly writing class and sometimes met a friend for lunch. But it was hard to relax away from home. I was distracted; I felt the pull of the apartment. Sitting at a restaurant table, it was hard to chat with my friend, to hear about the book she was reading, her trip to the mall to buy new shoes. I willed her to eat faster. Even though I was sure Roy was all right, I needed to get home.

One day on my way to the elevator I ran into Marigo, my neighbor down the hall. Her husband had died decades before, leaving her to raise two children on her own. "Don't look back and don't look ahead," she told me. "You have to live day by day."

If I'd heard this advice at any other time, I'd have thought of it as a cliché, simpleminded and impossible. Now I knew she was right. In this new world I was inhabiting, past obsessions had become nebulous, hard to hold onto. Will our son find a good job? Did our granddaughter choose the right college? I couldn't concentrate on those things anymore. The kids would have to figure out their own lives.

But with all my resolve, it was hard to keep my imagination from leaping ahead. What if he never gets strong enough to be on his own? What if we can never go out to dinner or to the movies or take little trips? What if the cancer comes back?

"I feel like I'll be lying in this bed for the rest of my life," Roy said one morning.

I smoothed out his blanket. "Oh, you'll be fine. You have to give it time. Remember what the nurse said, one week of recovery for every day in the hospital."

It was almost two months before Roy felt well enough to visit the oncologist. Conrad was gone, and so was B.B., the kindly aide from Ghana who had replaced him, coming to help us several hours a day. Now Roy and I were on our own.

We sat together in the oncologist's office as he laid out the options. Roy could decide to do nothing, but that would mean a 60 percent chance that the cancer would recur; he could be given a new, aggressive drug, but the side effects might be overwhelming; he could take a pill at home but it would cause severe nausea. Or he could come to the hospital once a week for an hour or so and get an infusion of two older tried-and-true drugs that would cause no side effects. That was the obvious choice.

The weekend before the chemotherapy was to begin, our son visited from Baltimore. He said he was worried; we'd both heard the horror stories—fatigue, illness, loss of hair, the treatment being as bad as the disease. "This may sound strange," I said, "but I wish I were the one having the chemo. I'd be less scared." My son nodded. "I know what you mean," he said.

If Roy is as anxious as I am on the morning of the first treatment, he doesn't show it. We eat our breakfast and page through the newspaper. I'm in the bedroom putting on my jacket when I hear "Jesus!" from the bathroom. In a panic I run down the hall and see Roy leaning over the toilet, trying to fish out the sheet of paper that lists his appointment schedule.

At the hospital again, up to the fifth floor, through a door marked Oncology Program. Roy writes his name on a sign-in sheet and the young woman at the reception window directs us down a wide hallway lined with bright paintings. Around a corner a nurse greets us and leads Roy away. I walk back to the waiting room and pick a chair that faces the door. I want to see what the cancer patients look like. I'm both curious and squeamish.

A tall woman, her bald head wrapped in a blue scarf, is putting on her coat. "See you next week," she calls to the receptionist and waves goodbye. A man enters with a glum-looking woman I assume is his wife. He appears to me like any normal sixtyish guy, flirting with the receptionist as he signs in while his wife sits down and examines her cellphone. Next comes a stocky man wearing a baseball cap who seems to have no eyebrows. "Hi, pumpkin," he calls to the young woman, and ambles down the hall.

The waiting room is large and pleasant, with a wall of windows and healthy green plants placed here and there. The chubby oncologist, wearing a sweater and corduroys, shambles past. He doesn't glance in my direction. I shuffle through the magazines on the table—Time, Sports Illustrated, People, Caring4Cancer. A plastic easel displays a flyer for a business called Tiffany Wigs. I take out my book and start to read.

Soon the blond nurse walks down the hall and into the front office, carrying a manila folder. On her way out she sees me. "Mrs. Potter, you don't have to stay here. You can come in and sit with your husband."

I look up from my book with what I hope is a grateful expression. "Oh, that's okay," I say. After awhile, though, I know I have to go in. I find Roy sitting in front of a window, the sun shining on his head and shoulders. The bald man is asleep. So is an old woman stretched out under a blanket. The man with the grumpy wife is reading a paperback thriller. I try not to look at their tubes and the mysterious places they lead to.

Finally the nurse comes in and unhooks Roy. "It wasn't so bad," he says on the way to the car. "I feel fine." I tell him the infusion room seemed warm and comfortable, the nurse competent and upbeat. "And the other patients," I say, "they're so relaxed they can't stay awake."

During his second treatment I sit with him the whole hour and a half, but I haven't done that again. Now we have a routine. I drop him off, run whatever errands I've lined up, usually the supermarket, the library, or a quick trip to the Gap. I time my return so I'll get there about 20 minutes before the treatment ends. I stop in the hospital lobby for coffee and a cranberry-orange scone and carry them upstairs.

When I walk into the infusion room, Roy always looks up from his book with a smile. He takes a sip of the coffee. "Mm," he says. "This tastes so good."

He smiles at me a lot lately. More than he used to, I think. It's an appealing grin, one I can see in a picture I took when we were newly married, as he sat shirtless on the bed in our tiny apartment. Now his voice is always gentle and he thanks me for every little thing I do. And in response, I try to be gentler, too, less like the often moody and argumentative person of the past, before the diagnosis, before the operation, before the Monday afternoons when I watch the drugs drip, drip, drip into his IV tube and wait for the plastic bag to empty.

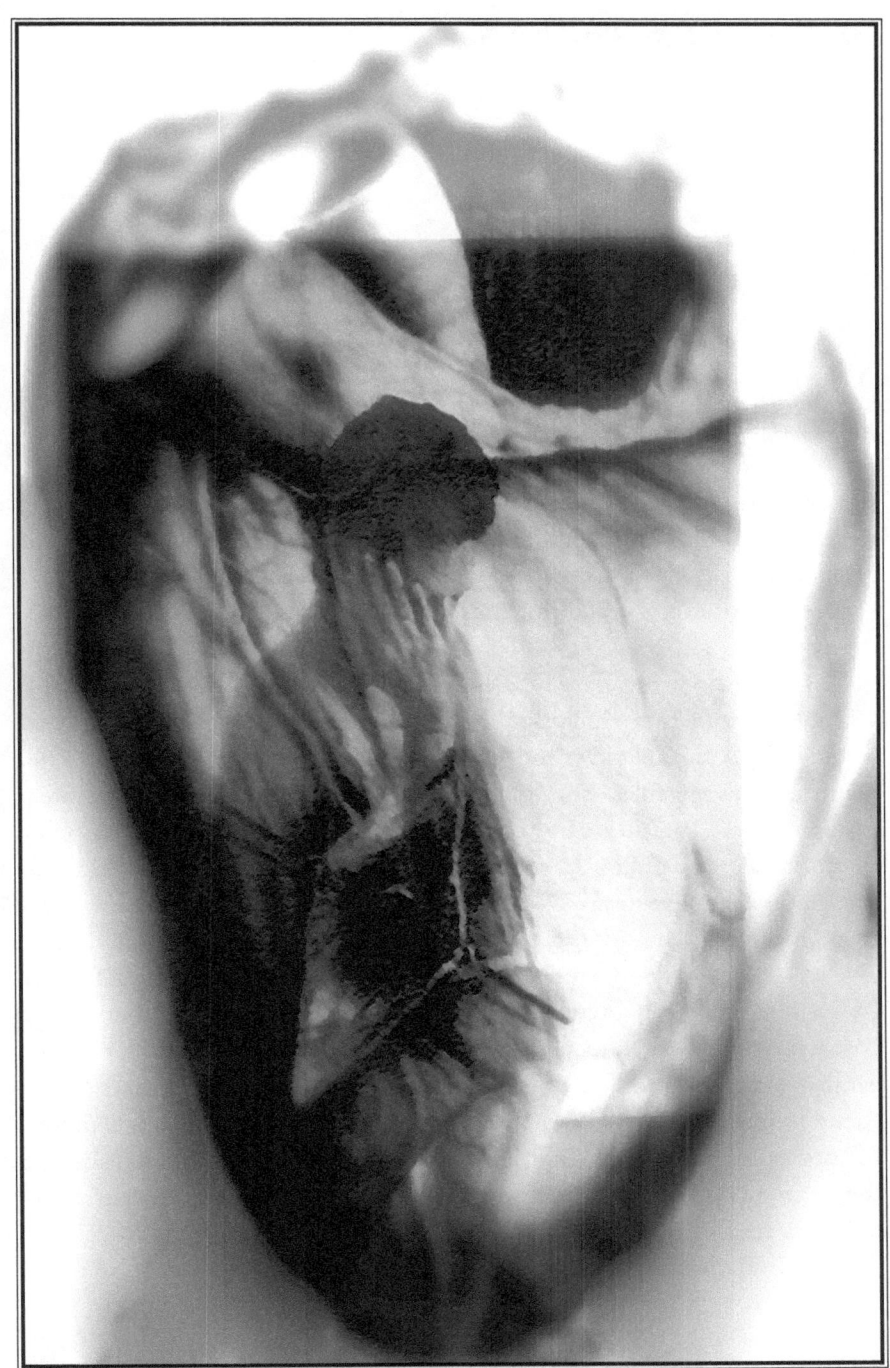

KIMBERLY K. FARRAR

"*Big C...little c...*"

Dr. Seuss's ABC

I want to eat that kiwi, Feb. 13th, 1998

I go into the kitchen and pour myself a cold glass of water. "Drink lots of water," says Dr. Lee, my oncologist. I believe the water will keep the chemo from burning out my kidneys and liver. Water is the opposite of chemo. Water is clean, natural, and refreshing; the chemo is the result of a shipwreck that exploded tons of mustard gas. So I drink lots of water to cool my insides.

As I pour my glass full, there it is. Resting on the cutting board is a beautiful, soft, fuzzy kiwi. I'm going to have a yogurt for breakfast and would love to dice that kiwi and stir it into the cream, but Dr. Lee said, "No raw fruits or vegetables. You don't want any fungi or parasites." My system is unprotected. Parasites that normally pass right through without stopping to see the sights would now set up camp, claim squatters' rights, build little fires and expand westward. No fruits, but I want to eat that kiwi so badly. I can imagine the beautiful green with the darker green in the center, those lovely black seeds, that texture only a kiwi has, the sweet tang of its soft flesh. I want that kiwi. If I could eat that kiwi, then I could drink another cup of coffee instead of water, maybe go shopping. This would be just a day off. I'd eat my yogurt and kiwi and go into the city, or go to a museum, maybe call a friend to meet for lunch. I'd be like I was. I'd slice it open and berate myself for not eating more fresh fruit. But I can't eat the kiwi, so I hide it behind the canned goods. 10:24 am. Normally, I would be correcting student essays in Room 150.

I fill my bowl with yogurt: plain, lonely yogurt.

The Diagnosis, Nov. 3, 1997

I rolled over on Dr. Choi's examining table. His jolly, Buddha face was gray and his mouth seemed thin. He said, "Well, Kim..." and I said, "Is it cancer?"

I finally had a diagnosis, after months of looking in the toilet and seeing blood and not seeing blood. One night it was blood, the next night it was tomatoes or undigested apple peel. I once sneaked into the Health aisle at Barnes and Noble and looked up "Blood in Stool." *The Handbook of Signs and Symptoms* told me it was one of the signs of cancer, but rarely did colorectal cancer occur in anyone under fifty. I'm 38. My husband had reassured me that it was probably just hemorrhoids and I put off calling the doctor another week until it was five months later.

You think the threat of death is going to profoundly change your life, that you will suddenly have the power to cure every weakness you ever had, to give up the okay job and pursue your hopes of being an artist, that your creativity will reach unparalleled heights, that you will be able to write the poem about The Void that you have always harbored in your heart. But the truth is, you cry and flag down a cab.

This is just the beginning.

Soon you start to fantasize about the future without yourself while skipping over the whole part about really dying. What is frightening about this is that it is not an entirely unpleasant daydream. Your passing away is so tragic, so dramatic. People talk about what a loss it is and say, "So young, too." You are exonerated from all the mistakes you ever made, the time you were a little drunk and rude. The time you slept with your best friend's boyfriend. The time you borrowed another hundred dollars from your mother knowing you would never pay it back. There are no more dilemmas about never having published that book. No more dread of laundry day. No more need to divvy up the chores with your husband.

You are omniscient. Your clothes still hang in the closet and your husband's arm is flopped across your empty side of the bed. Everyone misses you.

The one thing you cannot think about is leaving your baby.

The Surgeon, Nov. 10, 1997

"We need approximately two inches of margin on both sides and there has to be at least five inches of rectum..."

My husband, Jeff, and I kept trying to pay attention, but really I was staring at Dr. Imbaralu's face and listening to his accent. I watched his large pink lips moving up and down but it seemed like the words were blocked, as if my eardrums were too thick.

"The mass is about 5 centimeters so we'll make a wide-angle cut..."

Pay attention, pay attention, pay attention was all I could hear inside my head. My eyes wandered over to his model car collection. And I thought, if he does a good job, I'll get him a model car for Christmas.

"We'll take out some tissue..."

I wondered why the plaque on his desk had another doctor's name on it, Dr. Ducca, and why he didn't have his own plaque. I wondered if Dr. Imbaralu had any children.

"I need to take out the blood vessels..."

Pay attention, pay attention. The poster on the wall had two hands on it: One with the skin and one without. The hand is such a complexity of hinges and rubber tendons. The bones are so delicate and dancerly. I wondered if he practiced sports medicine or had a lot of carpal tunnel patients.

"There is no real way of knowing until we get in there..."

My husband was nodding so I decided to stare hard at the doctor. His eyes were round with a slight hint of Asian.

Then he pulled out the comic book of the colon. It was printed in faded blues and reds, bargain colors. I was sitting too close to his desk, so my knees were pressing up against the panel. I leaned over as he thumbed through the pages looking for...I didn't know what.

"Here. You can have your own," he said and pulled another one from the stack in his bottom desk drawer.

Understanding Colon Surgery. I curled mine up and kept looking at his. I didn't want to have to fumble through the pages trying to keep up. There were several panels for the colon. *Sigmoid Colectomy* was printed next to my row of colons. Box 1 was a complete colon, Box 2 had a triangular piece missing and in Box 3 the gap was closed with a dotted line.

"Here we have the upper rectum, mid rectum and lower..."

There was a courtroom type sketch of a crowd of seniors on the opposite page. One was missing, just a black outline, and the caption read, "1 in 15 people will develop colon cancer." The missing person was me. I had jumped out of the comic book and sat facing the surgeon.

"This—I'm going to remove," he said and took out a 59-cent Bic pen. Then he carefully cross-hatched a larger slice from the whole colon and I thought, that is NOT what you are going to remove. What you are going to remove bleeds and is wet, sealed in membranes, warm and living.

"Why so much?" I asked, looking at a smear of blue ink that went outside the frame.

"We need to get surrounding tissue to check for spread."

For spread? The pre-printed boxes had looked so neat and simple, but now there was ink and squares and smudges.

"But we got it early, don't you think?" I couldn't keep the desperate tone out of my voice.

He said, "We probably did, but you can only really tell once the pathology is returned."

No one gave me any definitive answers; there was always a *probably,* a *maybe,* or an *in most cases.* No one ever said, *we're sure, absolutely, no need to worry.*

They had to take out some of my healthy tissue surrounding the tumor to test for invading cells, and it hit me that what he was going to remove was trying to kill me, quietly, cell by cell. I stood up, stunned.

My husband handled the co-pay and scheduling while I stood next to him not knowing if I should sit back down or go to the bathroom or get my coat. Twisting my little comic book in my hands, I stared at the wood grain of the highly polished walls and noticed how it looked like hundreds of little mouths.

It was only 4:30 but already pitch black outside and raining just enough to be annoying. You didn't really get wet but it made you squint. Inside the cab we sat in silence. The roads were shiny and the windshield wipers only smeared the mist so everything was blurry, not enough water for those moments of clarity between swipes.

My husband took my hand and I said, "Imbaralu. What kind of name do you think that is?"

"I don't know, Spanish maybe."

I was bothered that Dr. Imbaralu didn't seem to obviously fit into any common ethnic category.

I wondered, "Is it Spanish? Greek, you think?"

"Could be Greek. Why?" Jeff handed me the appointment card,

"Stick that in your wallet, just in case..."

"In case what? In case it slips my mind that Friday I have major surgery?"

"Just take it," he said.

It was rush hour and the cars were backed up on Northern Boulevard. The red taillights shimmered for miles.

"I couldn't pay attention in there. I kept looking at his mouth but it was like listening to the teacher on Charlie Brown."

Jeff looked out the window. " I'm so worried. It's all weird and..."

"About what? I mean, what specifically?"

"The whole operation, everything. I want you to be okay." He leaned his head back and closed his eyes. Don't cry, I thought. I wasn't ready to think about *not* being okay.

" I know. You need me so you don't turn into an old man." He snorted at our old joke and his grip loosened on my hand. "Honestly, I don't want to think about it. I have two more good nights. Let's live in denial. What good does it do anyway? We'll have enough time to really feel bad."

"Let's get some wine."

"There you go. How about Greek wine in honor of Dr. Imbaralu? Greek is always good for a doctor, don't you think? Hippocrates and all that. The father of modern medicine. "

"I guess if there's anything you want your doctor to be, it's Greek," and he kissed the top of my head.

We passed Flushing Hospital where I would be getting operated on in a few days. I didn't like the way the ivy was rampantly growing all over the sooty brick walls. It looked like an old insane asylum.

"But I wonder what he is," I asked. "Maybe he's Turkish. I'm going to be fine. Hopefully the surgery will be it and—Look," I shook my comic book at him, "I have my little diagram to prove it. A souvenir. He can't be Chinese. Not with a name like Imbaralu."

"True, but Dr. Choi did recommend him and they all seem to be connected."

"The Chinese connection. Chinese would be good."

That night on television we watched a clip about New Yorkers who guide tourists around the city. The guide was Burmese and looked just like Dr. Imbaralu. Eureka! I pointed this out to my husband and we agreed. Burmese, definitely Burmese. I didn't know a thing about Burma and started to get a little worried.

The Surgery, Nov.14,1997
7:30 AM

I looked up at the huge lights when suddenly the sides of my face turned to confetti. I knew they had injected the anesthesia.

4:00 PM

A nurse across the room was flipping through notes on a clipboard. I couldn't lift my head. My husband whispered that he loved me and had to go pick up our daughter, Laura, from daycare. I mumbled, "I love you, too." Dr. Imbaralu was behind me, people were laughing, I closed my eyes.

Later, my husband told me the doctor was leaning over the gurney, practically resting his coffee cup on my head. It didn't surprise me. I was another fixed car, a mended piece of furniture, a successful repair job.

3:00 AM

I was in a room. The pain in my side was incredible. I thought it must be where they stitched the two ends of my large intestine together. The dotted line in Box 3. I pushed the red button for the good nurse to inject my IV with some extra morphine. I thanked her and slept for a few hours then woke up and rang her again.

The next time I woke up I was reaching for the hand of someone who was there and had let my hand slip out of hers. My arm was outstretched and my fingers were groping for the long robed figure that whisked behind the curtain. The spirit was soft and airy, like gray spun wool. I kept my eyes open for a few moments, hoping the shadow would reappear, but it didn't. The unit was perfectly quiet. In my vision I saw my friend, Alan, sitting cross-legged on the floor of my old studio in Tucson, I heard my Aunt Ethel's voice come over the phone, *the good Lord knows*...I held my mother-in-law's fragile shoulders as I hugged her. I felt the love of my friends and family and knew that somehow their energy had coalesced and come to tell me that it would be all right. I was comforted and unafraid for the first time since November 3rd. I slept well the rest of the night.

The next day I was relaxed. It was a visit from the supernatural, I was certain. I didn't tell anyone about the warm, gray figure because like all supernatural experiences it would have sounded hokey and trivial when put into words.

I was allowed only ice chips for three days. They were delicious and cold. Perfectly crunchy, like the crushed ice you can only get from industrial ice machines. It crunched just right so your teeth didn't hurt and it became food. The ice was the first step back to drinking, to eating, to life. I rang the nurse fifteen times a day for more ice chips.

I shuffled across the linoleum floor toward the bathroom, listening to the sound of my slippers sliding against the linoleum, shhh…shhh… shhh. Slippers are depressing. I tried to deny this by buying a pair that had a Dalmatian print, but in the end it made it worse. The black and white pattern seemed only to accentuate the gloomy pea green of the rest of the ward. My shoulders stooped as I wheeled my IV alongside me. The two of us barely fit in the tiny stall. I knew that walking would make me better. When I stood up, I felt my organs dropping and shifting back into place.

Bodily functions were most important. What you are taught never to mention at the dinner table suddenly became the only interest of all professional visitors. Did you go to the bathroom? Did you urinate? Was there any blood? Did you have a bowel movement yet? What color was it? Was it soft or hard? Did you pass gas? These were the hurdles to the hospital exit. They let me out three days early. November 19th, Laura's first birthday.

I could not buy her the Elmo streamers like I wanted. I could not have her little friend Ellie over. I could not make her a yellow cake or a card with lots of sparkles glued on it. We did manage to buy her a blueberry muffin and put one candle in it.

I kept telling myself that she didn't know.

The Follow-up, Dec. 5th, 1997

Dr. Imaralu cut out the tumor and stapled me back together. He left in a few clamps too so the staples would have some company—or so he informed me on my follow-up visit. He made a joke about going through airport security that I knew he had repeated to a thousand patients before me. I feel strange about having staples inside of me, especially being a teacher. I've spent at least three years of my life pounding the tops of staplers and now they have gotten their revenge.

There is a long scar that runs perpendicular to the stylish "bikini" cut used for my C-section. I lifted my shirt to show him how well the purple incision was healing and he said, "A work of art. It's a work of art." I flashed on Picasso's *Demoiselles* and believed that Dr. Imbaralu was right.

The Real Stories

What makes me the maddest about having cancer is the idea that I'm supposed to think and feel in a certain way. For example, everyone says, "Be positive!" All the books and articles talk about how what I *believe* can make me well and I get furious because I do not feel positive. I feel scared. I feel vulnerable and out of control. When did it start? How did I get cancer? I'm too young. What will happen? No matter how many New Age gurus tell me to *bathe my inner-self in a yellow purifying light,* I still have cancer.

After my surgery, my Aunt Ethel sent me a book called "Chicken Soup for the Surviving Soul." It made me want to bang my head against the wall and dye my hair purple. It was full of "inspirational" stories about people who had survived cancer: the man who had a barbecue which gave him the will to live; the kid who told Knock-Knock jokes about being bald.

I felt like writing a book called "I Have Cancer and It Really Sucks!"

It pisses me off, because the one thing these 'positive thinkers' never tell you is that before you can *choose life* you have to come face to face with the very difficult fact that you may die.

I couldn't talk about death until Christmas Eve when my husband and I were finally alone. We had poured ourselves each a glass of delicious red wine after the baby had fallen asleep, but the minute I sat down on the green pillow and looked into the tiny lights on the tree my vision began to blur. I was afraid to mention dying. Afraid, because every book and person we knew did not mention it. I watched the lights refract and shimmer. Because we had not openly discussed it, I thought about it more and more. Each time the thought of death passed into my mind, it was like trying to capture a stray cat with a pillowcase. The more I chased it, the weaker I got and the more vicious it became.

Finally I blurted, "You know, I could die." Jeff nodded his head and leaned against me. "I don't want to say it, but it's true. I don't want to die, but

I could and I won't and..."

"I know," he whispered. "I've thought it too." Then he looked away from me which made talking about it easier for both of us.

"I'm not going to die. I swear I'm not. I just have a feeling I won't and that baby needs me. I won't die, I promise."

Then he took both my hands and held them against his heart, "You promise?"

The Stuff

My delivery arrived and a nice man in a striped uniform with an embroidered name tag, Bill, set the big box on the dining room table. Every time I walked through the room I looked at it, re-read the label, shook it just a little, peeled the corners of the brown packing tape, hoping it might accidentally tear so I could peek in. This was the nurse's stuff and even though I knew what was inside, I couldn't help but get excited. It's some sort of Pavlovian reaction to parcels.

Lots of equipment comes with cancer. I have a chemo-port implanted just beneath my collarbone. A long IV tube is attached on one end to a needle that goes into the port. The other end is connected to the bag of chemo which is inside the pump I wear around my waist. The pump makes a funny Terminator type of noise that startles my daughter. She'll cock her head and look puzzled. We laugh. I prefer continuous infusion of the chemo to having to sit for treatments in a hospital. So now, I'm my own Sloan-Kettering.

The nurse comes to flush my line. One thing I have learned is that medical people lie about pain. They don't mean to, but never believe it when you know something should hurt and your doctor says that it won't—it will. The thing about pain is that you adjust to it. The more pain you have, the greater your tolerance. Things that once hurt me I no longer even notice. My chronic lower back pain, for example, has miraculously disappeared or perhaps the surgery just caused a shift in the pain continuum.

I still can't stand to get injections or get blood drawn. It doesn't really hurt, but I want to cry like a baby every time the nurse swabs the skin on my arm with a cold alcohol prep. By the time she says, "You'll feel a little pinch," I'm holding my breath.

The nurse digs in her big box of stuff. It contains a biohazard disposal jug, a biohazard clean up kit, a box of 9-volt batteries, some latex gloves (which I steal for cleaning), a box of alcohol preps, a couple of syringes, some heparin, some saline, and a few other little goodies. When she unwraps a new needle, I never look. It hurts when she changes the needle in my port, but what gets to me is the peeling off of the large, clear tape that covers it. After the surgery big pains are not so big; it's the constant small pains that keep reminding me that I have cancer. The skin pulls and then the port pulls on the muscle that it's stitched to. It feels like everything rips a little. I close my eyes and see streaks of white light.

She hooks me up after a flush of the line and a draw of blood from the port. She always says things like "A good return from the port," or "the port looks good" and I can't help but think of little ships aimlessly spinning in a harbor. For a moment, all I can see is royal blue ocean and tiny, white sails. Then she peels the latex gloves off her hands with a snap, washes up and cheerily says, "See you next Monday."

The pump spins and the chemo begins again.

The Side Effects

My doctor seemed to think I wouldn't get many side effects from the chemo but I'll list out the possibilities that I've read: nausea, vomiting, fatigue, hair loss, mouth sores, skin rashes, blisters, swollen fingers and toes, blood in the urine, blood in the stool, and in rare cases leukemia. You really have to wonder about a cure whose side effect could be leukemia. I asked Dr. Lee about the symptoms for leukemia and she said there are none. You just get sick one day. I know what that's like. One day you're drinking a beer and the next day you have cancer.

I have mouth sores and blisters on my nose. I'm losing my hair. But these aren't the side effects that bother me the most. It's the ones that aren't listed anywhere because they are my own personal reactions. I cannot tell the doctor that my eyes feel smaller or my body smells different. I smell tinny and harsh as if I have absorbed the air of the chemicals, the hospitals, the laboratories, the waiting rooms.

But I don't vomit or feel too tired and I can still take care of my daughter. I can still lift her up and tickle her, I can still wash her hair and make it into a unicorn with the lather, I can still read her *Dr. Seuss's ABC.*

"Big C…little c…what begins with C? Camel on the ceiling," I read aloud to her and to myself I think, Cancer in your colon, C. . .C…C. But I read the small board book to her over and over, keeping my joke inside. She turns the pages and when I'm finished she takes the book away for a moment so she can hand it back to me. When I hold her warm body, I feel the true heat of healing. All of this helps me more than anything. More than green tea, more than positive thinking, more than chemo, more than prayer, more than hope.

Begging

I have a talk show on the television and one of the hostesses just announced that Katie Couric's husband has died of colon cancer. Age: 42. And it all starts again. I can't believe it. My mind is wild. I could die. I won't die. He probably had the best doctors in the world and I have managed health care. I am 38. Did he die in the hospital? How did Katie Couric explain it to their two-year-old? Are his clothes still hanging in the closet? How does she sleep in the empty bed? What stage was his cancer? It must have been worse than mine. Why couldn't they save him? Did the chemo not work? He had his surgery in July and I start counting months. Didn't his friends and family pray for him too? I don't want to die, yet I could die, but I won't die. I can't die.

I'll eat right, I'll quit drinking alcohol, I'll do volunteer work, I'll be a better person. I'll do everything right. I won't touch that kiwi, I'll drink tons of water. Please, God, my daughter, she's so little. Please, please, please.

DARLENE MONTONARO

ULTRASOUND

This is what I see—
the shoals and rills
of moonscape, a cratered
valley littered
with imperfect stones.
Like an astronomer
I mark the territory
more awe than fear.
The frowning doctor
scans this aerial view,
finger tracing a dark sky
flung with stars.

I want to tell him
that I come by these scars
heroically. Every garden
has weeds, every life
its shadow that—
when illuminated— holds
its own dark beauty.

This is why I spurn
the smooth, weathered
surface of stones, search
instead the ley lines
of what lives beneath.
Scientists say
stone is always changing—
(though we don't believe it)—
that every object
holds within the seeds

of its own death.
Tonight I watch the moon
drag its shadow,
its cragged face spilling
silver light. I think of Coyote,
Navaho Trickster, his eyes
wild with mayhem, who,
legend has it
hurls stars into the sky

as an act of creation.

HEART MUSIC

I.
A branch of lightning
dances across my chest,
and I imagine my lonely heart,
its sad sorrowful flutter, the rope
of scar that will remain
if they cut me. My hand slips
beneath the crease of buttons,
fabric, fingers the rise of breast-
bone, the cleft of smooth,
unbroken skin.

II.
At the hospital, I comb
my hair for the camera,
sit fluorescent on a cold sheet.
The tech (cold, unsmiling,
silver as flatware) dims the lights.
On screen, my heart—
the squish and pulse a sad melody.

III.
Ebb and flow, fingers pressed
against wrist, my clock heart drums
thin as paper. I listen
for frilly beats, lost ones that skip,
do St. Vitus' dance against my chest.
But today my heart
is straight backed, little nuns
lined one after the other
across the EKG sheet,
heads bowed,
penitent.

IV.
At home I pull leftover tomato stalks,
prune herbs, furrow under
summer earth. I take my paper bag
of bulbs and worry each hole—
apricot beauties, peony tulips, angeliques—
sift dirt fine as sand over each scarred cut.
In this season of dying, when what survives
must turn upon itself, I kneel in mud,
listen to the heated rhythm
of the earth, leave my mark
on next season, next year.

A SMALL INHERITANCE

I know you would hate dying
in this pool of white,
a room that smells
of alcohol and floor wax.
Too sterile for lungs
that raked the mines.
Sucked clean of color
like your hands, fistless
against starched white sheets.

I watch your life disintegrate,
bubble into tubes
drip from plastic bags.
I am almost alone.

Dad, do you realize
that you never called me by name
unless I did something wrong?
That cold steel voice
at the top of the stairs.
Now you are an airless whisper
and I shape your halting breath
into penitence, and strain
in the stillness for one last summons,
some small inheritance.

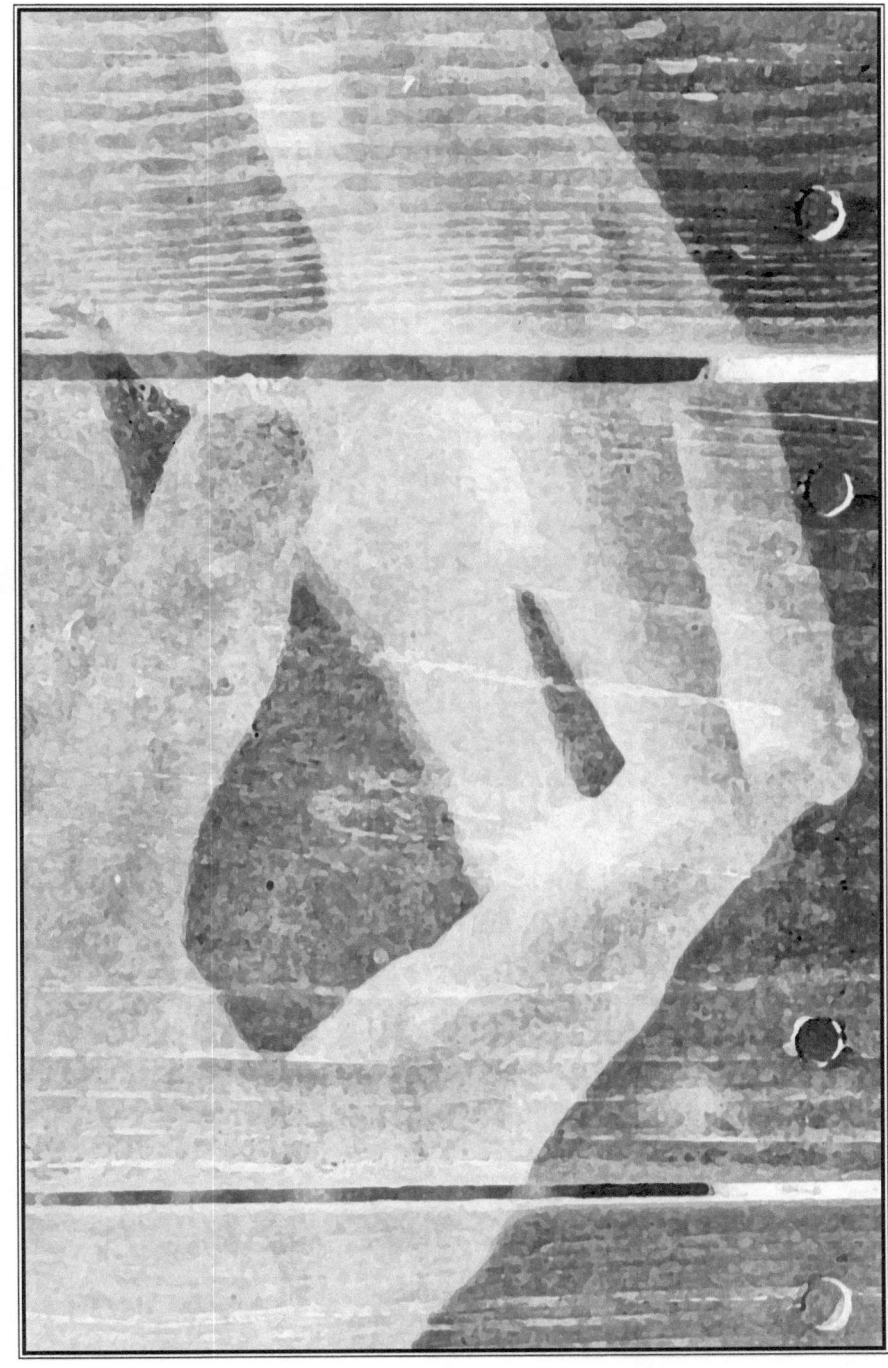

CINDA THOMPSON

TYPE I: ROOM 210

I can still see the inside of my own bare arm. The soft underside of the arm is stretched out in front of my face as I reach forward to try and catch another girl dancing out of my reach. Then the playground whirls in slow motion, and I fall.

Even before I woke out of the velvet dark of a coma in Memorial Hospital, Room 210, I'd somehow guessed what the condition "diabetic," meant. No matter many popular misconceptions, juvenile or Type I diabetes was not then, nor is it now, a diagnosis to be taken lightly. In the 1950's, I was only an eleven-year-old girl in a small town who could not understand why my parents, the doctors, and the nurses kept wasting their time in trying to console, lecture, or explain to me what I'd already understood in the waking. That my sentence was "for life," and the implication seemed to me to be a life that would now be different from all the rest. The rest being the apparently robust children with whom I'd been growing and thriving.

Before I woke up in Room 210 to the hush-hush opening and closing of elevator doors from across the hallway, I had attended my sixth grade class and been known as a good student. My biggest concern then was that I'd seemed to be losing my two best girlfriends. Rather plain, I'd had to struggle in order to keep up in the "looks department." Also a quiet girl, I'd had to work and play hard in order to keep myself even so much as noticed by these pretty girls who wore fluffy dresses with full skirts over "can-cans." These talkative girls growing into popular girls who were about to graduate into the seventh grade to find better friends, I'd been sure. On the day before I went into the hospital I can still remember being deliriously happy that I'd actually been able to acquire a boyfriend—not that the boy mattered to me so much as the fact that my girlfriends seemed again interested in me.

However, after I woke up in Room 210, my concerns became only two. The first being—why had I been singled out? There was hardly a diabetic in our whole town, much less anyone who was a juvenile diabetic, a child. There was no other child diabetic than me. More importantly I did not like what I thought people thought—that I'd been a bad child, one who ate too much candy! No, I decided that I did not care for this "being special." If not before, I now very definitely just wanted to be *like everybody else*. My minister, my parents, someone, everybody kept telling me that the God of my Sunday School classes was absolutely not angry with me, and that the same God never gave anyone more to carry than he or she could bear. An A-student, I did decide to be brave. I learned to give myself insulin shots daily. Indeed, my young life became a flood of syringes, needles, urine test strips, and alcohol swabs. Such gross and horrible things.

I could not help noticing that no one had asked me what I thought I could bear. When I was a child, the world of medicine was not what it purportedly is today. Back then, my doctors and my parents talked right over me in my bed, never asking me for a comment or question. No children, much less girl-children, went around then asking angry or inflammatory questions. Questions such as, "Why?" "Why not you?" "What have I done, or not done?" Or perhaps worse, "Does God have a mission for me? I don't get it, and I don't want it!" "Do you hear me? I don't want anything to do with God anymore!" I said this in silence.

My second big concern in Room 210 was the baby. The baby boy with whom I shared my hospital room cried endlessly. Alone in my room, but not alone, I gazed silently from my hospital bed over to his—over through the bars and into the bed in which his tiny body laid under an oxygen tent. I, myself, absolutely did not cry as I learned how to stick needles first into an orange, then into my own thighs, then my own stomach. However, the baby boy cried lustily. He screamed, and also, he coughed. The boy's mother and father took turns sitting with this child who'd been diagnosed with double pneumonia. The boy's mother, though, was surely not as old as I believed my own mother to be, and yet I reasoned she didn't look young—not with those dark circles under her eyes. And the baby's father, he couldn't be as old as my own father who still went to work everyday, while this man seemed to hang at the door of the room like a ghost.

I do not know now if I felt more concern for the baby in Room 210 or kinship. I do know that whenever the I.V. tubes were pulled from my own badly bruised arms and I could walk freely again, I'd wait until the boy's parents had drifted off to sleep or off down the hall to the nurse's station, and then I'd creep out of my own bed to stand over the baby's tiny body. Unlike my own, such a frail body caught in the murky, yellow light that shown through his oxygen tent. It was the boy's thinness that frightened me. He seemed so fragile. His tiny hands trembled when he coughed. His fingers curled. I, on the other hand, was strong. Of course, I was.

To this day, I've usually managed to block out memories of my own first trip to the Memorial Hospital's emergency room. I'd been told that the day I'd fallen on the playground, I'd actually struggled up and somehow gotten home from school. Then as my parents and even the doctor had thought I was still perhaps just fatigued from a recent case of the flu, I was sent to lie down on the sofa under the watchful eye of my father, ever intent on the T.V. news, while my mother fixed dinner. Only after I'd cried and pushed away not only my dinner, but my favorite—a chocolate milkshake, all the while complaining so about how my back ached, it hurt so bad—had I been rushed for a meeting with the our family doctor at the emergency room.

Then, I'd been surrounded by confusion in the emergency room— bright light everywhere, the fall of footsteps and voices calling, the clank of silver metal. I still hate the sound of clanking metal and bright light. I remembered in Room 210 how my own parents' faces had seemed so far off. Why, they were floating so far off, I, as their child, did not have to worry anymore about their fright, did I? What I remember now though is sound of my mother desperately crying, the sound of my father praying. The deep shadow that had become, to me, my parents' faces. Or has my memory made such things up? If so, why?

I have always remembered easily that the faces of the baby boy's parents had finally become happier. The two smiled tremulously as their baby began to grow stronger, as his tiny body became finally free of its filmy tent. Of course, back in Room 210, I did not really worry for my own parents well-being. They were all right by then, after all, because I had taken great, even grown-up pains, to reassure them. I told them clearly and more than once that I was all right. I would be fine. Never mind my real feelings, if I had to take shots every day, no problem. And no, nobody had to worry about me filching sweets or candy, a piece of pie or birthday cake. If "the authorities" said I couldn't have any, well—I wasn't weak, and I didn't want any. So there! I began to assure every adult with whom I came in contact— parents, neighbors, teachers—we would all go on exactly, exactly as we had before. Did they understand me? Except for the not eating sugar thing, we'd go on as before.

Now, I know I was experiencing a totally new feeling, a most unchildlike feeling. I actually felt sorry for my parents. To me, they seemed to need reassuring. "This thing" evidently simply must be made easier on them. They who very carefully did not blame each other, but themselves as a unit for "the condition that had befallen me". Our family doctor had assured my mother that no, no, it was not too much sugar in the diet that caused Type I diabetes. Perhaps it was an inherited trait, but no one really knew for sure yet. The doctor assured my parents that getting me to the hospital in time had saved the day as then the staff had be able to ease my blood sugar down, ever, ever so slowly. He stressed that my child's heart had been saved any lasting injury, any lasting weakness. In Room 210, I sensed somehow that I was not alone in asking why about life, why and what now.

That first time, I had to stay in the hospital for nearly a month. Again, the world of medicine not being quite what it is today, the doctor or staff wanted to get my blood sugars balanced, wanted to observe me. I grew stir crazy, bored and even disappointed when the baby boy was discharged and his uncle no longer visited. The boy's uncle had come sometimes to relieve the exhausted parents, and I'd grown interested when he'd informed me that he was a teacher, a teacher of children near my own age. In fact, the man said he'd have his students write letters to me. At first, I hated these letters as I felt I'd been "singled out" as the recipient *just because there was something wrong with me*. Of course, as the teacher was being so nice to me, so adult in his conversations, I could not bring myself to tell him to stop his students' unwanted attentions. Actually, I even began to enjoy the letters. Not their contents, so much as the individuality of each student's handwriting— sloped and awkward handwriting so like my own, yet not my own. Letters not only from another school, but from a whole other small town. Again, a small town like my own, but not my own. Letters from a world beyond my borders.

I took up my own pen and wrote. I wrote back. The point being, simply that I wrote. My hand moved quickly, as if feeling some desperate need to communicate. At the same time, I took to bargaining with God as it seemed to me that this writing thing could become very important, could become a bargaining chip. What I bargained was that if I had "my condition," for say, an interminable six months of daily shots and "gross" urine tests, or okay, for maybe even one whole year, could I not then use my knowledge, my experience to write a book. I promised God I'd write a book about a child with diabetes. A book to help people, I reasoned as if in God's presence. Surely then, I implored God, I could then again grow to be "well"?

The truth I was not about to tell anyone was that I felt I simply could not bear thoughts of my future. Not a future of no more chocolate cake, no more cookies and brownies. Not a future of shots and more shots, needles, blood and urine, and more needles. A future of high and low blood sugars dwindling down to blackouts and unconsciousness, true *panic*. Panic while friends stared in pity at me as I tried to glide unseen down the hall. Friends who hid sacks of candy behind their backs, and friends who apologized endlessly to me while they cut their respective birthday cakes. I dreaded a future in which I'd have to go around *confessing* my condition to all I met. Wouldn't I have to tell boyfriends too? No, I'd have to hide my syringes and needles. Only test my urine in deep and dark secret. I scrambled inside myself to throw up a wall around myself. A shield of calm. I wrote no one about this. Not only did I have a secret, I had no words.

A child from an isolated town, a girl child from whom "the usual" was expected—the usual being a husband and "healthy" babies, but even more, an easy smile and an uncomplicated attitude—just a child, I realized I was in quite a predicament. Why, girl children were not supposed to worry their "pretty little heads" at all. They were not supposed to worry about anything at all. Yet here I was, wandering around in my head already. I was wondering if I could carry off this "life thing" at all. I hated being a diabetic. Therefore, I hated my life. Couldn't we call the whole thing off?

The death of a child occurred while I lay in the hospital. That hush-hush sound of the elevator door opening and closing across the hall from Room 210 is forever the sound I will associate with her memory. Not that I was supposed to see the girl or hear her story at all—the story about which all the nurses, aides, and even my own parents, buzzed. This particular little girl, it seemed, had evidently been beaten to death. I strained to hear details, but all I gleaned was fragmented talk of ropes and kerosene oil. Of blistering. Evidently, the girl had been beaten to death by her own parents. Beaten or burned. In the whole of my short life, I'd never heard of such brutality. Never.

I can still hear that elevator door opening and closing. I've crept from my late-night bed to peek through the crack in my door, and I hear the man from the funeral home telling my mother that he's come to "collect" the girl. The voice says that now, at least, the child's pain will be over. Her "final journey" can begin. As the gurney is pulled back into the elevator, I glimpse a bare, outstretched arm. A bruised arm. The inside of my own bare arm is bruised purple from wrist to elbow due to intravenous feeding and blood testing. I run back to bed before anybody catches me.

Finally, I am discharged from Room 210. My blood levels "balanced," I am released back into life in the sixth grade. To what I've insisted to all will be no more and no less than a perfectly "normal" life. True to my word, I think I act outwardly "the same." My two girlfriends and I steal one of the encyclopedia carts and take rides up and down the hall. My life hurtles toward a new school year, a new school. However, my concentration on boys, the use of makeup, and my own popularity seems at times disturbed. I do not know if I knew then that it was I who left my girlfriends behind. What I knew was that I was not the same.

Whether I admitted it or not, I had become a different person. A child no longer wholly a child, and in fact, one who felt and still often feels very separate from others—someone who feels as if some important part of herself is forever stealing away from her own body in order to observe family, friends, a town, a whole world. Decades later, one part of me can still see another who lay in a hospital bed, the elevator door hush-hushing outside, while she scrawled one word only in large capital letters across the first line of a new notebook.

WISDOM. I have no idea how this word entered into my childish vocabulary, but I guess I'd hoped, even as a child, that if I found wisdom, I'd have some sort of remedy or answer to all I now felt as pain. Maybe I'd at least have some answers to all of my whys. Until recently, I'd never wanted to return to the subject of Room 210, Memorial Hospital because there, I now know I felt robbed of my childhood. Before Room 210, I'd not dwelt on even the possibility that there were difficult, perhaps unanswerable questions in life. In Room 210, though, I became the A-student without the answers. Years later, after a lifetime of learning and unlearning, I can still only change the period I put after the word in my child's notebook to a question mark. WISDOM? Could it have, can it ever really help? Or is it simply what we hope will grow up around our pain, our difference.

A formerly unconscious child "came to" in Room 210—not so much seriously ill as seriously wondering. Why pain, why fragility and why suffering? And why did death feel closer now? I even began to question everybody's "good intentions." Why "the fuss," such "a stew" all around me? The child in Room 210 awakening from the velvet dark of a coma not-so-simply, and rather too suddenly, simply came "of age." However, at this point in her life, she had no words to express or describe the sudden deep river she felt sweeping through her. The might-be-meanings of my "diagnosis" seemed beyond me. Indeed, I began to toy with the concept of "meaning" altogether. Meanwhile, the whisper of elevator doors opening and closing to shafts of light, shafts of dark gave me a rhythm for "recovery," and one day I bolted from my bed to run through them. To be carried down to the outside world. The world as I'd known it, now on some other level.

As an adult, I sometimes feel haunted, and in fact, I've had to learn to stop "the garble." Doors open. They close. Doors breathe open, and though a human being be wounded to the root by shaft after shaft of darkness, or wave after wave of living, that same human child, for no foreseeable reason and with no recognizable path, can rise to live raggedly on. To grow toward the light. Now there's the miracle.

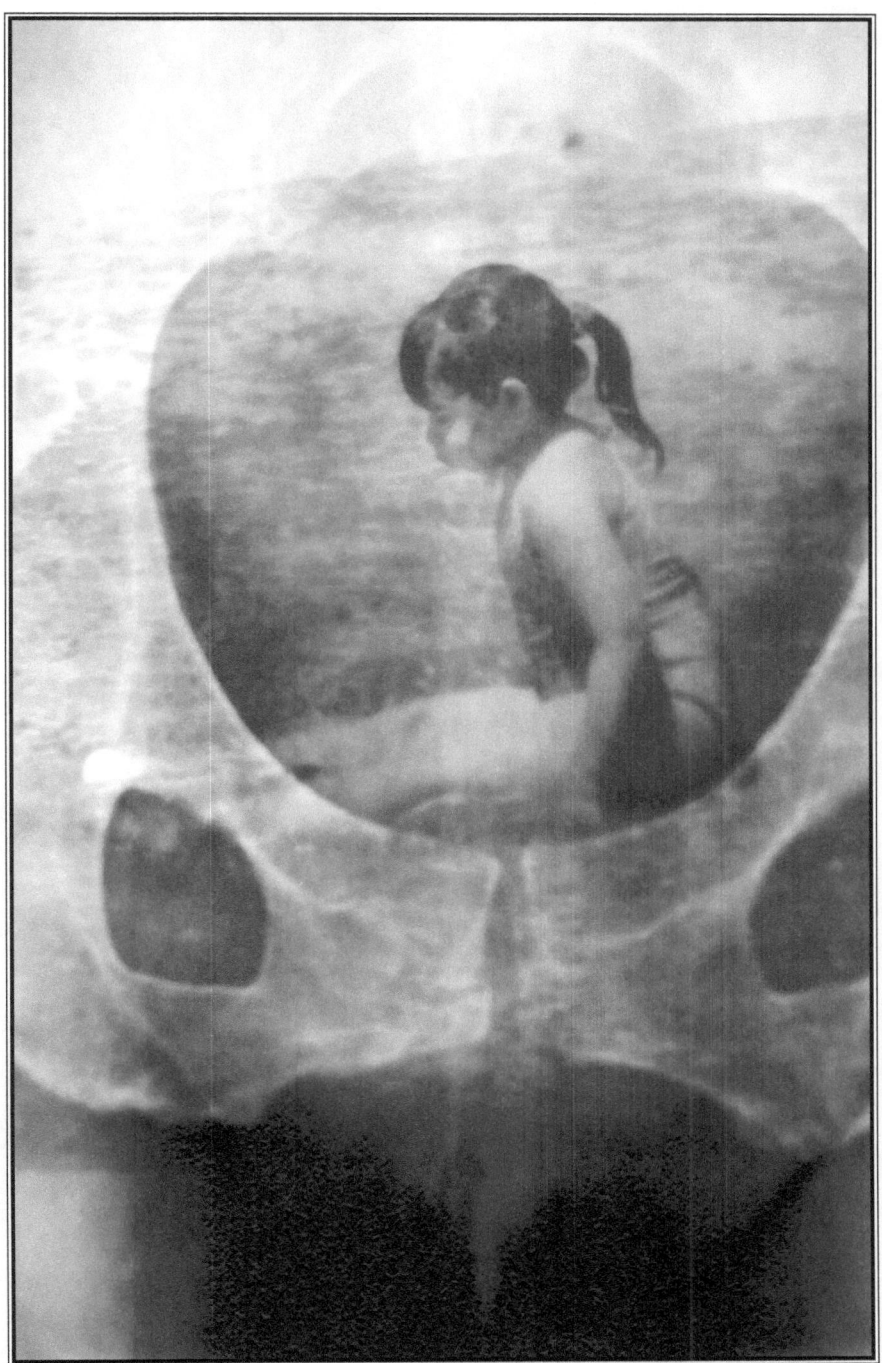

CAROL V. DAVIS

THIS ILLNESS, THIS CHILDHOOD

What will you remember from childhood?
Propping up your small body last night
as the sky cracked with midnight rain
mask slipping down your chin, mist
escaping as you cry with exhaustion,
your chest concave as aluminum siding
flapping in a desert wind.
It's no consolation to name those worse off
racked with diseases more deadly than this
when I can line up the medicines
from one end of the house to the other
like a dancer who crosses stage on pointe.
All three of you, before you could walk,
yielding to coughs and ungodly whistles
as if possessed by a *dybbuk** wrapped
around your lungs and squeezing.
By the time you came I knew what to expect,
though foolishly hoped the girl would be spared
(boys twice as likely to succumb).
Your brothers lead the way
like Moses crossing the Red Sea.
Each Passover we reenact this journey
as I did with you: recognizing the signs
in first cough, first infection.
They'll grow out of it people say
and I nod, without strength to disagree.
You'll carry the scars in your lungs
like a memory of childhood poverty
the wicked seed lying in wait.

* a wandering soul (in Jewish folklore) that enters and controls a living body

ILLNESS

To have your breath confiscated,
something you always took for granted.
The easy in and out, obstructed only by
surprise or full passion that sweeps through
the body, suppressing all normal function.

It is as if your lungs turn to soft sand,
where, on some obscure holiday, villagers sweep
down from the hillside to perform ritual dances
under the night sky and partially realized moon.

Or as if a pogrom had finally struck big city
America, as your grandmother always feared,
her packed suitcase kept hidden under her bed
and giving her daughters names no one could
possibly mistake for Jewish.

And now it all comes back.
The fear of nighttime knocking, never experienced,
but circulating in the blood like some gene
gone bad, the questions that linger
in the dark spots behind the eyes.
What we thought we had, now taken away,
so abruptly, so brutally.

MARY V. DAVIDSON

THE BIRTHMARK
For Julia

"You didn't tell me, Mom," chides Julia,
my third-born springtime child,
"that the needle would stay in *long*. . ."

Eyeing the week-old scar that wraps around her tiny leg,
her eyes, cloudy still with pain and doubtful memory,
she numbs me to silence for my well-meaning but certain betrayal.

"You said it wouldn't hurt so *long*."

She's assumed I would know such medical facts
as well as I know the name of her favorite stuffed toy,
the day of the next full moon,
when we'll make chocolate-covered strawberries,
where she's abandoned her other new sandal.

Disappointed in me, she perches on the kitchen window sill,
her post-op pain judged even now by its duration,
not its intensity;
the length of the scar on her calf,
not its permanence there.

I feel my bones' marrow tremble;
I skip a breath.

Later, Julia chuckles at her "new leg,"
displays the stitches' trace to her friends
as though she were her own doll,
the operation a rainy-day diversion she's invented,
the scar a tattoo she's drawn upon herself.

But in the night, alone in her big bed,
she brushes the spot tenderly
as I sometimes touch it myself,
fingering the place where the birthmark once was,
aching deep inside for its irrevocable disappearance.

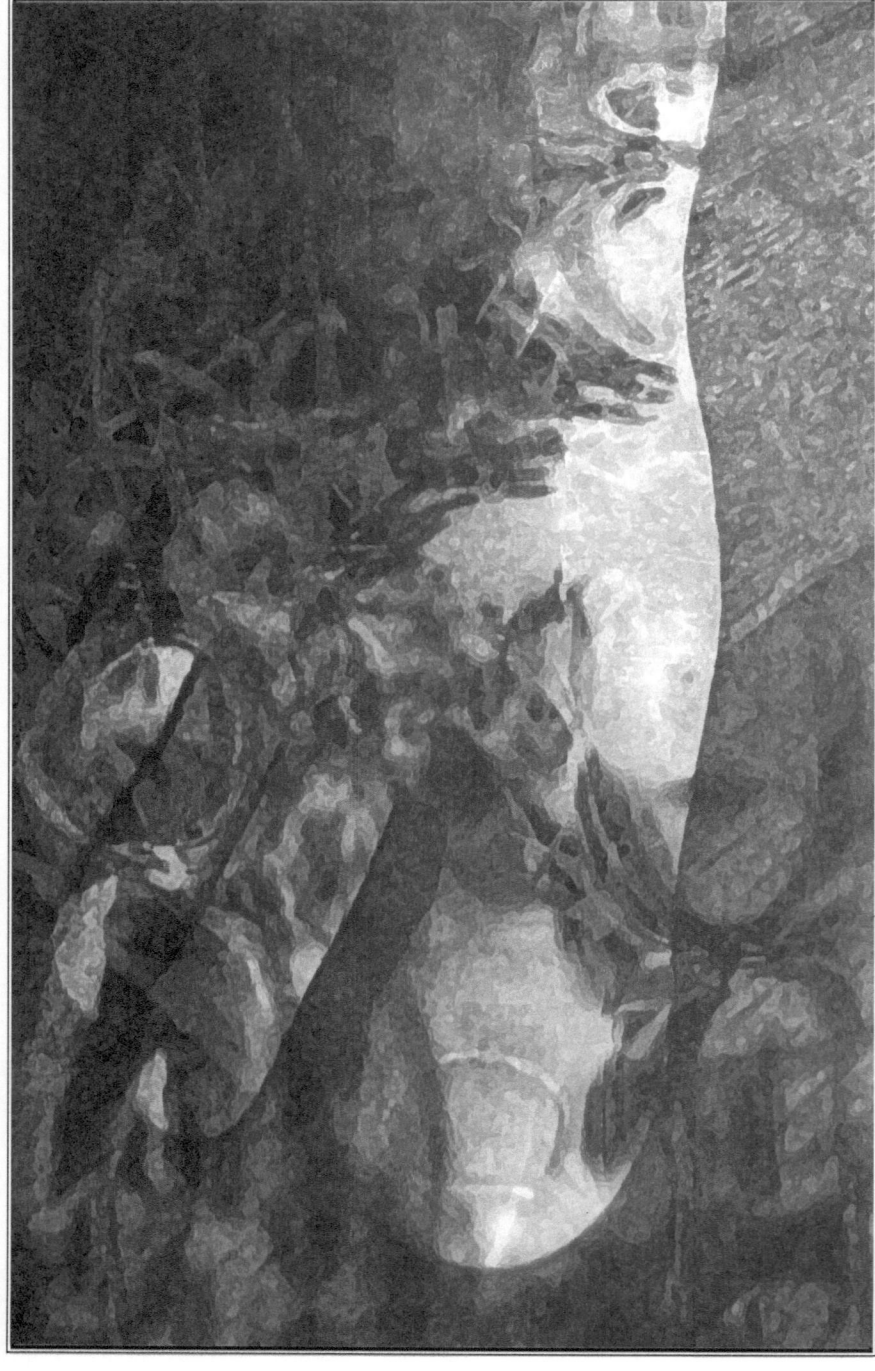

MICHAEL ONOFREY

RAIN

Tapping at the glass and drizzling down. Dark outside. Jack propped up on a hospital bed with a window to his left. The rain calms him, relaxes him, takes him away and makes him think of other things. Not necessarily pleasant things, but somehow comforting, as if Jack were part of a bigger picture.

His wife left an hour ago. She had to take the bus and then the train and then have a friend pick her up at the station. Jack thinks about her on the platform, wind blowing, rain coming down, December-twenty-sixth rain. He hopes she isn't having too much of a problem with it, but at the same time Jack is thankful for the rain. He sees the platform. He sees the overhead. He sees rain slanting in from the side. He sees rain on the streets and cars splashing through it.

With his head turned he watches and listens. Indifferent pitter-patter, eddies of moisture on glass. The pain pill did something but not enough. They told him that there wouldn't be another pill for eight hours. Until 2 AM.

A modern hospital in central Japan, farmland surrounding it, a town not too far away, competent physicians and nurses, everyone kind, excellent facilities, four people to a room, two beds with window views, two beds without, curtains separating patients, central heating, temperature comfortable, a plastic bottle of mineral water within Jack's reach.

Jack thinks about his mother, thinks about her pain, thinks about his witnessing it for the two years he took care of her before she died in a hospital in Los Angeles. Pain and old age, how could he have understood it until now?

The nurse said to use the buzzer if he had to go to the toilet. She'd help him get out of bed and make the journey. Each four-patient room has a toilet just past the sliding doors of the room. It isn't far. Is Jack feeling something, some pressure? Perhaps he has to urinate. But that's how the pain began—pressure as the anesthesia wore off, as the lower half of his body came back to life, as he wiggled his toes and raised a leg while everyone watched.

He buzzes for the nurse and she comes. She stands next to his bed and watches as he struggles to bring his legs over the side of the bed, an IV connected to his left arm, a plastic bag of fluid hanging from a steel hook, a movable metal tree with a handle. Jack slips his feet into his slippers. He stands and feels his legs, weakness and strength. He straightens the surgical gown. The nurse watches. He pushes the IV tree in front of himself. The going is slow but he's moving. The nurse watches. He enters the restroom and closes the sliding door and then stands before a toilet. The nurse waits outside. There's pressure but he can't pee. He stands. He feels pain. He's surprised to be standing. He's surprised to be walking. Pain. He understands that it's part of the deal. He wants to tell himself that it's only pain but he knows that that's bullshit because pain has its own dimensions, which are always current. On a scale of one to ten, seven is only seven until fifteen is discovered. It feels like someone has stuck a knife in his right-side-middle about three inches above where his right leg meets his crotch. He thinks about the nurse standing outside. He thinks about her waiting. He urges himself to pee but nothing moves.

Jack opens the door and goes out and tells the nurse that he couldn't urinate. He knows he is supposed to report urination and bowel movements because he has heard the nurses asking the other three men in the room about these things. The nurse nods. Jack starts back to his bed. The nurse follows. When Jack's in bed he asks the nurse if he has to buzz her again if he has to go to the bathroom. Both Jack and the nurse understand that Jack has made this initial trek unaided. She says he doesn't have to, but if he thinks he needs her he can buzz.

Rain against the window, rain tapping at his senses, rain drizzling over his thoughts. He dozes.

At 2 AM he goes to the restroom and urinates. At 3 AM he makes a return trip and urinates again. At 3:10 he buzzes for the nurse and asks for a pain pill.

The day nurse, the one who mostly attends to him, is helping two other nurses push Jack's bed along a corridor. Jack's wife is hurrying to keep up. They turn a corner and then turn another corner. The ceiling is whizzing by. The nurse pushing the bed near Jack's head asks if he is nauseous. The thought's crossed his mind, but no, he isn't nauseous. And then the hurrying stops at an elevator, everyone standing around. When the elevator doors open Jack says good-bye to his wife.

Down four floors while stopping at each floor, staff entering and exiting with machines. It's a short roll from the elevator to where automatic doors open, first one small room and then another set of doors to another room. This room exudes serious business. As it turns out, it's a transfer room. Jack's bed is raised and he is told to roll onto his side. A plank slips under him and he's told to roll onto his back. Like a piece of cake slipping from one plate to another with a spatula, Jack is transferred onto a table and then shuffled onto another bed, which turns out to be a hard gurney. The IV is transferred and a blue puffy hat put on his head, a pillow shoved under his head. Another set of doors open and he's moving.

This is it. Jack can tell by the lights. A cluster of lights that somehow resemble the lights in a football stadium. A switch is thrown and the lights come on. Jack is under the lights, his body the focus of attention. Everyone in the room is young. Jack is the oldest person.

Jack is told to roll onto his right side. Then he's told to bring his legs up. He understands that he's to get into a fetal position. There is a woman with a mask and a blue cap and she is right next to Jack's head and she tells him what is going to happen and what is happening. She also tells him that everything is okay. She holds him while his back is swabbed three times. A man with a beard tells Jack that they are going to put a thin needle in his back. And they do. They put it in his spine. It doesn't hurt much. More than anything, it's the idea that hurts.

Jack is told to lie on his back and straighten his legs, which they help him with because funny things are already happening to his legs. There is a rush of warmth that borders on hot that spreads downward from his thighs. The man with the beard asks Jack if his legs are warm. Jack says they are. The bearded man says that's good.

A small towel is hoisted in front of Jack's face so that he can't see what's going on below. He can look up and he can look to the side. He can hear and see and speak. His arms and his head have mobility, but his arms are loosely strapped to supports that extend out from the gurney. His posture is that of a man on a cross, left arm with an IV, right with a belt around it that contracts and deflates slowly as if his blood pressure were being taken. There is a beeping sound in the room. A regular beeping sound with space between beeps. Jack wonders if it has anything to do with his heartbeat. A woman swipes at his shoulder with a piece of gauze that is cold. Perhaps it's soaked in alcohol. The woman asks Jack if it's cold. He says it is. She swipes his waist with the gauze and asks the same question. By the third time Jack can't feel anything at his waist. Jack is told that they are removing his jockey shorts.

Jack's doctor leans over the towel and looks at Jack and says that they are beginning. The doctor's face disappears.

Jack smells burning flesh.

The lights come on. It's dark outside. The rain has stopped. A few headlights move on a road in the distance. Jack looks at his wristwatch. It's 6 AM.

The day nurse shows up and records his temperature, blood pressure, and looks at the incision. She smiles and tells Jack that everything is fine. She's in her mid to late twenties.

The other men in Jack's room are served breakfast but breakfast doesn't show up at Jack's bed. The nurse apologizes because there's been a mix up. Jack's breakfast is in the dining room down the hall. The nurse will fetch it for him. Jack asks if it's okay for him to walk to the dining room and eat. The nurse's face brightens. She says that's fine.

As Jack shuffles down the hall there's pain all through his lower belly and crotch. He's got his IV tree alongside, his slippers on, and his surgical gown on. No one pays him any mind. In spite of the pain Jack finds himself buoyed by this meager excursion. He's mobile and that somehow spells independence, and perhaps recovery.

When Jack reaches the dining room he shows his plastic wristband to a middle-aged woman behind a high counter. She places Jack's breakfast tray on the counter. She asks Jack if he can manage. Jack tests the weight of the tray with his one hand and says that he can manage. The woman watches as Jack makes his way to a table. There are other patients in the room. Two of them have IVs, but Jack is the only one with a surgical gown. The others are in pajamas. When the IV comes out of Jack's arm in the afternoon he'll attempt pajamas. That's what the nurse told him. Most of the patients having breakfast in the dining room are men. Two are women. All are Jack's age or older. The room is spacious, plenty of tables and chairs, a view toward the west.

After Jack has set his breakfast tray down on a table he makes his way to a vending machine. He's brought a change purse with him. He buys a cup of instant coffee and returns to his table. He drinks his coffee slowly. When he's finished with his coffee he starts in on his breakfast—fish, rice, miso, a small carton of milk.

On the way back to his room from the dining room, Jack stops at the nurses' station and writes his name on one of the two whiteboards that are on the counter. He schedules himself for the bath/shower room for five o'clock. There are two bath/shower rooms. Jack signs up for room number two. His allotted time is thirty minutes. According to the nurse, a shower is on Jack's list of things to do. Jack prefers showering before dinner, but he can see from the whiteboards that most of the patients prefer to bathe after dinner.

Back in bed, the idea strikes Jack that he'll keep his surgical gown on until he takes a shower. The IV will be out by then. He'll change into his pajamas in the shower room. He'll also shave in there. Jack has a lot on his agenda. He feels tired. He arranges his body to where there's the least pain. He falls asleep.

His wife is upstairs sleeping. It's eight in the morning. Jack's watching wind-driven snow as it races down from the sky, a cup of coffee in hand, a sliding glass door in front of him. His recovery is measured in action—what he's able to do. Each day it's more.

But the pain. It lessens each day. Its area shrinks. But it's not a steady decline. It's up and down throughout the day and night. In addition there's a new kind of pain that began the night after the operation. It originates where his shoulders meet his neck. It feels like two clamps tightening, one on each side of his neck. It's not all the time. It's only sometimes, but when it occurs the clamps keep tightening. Pain goes up his neck and into his head. It causes a headache. The doctor told him to lie down and put his head on a pillow and that will help. And it does. And so do the pain pills that he has brought home from the hospital. This pain is a side effect from the anesthesia. Jack supposes it will go away in a couple of days, but he doesn't suppose all the pain will go away. He's too old to suppose that. He's fifty-nine years old.

Inguinal hernia, the most common variety of hernia, not a big deal. Minor surgery can correct it. Actually, it's the only thing that can correct it. It's billed as a walk in the park. But for Jack it's a rather strange park, one with twists and turns.

Jack sips his coffee and watches the snow. He's glad it's snowing. He's glad he's out of the hospital. Three nights was enough—one night before the operation, two nights after. He couldn't wait to get out. When he walked out the doors downstairs it felt as though he had gained his freedom, a bird let loose from a cage. He was so happy, so fundamentally happy—brisk air at his face, sky overcast, his wife at his side. Yet there was something else, for at certain times during his hospitalization he had thought that he might not get out. When they were putting that needle in his spine thoughts were pinging around inside his head like errant electrons. Minor surgery, a simple operation. Done thousands, perhaps millions of times annually. Yet Jack knew that there were no guarantees. But he also knew that the numbers were on his side, and that's what he kept coming back to—numbers. They eased his doubt, eased his fear. He slipped into a statistic. But statistics were only numbers, numbers that describe chance. The numbers were well in his favor and he was aware of it. Yet numbers do not define an individual. They offer a handle; they offer a degree of assurance; they offer a way of getting through the tough parts. And something more. Numbers and their correlations create a logic that is so prevalent that it's become belief. At the beginning all Jack had was a bump in the area of his right, lower abdomen, no pain, no restriction of movement, no interruption of bodily function. He felt fine, or at least normal. What led him to the hospital and then to the operating table was belief, belief in statistics, numbers, and percentages—people with hernias and all the operations that corrected them. But at the same time the skin of this belief became transparent while they were slipping that needle into his vertebra. Once Jack was behind the skin of this belief he was left with two things—chance, and himself. Numbers and percentages describe chance, and chance became a gamble when Jack stepped into those numbers. In turn, gamble forced Jack to be alone with himself. No matter how much support he had, and there was plenty, and no matter how powerful the statistics, Jack was alone in this. This was his experience, an experience his body would deal with in its own individual way. Pain was evidence of this truth.

Snow falling, wind blowing, two sheets of glass separating him from that weather. The room is warm, a hardwood floor beneath his slippers. His thoughts linger. They linger at the doors of the hospital, for when he was leaving he was not only struck by his newfound freedom, but he was also struck by the sight of people streaming into the hospital while he was walking out. He was so happy to be on his way home, yet he couldn't help but to notice that most of the people entering that hospital were his age or older—another glaring statistic, another set of numbers.

Snow builds on the ground, a couple of inches on the wooden deck abutting Jack's house. Jack's two cats are clamoring at his feet. They want out. Jack pulls the sliding glass door back. Cold air rushes in through the gap. The cats shy. Then they put their noses to the air and work up their courage. The one goes out, a tentative paw on the snow. The paw sinks through the snow to where it finds purchase on a wooden step. The cat's face is all screwed up with curiosity and hesitancy, but now a wedge of familiarity enters its furry countenance. It brings a second paw over the threshold. The second cat wants out as well, its body rubbing up against the first cat, who now takes a step down by testing the snow on the deck proper. In short order both cats are on the deck, each high-stepping in an animated expression of dislike. They are on their way to the steps that lead to the yard. They look like puppets on strings, marionettes. Jack starts laughing. Pain knifes through his body. He stops laughing, his one hand going to his abdomen. Laughing, sneezing, blowing his nose, coughing—all painful.

The cats are at the steps of the deck and they are descending, wind tweaking their fur. They slither off the sides of the steps to the ground and quickly disappear under the deck.

Jack closes the sliding glass door and stands, snow falling, wind blowing.

ADELE STEINER

FEVER HEALING

You offer to say a prayer for me,
but I don't know what prayer is.

I hear no words, only sounds your voice makes.
It quivers and shakes as if afraid

of its own rising, and I know that you
are frightened by heights: The farther

you distance yourself from the earth,
the more aware you become of its turning,

of time passing and your inability
to slow either of them down.

Heights place you face to face with your
other fear too—falling toward the ground

at speeds high enough to skin your elbows
knuckles, or knees because flesh in those

places grows so thin over bone that
it tears whether you shake your fist or

flail the full length of your limbs against
the wind. So, you tend to your old wounds

instead: Your hands rub the bruises hard
enough to let you know that each new pain

they bring cancels out the old and that
pain-on-pain makes a balm. I can feel it

in your fingers the moment they reach out
and begin to stroke the side of my face.

From the tip of my brow, past one eye,
and along the jawbone to the center

of my chin, your fingers follow the same
path over and over again until

they wear it deep and wide enough for me
to rest my head in, close my eyes, and sleep.

TELEOLOGY
(For Kevin)

The tumor weighs on that part of your brain
controlling emotions, but it doesn't hold
them in. Releasing them, instead, it's like

your hand when it squeezes blood from its
fingers back up your arm so you can make
a tight white fist, a wrecking ball with

enough swing in it to throw a punch and
destroy your pain. It comes as no surprise
then when you ask for your morning slice

of toast burned and milk from a bottle so cold,
cream thrusts its back up against the lid. Pouring
smooth over your bread, it proves in one swallow

that healing is possible before breakfast:
It's then you can catch a glimpse of the mummer's
moon dragging the back of one hand over

water to slow its departure. When all five
fingers reach down, they stir the deepest
oceans up into waves. Frothing and

spiraling out, they wash up on distant
shores and wear down their hard edges until
only lands' insides are exposed: Soft

and new enough to give in to rushing
rip tides, they embrace the water, and
learn through bending, that they are still

able to corner the undertows, turn
each treacherous pull in on itself, and
leave it to spin round and round in eddies.

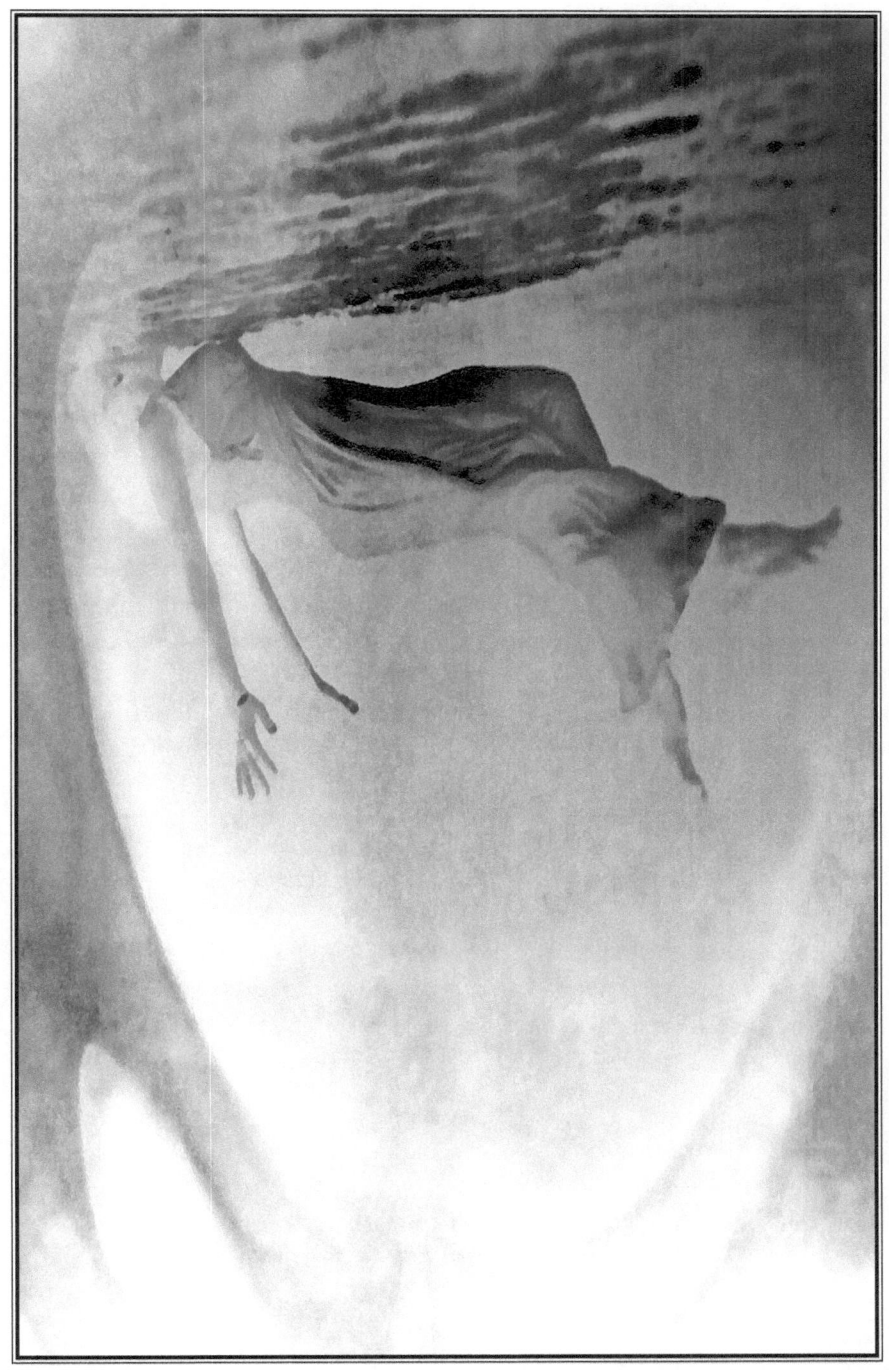

MERRY SPEECE

SICK

When I close my eyes, a pink angora sweater in a landfill, a creepy thought.

I've been lying here a long time. In this bed where I have, through the years, turned adversity to my pajamas. Every morning when I wake, I ask, what will a new day bring? A newspaper. Besides *that*. No, just a newspaper.

So in the early hours I lie in bed longing for the day's newspaper. My energy reserves in thimblefuls, I hoist one up and rise for the news. At the front door's the paper, and in the sky my moon's still there. Moon, when are you ever going to help?

I step back from the door, the morning, and the world. My hip joint gives. So, it's one of *those* days, when a leg doesn't want to stay in the socket.

Back to bed. Now :

> Housed. Laid down inside.
> Sharpening stone in dull water.
> Or—No. 0 biscuit in its slot.

I take up the paper. The sentences of the newspaper swim, the news washes over me. Other people's lives. Humanity.

Lay it down, all too much, to rest.

And now for the Poetry Minute, about all we can stand.

Timepiece

Look at the little clock that's been
Fucked to death.
Wind-up watch, pocket watch, body heat.
In the desert, I am Dali's, not upright.

If only I could get a message to Emily Dickinson through that messenger boy God. That's what I do as I lie in bed. Think of my pretend friends. Right into the future I chase Cesar Vallejo trying to make him wear a condom.

Welcome

> *Death*
> *the boy unrolls the long white condom for me*

When the phone rings, it is, as I figured, my daily wrong number. People try, day after day, to reach Human Services. I'm glad enough to hear a human voice, and yet how anxious and baffled and ashamed the poor sound caught trying to go on relief. If it weren't for the grudging support of next of kin, I could be one of those calls myself, and I could dial wrong just as easily as anyone and get my own busy signal.

I used to have a beau, and he called. That was so long ago, however, I can hardly remember. It was another life.

And yet—I still love him. And I might be able to say just how much if only I had that *Software Classic* MATH RABBIT.

> Your promise to me was
> the Krispy Kreme Promise.
> I could always count on you
> for freshness.

To him I used to write the most passionate letters. But I gave up writing when I couldn't do it, too much in love, without getting that telltale sore throat on the right side.

> *Double my grief*
> *Like a wedding*
> *like Death the Bride*
>
> *I feel as if*
>
> *once I held a sack*
> *of grain*
> *and spilled the seed*
> *and we both sagged down*

Love for me in the millefiori.

To be honest, a man did call for me—what was it?—two weeks ago? Woke me from a dream. It was the loveliest dream of my beloved kissing my fingertips and opening my palms to his lips and then down the insides of my wrists and on to the tender skin of my forearms.

On the phone was the heat pump repair, Elbert "Pee Wee" Sweat (real name, as it appears on his card), and shortly Pee Wee stood at my door, come over at last to add freon. "You put that stuff on your hands, and your hands'll drop off," he said, proffering the tank—threatening. Then when I walked out to show him where the unit is, and I leaned close to the machine, he growled, "Keep your fingers away from there, or you'll git your fingers cut off."

When he'd called, finally, to respond to the pleas I'd left on his answering machine, I'd heard this strange voice say, "This is Elbert Sweat. Remember me?" though I'd never met the man. *Remember me?*—the question in a bad dream and *your fingers'll git cut off, your hands'll fall off.*

This makes me think of a dream I had the other night. The key to the dream was a German word, but when I woke up I couldn't quite remember and struggled for the right translation. The place in the dream—what was it called? The place, no it wasn't Liebestraum, Love's Dream

on the summit of the wooded hill   this castle no
monastery   no now that my time has come   and
I am inside and see nuns   we are obliged to call
it what it is   convent

Lebensraum   in the history of cruelty some people
have become a cliché   these nuns just as bad   I
am a prisoner   in the Leben the Leben something   and either this is the 90s or I am in my
nineties   I am old and on the shelf   with
yellowed scrolls one of which is mine   that a nun
will draw out to read the expiration date   on the
day she and the others will facilitate my death

I must escape my old bones ache   my aching bones
the pain   thank God for the tunnel Pain   this
way the quickest exit out of   Lebenstraum

In another dream I was looking for a grave marker. I mean I was shopping for one and trying to see what I could get for the fifty dollars in my pocket, all I had. The one I found was slight and brass and competently bent 'round rather in the shape of a music stand. The grave marker was for my own grave.

Let the music begin.

An alarm! I am reminded of the world out there. Someone's security's gone off.

No, crazy, that's a chickadee, the way chickadees *insist*. God, and sometime last week the sound of a cricket I mistook for a disk drive going bad.

The weeks go by, long, like eels, and unelectric.

I'm bored to death, and I may get up in a moment and turn on the lava lamp to watch. At last night's viewing, the lava flowed up in a staircase to the top. When the heat rose, and the stair collapsed, at the bottom was revealed a one-armed person with their head against the glass. Apples fell and piled around the poor thing. The apples rotted or melted and lost their shape, and then yellow fluid bubbled up under the red lava, and red balloons rose and blistered in the liquid sky, and the blisters broke, and the red balloons shuddered, redder and more perfect, and continued to rise. Down below, the person collapsed in the heat, lava pouring from pelvis or big leg stump.

Other times I lie on my back and look up at the reflection in the globe of the floor lamp that leans in over my bed. I meditate on the life of The Girl in the Globe of the Gooseneck Lamp.

She lies there in the white iron bed that curves around her. A door and two windows, a bookcase and many books, lean. She's the center of a cell, sealed off, waiting for a miracle.

Waiting, more like it, to meet her Maker on the Day of Poor Judgment.

Her mouth is small in sorrow. Eyes recessed in dark hollows smolder. Her face could hardly be rounder.

Her head is big, her feet, so far away, barely there. When she reaches out, the arm that appeared normal at her side, fattens, bruises swell, the ragged patch of rash erupts, and here's a hand huge in your face.

It's one of those days when she feels as if the flesh is coming off the bones of her forearms. Her bones sing Klingon opera, aria of warrior's torture. She's short of breath and coughs.

She made the mistake yesterday of trying to escape into the world. And in the middle of the night she woke with shirt drenched. Later intense itching on her back and fingertips disturbed sleep again. At dawn when she came to, both little fingers and both little toes had lost feeling.

Now she tries to collect her thoughts through pressure in her head.

She lies there and what does she worry about, how terrible it would be if an asteroid hit Serpent Mound.

She lies there and daydreams about living in a little house on a bend in the road and feeling each traveler take her curve slow.

She writes in her head: I am as leaden as a Roman General. Gone down. In armor. Under horse hooves. *Landslide.*

Sometimes she cries a little.

Chernobyl, we are sick.

And what, you ask, you foolish person, what about a miracle?

Thusly, said the magician.

LUCILLE LANG DAY

INTENSIVE CARE

My left arm a lead weight,
my skull a swollen gourd filled
with stones. My pillow, small,
hard, offers no comfort; my limbs
are cold. My life recedes
like a road in a rearview mirror
as I rise into another element,
a green cuff squeezing my arm,
suction cups gripping my chest.
Needles and wires everywhere,
my fingers find no surfaces;
my tongue can scarcely move
in the thick air. Breathing sand
on a dark street where a woman,
gaunt, with papery skin, rips
the tube from her arm, I say, "Yes,
I understand—no more pain."
Queasy now. My back aches,
head thrumming relentlessly,
pressure two hundred ten on the red
digital display. A soldier
lies in a trench, his right leg
ripped from his hip, his blood
mixing with dust, red and gray.
He is thinking of summer, the shade
of a tree with long green leaves,
the cool white crest of a wave,
gentle hands. Someone is lifting him
into a plane; the steady roar
of the engines is all he can hear.

Alone. Concentrating on stillness.
Each movement is the center
of rings of pain, waves, expanding
in the brain, a dark lake.
But blue lights rim the runway,
bread is rising in the kitchen,
the baby asleep in her crib.
From a distance far as tomorrow,
someone whispers, "You're okay:
you're going to live."

MRI SCAN

I am trapped in the center
of a huge electromagnet.
A plastic mask
clamped over my head
holds me in place.
It's an antenna, they say,
to knock my hydrogen nuclei
into disarray.

All I can see is my face
suspended in a mirror
a few inches above me, framed
by a blue hospital cap
and the top of my white gown.

The machine buzzes like a saw,
then rapidly taps
like a jackhammer. A slower beat
reverberates in the background.

Don't swallow. Don't swallow.
I repeat the doctor's order
to myself, while he
examines the curling and folding
landscape of my brain
and the rungs of my spine,
which must look like a chain
of shallow hoofprints
in sand, made by a strange,
one-footed creature
searching for an oasis.

The tapping continues.
I think it's coming
from inside me.
I am filled with sand
that shifts over bedrock
in a terrible glare.
No lucent pools
or palm trees
are anywhere near.

THE HOT TUB
For Gene

In the light of a yellow bulb
above the redwood planks
where we stripped for the hot tub,
we slip into each other's arms
like two aquatic creatures
with smooth white skin, except
for the red scar on your belly,
gelatinous in the glow
of that bulb, gleaming
like an egg yolk. We float,
caressing each other's limbs.

The last time we made love
was New Year's Eve,
your sixtieth birthday,
after eating cracked crab
and overcooked broccoli—
before the surgery.

But maybe the last time
isn't the last. Out
of the tub, on wet planks:
urgency. Power lines
crisscross the overcast sky
like lumbar nerves, humming
with energy. A star
pokes through clouds. Hot
and naked in the steam,
we throb like that star—
our molecules fused,
our light set free.

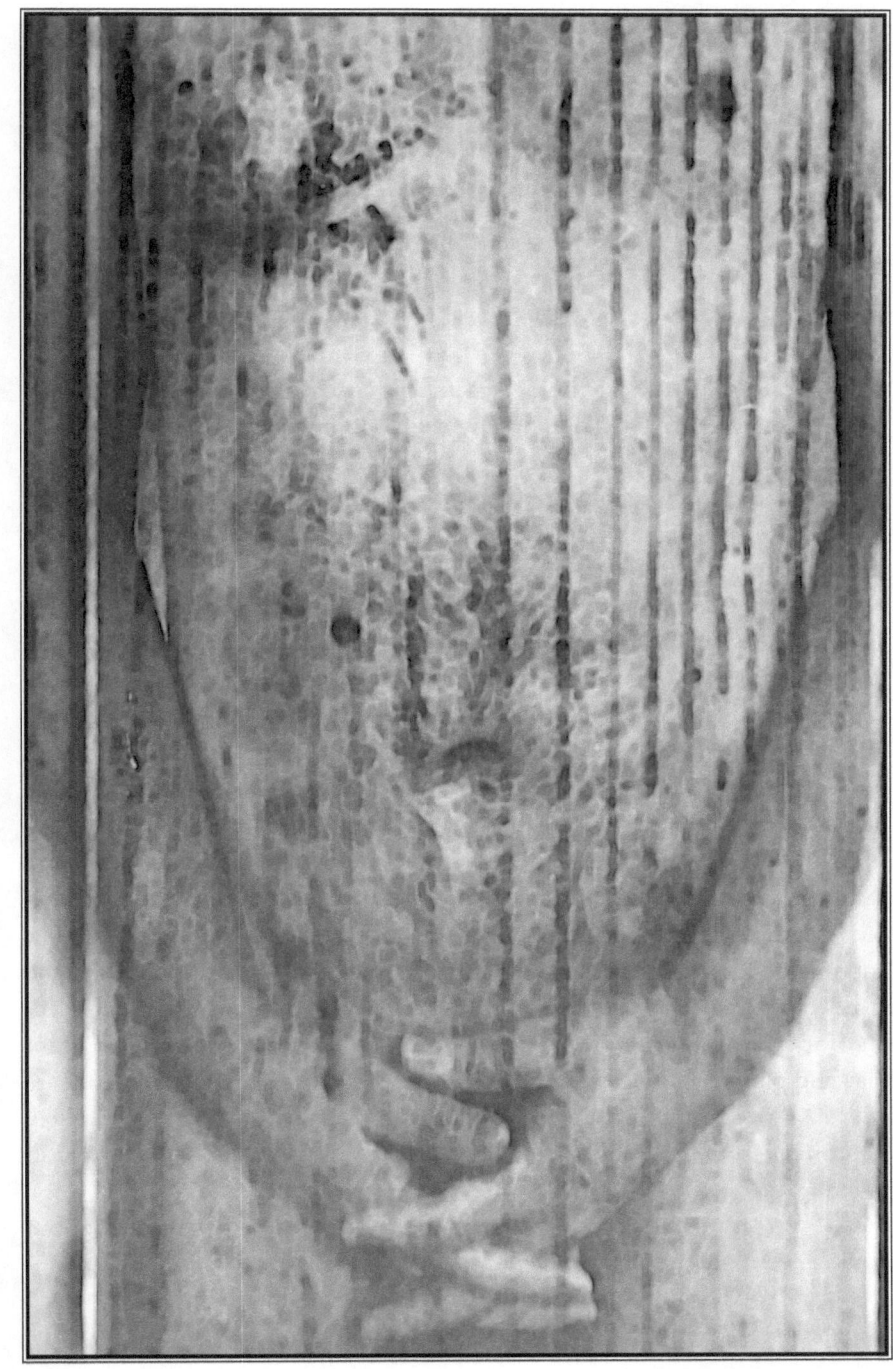

TERRY SANVILLE

BLUES FROM THE STEPDOWN WARD

I think it was nighttime when they moved me out of the ICU. I stared up at overhead air conditioning vents slipping past. My gurney turned into a huge dark room. Two nurses slid me onto a bed near the far wall, hung IVs, handed me the call button with the TV controls, then vanished. Golden light filtered in from the hallway. The ward was quiet, the first silence I'd enjoyed in a week, at least I thought I'd been there that long.

The sheets quickly became sodden with my sweat. The nurses said I had a fever from an infection of the surgical incision in my gut. The doctor had been called. I waited for him in the darkness, trying to focus on something other than recent events that landed me in the hospital. But those images were too vivid: vomiting clotted blood all over our kitchen, bleeding out from a huge stomach ulcer. There'd been no warning. If it wasn't for my wife's quick actions, if I lived alone, I'd be dead.

I wiped sweat from my eyes, clicked on the TV and surfed the channels. On some public station two guys clutched acoustic guitars and sang old style blues. I recognized the songs as those written by Robert Johnson and one of the guitarists as Eric Clapton. I studied his hands, listened to the sweet blue notes, and sang along. The music seemed to meld with my fever and for a few moments I was sitting on a stool next to Eric, watching him play and plunking along on my L-4 Gibson. Then the lights blinked on.

"Ya know why they call him 'slow hand?'" my surgeon asked, motioning to the TV. He was a short stocky Asian who spoke without an accent.

"You mean Clapton?" I answered. "I've heard that nickname but could never figure it out 'cause a lot of his playing is really fast."

"You're right. But he takes time to add just the right touch to each note he plays."

The surgeon leaned over me and stripped away the square white bandage covering my stomach wound. I groaned as the tape pulled up hair and skin, focused on the TV, and watched Eric's fingers, trying to memorize what I saw. This doc was definitely no 'slow hand' physician.

"Your incision is infected," the doctor pronounced. "Got to open it up and let it drain."

"You gonna do that here?" I asked. "You gonna give me something to knock me out?"

"Won't take but a minute," he answered in a soft voice and reached for a device to remove the surgical staples. "This part shouldn't hurt."

Removing the staples from the five-inch incision actually tickled. I stared at the TV as Clapton and his partner began the introduction to Johnson's "Crossroad Blues."

"Okay, now, on the count of three I'm going to open the wound." The surgeon placed a thumb flat against my stomach on either side of the vertical incision and drew the skin tight. I began to softly sing along with Eric.

"I went down to the crossroads, fell down on my knees."

"One."

"Went down to the crossroads, fell down on my knees."

"Two."

"Asked the Lord above have mercy, save poor Terry, if you please."

"Three."

I grunted, held my breath, and felt the barely-knit skin pull apart and the wound open up. Blood and pus flowed down my lower abdomen.

"Standing at the crossroad, tried to flag a ride."

"I'll be done in just a minute," the doctor said and quickly dabbed at the drainage with a sterile dressing. "You did great, a real trooper."

"Standing at the crossroad, tried to flag a ride."

He wadded up a piece of gauze and poked around in the inch-deep incision. I waited for my guts to come popping out, but they mercifully stayed put.

"Didn't nobody seem to know me, everybody pass me by."

"That's one of my favorite blues songs," the doctor said and stepped back, stripping bloodied latex gloves from his hands. "The nurse will be in to redress the wound. Rest easy and enjoy the music."

I continued staring at the television, not wanting to look anywhere else. I felt like I'd just been in a knife fight and was laid out on the hard plank floor of some Southern juke joint. Black people stare down at me as the band plays on. The place smells of sweat and reefer. In one corner a slender, full-lipped mulatto wipes his jackknife on an immaculately white handkerchief and slips it into a vest pocket. A lit cigarette precariously dangles from his mouth. A golden-skinned woman sits on his lap and nuzzles his neck. He grins at me and sings along with the band.

"Standin' at the crossroad, baby, risin' sun goin' down
Standin' at the crossroad, baby, eee, eee, risin' sun goin' down
I believe to my soul, now, poor Terry is sinkin' down."

A heavy-set black woman with a stethoscope draped around her neck stood over me and stared at the surgeon's handiwork. She tsked to herself and poked at my incision with a gloved finger.

"Looks clean, nice and red. That'll heal up fine once we get the infection under control." She hung an IV bag of Cipro on the stand, tied a tourniquet below the elbow of my right arm and went searching for a vein, finding one on the third poke. I focused on the TV and continued to sing along with Eric and the boys.

"And I went to the crossroad, mama, I looked east and west
I went to the crossroad, baby, I looked east and west
Lord, I didn't have no sweet woman, ooh well, babe, in my distress."

"What's that you're singing?" the nurse asked. "Sounds like somethin' my Grandpa would know." From a needleless syringe she dribbled a clear liquid into my open wound and swabbed it out with gauze. I groaned and drew deep whistling breaths through clenched teeth. The nurse was quick and efficient. She placed four-by-fours and a new white dressing over the incision and taped it down.

"You're not from the Delta, are you?" I finally asked, breathing hard.

"You mean Mississippi? Lord no, born right here in LA. But my grandparents sharecropped outside of Clarksdale, years before the war."

"Yeah, well, that song was recorded in 1936."

"I don't pay much attention to old blues music. But I sing gospel in church."

"Close enough."

"Yes, but in church, we sing to rejoice and praise the Lord, not to complain about losing a woman, or some such notion."

"For me, singing sweet blues is the same as rejoicing—just a different way of doing it... helps me know what I'm feeling is real."

The nurse stared at me for a long moment and nodded. "Yeah, I can see that. If I had a hole in my belly, I'd probably be doing the same." She chuckled and turned to leave, humming. Her deep contralto voice blended perfectly with the tinny sounds coming from the two white men singing on television.

> *Sometime after midnight my fever broke. I drifted off to sleep and dreamed about singing with long-dead blues men, learning even more lessons about suffering and rejoicing, learning till my fingers felt thick and full with all of it.*

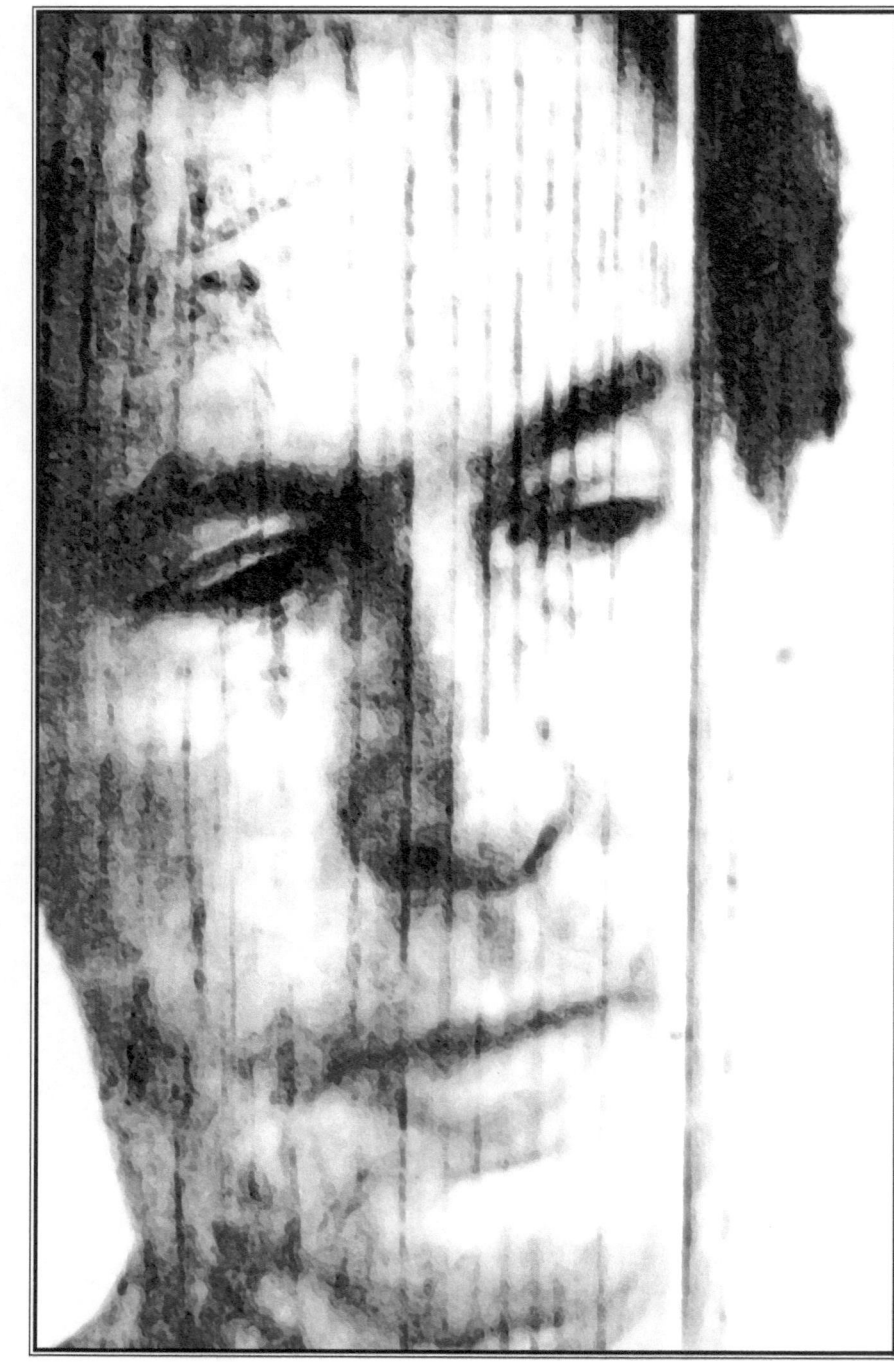

PATRICIA SMITH RANZONI

HUSBAND CUT MY HAIR

I cannot reach it anymore. Fetch the wedding-dress scissors
from my sewing chest, my good pair to be used only for cloth,
from their blue velvet case. I know it shocks you I would ask,
the way I've guarded it these years letting and letting it lengthen
just for us to dance around my round hips if you still love it lie
with me now and help me let it down as long as. . .

and weave your fingers through these threads of me husband
if you have loved it slip again into my waves let me be your rings.
Show it as it has shown you. Dip again into its flow is it fabric
or water it doesn't know itself or what it means.
Lift it to your lips and thank it as I have every day.

These tears. . .*oh*. . .because of where these fibers of my being
have been what vision settled into them what shine
they may not know again *I cannot reach it anymore.*

If you've loved the way I've carded and plied it by hand
until it's spun a stellar spray down our backs, give your hands
for it to tremble into and look upon it the way a man sighs as if
he will die unless he does. Cup it like our brook being swept away
if it is that and drink it with me as it goes.

Have you loved the way the silver has swirled through the last
of my girl-black silk *whisper that*. The way I've fluted it up
into fountains being my own kind of lady if I have been yours
        hold me
        cut my hair my strength

          I cannot reach it anymore.

from *ANOTHER LONG*

26.
thirteen years
running on infusions
rationed time
how she's used it
how it's used her

27.

> *when she asks why*
> *the quiet weighs*
> *so much*

28.
five tries sometimes
to stitch the catheter
into some thin vein
after cutting costs
they cut the I.V. team
five piercing probes
like sewing shoes
what's a mistake
if not human
even when she cannot speak
they learn to know how she feels

> *in their hands*
> *she is a garment in their hands*

29.
how Brenda, good at it, zaps the lightning that struck her
(and each brother and sister down the line
picking potatoes in a County storm)
into prize flower beds now, the grind of tractors echoing
in hospital beds raising her patients to her conductive care

how Amy, good at it, with the latest Patriot scores
laughs and coaches and counts down the drops per quarter

how her sister's way-back schoolchum Marge, good at it,
neighbors while wrapping her arms in steaming pads
to raise the veins
what it used to mean to be home

how Peg (talking symphony), and Kay, Ann, and Kathy,
good at it, bring in pictures and stories of lifetimes to swap
infusing her with the old kind of care, bringing her back

balloons and songs for her birthday
she makes them caftans while she still can

what *hospital* used to mean, *here*

all shifts, good at it, names she's tried to hold these years
keeping more their eyes and kindnesses
entering her bloodstream and brain again and *hundreds*
of agains giving more than work against money constraints
to practice their science their art entering her heart *for life*
fleet of mothers, grandmothers, daughters, sisters, aunts
not that gender has anything to do with it   (Gary, Bob)

what *nursing* used to mean, *here*

43.
(she lists her at leasts)

open to dawn meaning morning
keep still to know what night has left   *reach*
read   write
cleanse in every sense
dress for ease or work or art
think apart
read   write
refuse unworthy use of voice
note what it is you miss
read   write
send whatever way some peace, gratitude, comfort, delight
read   write
work as much as . . . *push*
    try to play the same
dance in every sense
rest if need be retreating as must
read   write
drink enough good water
laugh
be outside all weathers as much as. . .get into dirt
eat one green fresh-picked thing even if in winter pine tea
save something let something go
cry if need be if not don't
make or take in music preferably both
read   write
consider the heavens consider earth as much
cleanse in every sense
be still to take in the day
forgive (self, others, God)

praise (the same)
share as much of this as wise with children
sleep in touch   *reach*
read   write (if need be)
    sleep deep sleep
    swim in dreams to poems
    sleep high sleep
    fly dreams to poems come home
    sleep sleep
begin again

MARION DEUTSCHE COHEN

ON READING TO SICK PEOPLE

When you're reading they don't ask you to scratch just below the left nostril
Or wipe the outside corners of both eyes
Or range their lower right leg slowly twenty times.

The more you read the less they itch.
The more you read the less they ask.

Who was it?—Scheherazade?—
Tale after tale
To hold off her enemies
Distract her friends

Escape her dying, her dead.

MARCH 6, 1998

Maybe equations DON'T take care of themselves, maybe I have to keep
        checking on Them
Make sure the x's don't change into y's, make sure the epsilons don't change
        into Deltas, make sure minus-signs don't keep poking their way in.
Even my new favorite equation, the one about F-bracket-x divided by the
        ideal general by p of x, make sure that homomorphism still works,
        make sure the First Isomorphism Theorem doesn't become the
        Last Isomorphism Theorem.
And maybe the two sides of equations will become wings and carry it away,
        maybe the equal sign will spin ninety degrees and become too tall,
        a barbed wire fence, block the two sides from each other, make it
        impossible to cross over.

Or maybe it'll all fly away, no such thing as math, math gets outside, gets
      physi-Cal, become physics.
I have to lift it, toilet it, wake up at 2:00 A.M. and stretch its legs or scratch
      its Nostrils and I think I hear it calling Mar.

ONE WOMAN SHOW

I, the one he began with
And the one he'll end with
Am acting out this deathbed scene.

I pretend to say "Hey, I just took Devin to visit the various colleges.
   Yesterday we went—"
And then I pretend to pause.
And then I pretend to ask, "Do you want me to talk about this kind of
thing?"
And when he nods, I pretend to continue, yesterday's Temple, tomorrow's
   Drexel.
And then I pretend to fall quiet.
I pretend to hold his hand.
I pretend to be the only one not bustling about

Just being there, the one he began with, the one he'll end with
The one who's been too much in the middle.

CALLING A SPADE A SPADE

Because I might have regrets
And because he was so unwilling to die
I lift up the spade
Fill it with dirt
And gently trickle it over him.

The spade is heavy.
The dirt is heavy.
But not as heavy as HE was
During those six years.

I lift again.
But not again.
And not as high.
And not only the toilet.

And not in the middle of the night.

PHYLLIS LANGTON

MISSION ACCOMPLISHED

Dear Gentleman George,

Death hangs in the air on September 11, 2001. I drive us to our new four-story townhouse in McLean, Virginia, twenty miles from the Pentagon. This morning, terrorists have flown airplanes into the Pentagon and the World Trade Center in New York City, killing thousands of innocent people.

Although you hold the hand railing tightly, you walk in the front door with a faint smile and little assistance. After we walk around the first and second floors, I hear you sigh and your face turns gray. You take my arm and say, "Where's our elevator? Let's explore the other floors."

You comment on the sparkling chandelier giving off soft light in the elevator, the hardwood floor, and the matching stained walls. You begin to explain to me how the elevator works on a hydraulic system. However, I see your legs begin to tremble. Quickly you grasp the side rails.

"When I die and leave this house, I want to ride down in this elevator standing tall. A fighter pilot doesn't want to leave his loved ones and his world feet first. I want to complete my mission with dignity. I want to go out of this house the way I came in, standing on my feet. Do you think you can manage that, Phyllis?"

Is he serious? "Yes." I say it so quickly, with no idea of how I will manage or what it is that I am supposed to manage. "I can do it, and furthermore, I will."

On March 20th, 2003 at 3:15 am, you die peacefully at home after you talk to me while I hold your hand. I have no energy to move. I sit by your side and revisit some of the memories we built during these last three years. The ceiling fan whirls above my head. The only sound I hear is the heater when it recycles. Life has left the house.

I feel chilled and run the bath water especially hot. I crave all the bubbles and sweet scents of lavender. I sink into the tub and weep.

Suddenly, I remember that we have seven dear friends coming to lunch at noon. Do I cancel or have them come anyway? I know what you would do. You would not cancel. I decide that their company would be comforting to me and them.

In a daze, I realize that I have to call the hospice nurse to come and officially pronounce you dead. After the nurse examines you, we review the necessary hospice protocol for discharging you from their services and the legal issues of declaring you dead, signing papers, discarding down the toilet your unused narcotic and other medicines, and selecting a pick up service to transport your body to the funeral home in Arlington, Virginia. I thank the nurse for all the services that hospice so graciously provided us for over a year. You and I have said on many occasions "Hospice people are true angels of life, not angels of death."

You are dead and will be leaving the house for good. I will be alone.

I wait another hour and call the transport service to take you to the funeral home. On the telephone I instruct the drivers to back their vehicle into our garage which I will leave open, for them to close. This way the neighbors would not be disturbed with vehicles doing strange things during the night. I know you would want me to do this. You enjoy the neighbors so very much. You visited with them yesterday.

In the meantime, I call Dianne and Harvey who arrive shortly before the transport drivers. The drivers pull their SUV into my garage, and close the garage door. I note the senior driver, who wears glasses, doesn't resemble anything I remember about funeral drivers. He wears a wind breaker jacket, and a lack-luster shirt. The younger driver is in non-descript casual clothes, and he appears to be a trainee because he doesn't seem to know what to do with himself or his hands, which remain in his pockets during most of their visit. He is clearly very sleepy.

I say to the drivers, "Hello, I am Phyllis Langton and these are my friends Dianne and Harvey Kammerer." I stretch out my right hand to shake theirs. They introduce themselves, and offer weak, limp handshakes. You used to comment on people's handshakes, especially men's, and your comments weren't always nice. But I have only one mission on my mind and that is to meet the promise I have made to you. I'm going to be sure you ride down the elevator standing tall.

After telling them where George's body is to be taken, the senior driver asks "Would you please take us to Dr. Thomas and tell us the best way to carry him out?" I imagine all kinds of thoughts are going through his head like: how much does Dr. Thomas weigh (they are not robust men); will he fit on the little stretcher we have brought; what floor is he on (hopefully not on the fourth); and how much work is it going to be to get him into the SUV?

"Yes," I answer. "He's on the third floor. We've an elevator and I'd like him brought down in the elevator. My husband wants to ride in the elevator one more time, standing up."

They stare at me with wide open eyes and blank faces. He wants to do *what?* I wait but they say nothing. So I tell them my plan. I ask them to wrap you securely so you can stand in the elevator leaning against the wall with my arms wrapped around you to keep you from falling. They are to put ties around your waist and secure these to the elevator wall railings. I ask them to leave your face uncovered so that I can see you and talk with you during your last ride out of the house, and our last ride together in our physical bodies.

The senior driver's pale face begins to show some strain. He appears to be middle-aged but doesn't look in much better health than you. He now has his hands in his pockets and begins to shift his feet back and forth. He says tentatively, "Mrs. Langton, we can't do that. It is too dangerous. He might fall."

I want to say to him, So what if he falls? He's dead. He can't hurt himself. What are you worried about? So instead I say, "I'll wrap him myself."

"No, no that won't work. We just haven't been asked to do this before, and we don't know quite how to do what you are asking."

"Maybe we can work together," I say. "He won't fall if we wrap him carefully and then tie him to the handrail. Besides, I will be holding him during the entire ride. So what's the problem? I don't think you understand how important it was to my husband, who was a test pilot and fighter pilot in three wars, to accomplish his mission of leaving the house standing tall on his feet, instead of leaving feet first."

They nod what seems to me to be agreement. We will work

together.

Slowly we begin to prepare you for your ride. We reinforce the wrapping around you so that it will be firm enough to support you. We finish our work and walk you to the elevator. The men lift you to your feet and hold you steady with their arms securely around you. When you are standing and secure in the elevator, I ask Dianne and Harvey to escort the drivers to the first level where we will meet them. I close the elevator door.

So that I can have more time with you than it takes to travel three floors, I do not push the button to start the elevator. You told me when we first moved in how the elevator light is timed to go off in about 3 seconds if the elevator doesn't move. So I switch the light to "on" so we can talk awhile with the lights on before we begin your last ride to the bottom floor, standing tall.

My own feelings are fuzzy at this point since I am so mentally and physically exhausted, and I am focused on keeping my promise to you for your last ride. We are surrounded by your favorite pictures. I remember talking and reminiscing with you about the many pictures which I keep on the elevator walls so you can enjoy them during your daily rides. There are many of our Ireland trip when I surprised you for your 73rd birthday. You had no idea where we were going until we stood in line at Air Lingus Airline in Boston, and I handed you your ticket and you said, "But, Phyllis, I have appointments." "I know," I said, "I cancelled them."

And the funny pictures of our daughter's wedding. When you were walking her down the aisle you had difficulty keeping her from running. She was so nervous. When you arrived at the railing, you told Bishop Eastman, "Hurry up and marry them before she gets away and runs out of the church."

Pictures of two of our darling granddaughters, Claire and Lorna, playing soccer, are close by your face. "Coach Edward", their father, arranged a special game in your honor after the May 2001 season was over. We drove to Nashville for the game and tears were in your eyes as 5-year old Claire made five goals against the boys: 6-2 the game score. And Claire was so excited and proud of herself and you, she ran into you at full speed to hug you, after the game. She grabbed your legs, and you both fell over, laughing all the way to the ground. And, look at Lorna, almost two years old at the game. She got into the game by chasing the ball after it left the field with her box of animal crackers waving on her arm, plus a back end full of diapers.

She wouldn't give them the ball back to finish the game.

Here is a picture of you checking out your airplane in Viet Nam where you were a squadron commander and fighter pilot during the war. I also have one of you in World War II in the Army Air Corp and you as a fighter pilot in Korea. You look tender as though you are touching a baby's bottom when you touch your airplanes, so gently and with such reverence. These planes brought you home after some terrifying, but successful missions.

One of my favorite pictures is of you and me at the Army Navy Country Club in Arlington, Virginia in 1991. You had just assumed the presidency of your West Point alumni class of 1948. You looked so dapper in your Brooks Brothers silk jacket, with dark grey slacks and highly polished black shoes and black socks. You were happy and proud to be class president, to work with your classmates. You used to say "...the best thing I got out of West Point was my classmates." Then you would look at me with those devilish blue eyes and add, "And, of course, their wives."

These pictures break my heart. We have shared our life; we have shared your death as you trusted me unconditionally to make this journey with you. You gave me the gift of caring for you until you took your last breath, and I reassured you that you were 'home', a true story of "till death do us part."

But now you are in a distant place where I can no longer reach you. As we approach the ground floor, I can see the weariness fade from your face. You are completing your mission to stand with dignity and leave your home the way you came in. I did not close your eyes when you died and to me your eyes are sparkling and you have a smile on your face. As the elevator door opens on the ground floor, your blue eyes still twinkle at me, and I will always remember you that way.

As the SUV bearing your body pulls out of the driveway, I remember a poem I read a few weeks ago by Emily Dickinson, "To live with constant weariness takes forever; to die, takes just a little while. It's only fainter by degrees and then it's out of sight."

"Goodbye, sweetie. Rest your arms in peace, my love."

Your loving wife,
Phyllis.

MARY-LANE KAMBERG

ARTIST'S EYE

At St. Luke's, Barbara's mother
sits propped with pillows
Out the window, rooftop air conditioners
obscure the park across the street

Oh, mother,
I wish you could see the oaks,
the fountain, the lawn
Not this

Barbara's mother shakes her head,
frames the scene with thumbs and fingers
But, Barbara, look! Look at the angles!

SUSAN R. NORTON

WATCHING MOTHER GO

Words that scissor
a mother and daughter

apart are forgiven so that
in these last few days

Mom can spend her hours
trying her hardest to let go.

She speaks little, eats less, puts
aside her book of memories.

And with all this letting loose,
she cannot quit my hand,

her last tow line. She clutches
at it sometimes, other times

her fingers flutter,
butterflies against mine.

I wonder if it would help
if I loosen my hand from hers,

pull away like she had always
done from me or does she need

time to separate from a world
that never seemed fair and those

of us who disappointed her.

HEATHER TOSTESON

ONCE MY MOTHER KNEW MY NAME
For Penelope

Once my mother knew my name
as she did those of violet, trillium,
cinquefoil, the poppies in Flanders' fields.
Nothing will ever feel the same.

Surely what sustains us is just this simple.
A shadow racing across a pasture
faster than thought and then we are caught
in a hot pure light. Once my mother knew my name.
I heard her, like an answer.

These nights I watch the moths cicade
through the light's halo and dream inside
the moon's perfect globe a flower unfolds
furtive and luxurious as womanhood.
Petal by petal, I assume my mother's myth
and begin the unraveling designed
to transcend time. First my name, then hers.

As a child, enthralled, bewildered,
I would watch for hours as Japanese flowers
bloomed from clam shells no larger than my thumbnail.
Mute. Huge. Blazing.
Names I believed were transformations.
I stared into the water glass as if into God's face
the equation was that exact.

Now I am left with a sensory trace deeper
than memory, the pressure of my mother's shoulder
as wordlessly we watched together. Like homecoming,
to name is to lose, reclaim. The thought threatens
to tear my mind as if it were flesh:
She knew me before I knew myself.

 She doesn't know where she is any longer.
She doesn't know what makes her face clammy, wet.
As I stroke her forehead beads of sweat break inside my hand.
Glass. Water. Mother. Daughter.
Once she knew my name.
I hurt her like an answer.
Now I hold her because it is the language left to us.
It is the deepest form of worship.
If the past were a glass, enough grace settles here,
petal by petal, to define a lifetime.

THE INTELLIGENCE OF LOSS

1

When I first cupped the print in my hand I felt the simplest
relief. My mother in my red coat. She keeps recognizing
it as mine and offering to give it back. She who has always been
a relentless succession of desires so intense
you couldn't call them selfishness.
And now there is this effacement almost mystic
in its completeness. Red, she cries out.
And with each rush of sensation, like a receding tide,
remembers less. I feel a mother's rage. I want to shield her
from herself. It is an old story, inexorably
transformed.

2

Waiting for the movie to start, sitting together in the dark,
I repeat over and over the names of her children
and the order of their birth. I never seem to tire of this.
Stop only when the screen fills. But the movie makes her restless,
people appear, disappear. Weird, she says firmly as she dips
her face into her cupped hands, cheerfully meets
the eyes of the woman washing beside her in the mirror.
As we leave the theater, she looks at me sweetly and asks,
Who was your mother? She uses my given name.
She is pleased by my answer. *Did we ever live together?*
Where? I take her arm as we cross the street.
She does not brush me away as she used to.
To be abandoned and denied are different entirely.

3

All I can think about is getting us near water. I think
if I do not have something vast like that to rest my eyes on
I will die of grief. Seated there, staring out with me
at the shiftless horizon, she asks again, *Who were my children?*
I return to the car to collect the camera. From there,
I am careful to position her, in my red coat she keeps exclaiming over
and offering to return, along with the three birds in the grass,
the striae of seaweed and sand, the surf and the clean horizon
dividing the vast sea from the monochroic sky, all the elements
in such perfect internal proportion the image hums.
As I hear the shutter close, I know I am giving up something,
all those stories I have been making and remaking all my life
to try to understand why her life has been the way it has.
All this time and thought on my part and I can't give her back
the simplest thing, what it felt like to breathe deeply
on a June morning in 1950, or what it feels like
to do the same here on a California beach in September 1992.

This is a picture of what it might feel like if she knew
what was happening and could put herself in my shoes.
What haunts me is not the scale of the photograph, that feels natural
to me, the world falling away from us infinitely on either side,
but the acceptance. Can you understand?
If I had my deepest wish, we would stop right here.
She wouldn't slip an inch further away.
I would never ask anything more of her either.

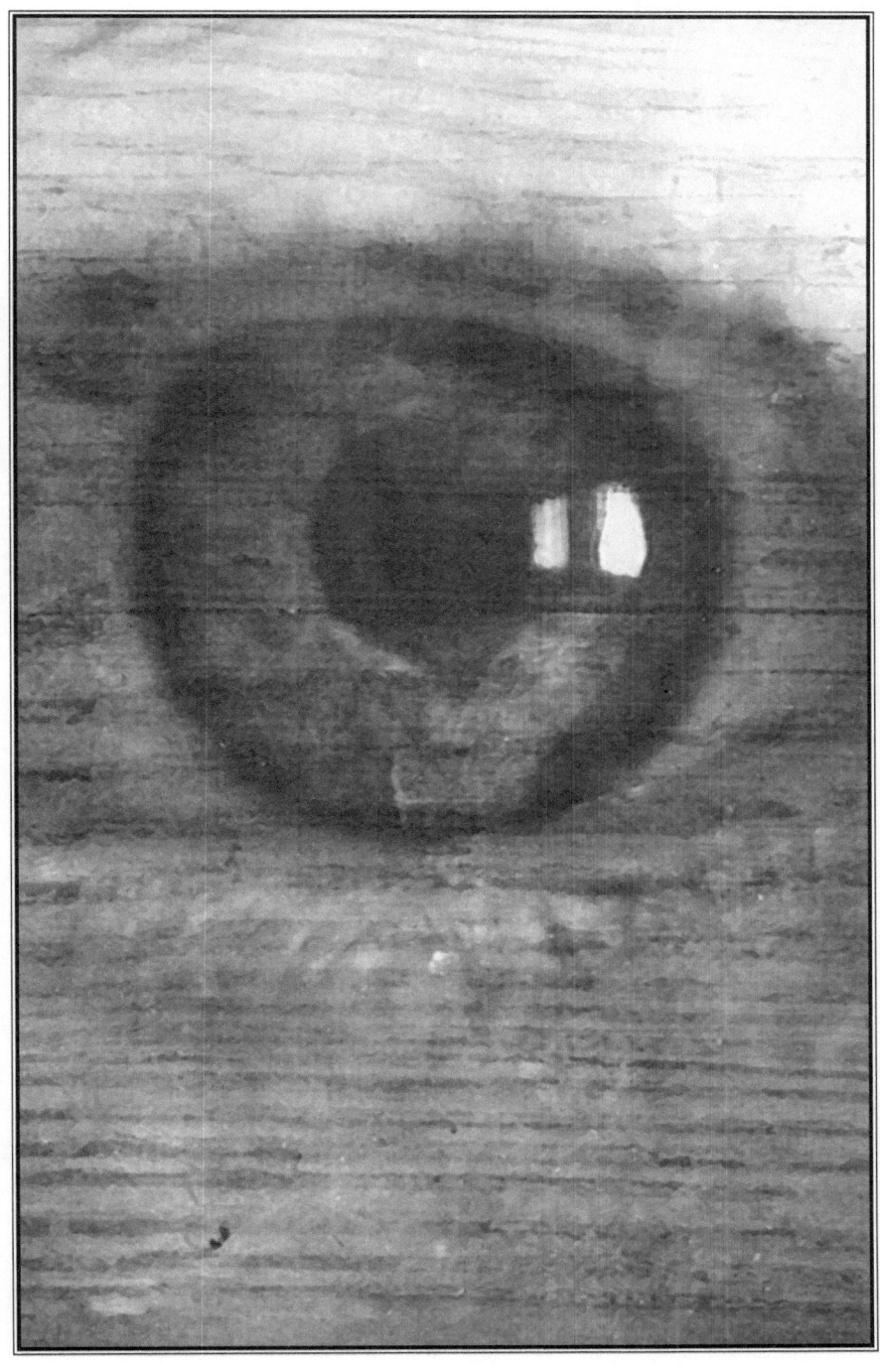

SUSAN HODARA

AFTER THE ACCIDENT

Before The First Visit

I am compiling mental images of my father since he was hit by a car on Monday. They are composites of the information my mother is telling me, and now there are three. They are distinct, and they keep repeating in my mind. Each one leaves me feeling helpless and heartbroken, both of which I am.

The first is of the impact itself, and it is cartoon-like, flat. It haunted me Monday night after my mother called, and kept me from sleeping. They had been walking in the crosswalk of the parking lot of the hospital where my father takes an exercise class, when a car, moving fairly slowly, just didn't stop. It was driven by a woman in her 80s, not much older than my father, come to think of it, though my father lost the confidence to drive several years ago already. My mother told me she was so angry that she threw her gloves at the woman's car and yelled, "Didn't you see us?" She had, the woman stumbled her reply, but she thought they were further away.

My father was knocked down. He hit his head on the pavement and his leg was badly broken. He lay on the ground, my mother told me, shouting, "I can't move my leg! I can't move my leg!" Later, he kept asking her whether it was his fault, and what had he done wrong.

The moment of my image is of my father falling. The car isn't visible; it's just my father sort of rolling on the ground just inches from the curb of the sidewalk. He's wearing a light blue short-sleeved shirt tucked into darker blue trousers, and his graying hair is combed neatly back over his head. He has no coat, and in my mind, his brows are furrowed and his face holds the worried look he has when he's displeased or angry, or about to complain. He is flat, two-dimensional, and I'm seeing him from the side. His back is rounded, his shoulders hunched forward, his knees bent and brought up, so he almost forms a half-circle. He stays rigid in that position as he falls. If he fell backward, he might actually rock back and forth on his spine. When he hits the ground, he is on his side, his body held firm in the same position.

My second image comes from the next day, when my mother tells me about the night and the following morning awaiting surgery. I can only imagine how drugged he must be, waiting all that time with a broken leg. "He's only semi-conscious," my mother says, but I don't know what that means. Then she adds the information that forms my second vision of my father. "He's been acting kind of weird," she says, downplaying the way she does any extra concern but obviously disturbed nonetheless. "He keeps saying it's too hot and trying to take off his clothes. I tell him, 'Don't do that. Don't do that.'" So I picture my father now lying on his back in a hospital bed, rails along the edges, wearing a light blue hospital gown now untied in the back. He has pushed the thin but ironed white sheet and some overly used, pilled wool blankets to the bottom of the bed, and he keeps tearing at his gown, pulling it away from his naked body underneath. His head is thrown back, his chin pointing towards the ceiling, his skin a little shiny and pinker than usual. The word that best describes the way I see his face is 'anguished'. If I were there, he wouldn't even know it.

My third picture is from after the surgery, and it includes sound. He is in a private room now in the pulmonary ICU so they can keep a close watch on him for a few days. I couldn't speak to him yesterday because he was still blurry from anesthesia and trauma. It seems I can't speak to him today either. "He's still kind of out of it," says my mother. When I press her, she tells me he's having trouble breathing because of congestion accumulated in his lungs from the anesthesia, "which," she adds, "is to be expected." He is uncomfortable, she says. Then I can hear it in the background, a sawing sound, breathing as if it were being spoken as well as breathed, in out in out with little bubbles of phlegm making popping sounds along the way. It goes on and on. "He's trying to cough something up but nothing is coming," explains my mother. What I picture now is my father in about the same position in his bed, still on his back, still wearing the blue gown. The bed has been remade, and the sheet and blanket are undisturbed over his chest. There are tubes now; he's having a blood transfusion and there must be some kind of IV to feed him. His head is still looking back, his brow still furrowed as he breathes out loud. The sound holds his voice in it; it couldn't be anyone else's breathing, and I can imagine him talking to me using the same tone. Only now it's the most of him that can be expressed, the need to clear his chest.

I see these images within the first 20 seconds of waking up in the morning. At first it's just an uneasy feeling, then my pictures rush in and with them the high-strung queasiness that stays with me all day. I carry them with me, waiting to hear if there's been any change, if he's getting any more comfortable, any more like himself. I rely on them as my only connection to what's going on there before I travel this weekend to visit, snapshots like the ones you're shown after someone else's vacation. I see the accident and the hospital, and I recognize that this will not be an easy recuperation.

It is only briefly, however, a few times each day, that I allow myself to feel the emotions that are attached to my pictures. Then it's like a wind whooshing through my chest, emptying it with a great force, then ushering in powerful combinations of anger, pity, sadness and fear that make me have to sit down. Then my three images come back, all vibrant with these emotions, and I'm filled with what I keep wanting to call 'dismay'. Some say, "These things happen." Others express their temporary horror and offer their sympathies. I just seem to go about my daily business, overcome with all the terrible parts of my father's accident in those moments when I feel them, and otherwise just flipping through my pictures and shaking my head.

The First Visit

I finally make my way to the ICU on Saturday morning, where my mother and two brothers await me. By now my father's condition has deteriorated from a broken leg to a fat embolism that has traveled to his lungs and caused respiratory failure. Overnight, he has been intubated and sedated. When I see him, I realize that though his condition has become more complicated, my images weren't far from reality. His hospital gown is blue and white, and there is an ironed sheet covering him, pushed down to his waist. He is on his back, his head tilted slightly upward; his eyes are closed, but his eyebrows angle down towards his nose every now and then in some expression of discomfort. I am afraid he is having bad dreams, the way he seems to struggle in his drug-induced sleep.

It's the medical instruments I hadn't thought to picture. Every part of his body seems to be invaded. There are tubes everywhere, some carrying drugs and nutrition in, others delivering waste out. The biggest is the respirator that is fed down his throat and is now breathing for him, held in place by white tape wrapped several times around his head under his nose. The skin of his cheeks and neck bulges slightly under the tightness of the tape, and I worry for a moment until I realize that in the scheme of things now it hardly matters. His feet are encased in oversized pink foam rubber "booties," they call them, through which electrical current is sent to stimulate his blood flow. His wrists are restrained so he won't unwittingly hurt himself in an urge to yank free. You almost forget that his leg is in a cast.

What strikes me first, though, is how small he seems and how still he's lying. Although he's sedated and can't talk, we're told he can hear us and register what we're saying. Still, I feel awkward, unsure of what to say. "Hi, Dad," I begin, "it's me, Sue." My words sound stilted but now they're all I have. I stroke his hair, smoothing it away from his forehead. His scalp feels greasy and rough, but the skin on his face is remarkably smooth. There is dried mucus on the side of his nose, and gathered in the corners of his eyes. Suddenly I think of his mother, my grandmother, and wonder if he longs for her now.

I talk for less than a minute, it seems, not long enough, I berate myself, thinking fast for more to say. "We're here with you," I tell him. "We love you." I stand by him a while longer in silence, still stroking, studying his face, the whiskers that have emerged around his chin, the yellow stain of Betadine that has dripped down his neck, the whiteness of his shoulders that I haven't seen for years. When I talk to him, I'm afraid my voice will betray the fear and sadness that are filling me.

I look over at my mother, who is bolstered by her children's presence.

She's small and solid, her shoulders slightly rounded with her 74 years. Though her face is more lined than I remember, she is remarkably stoic, sitting now with her knitting, a banana from home blackening in a napkin by her side. The only time she cries is when she tells us of her own father, who died when she was 10 during a botched hospital stay. The whole day passes quickly, though we've done nothing but sit and stand, and we're all tired when it's time to leave.

After the First Visit

I'm staying with my mother in the room that used to be my brother's, the room with the double bed that Paul and I sleep in when we visit. It's unsettling to see reminders of what my parents had been in the middle of. In the bathroom, a *New Yorker* magazine folded open to an article about Rembrandt. By my father's side of the bed, the top of a pen sitting next to a crumpled Kleenex on a stack of books. In the kitchen, the blanched almonds my mother had prepared for the ginger cookies she'd planned to bake the afternoon of the accident.

Then I become almost giddy when I realize my father won't be hovering over every dish I leave unwashed in the sink, every chair I pull out from the table and don't push in when I get up, every crumb that drops from my toast to the floor. In the shower, it occurs to me that I don't have to worry about the hairs I might leave behind, but then I automatically wipe them away with the dry yellow sponge that sits on the edge of the sink, quickly scanning the bathroom for anything else askance, not out of habit, but in deference to my father.

Since the weekend, it's just a single image I'm holding of my dad. It's the one I have taken from the visit, in the hospital bed with all the tubes, the one with his eyes closed in sleep. My mother tells me he's more alert now, feeling more pain as a result, but in my mind he's still asleep, until the next time I visit.

As for me, I'm restless. I take all of my husband Paul's shirts to the cleaner, stock up on milk; my approach is a just-in-case attitude, where nothing should be left undone. Even though I don't think I'm worried, I'm not sleeping well, and my eyes have a constant stinging sensation that I know is exhaustion. Yesterday I called upstairs to my younger daughter, Ariel,

"David," my brother's name. I just said it right out loud, checking to see if she was almost ready for school. "David!" I yelled, saying the whole name before I realized my mistake.

Sometimes it comes to me that my father is in this predicament because he was hit by a car, and I conjure the old woman and wonder if she has any idea what she's done. Then I get so angry I feel like shaking, so frustrated I want to just push that part of the story away into the background where it usually is. After a while, I'm back to wondering how my father's doing, and I'm waiting again to update my vision. The phone calls tell me things like, "There's not much change," or, "They're still giving him blood," nothing I can really use, nothing that affects the picture. What I need, I realize, is my father himself, and the way I see it, I may have a long time to wait.

The Second Visit

We return to visit my father the following weekend, Paul, my daughters Sofie and Ariel, and I. I have warned them about the tubes and repeated to the girls that he is unable to talk and that he might not wake up at all. But when we enter the room, his eyes are open. 'Oh, look! He's awake!" Last weekend he hadn't opened his eyes once. I am like a little girl filled with excitement.

Everything else about him is the same—the tubes, the regular hiss of the respirator. He is lying on his back and he is still. He is looking straight up, and when I go to the side of the bed, I see that his eyes are different from his healthy eyes. They are smaller and his left eyelid droops a little lower than his right. It's hard to tell where his eyes are focused.

I lean forward against the bedrail. "Dad, it's Sue." Slowly his head begins to turn towards me, and I am thrilled. "It's Sue," I say again, this time a little louder, and his head continues to move. His eyes stare above, aimed at the ceiling but leaning in my direction. "Can you hear me?" I ask, and see that his head gives the slightest nod in response.

A week before I wondered if he'd ever awaken again. "Sofie and Ariel are here," I tell him, enunciating slowly as if he spoke another language. Then I usher them in front of me, believing their voices can heal him as well as any drug. They speak to him one at a time. Sofie is confident, but Ariel speaks too softly and doesn't know what to say. "Just tell him you're here," I urge. "Tell him you love him." Then his eyes close again and he drifts away.

It's like that throughout the day. Mostly his eyes remain shut, but we speak to him on and off anyway, taking turns stroking his hair and holding his hands. It strikes me that we are at a point when the fluttering open of my father's eyelids and the slightest movement of his head have become momentous events, and we hesitate to leave for dinner in case we miss another short period of this hazy wakefulness.

We return later to say goodnight, and it's then that I snap another image to add to my collection. My father is awake again, and this time when we say hello, he tries to lift his head. It is too much. His cheeks turn pink and he grimaces; a beep sounds from some piece of equipment, summoning a nurse. I step back for an instant in alarm, then approach him again and tell him, "Calm down, calm down. You have to rest and be still. It's okay." My anxiety dissolves into a strong caring instinct that I recognize from the way I comfort my daughters, and the way I responded to our cat right before she died. My hand smoothes the top of his head over and over, while across the bed, Sofie has taken his hand and is whispering, "Shhh, shhh," like she's talking to a baby. His head relaxes as we speak. "Good, good," we coo, so relieved when the signals stabilize.

But now he is more awake than before, and as I speak, he turns his eyes to find mine. "He's looking at me," I say to the room, nearly breathless as I peer closely at his eyes to see if they're really seeing me. "It's okay," I tell him, believing that they are.

What I see next touches my heart. There are tears. I'm sure of it. Not flowing, but there, cupped in his lower lids, gatherings of tears. His eyes have reddened just a little, and I am sure he is telling me his anguish, his love, and the flow of emotion still stuck inside him. "It's okay," I repeat, and he closes his eyes.

No one else sees my father cry, and when I tell them, they say you can't be sure what he's doing. But I believe in that moment he was letting me know how he felt, and though all he had were his eyes, it is an embodiment of my father that is branded in my mind and that I will never forget.

After the Second Visit

It was a turning point, that visit. I tell Sofie and Ariel it's because of them, that the sound of their voices gave him strength. By Monday night, the respirator was out, and now my father, though still very weak, is breathing on his own, eating, and talking. He has been moved off the ICU into another ward, where, my mother tells me, he has started to complain. "He wants to go home," she says. "When I told him I was going home to bed, he asked me, in all seriousness, 'Why can't I come with you?'"

The healthier my father gets, the unhappier he will become at having to stay in the hospital. He will complain about the food, and he may not like his nurses. He will be angry about his broken leg, and annoyed when he realizes how much work he has to do before he is able to walk.

"Now comes the hard part," my mother confides. For two weeks, she has sat by my father's bedside from morning till evening, knitting, reading the newspaper, taking short walks down hospital corridors, or, if it was warm enough, along the pathways outside that meander around the complex. She has had unexpected visits with her children, and more phone conversations with friends and relatives than she is used to.

With my father's healing comes another chapter, one in which my mother will be required to look out for his welfare in the hospital now that he doesn't have the immediate care of the ICU. It is one in which she'll have to calm my father's anger and impatience, and failing to do so, bear the brunt of it. She will come earlier in the morning and leave later at night, perhaps feeling a guilt now that she didn't worry about when she left him drugged and sedated. For two weeks she sat with quiet purpose, unable to do more than speak softly and touch gently every once in awhile. Though she is relieved, as we all are, and anxious for my father's full recovery, I wonder if there isn't a tinge of nervousness, maybe even of regret, as she bolsters herself to go through what must come next.

My father is still being given morphine for pain, and my mother confesses, "He's really out of it." When I press for details, she tells me he says things out of context. "Let's go for coffee," he'll suggest, or, "Let's get out of here and go home." Sometimes in his sleep, he smiles and gropes at the air in front of him.

"It's the drugs," I tell my mother, but we're both not sure where the man who was my father is now, and if he'll ever return.

The Third Visit

I fly to Washington for just the day. I am excited to see my father awake, to hear his voice again, but when I arrive in the morning, he is sleeping soundly, an oxygen mask covering his nose and mouth. I want to awaken him, though he looks so peaceful, and, watching him closely, I approach the bed. "Hi, Dad," I say, "It's Sue," but he doesn't respond and I don't have the heart to speak any louder. Later, when he opens his eyes, it's just for a moment before they close again.

A nurse sits in the room in a chair by the window. Her name is Shelley and she is studying from a chemistry textbook, her large cloth pocketbook perched on the wide sill next to a pile of sheets and blankets. "He has such a beautiful smile," she tells me, an odd comment, I think to myself, given the circumstances. She is there to keep an eye on him, but I feel awkward talking to my still-sleeping father, and I wish she would leave.

A few hours pass before he wakes again, and now his eyes are wide, startled, frightened above the mask. He stares at me as I talk to him. I tell him who I am. I want him to melt with pleasure, to smile with relief, but he just stares unknowingly. "Do his eyes always look like this?" I ask my mother, feeling alarmed myself, and she shakes her head no. I take my father's hand to calm him. As he falls back to sleep, I decide I was just part of some mysterious dream, a blur of drug-shadowed conscious and unconscious which is his private world now.

In the afternoon, though, his head clears a bit. His eyes look normal now, as if they're looking out, seeing what we're all seeing, instead of barring any access the way they appeared when he was sedated, so small and inward. His eyes are hazel the way mine are, though dimmed, duller, as the whole of him seems to me. The nurse removes the oxygen mask so he can talk, and then I see why she'd mentioned his smile. His face lights up when he recognizes me.

"Sue," he says. This is the first time I've been able to talk with him, and I notice that his words are slurred like he's had too much to drink. His voice is husky and hoarse. I take his hand and he keeps smiling. He is like a child, looking up at me with a mixture of awe and confusion, his eyes happy and free of anything but love.

My father used to confess over and over that when my brothers and I were small, my mother would have to remind him, "You have to show them love."

"'Love?' I'd say to her. 'What do you mean, love?' You see," he'd confide, "I didn't even know what she meant." My father would tell me this to explain what he felt were his shortcomings as a father. He blamed his own parents, who, he says, raised him with no expression of love whatsoever. He lived with his guilt at being unloving to us when we were young, and at not being a good-enough father.

Now, lying in his hospital bed, he is nothing but love, love in a world all his own. He is smiling and touching and telling my mother, then me, then my mother again how much he loves us. Sometimes I see him watching my mother as if he's just fallen in love. When I speak to him, his eyes gaze at mine as if rapt with interest, like a baby whose whole world is his mother's voice as she speaks to him. He nods and says, "Is that so? Is that so?", then smiles his broad smile again. He kisses my hand, which he can barely navigate to his lips, and I kiss his forehead more easily than I've ever been able to kiss him before.

Hours pass and I am staring at him, holding his hand. His skin is smooth, his graying hair longer than usual and thick. "You look young," I tell him. "You look good." I see the boy I never knew, the handsome young man who married my mother, the father I never thought of as old. They are all layered there on the man who now can barely move, and still cannot comprehend why. When I glance at my own reflection in the bathroom mirror, I am struck by my own resemblance to him.

My father has been lying immobile for almost three weeks, and now it's time to start physical rehabilitation, not just to teach him to walk on his broken leg, but to strengthen the muscles that have atrophied from disuse. The physical therapist has shown my mother exercises she is to do with my father.

"Let's do your exercises," she suggests, and my father nods compliantly. She removes the blanket that cover his legs, and I see for the first time the brace that protects the break. It is the other leg, though, that is more shocking. It is white, hairless, and so very, very thin as it tapers to his ankle, which seems no bigger than my wrist. I see that the skin of his calf seems empty, a bag whose contents have been removed, as if there isn't any muscle there at all. It is so unnatural that I have to touch it, and when I do,

I am struck by how soft it is, but how odd, how un-leg-like. Two more times during the afternoon, I touch his calf, just sticking out my finger and poking gently. I know he won't even notice and I am fascinated.

His body, though, is healing the way the doctors assure us it should. It is his mind that concerns us more. The doctors call it "lucidity," and the nurses test him by asking questions whenever they come in. Then it's like a quiz show, and we hold our breath to see if he'll say the right answer.

"Do you know what year it is, Mr. Rubin?"

My father glances up at the ceiling in thought. "The year is. . . the year is one thousand nine hundred and thirty five." They never tell him he's wrong, but when he answers correctly, we all exclaim, "Good! Good!" like we're talking to a small child.

"And do you know who the President is now?" He tries to think but doesn't say anything.

We tell him about the millennium. We tell him it's now 2000, and he looks at us with sincere interest.

"2000?" he says with surprise. "Really!"

"Yes." I am determined now that he can know this. "It's 2000. 2000." I repeat it slowly. "Now, what year is it?" I try.

"The year is two thousand . . . eighty four." My heart sinks.

But mixed in with the confusion is the sense of humor my father was known for, and it pops up unexpectedly and makes us all laugh—a mixture of relief, familiarity and hope. Later, another nurse points to my mother and me sitting by my father's bedside.

"Do you know who that lady is?" she asks.

"That is my daughter," my father replies now without hesitation.

"And who is the lady sitting next to her?"

"That's no lady," quips my father. "That's my wife."

Sometimes he seems to drift away from us into another consciousness. He lifts his left arm again and again, studying it and turning it slowly as if looking at a watch. But there is no watch, only an IV line and bruises from so many needles. He scrutinizes his fingertips, rubs them together a little and looks puzzled. Once he turns to me and asks, an open and questioning expression on his face, "So have you pretty much completed your secondary education?" It is this part I find most distressing. We don't know where my father has gone, and though we've been told some disorientation is common after sedation and trauma, we worry that he won't come back.

A little later, he looks up at me and says, "Where do *you* come from?"

"It's me, Sue," but he doesn't seem to register. "Do you know who I am?" I ask.

"Yes," he replies. He does that. You ask him a yes or no question and that's the only answer you get. You have to ask further: "What?" or "Who?", which I do.

"You're one of the Levinson girls," he answers.

"I'm Susan, your daughter," I tell him firmly, a smile still fixed on my face. I glance at my mother. "Do you know who I am?"

"Yes," he says confidently. "You're one of the Levinson girls."

This is the only time I need to leave the room. When I return, he looks surprised and delighted again, reaches out his hand and says my name.

Interspersed with these periods are times of great agitation, when my father is angry that he can't go home.

"Shall we go home now?" he asks my mother, sometimes persisting for hours.

"Not yet," she answers again and again, trying to remain patient.

"Why can't I?" he'll ask. "Why not? Tell me why we can't go home?" Sometimes he hits the bed in frustration, and once he told my mother he hated her because she wouldn't let him leave. After a while, he quiets down and stares ahead of him, then slowly his eyes close and we are relieved.

Late in the day, we're tired and no one is talking. The hospital television is tuned to a series of cooking shows, which we all stare at without the sound. I am sure my father isn't following the recipes, and neither am I. Suddenly he looks at me and says, "Life is sad." "What?" I ask, because I can't be sure. "Life is sad," he repeats, and at that moment I feel nothing could be truer.

When I am home again, I wake up in the middle of the night from a dream about my father. My family is there and we are all concerned because someone is ill. My father is worried, the expression on his face serious. Then I see it is the same face I've been staring at all day, the one with the smooth skin and the thick gray hair, and I remember it is my father who is ill. When I awaken, I miss him and wish he could still be one of us.

I can talk to my father on the telephone now, so I call the hospital each day. I visualize him laying there, his face serious, the phone pressed gently against his cheek.

"Hi, Dad," I say with cheer and enthusiasm.

"Hi, Sue," he responds, his voice gravelly and airy. I still hear the slur in his words.

"How are you?" I ask, and he says, "Oh, not bad today," or instead, in a much quieter voice, "Today I just feel down, so down in the dumps."

I try to reassure him; I think fast for things to say; I make my comments in the form of questions: "Are you more comfortable today?" "Did you have physical therapy yet?" "Did you sleep well last night?" His answers are short, but always full sentences: "Yes, I am." "Yes, I did, Sue." "Last night? Last night I slept pretty well." If I don't keep talking, I'm afraid he'll just be silent, but once, after a pause, he says, "All's well that ends well." I'm not sure I heard correctly, but he says it again: "All's well that ends well." "That's right," I say, "All's well that ends well."

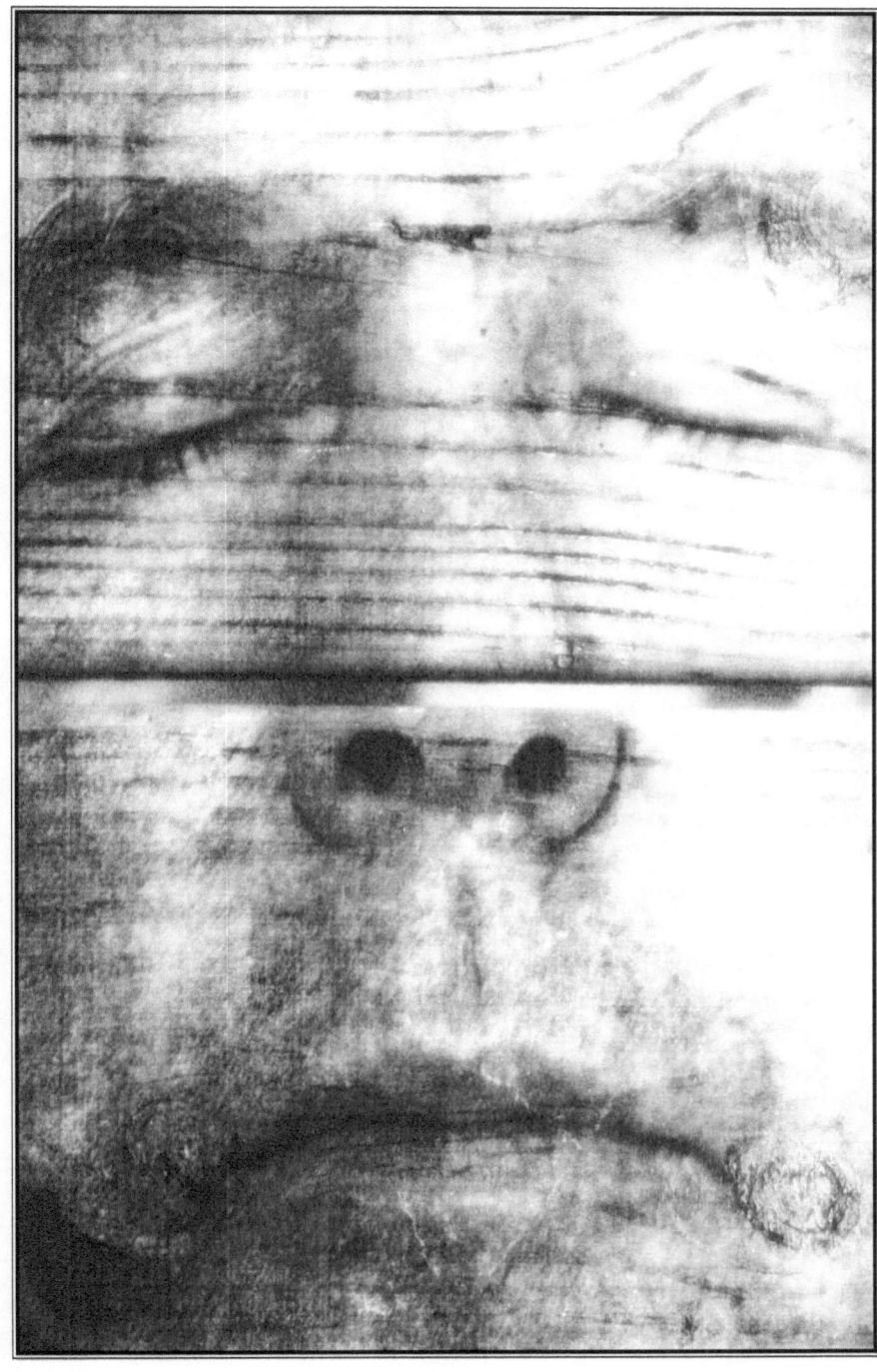

SUSI GREGG FOWLER

AFTER THE STROKE

For Jane

I watch you struggle
to form words,
taking your energy
and funneling it
into phrases.
I never before
recognized as art,
this sculpting of sound.

You blow your breath upward,
lift strands of gold and silver
off your brow –
the one hint of pique.

Mostly, you seem to leave
frustrations in the pile
of things outside your
hospital door, the cast-off
inessentials:
          false modesty
          resistance
          defensiveness
          self-protection.

Before, I sometimes felt
you holding back,
playing in shallows.
Now I see the banks defined.
The river runs deep.

You are teaching us all
to swim.

JOHN HOLBROOK

ENVISION

After the doctor calls to tell you
your mother's suffered a catastrophic,
at the base of the brain, main stem stroke,
that she is conscious but paralyzed
from the neck down, that she can neither talk
nor swallow, that her vital functions are fading,
that she will be given no oxygen,
food, water, only saline, but be made
comfortable and as the dying process
bears down on her be given morphine
to ease the pain, to let her rest
between each breath
as her breathing's sure to become labored. . .

—What is it you imagine of her last moments
lying there, unable to cry out,
to respond only with the blinking of an eye
to questions from family members concerned
with her comfort, the priest administering last rights,
a sister placing my phone call
from Missoula to Flint up to her ear
so that I might offer words of love,
news, the Holidays, and of her granddaughter Karin,
home from Alaska with her boyfriend Sean,
who've been away a whole year working,
whom she saw last when still a child?

—What is it you envision
with a stroke someday of your own
with nothing so much
as a blinding bewilderment to help you cope
with a sense of helplessness

unprecedented in scale,
while the animal-body part of you
breaking down, begins its awkward
sure passage back to humus, mineral in soil;
where one good eye closes then opens
to a blur of faces praying you see
and remember them but can't be sure
what the slight tremors
in a corner of your mouth might mean
or what sense if any to make
of sounds coming from your throat
so unfamiliar that not even you
can dream them intelligible
anymore that your physician himself,
with all his training, can,

—except, later on, when
long past midnight, the family having
left quietly for a little rest back home,
the nurse, stethoscope back on her shoulder,
slowly folding your hands in hers,
the doctor listening over your mouth,
his hand on your same forehead,
thumb and forefinger sweeping down
your descending gaze. . .
how rarely he verbalizes anymore
but you're sure he's thinking:
the coming in, the life going out,
the small epic struggles for and against its loss,
our flesh, blood, our bonding with each breath,
the pain, our gains, steady, up until death.

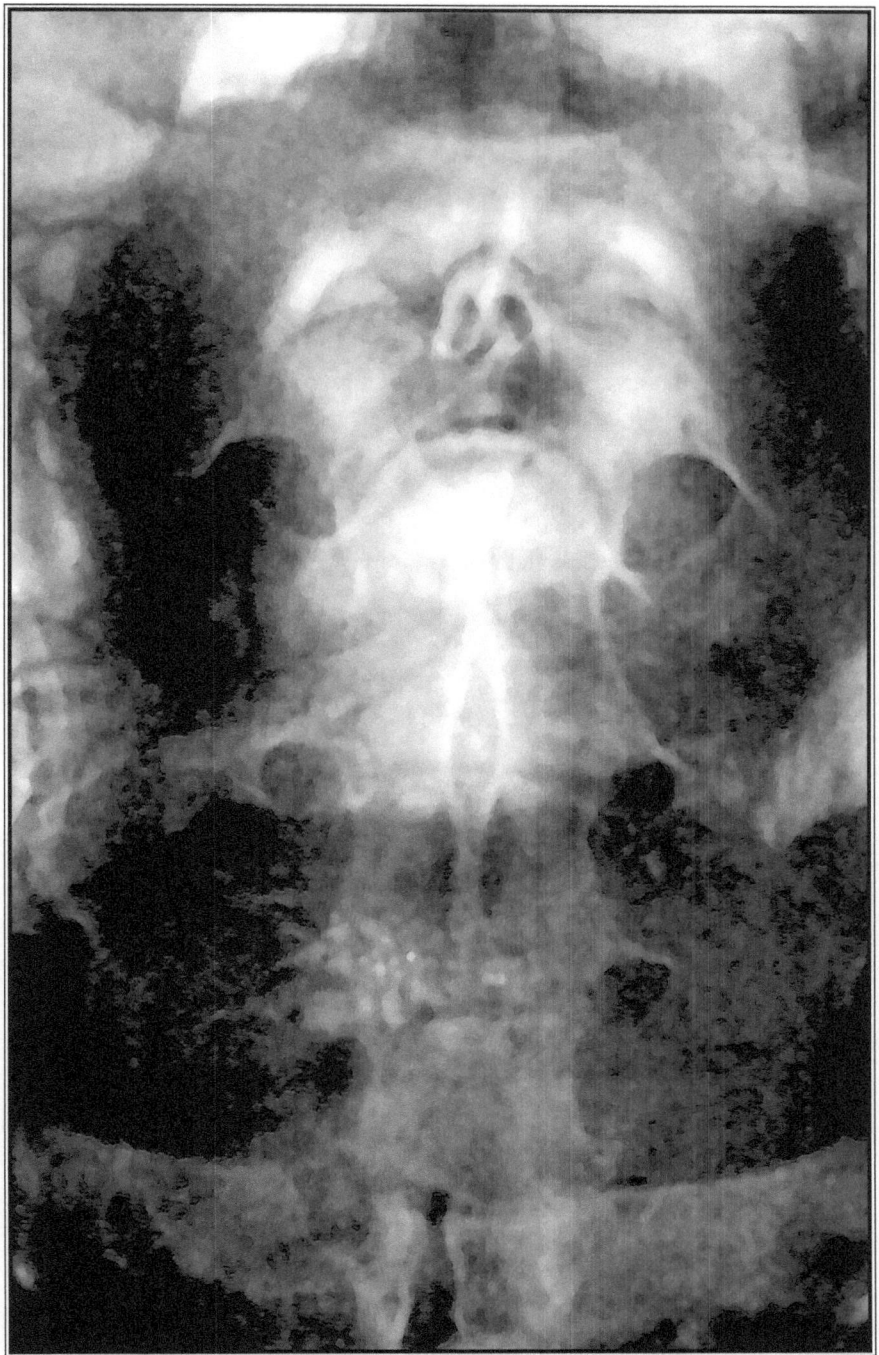

SARA LIPPMANN

THE DYING TRADITION

Long after everything, I will remember the smells: Cabbage soup and rotting lilies. Accents of indignity. I will remember her signature 4711 eau de toilette and her pride of all things European. Her room I will have less trouble forgetting. It is spare, unremarkable. Today, the partition is drawn, revealing a lone window that overlooks the George Washington Bridge. A barge inches along the dull slate of the Hudson. The day is overcast. The radiator clicks.

"Sit on the chair."
"Sit on the pillow."
"Sit on the chair."
"Sit on the pillow."

My grandmother's neighbor is performing morning calisthenics. Her commands spill out in a blunted, vibratory string, as if uttered from the back of the Bronx-Manhattan express bus. Her routine is undistracted by my presence, much less my grandmother's; my grandmother has conked out again. I stare at the stranger. There is little else to do. My grandmother could sleep for weeks. I cannot stop staring: at this woman's plastic ferns and array of Hallmarks; at the recent wedding photos on the wall, satin gloves embracing the sloped shoulders of this woman with the far-off look, for she too is someone's grandmother. I study her movements as she shuffles from the head of her bed to her chair, I study the trembling of her lip, her bosom consuming the entire expanse of her torso as she catches her breath and shuffles back again, her bottom flat and padded, her beige trousers coveting crumbs, her blue sweater in need of a bib.

"Sit on the chair."
I think of Dustin Hoffman in *Rain Man*.
"Sit on the pillow."

This woman is no autistic savant.

"Sit on the chair."

She is a resident at the Hebrew Home for the Aged. Such behavior is run-of-the-mill here, where my grandmother lives now, where she will die. It's not bad as places go. The campus remains true to its brochure: There are multiple wings and activity rooms, a gourmet restaurant, artwork worthy of its celebrity donors, an antique Lionel train exhibit, sculpture gardens; you can even spot swans feeding along the pebble-strewn bed of the river. When we moved her in on Christmas Eve, we said, "Think of it like an Ivy League university" and she threw back her chins and winked at the orderly, "My family knows how to spoil me," as if we were treating her to an all-expenses-paid luxury cruise vacation.

The dying starts in December:

"Can you imagine," she tells the doctor. Bolstered by pillows, my grandmother looks as if she's awoken from a regular afternoon nap instead of a twenty-four hour coma. The doctor, a third year resident, flashes his penlight; her lids flutter in response. He's here to collect her patient history. My grandmother is ninety-four years old. How much time does he have?

"I am sitting in the Corner Café, right off Johnson Avenue, on the corner of. You know. You don't know it? You should go. It is such a nice little café and I am sitting there with my son, Larry, my youngest, you know, and every Sunday he comes and we go and he orders the potato pancakes, like bird nests they are, so light and crispy, and the strangest thing. I have the donuts. It was Hanukkah already, which came early this year, don't you know. *Sufganiot*, for that is tradition. And they are the most delicious donuts you've ever had, with a dusting of powdered sugar, the warmest gift of strawberry when you bite in."

"And then what happened, Mrs. Lippmann?"

"We ate."

He makes a note in her chart.

"Do you know why you're here?" he asks and she shrugs. He snaps his pen and hooks it to his shirt pocket. The resident crabs over on his stool and checks her vitals, taps the bags dripping life into her veins, and feels for her needles. They have been secured with gauze and taped to her arm. When she speaks, condensation fogs up her oxygen mask. Electrodes monitor the beating of her heart, which had shut down entirely the night before.

She gazes up at him and blinks.

"The donuts?"

"Mrs. Lippmann, I doubt it was— "

"You cannot imagine until you've tasted them," she says, her blue eyes clouding over in memory.

She is in intensive care and she is sleeping. She is sleeping most of the time. I press my lips to her forehead. It is damp. Her hand clutches mine like a child.

"Sarala," she smiles; her voice, muffled by that mask, is every bit as German as the day she arrived in this country over sixty years ago.

"Do you know?" she asks.

I wait. Her oxygen wheezes.

"I am in the hospital," she announces as if she were joining the circus.

"I know," I say, and then I say, "Omi." Omi is grandma in German.

It's been four days and my grandmother is not listening to this hospital nonsense. Any bird brain can see she is quite clearly lying in her twin bed at home; home being an assisted-living facility and not a nursing home, not the Hebrew Home, not yet, but on Henry Hudson Parkway, down the street from the apartment in which she'd lived for the last thirty years; home is room 919, a one-bedroom unit with a modest living area and a kitchenette with a stuffed-to-capacity mini-bar fridge.

Pheh, my grandmother says.

My father prepared me for this: ICU psychosis, the disorientation and delirium that stems from living where it is always day and never night, where the machines bleep and the nurses draw blood and doctors probe and the fluorescents are humming round the clock. Every fifteen seconds my grandmother tries to spring out of bed. Pushes up her body like a baby discovering its legs only to redden and grow short of breath upon realizing she is attached to a complicated network of tubes and machines and needles. Bring me my walker, she demands. We are going to be late. Late? I ask. Late! She cries; she is beside herself. Tardiness is a terrible sin. My walker! She thrashes from side to side. Let's go! Where are we going? I ask. To dinner, she says. Salmon fillet, tartar sauce, sweet peas. Get with the program. Hop to it, she says. That a way. Let's get out of here before the slobs steal all the good seats.

Sentimentality has no place here: she is not a young woman. She has lived her life, had her children, she has suffered her ailments: broken hips and a broken wrist, uterine cancer, two bouts of colon cancer, a handful of myocardial infarctions as well as a brief stint in a mental hospital, postwar and postpartum and never discussed. Despite physical limitations brought on by severe osteoporosis, she runs laps around our memories. We should all be so lucky. And yet. She is the matriarch, our family's glue. How can she *not* live forever?

My grandmother is drinking the Atlantic Ocean. This is what she tells me and I commend her for it. In the next hour, she must polish off four pints of bug juice from a straw. I fill up the pitcher and hold her cup as she drinks. Enough, she says. My grandmother never has drunk this much in her life. A thimble-sized glass of orange juice in the morning, one of cream soda at day's end, a cup of tea in between. Enough, she says, as I keep pouring. I ask her to drink more. I tell her it would make me happy. More importantly, I tell her it would please the doctors and she is not one to disappoint. The doctors are running tests. They have scheduled MRIs, full-body CATs, X-rays, blood, urine, the works. She has to bloat her belly like a pregnant woman only the doctor plans to search for cancer and not for a fetal heartbeat. Enough, she says as she drinks. Water drips down her chin. Enough, I'm drowning here, enough.

The ICU waiting room smells of apple juice and French fries; it is filled with married couples and families. They pace the linoleum and sink into chairs, they bury faces into necks, they blow noses, they have begun the long slow process of grieving. Children kick over towers of blocks. A woman sobs into her cell phone. All of them have been robbed, their loved ones stricken abruptly by accident or prematurely by disease. I stare up at the television monitor. The picture quality is poor but through the static I can still make out the soap opera I knew well in childhood. My grandmother is ninety-four years old. She has seen me fall in love; she has seen me get married. I am the luckiest girl in the world.

My father drives up from Philadelphia. It is a weekday. His face is haggard, his jaw slack and unshaven. A three-sphere cluster has been found in my grandmother's brain. That's what the X-rays indicate and the MRI confirms. I picture a model of a water molecule like the kind we constructed from Styrofoam balls in high school chemistry class: two oxygen atoms stuck to a red ball of hydrogen. This much the doctors know. What they do not know is what caused this mass or where it's coming from, if it is cancer, and if it is cancer then where did the cancer (not that they've sworn it's cancer) originate because they seem quite confident that the cancer, if it is cancer and they are not swearing by it, first took root elsewhere in her body before blooming with such admirable symmetry in her brain.

My father has a theory. He is also a doctor (as per the rule of the firstborn of immigrant parents) and he has done his research. Citing some medical journal, he explains a phenomenon among religious New York Jews who have presented similar cerebella formations following unwitting and repeated exposure to non-kosher food. Their systems, it appeared, couldn't fend off the unfamiliar—and ultimately, toxic—presence of *treyf.* It is only bacteria, my father declares, an infection spawned by the well-meaning gentile hands of the kitchen staff at the place where your grandmother has lived for the past three years. There is righteousness in his voice, the vestiges of his orthodox upbringing. There is hope too in his voice as he says it: With a proper regimen of steroids and antibiotics, this little matter will all go away.

It does not go away.

My grandmother remains in intensive care because every week or so she has an episode. One minute she will be kvetching about the consistency of the Jell-O and the next minute she will be out cold. The doctors have called these spells of unresponsiveness seizures, mini-strokes, pseudo heart attacks, but it is likely the three-ringed-circus in her brain has something to do with it. Today she is wide-awake and trying to yank out her IVs. She is agitated. My grandmother has not been out of bed for two weeks. She kicks at her sheet.

"There is pain in my vagina," she wails.

My grandmother has never uttered the word vagina, *ever*, in her life.

The doctors work their wonders. My grandmother's is a special case, which means specialists stop by all the time. They round; they consult. Professional, well-mannered, nice-looking enough; to my grandmother, they all might as well be Cary Grant. Her eyes brighten upon their arrivals; she sits a bit taller in bed. When they lean over her, she caresses their white coats and fingers their pockets, taps their stethoscopes' icy diaphragms with brittle nails.

This specialist has blonde curls and light eyes and an Irish last name, which means despite his virtues, she will not be trying to make a *shidduch* for my younger most eligible cousin. Nonetheless, she introduces him to me proudly, her granddaughter. He is drawing bull's-eyes all over her scalp, in nineteen places total, at equal distance apart. The specialist (a technician, but the white coat is misleading) calls her a punk rocker. My grandmother shows off her wattle and laughs. This is flirting. She asks him if she is a good patient, and he tells her, the best, as he places a white saucer over each circle to which he hooks up different colored wires and connects them to his EEG machine. The questions go like this:

Do you know your name?

Do you know where you are?

She answers: I am not some kind of idiot, you know.

There will be red streaks in her hair for a week.

They are not always good days. There are days when the oxygen straps slip off her ears, small and withered as dried apricots. Days when the gas hisses in mockery, when my grandmother gasps for each breath. On these days, I lift her head and readjust the tubes, fitting the green capillaries back into her nose, but she is unaware of the difference. She picks at the skin on her lips. They bleed. The straps fall. I tighten them. I adjust. I press the tubes into her nose. She pushes my hand away. It becomes quite a game except that neither of us is laughing. When her lunch tray comes on such days, she is not hungry.

My grandmother wants to see the baby. Her eyes a watery glaze, she is clear about the pickles and horseradish; she is foggier about the baby.
Whose baby? We ask, my uncle and I.
The baby, the baby, she mumbles.
Ma, my uncle calls, squeezes her shoulder.
Omi, I say.
She crooks her arms like a cradle. There hasn't been a baby in our family since my first cousin was born and that was twenty-five years ago. My grandmother clucks her tongue. Pockets of spittle gather in the creases of her mouth.
My uncle signs the do-not-resuscitate order.

Later we will learn it was nothing to worry. She had been dreaming with her eyes open. People actually do this. My grandmother does this. It is perfectly normal. In dreams, my grandmother is a young woman; deli is served fresh; she attends a ladies' luncheon in dreams; there is a kosher feast for a baby of unknown face and origin because, after all, dreams are like that. The most delicious tongue sandwich, she will say and we will smile and exchange I-told-you-so glances at this sound, reasonable dream. See? Despite all the attention to that region, there is absolutely nothing wrong with my grandmother's mind.

The cafeteria reeks of slop and industrial dish washing. I drink Coca-Cola and eat Asian rice snacks. This much my stomach can handle. From now on, I will pick up these items every day at the lobby's gift shop along with the newspaper, which I will read to my grandmother even though she tells me she has heard enough of the lousy cowboy and his rhetoric of war. The rice crackers come in different shapes and sizes. I suck off their soy glaze before crunching into them. I eat them one by one. I will eat them like this for the next three months and then I will eat them never again.

They've decided to lay off all the invasive tests; the results would solve nothing but medical curiosity. Since the first night of Hanukkah, it appears my grandmother has also suffered two heart attacks and a urinary tract infection. As for the inconvenient situation in her brain, the doctors opt for metastasis. It is the most popular deduction although it remains unknown exactly where the primary cancer first flared. The CAT scan was clean. Must be melanoma. Even though her skin is no more mottled with sunspots than any ninety-four year-old, she did spend summers in Zurich and winters at Daytona Beach without proper UV protection. No one is suggesting treatment. We raise the question of time. There are arrangements to be made. Her heart is weak. But she is a stubborn German woman, a fighter to the core. And malignancy, like everything else, we are advised, progresses at a snail's pace in the elderly.

My grandmother has been transferred to a step-down unit. Progress!

She says, sitting tall (for four-feet-nine-inches) in her narrow hospital bed. I am the Patient of the Year. We bring so many bouquets the windowsill looks like Easter. Out the window, snow melts into the Hudson. The flakes fall and dissolve, but when they stick to the banks she knows not to expect visitors. It snows more than average that December.

At lunch, my grandmother makes fun of the food. This is her specialty. Her meals come wrapped like airplane rations. How can chicken soup be made without chicken? This fish looks like an old shoe, she says. I pull up a chair and push down the bed rails and cut up her Salisbury steak, her chicken a la king. She always chooses mid-chew as a good time for stories but I am a stickler. I tell her she cannot talk while she's eating. There are no exceptions. She will choke just as her friend's husband, Benny, choked on the hot string of his cheese pizza, and we all know what happened to him. She nods soberly as she chews and her bridge slaps away. She eats and she eats on account of the steroids and when she isn't eating she's laughing. Her euphoria too, is on account of the steroids. For dessert, I bring chocolate glazed donuts. She shoves an entire Krispy Kreme in her mouth and I worry she may bite off her fingers.

I visit my grandmother in the hospital for the last time. Tomorrow is Christmas Eve and she is moving; she will be transferred to the Hebrew Home; she is not going home; she will never go home; she will die in this nursing home, which she does not know. She does not know this because we have not told her about the billiard balls clinking like a wedding toast in her brain. She knows about the seizures and she knows about her uncooperative heart but we have left out the part about the cancer (there is, we assure ourselves, reasonable doubt) and we have sidestepped the impending reality of death. After all, from the day we are born we start dying; we are all always and all the time dying; there is no point in underlining this. Over the next two months we will question the ethics of this decision. She will ask us what is wrong with her and we will lie to her, our mother, my grandmother. We will convince ourselves that we overlooked the particulars because we did not want to break her spirit. When she muscles her way into January, February, and then, March, we will remind ourselves that the doctors predicted it would be otherwise—weeks, not months!—and we saw no reason to frighten her. We will tell ourselves we had her best interests in mind. We will tell ourselves that no one wants to stew in her own mortality. Regardless of what we tell ourselves, she will die knowing she is dying and somewhere in the dark, murky reaches of her brain, she will die knowing her family knew the truth all along and looked her in the eyes and showered her with kisses and refused her this information.

But not today. Today she is convinced nursing homes are the places for short-term physical therapy and who are we to argue. She will go, stamp in her time card, do her leg lifts, get behind that walker and push away. I am doing her nails for the occasion. My grandmother is gushing about cream puffs and pink lacquered furniture and an uncle who snipped the buttons from dinner guests' overcoats. Her eyes light up like the streets of Berlin. Images pour out in a wash of parquet floors and starched pleats and river cafes. If it weren't for the mention of a militant schoolteacher or snotty classmate that stole her apple there would be way of knowing that she escaped Nazism and that she was practically the only one in the family who did.

In the beginning, I visit the Hebrew Home daily, but anyone who's ever started a race sprinting knows it's tough to maintain the momentum. Once the curtain falls over my grandmother's left eye optimism does not come easy. The hour and a half travel time feels like eternity, so I cut back to two or three times a week, depending on how many other visitors are expected on evenings and weekends. The winter is unrelenting, so I've taken to running the half-mile from the bus stop to the Home, but it's often icy and today I slip and break my fall like a child, skinning my palms and knees. I've torn my gloves and tights and the wind stings my cuts and I stand there in the middle of the road crying, tears forming ice on my cheeks.

There are hardly any men here, not like my grandmother is on the market. In the lounge there is a double amputee, a caged parakeet, and a youngish widower dressed in khakis and red shoes who demands his supper every five minutes. Of women there are plenty. One slouched like an accordion is declaring her love for all passersby; another is calling the same passersby "cunt motherfuckers." A third woman claps her hands in her wheelchair. The rest in the lounge are asleep, heads slumped to their chests like unused puppets, mouths agape, drool leaking out onto their sweaters. My grandmother and I decide to spend our visits in the privacy of her room.

"Sarala," her voice is strained, the pitch unnaturally high. My grandmother sits, knees splayed, in her wheelchair. When she moved in, the nurses requested that she buy cotton trousers with elastic waists precisely to avoid this kind of peepshow but my grandmother explained she was a lady who had no use for garments that did not require dry cleaning. She wears a wool tweed skirt and a silk blouse with a large sauce stain. Her nylons are donuts around her ankles; her hair has been cropped and hugs her face like a flapper. I tell her this. She laughs and says, "Right," but I'm not sure she hears me. Right is what she says now to assure us she is not missing a beat. I gently close her legs. "Right," she says. I walk over to her good side, where she can still hear and see. I hold her right hand.

Did I mention the eating? This is what we do. We eat. It is always lunch and when it isn't lunch, it's snack time. Who can keep track? Nothing spoils her appetite. I bring chocolates and marzipan and ginger cookies and smoked salmon and creamed herring and soft rolls. She eats. She eats without chewing (why be slowed down?), and even though she says the Home's cooking is inedible, she does a fine job of polishing that off too.

The nurses have it in for her. My grandmother whispers: They are rough and fierce and mean. You've got to get me out of here, she says. Tears wet her blouse. She has given up therapy. Or rather, therapy has given up on her. What is the use? Her coordination has been cut like electrical wire;

the therapists fear she will fall. So that's it. Discharged from therapy, she must give up the dream of once again dressing herself and tying her shoes. She must relinquish any hope of ever using the bathroom alone. There are accidents. Diaper rashes. Upset stomachs, insufferable smells.

I am a big baby, my grandmother sobs.

The rabbi comes on Friday. For twenty years, my grandmother has walked to his shul and occupied the same seat beside the *mechitza* separating men from women. Sabbath is not something she misses. The congregation has learned to count on her like a Swiss watch. In his black suit, the rabbi sits and asks her for a story. Right, my grandmother nods. Right, right, right. Margot, tell me a story to carry me through Shabbas. But my grandmother no longer tells stories. She holds her head with her hand. The rabbi holds her other hand and leads us in Shalom Eleichem but she does not join in because the words do not come to her. Her nails are crusted in food. He wishes her Good Shabbas and she nods so he puts on his hat and after he leaves she sits proud and mutters, what a busy man, that he should find the time to see me.

We have parties on weekends. My parents come, my cousin, my aunt and uncle, my maternal grandmother, old neighbors, a lady from the temple. There is always a celebration: a birthday, another Saturday, the Ides of March. We wheel my grandmother into the elevator and down to the sitting room; we adjust my grandmother so she does not slide out of her chair. We say: Look at this thick marbled corned beef! Rye soft as pillows! Hot knishes, your favorite! Frankfurters, what a treat! We smear piles of egg salad and liverwurst on black bread. My grandmother chews with her mouth open and when she is finished she cups her eye and then she bows her head.

Open your eyes, Ma.
"Sit on the chair."

Omi, look at me.

"Sit on the pillow."

Yoo-hoo. Peek-a-boo. Over here. We clap. We wave. We stamp.

We say, Do it for me.

I am, she says but all movement has stilled beneath her lids.

We sit vigil. My grandmother is curled up in her smock and hugging the rails; she has stopped taking food or water but she is not quite finished with air. We gather around her bed and talk to her. We read the paper aloud; we listen to *La Traviata* on public radio; we watch the nightly news. We watch her. For 48 hours she breathes. No tubes, no oxygen. Her body rises and falls, gently at first, becoming more labored with each passing hour as you'd expect from a woman wrestling the angel of death, but she holds on, my grandmother, until my sister's returned from Africa and my uncle's navigated rush-hour traffic, and when all parties are present, she gathers up the last wisps in her lungs and draws her nose to her lips, exhaling with the fierce conviction of her ninety-four years: HA.

Her funeral is small. My grandmother has survived most of her friends. Women from the Chevra Kadisha, the orthodox burial society, have been taking turns keeping watch over her because she cannot be alone. They have washed her, first her head, then each side, they have run a toothpick beneath her toe- and fingernails. They have dressed her in clean white linen. Although I cannot see her, my grandmother lies in a pine box punctured with holes to expedite decomposition, for that is the goal: from dust to dust. As her body is lowered, I picture worms despite my best efforts. It is a beautiful March day and we shovel. This is the tradition: We shovel and we shovel and then we eat.

MARIAN KAPLUN SHAPIRO

MEMORIAL SERVICE FOR A QUAKER

In the end she wanted you to know
what mattered. So she spoke inhabiting
the tender shallow spaces between the keys
of the clavier, between
the shards of grass, the in-
and-out-breaths in this Meeting
House. Here we wait,
patient iambs, graceful anapests
of faith, of awe, and witness, and of doubt,
the steady heartbeats of a sonnet thrumming
to the easy laplap of a summer
lake.,

In the end she wanted you to know
it had been hard: Holding truth still
against the executioners, when
their blades were rusty with old blood. Coming
back. And back. And back. And back to tortures
untallied, terrors indescribable,
unforgettable. Therefore
forgotten. After, she insisted upon
apple trees. She mined for love, exalted
in the precious metals of her friends,
her family, the stunning souls of strangers.
She panned for joy. You were surprised to find
her in the cracks of driveways, springing up
yellow in fortunes of stubborn dandelions.
In summer she swayed purple in panoramas
of loosestrife, vibrated in fanfares

of red wild roses. You saw her soaring
with startled seagulls and the common Canada
goose. In the end, she wanted you
to know she was afraid to die alone
in the aftermath of ancient arrows,
knives, and hatchets. Forever, it seemed,
the butcher waited with the violent, vicious
ax.

In the end she wanted you to know
what matters now: glimpses of baby moose,
prancing silver in your headlights.
A grandchild with your toes.
An arm flung on your belly
in mid-night. Stars
that shock your skin, like lemon
ice exploding on your tongue. A prayer
hurled into silence. A kiss that loves you into
morning. A certain song: *Sometimes I feel
like a motherless child. Sometimes.*

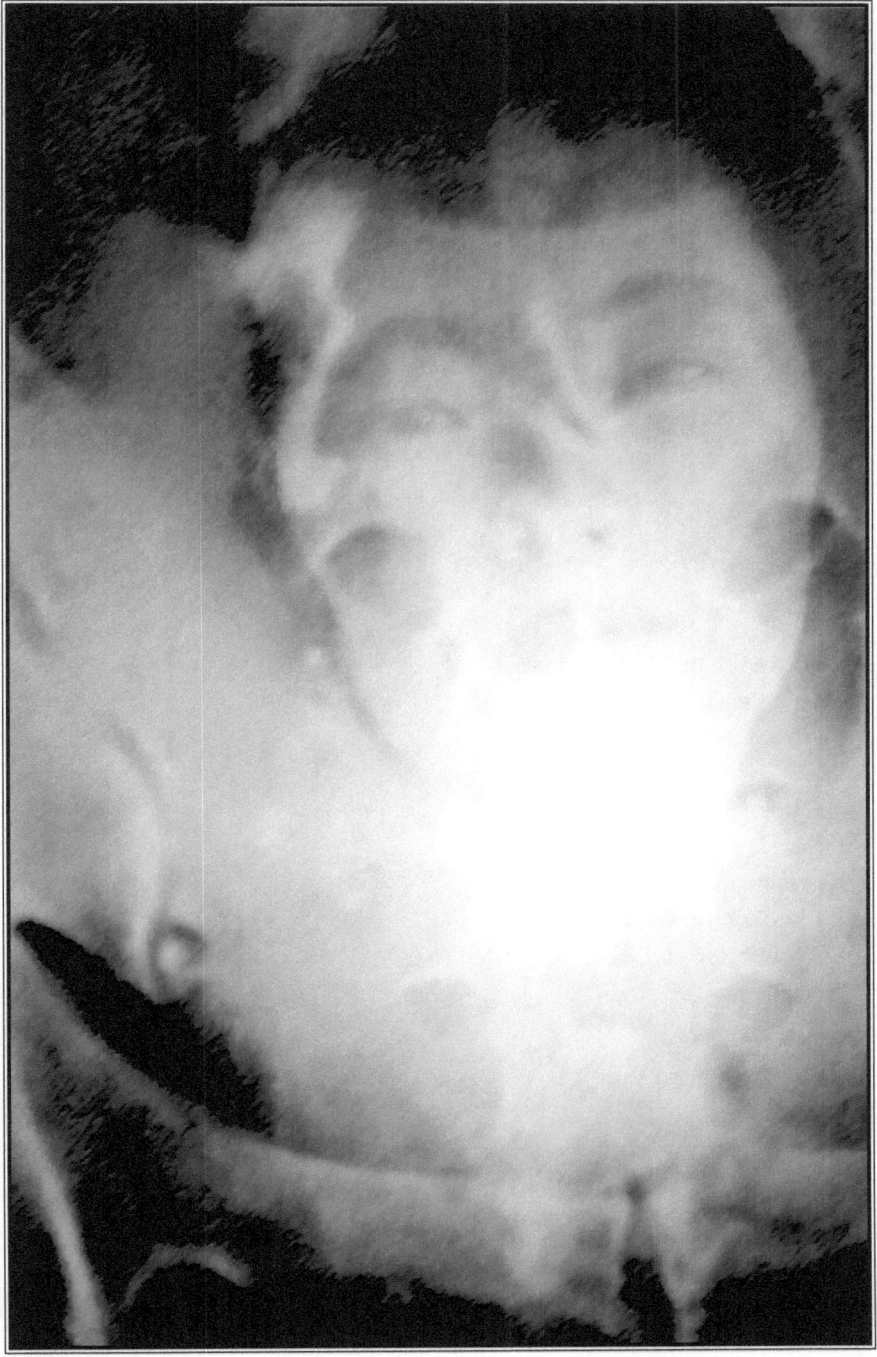

MERRY SPEECE

SWEET FACE OF THE KHMER WOMAN

1.
Reveal thyself, reveal thyself

but I am the one
from whom God's face
remains hidden.

2.
In every field
I searched
and into the woods
and cried,

Where are the pink rimmed eyes
of that white faced cow?

3.
By night
with fever
I dreamed a dream full of longing
and I know God came to me
and lay with me and when he turned to me
he had the face of Brando.

4.
God thought
an emissary, cool Death,
clean shaven man in a suit,
patient at my computer while I slept,
would do.

5.
I read:
to the Australian reporter
the Vietnamese said
the soldiers knew what day
they would die, the day the Woman visited:
"Death she is a Lady."

6.
Grace is bestowed
and there is immortality of the soul.

At the home of my friends, the So brothers,
I see for the first time another visitor, their mother,

and I bow to her sweet countenance
and she hurries over to embrace me.

TERROR AND TRANSFORMATION

GREGGORY MOORE

DIRTY, PINKISH SKY

It's flat and turbid. The rain clouds are an amber-brown, collecting dust and
not parching this desiccate basin. The air is close and full of heat, slightly
smothering everything. The birds don't seem to want to fly, even though the
onset of dusk is when they like to play around here. Someone's coughing
underneath all of this, and I realize it's me, I'd forgotten for a minute.
There's a pink behind everything, the sun must be going down somewhere
behind those clouds. They must be huge to hover over everything that can
be seen from here. I look behind me, but there's no sun, just worthless
clouds.

    I keep walking east. I've been walking east for an hour, walking
in between coughing fits, and I don't know how far I've gone. I spit on
the dusty sidewalk and look at the wad of brownish phlegm, disgusted by
myself, disgusted by my dying, the way it's happening, the decay, the rot, the
deliberateness. I want it to rain, but I know it won't, I know this place too
well, I know that fucking sky.

    It's been so long since I've been here. Why did I come back? I
hate this place, I always hated it. I think I just didn't know where else to go,
what else to do, and there's an instinct to want to make a pattern of it all, to
describe an arc or circle instead of a random, inscrutable squiggle of a life.
Dumb.

    I look up at the hills, at the faux-adobe houses up there. They're
all pink, vibrant and alive, illuminated, although in my memory they are
a uniformly nauseating yellowish-cream. The clouds seem to glow from
beyond, and I realize it's the sun. I look back, but I can't see where it's
broken through, can't see where it could have descended beneath the cloud
cover before dropping off the horizon, a horizon that in any case I couldn't
see for the ugly urban sprawl. But up there the houses somehow are
beautiful, the hills, they visually sing. I knew a girl who lived up there once,
50 years ago, I wonder what she's doing now.

CATHRYN COFELL

WOMB, BELLY, GUT, CAVE

1982

Dead night. Your brave mother's face looks down on you. Already you
sense

someone missing even though she fills you like a bucket so full you spill
wild

as flood. She comes for you, sweaty and pale. Her beach hair tangles in the
crib

joints, her hands tangle in the sheet, her unsteady fingers tangle your tiny
body,

pressing for an answer to what makes you scream, to what makes you
stop.

1991

A school picture, poorly cut, hangs from a magnet. You did not grow into
these features

fast enough. A friend's father has touched you in damp places, denies the
ruin. He

does not stop growing. Every one whirls in circles: the stepfather who
threatens spray

paint and bullets; the mother who covers all the mirrors, sculpts pots for
this saltwater

and ash; the witch doctor who sold you out. Indian throat singers once sent
songs

across the Canadian prairies to show a path to the next village. *Where are the
lyrics?*

you question in red chalk around the sidewalk of your body. *When is my voice
the road?*

1995

You are fifteen and thin as a pressed weed. Your wild breath screams *woman,*
   your body
screams boy. You are that weed in a garden filled with raw compost.
   Absence moves you
like a worm. You dive head first into the shallow end, split like a peach,
   explode in all
directions. Acrobat, astronaut, albatross, assassin—you are a blank canvas
   but have hidden
all the brushes. Your mother checks the water for sharks, finds wads of
   tissue soaked in blood.

2002

You are alone in a hospital bed, waiting. You can count on both hands the
   times since
you were five that have been spent alone like this, yet you can't help to look
   out the open
door, and look again. In two hours a doctor will scrape your womb clean as
   a gourd,
scrape you raw. Split you like a nail. *Move on,* you write 500 times on the bed
   sheet,
take this and move on. Pack the thrift-store jeans, the breadmaker, the pills
   that keep you
from bleeding to death. Bring that old saxophone. You will find yourself
   alone and want
to hear the blues. Kiss your mother goodbye. Leave this place. Take this
   place with you.

2008

You marry a man who does not need your name tattooed on his back. Who encourages you

to keep your own name on a business card in your wallet. Today, we are having lunch.

An old woman with an old friend who have not seen each other for a long time. People pause

to watch us drink tequila and chitter like finches. They think of their own secret daughters.

It will make us think of our own mothers, of the secrets we hide, of the secret layers of skin.

We will touch our empty wombs hidden under the tablecloth. Lock our fingers tight.

ANXIETY ATTACK

Then the creeping starts. Teeth marks in the back
of a hand. Furry scuttle around bare toes. Cramps
deep enough to break a sweat, to drain the blood pale.
You sit on the edge, head down until the buzz stops.
Sit up slowly. Look behind, then look again.
Only the cat, her black tail swishing.
Down the street, kids should be shooting cap guns,
old women should be plopped on porch rockers
fanning their dresses and everyone's flaws, and
in the distance, a lawn mower drone. But only the cat,
her black tail. And you, looking behind.
You open a bottle of wine, no glass. Run barefoot
to the gas station to buy cigarettes, even though you haven't
cracked a pack in six years. You light one on the run back,
heart a roaring tornado. It comes. Hard.
You have never been close to death, never touched a cheek
in a coffin, yet you are certain this is how it feels
before the calm comes and the light comes—
when your car flips on the ice of a deserted county trunk
and you wake much later with your ear in your hand,
something metal running through you and the car
smelling of mercury and gasoline, and you know
everyone else is safe at home watching the weather,
waiting this out, waiting for the plow to pass.

CHRISTINA GOMBAR

IN THE COMPANY OF GHOSTS

I am a ghost. You may have seen me in the supermarket, on a park bench, standing in line next to you at the library. I walk beside you. But I am not really in the world.

I am still on the organizational chart at the company where I used to work, but someone else sits at my desk. My name still appears in the address books of friends, though most no longer call. If I publish an article, lawyers advise, I must use a pseudonym and refuse payment, though my financial situation is dire. Occasionally, a van with tinted windows parks across the street and runs a camera on my house, or trails me to the supermarket and reports back to my employer. But most of the time I am invisible.

They say that ghosts wreak havoc because the spirits don't understand that they are dead. This is how I feel. I have had some version of Chronic Fatigue and Immune Dysfunction Syndrome, or CFIDS since I was 31, but it wasn't until three years ago, when I was 39, that it caused me to drop out of the world—leave my job, shut down my social life, put all plans for the future on hold, change from living as one type of being to living as another entirely.

When that devastating attack came, I didn't quite understand what had happened. Like a spirit with unfinished business, I continued to knock around, angrily attempting to do the normal things, insisting on my right to be in the world. Remembering those first months, I have an image of a headless horseman, wandering the aisles of the supermarket, furious that they'd rearranged the shelves, were hiding things from me, wondering when someone had broken into my car and changed the control panel, why the world suddenly moved up ten speeds.

In my case, the overwhelming and most incapacitating symptom of the illness is brain dysfunction. When I get sick, a vein in the back of my neck seems to constrict, something seems to invade and inflame my brain and central nervous system, and everything freezes, then crashes, like an old, overloaded computer. In this state, I used to get up, dress, drive myself to the train station, board and settle in for a half hour of rest, congratulating myself for simply getting myself out the door one more day. I shakily navigated Grand Central Station, weakly gathered my food, and walked the four blocks to work. I sat at meetings and at my desk, in makeup and full business attire, with the appearance of professionalism, but the intelligence of a department store dummy. Even after I couldn't go in to work anymore, I would take advantage of small bursts of physical energy, or simply push myself, as I had been pushing myself out the door to work for the seven years since I first started to change, and ride the bicycle at my health club. Though it took me three tries to *find* the health club, a short simple drive from my home. But I was sick for many years before I got to that stage.

People Don't Believe in Us

Most people don't believe in us ghosts, and I understand why. For many years it was hard for *me* to admit or even register my symptoms; they came on and increased so insidiously. During my initial attack of Epstein-Barr, which is often but not always associated with the onset of CFIDS, my nice, old Jewish doctor said, "Swollen glands, mono? That's nothing! I used to get that in med school. Stay home! Have a baby! Take it easy!"

This was not an option; I've always had to work, even now, I have difficulty explaining to people why I don't just do some easy, part-time work: I have always been the only benefits provider, and even on disability, remain the breadwinner of our home.

The problem with diagnosing the onset of CFIDS is that the initial symptoms are often the same signs of stress and fatigue everyone has—tiredness, mental fog, headaches, irritable nerves, fevers, a feeling of general heaviness—in fact, just an extreme version of life itself. The difference is, I used to be able to push through the fatigue to resume an energetic state. Now if I do that everything gets worse. As my body demands I slow down, I keep commanding it to move. An intense distress, both physical and emotional, descends as the virus—or whatever it is —takes over. I know I am ill, though apart from the fever, I can't locate where the problem lies, because it's in the nerves, the brain, the registry system itself.

This neurological vulnerability is the aftermath of a brain infection I well remember suffering, but which was dismissed as "yuppie flu." Later, MRIs and other brain scans showed up lesions; a radiologist who didn't know CFIDS from measles deduced from my X-ray that I'd had encephalitis. Blood tests show up irregularities, elevated antibodies to the Herpes VI virus, which is also associated with Multiple Sclerosis. I have tried antiviral drugs, drugs taken by epileptics and MS patients; I try every new and improved anti-depressant that comes on the market. I make use of yoga, meditation, Reiki healing, acupuncture, acupressure, massage, holistic medicine, Aryuvedic medicine, elimination diets, vitamin and mineral supplements, organic living, religion and psychotherapy. Everything helps incrementally. Nothing has gotten rid of it.

Becoming a Ghost

It is tempting to believe that ghosts deserve their fates, that they are simply suffering for the sins of their pasts—the greater the previous plunder of our bodies' natural resources, the longer the stay in the purgatory of ghost life. I used to work a tough, management job on Wall Street, and then do other writing until two a.m. I lived in a small space, literally and figuratively—not enough light, leisure, freedom, spiritual sustenance, sleep, fresh air, or exercise. I didn't know I was doing anything to harm myself; I thought I was paying my dues.

When I was young, I enjoyed an excess of energy—I used to *annoy* people, with my insistence on incessant activity—talking, running, biking, swimming, working, socializing. But I seem to have overspent my energy, splurged it foolishly, thinking the fountain would never run dry. Now I must be parsimonious until the wellspring naturally, miraculously replenishes itself.

Ghost Rules

Ghosts must live by new rules from their previous, Normal selves. Over the course of many years of trial and error, I've learned to counter everything I ever taught myself. Exercising discipline is often counterproductive for ghosts. While I once ignored fatigue and other warning signs of strain, now I'm forced to take heed. I know that pushing on to complete a task, or series of tasks, when I'm already tired will lead to further disability and perhaps a car accident. In order to do anything at all tomorrow, I may have to stop myself from doing all I'd like today.

Ghosts must treat themselves like newborn babies, eating nourishing meals at set hours whether they're hungry or not, resting after eating or any exertion. Like any other kind of child care, it can be boring. In order to avoid days of serious as opposed to moderate or minimal illness, ghosts have to stop at the first sign of fever, fatigue, mental confusion, or even emotional upset.

Yet, it is not as if we ghosts do nothing at *all*—it is more that we exist on another plane, and run on an entirely different voltage from our previous, Normal selves. We are not so much sick all the time, but healthy, or at least functional, within very restricted limits. In other words, we do things only when we feel like it. (Ghosts are notoriously capricious.) This is probably at the root of why people see us, but don't believe in us.

Ghost Shame

Ghosts are often ashamed of being what they are. It is embarrassing to change so drastically, hard to acknowledge loss of mental functioning and emotional equilibrium. Because on our different energy current, these things are always in a state of flux, almost as if we were starting to break apart— something that's only supposed to happen *after* we die. Ghosts retain some of their former mental capacity, but lose others as they metamorphose into the next stage. Tests show my IQ is down to 77, little more than half what it once was. While I can still interpret a metaphor or describe a painting, I cannot remember a list of six words dictated to me, follow a set of simple instructions, or figure out a puzzle. I can no longer execute the complicated mental pyrotechnics of my last financial writing job, no more than my body can tolerate the strain of commuting. I read and write at a small fraction of my Normal speed and comprehension. I recently took a test for an online, work-at-home news digest writing job; I could only finish two of the five stories in the time allotted, and those badly.

A ghost might have to do a simple budget over six or seven times because his disintegrating ghost-brain can no longer handle basic math. (Are these skills irrelevant in the next stage?) Some ghosts I know can read newspaper articles but can't follow the plot of a novel or film. Some ghosts I know can't read at all.

Conventional jobs are often incompatible with the ghost state, though most of us fight against that truth for as long as we can. I have been out on disability for six years now, twice as long as I held my last job. Without a career, I lack an identity. To be idle is to be worthless—this is the message I get from Normals. No job? No kids? (my health/money situation disqualifies me from adoption.) What is the point of you?

When I first went out sick, I lived in suburban New York, where my local grocery is run by Croatian immigrants. The father worked a seven-to-three shift at a factory, then came home and ran the shop. When I tried to explain why I was home, he seemed personally disappointed: "I have people on my staff like that," he said sadly. "I don't understand. They stay out for a week, a month ..."

I haven't figured out how to tell him I'm a ghost now, and that jobs aren't always part of the ghost life. Before, when he used to see me rushing in at 8:30, having worked till six or seven o'clock, he'd say, "You're so good. I hope your husband appreciates you—*you do so much.*" Now I've learned to lie; I tell people I work at home.

Ghosts hate not being part of the world. It is conceivable that ghosts could work from home, following the whims of their restless incarnations, that might, for example, dictate the hours of three to eight p.m. the prime working hours, rather than nine to five. But it is too much trouble for companies to deal with ghosts on their own terms. They miss us and our contributions at first, but they forget, they move on.

This ghost would like to go back to freelancing, but able to write at a variably small fraction of the speed I once did, and out of commission completely for unpredictable stretches of time, I would be unsuitable for this deadline-driven occupation. Furthermore, it would provide no secure income base. Although ghosts feel invisible, that we exist on another plane, we still need shelter, food and all the other material things our Normal selves needed.

We are trapped in a world for which we are no longer suited—still alive, but cramped by poverty and disability, and rules made for Normals. My company and Social Security insurance payments add up to less than a quarter of the income I'd make if I were still working. Both organizations subject me to annual, months long medical interrogation and documentation drills, accusing me of mental rather than physical disorders, insinuating I am either an alcoholic or addicted to street drugs. I have been spied on with hidden cameras. If I'm well enough to get the mail, they may reason I'm well enough to work 40 hours a week, plus drive, commute and take care of myself and home. If I can brush my teeth, I should be working in a factory. Pressed by the costs of war, the Social Security Administration is thinking about means-testing *all* disability recipients, meaning I could become homeless. (Unable to meet my mortgage payments, I have already sold my condominium and moved to a home half the price in a cheaper part of the country.) The powers that be begrudge the few hundred dollars I receive from a system into which I paid for over twenty years, to ensure I wouldn't starve if I became too ill to work. Which I have.

My company has farmed out its disability administration to an insurance company that does not believe in my illness, and puts a limit of two years on payments, though the illness is forever.

My employer continues to contribute to a pension. But if I try to start up a career again, make any outside money at all, the disability insurance, medical coverage, pension—all of it will go away forever. While my health condition shows every indication of staying. I have to look at the big picture. It's too risky. I remain invisible.

Ghost Losses

One of the worst things about the ghost life is the isolation.

"You're not really sick," declared a former friend, a high level executive who attends law school full time and sees her baby son two hours a week. "Maybe some day you'll decide to go back to work..."

Said another, "Mary had Epstein-Barr, too, but she has it under control, she has to, with those kids ..." Despite the fact that my own life, as she well knows, has been thrown into complete personal and financial disarray by this. I cannot afford to be sick any more than her friend Mary can.

It is the case with many ghosts that people stop believing in them—their friends, their families. I recently frightened my old boss by calling her on the phone. Don't be scared, I said, I'm just a ghost. But I could see my intrusion, this declaration of my continued existence, albeit in changed form, was unwelcome. There are strict boundaries between the world of Normals—which I can still observe and understand, and the ghost world, which is invisible to them, and feared.

The spouses of ghosts see themselves as bereaved. I have many ghost friends whose spouses stopped believing in them, and left them for a Normal.

Because we are invisible, it's hard for a ghost to stand at the sidelines, rejoicing in others' good fortune, pay the constant tributes the Normals seem to demand for reproduction, for career success, for enduring marriages. At weddings my cousins look at me oddly. Why haven't you moved on in life? Published your next book? Had a child? It's too complicated for polite conversation. Saying you have Chronic Fatigue Syndrome is like saying you were raped. *You* are the one who is immediately suspect. Because if it happened to you, it could happen to them, and they don't want to think about that. Likewise there are no visible marks. If you lived to survive, then you must not have really suffered, you must be guilty, you must have brought it on yourself. If you're still alive and semi-functional, if you're still trying to put on a good face, then who's to say anything really happened to you? Unbelieving, puzzled, their eyes and attention rest on me less and less. I am an enigma not worth solving. I feel my apparition grow a shade lighter.

Ghost Emotions

Ghosts lose the intermediate shades between extreme pleasantness and passivity and extreme irritability and anger. The seeming passivity and pleasantness are a result of letting go of the pettier concerns that consumed our former, Normal selves. The anger and irritability are an outgrowth of constantly feeling ill and out of sorts, stressed and desperate. You are angry at an illness without a cure, or even, sometimes, a central symptom.

Though ghosts lose much of their physical stamina and mental acuity, they often develop a compensatory sense of heightened awareness and perception. They do not suffer fools gladly. I have developed an allergy to certain people—needy, whining, demanding, and especially overbearing and pushy women. Like any other source of stress, these must be eliminated for my own self-protection.

Because I felt useless in my ghost state during my first year home on disability, because I didn't really understand how I had changed, I thrashed around for other ways to be useful besides work. Instead of figuring out how to adjust to being a ghost, I filled the most urgent need I saw—I became a"wife" to my girlfriends. I listened to tales of their daily struggles, I made sympathetic noises, I offered advice to take better care of themselves, lest they suffer my fate.

But eventually, this stratagem ran out of gas. My friends and I were together in a struggle against life and time—the long struggle to earn and save enough to buy a home, then the struggle for motherhood. To my friends, my physical collapse looked like simply giving up, a betrayal of feminism, even. They looked at me not working and saw self-indulgence.

Within two years, two of my best friendships ended, friendships that I considered enduring and deep turned out to have been built on foundations of sand. The gaps between my ghost life and their Normal life became too vast.

Ghost Denial

As with any other unpleasant or disturbing experience, it is easier to minimize the ghost state by denying it. After I was forced home, I couldn't bring myself to tell anyone, to name this disease I didn't want. This was easy because I've never looked sick. Many people with CFIDS actually look better than Normals, as if, like spirits, we have reclaimed our essential selves. We get more rest, eat better, tend not to drink alcohol or caffeine, or smoke. (Our unstable ghost bodies tolerate less and less as time goes on.) We keep early hours and don't strain ourselves. If we had to stop working, we probably look better than when we did. We appear as deceased loved ones do in dreams, or people are said to appear in glimpses of the next world.

I can understand that to others, CFIDS and the similarly mysterious illnesses of Lyme disease and fibromyalgia just look like a bad attitude, or depression. If you have one of these conditions and can still work, chances are you are so tired you don't have the energy for the normal office chit-chat. Ghosts can't waste their limited energy on enthusiasm; they need all their limited resources for the task at hand. A woman at my last job appeared withdrawn before she crashed and went out for good. (There were, including me, four cases of CFIDS, all women, in my then sixty-person department.) Even to me, this woman seemed merely unhappy, overloaded, a working mother with a long commute. I must have appeared the same, dragging into work ill for several months, going in and out for several week stretches before I bottomed out.

Ghost Style

In his memoir, "Intoxicated by My Illness," the late writer and critic Anatole Broyard said, "We must develop a style for being ill." He recommended all cancer patients buy a new wardrobe of casual, yet elegant clothes.

When I became a ghost, I became a blonde. When I first went home sick, I knew I would be home for a few months. Free to diverge from the seemingly mandatory short dark hair style of my office, I gave the go ahead for an auburn shade, which came out a jolting firecracker red, surprising even the girls in the salon. I looked at my reflection with alarm. Yet my altered appearance, though undesired, reflected the disorienting transformation of my mind and body.

A few months later it became a light auburn with blonde streaks. This incarnation seemed to suit my changed self. I tried going back to brunette again, but looking in the mirror, the gap between the dark-haired, young, strong person I used to be, and this changed person I had become was too depressing. Lighter hair projected a more accurate, if more fragile persona, but also encouraged a more cheerful state of mind, which seemed contagious. Don't take me seriously, and I won't take *you* seriously. Beckoned by my hair, people turn their heads, shop attendants wait on me first—a tremendous advantage for a person who's been known to collapse while standing on line. In this way I defy the invisibility of my ghost state.

But being blonde can be misleading. Blondes have more fun, and ghosts aren't supposed to enjoy themselves. People may mistake me for an idle, rich housewife, and it is hard not to internalize this fantasy, despite the state of my balance sheet. Seeing is believing, however, and Normals resent the illusion, resent my apparent leisure, not seeing that, though I lack their worries of children and jobs, I have a host of strange and difficult obstacles.

To say nothing of disappointments and losses.

Ghost Warnings

Voices from the ghost world are relatively rare, and somewhat unreliable. There are a dearth of good memoirists. One of the best is Floyd Skloot, author of *The Night Side* and *In the Shadow of Memory*. He is a poet, a fine literary writer, who frames his insights elliptically around well thought out themes. I envy the fact that he seems so sure of himself and his position, his status as ghost; he gives absolutely no time to detractors. But his illness descended on him abruptly. He went from being a marathon runner to a cripple in a matter of days. I went down by degrees. Hit with succeeding blows of illness, like a prize fighter I kept getting up off that mat and coming back. It was harder for me to tell when I actually crossed over.

Skloot doesn't seem as angry as I am to find himself a ghost. He skims over the fact that the illness ended his first marriage. He doesn't seem afraid of the future the way I am. His illnesses descended on him when he was in his forties, had already established family and career. Mine hit me at 30, when I was struggling to start a family that never materialized; my continuing struggle for work, to this end, further compromising my health. Skloot seems to have adjusted better, living far out in the wilds of Oregon. Perched until very recently within view of the Manhattan skyline, I've been struggling to get back in the world like a moth beating
at a screen door.

In her memoir, *The Alchemy of Illness*, Kat Duff combines traditional and New Age philosophy, history and spirituality in her uplifting analysis of the illness experience. In the last chapters, the author attributes her illness to a sort of inherited bad karma, retribution for the fact that her ancestors confiscated Indian lands and may have committed atrocities. What does that say for the many minority women I see crowding my doctor's office? The young Orthodox Jewish women? Whose bad karma are *they* paying back?

There are a plethora of books by non-ghosts offering bogus cures. Dr. Bernie Siegel says that it is in your power to heal yourself, that it is only a matter of life style change, of communicating your needs to others. Although from the first serious attack at 31 I knew I would have to change my life, and began to accept certain limitations, others couldn't, or wouldn't. In one book on "coping" the author talks about stress management, but not about how to make a living if your body can't handle a normal work load. "Ultimately, it's not important if you can't meet a certain work deadline." I wonder what world *he* lives in?

It took two and a half years for me to accept the fact that I was a ghost. I did something I'd avoided before, sought out the company of other ghosts. I traveled to Washington to lobby Congress for CFIDS research funds. Seeing a large room full of people, all damaged in slightly different ways, brought to mind the robots marked for an orgy of public destruction in the film *Artificial Intelligence*. Some of the robots were little more than joints and wires, while others seemed at first glance fine. One robot had a stunningly beautiful, perfectly intact face—Juliet Binoche's—but her neck was a shredded metal skeleton. Likewise at the CFIDS gathering. My lobbying partner could only make her way with a sturdy metal cane. She holds an MBA from the University of Chicago, held high level government posts and ran her own business. After she got sick she was reduced to living in her car, then women's shelters. She is now in public assisted housing, and has so much neurological damage she has great difficulty even speaking. Another woman's lean contours told me she was well enough to exercise. Thirty seconds into our conversation, her expression told me she had forgotten what I had just told her.

The only poster-girl for CFIDS is Laura Hillenbrand, author of the best selling *Sea biscuit: An American Legend,*. She lives in D.C., and I met her father, who lobbied in her stead. Laura has done a great deal to put a different face on the illness, but I have mixed feelings about this. Like her, I turned to writing as my last hope for an income source—unlike her, I have not yet sold a bestseller. When I tell people I write, their immediate response is: Well you should be able to make a lot of money from that, citing the Seabiscuit girl. The vast majority of ghosts live in obscurity and financial disarray. I would love to read articles about how ordinary people struggle, but the media has the mistaken idea that I am interested in celebrities.

Money is the great determinating factor in quality of life and medical treatment, for ghosts and anyone else with a chronic illness. I have met girls in my doctor's waiting room who live and work "on the street." Others are pampered housewives. My friend Hal, a former high earning sales executive, lost his wife, who wiped out his 401K, and lives on Social Security and what he earns from one night a week of bartending, which costs him three days of recovery time. If he can work two nights, he can afford the six hundred dollars for experimental drugs that seem to help. But this extra work itself floors him; it is a Catch-22.

I am luckier than some ghosts, unluckier than others whose families recognize the gravity of their situations. A few years ago, I was the object of a temper tantrum by a relative who was furious I couldn't make a Bar Mitsvah; I had told her I was attending a weekend retreat (which took me a year to pay off) led by a doctor who specialized in my illness. I was lucky to get in, it was tremendously helpful, people traveled from all over the world to be there. Hundreds of others attended her son's event; I'd sent my apologies. Still she took offense.

I still look for a way to be in the world as a ghost. If I don't inform people of my condition, they take me for well, which eventually leads to misunderstanding and disappointment. If I decide to eschew makeup and hair dye, and become one of these people who bore you with a litany of their health complaints—no, I won't even go there. Yet attempting to be happy, appreciating whatever I *do* have, leads my overstressed contemporaries to the conclusion that I'm enjoying myself and my condition.

And so I remain a ghost, in limbo. One part of my life is over—jobs, friends, goals—and the other hasn't started yet, or at least, has not started in the way I expected it to, with a full recovery and return to my old routine of wage-earning work and activity.

Ghost World

When the country underwent a change, experienced the shock and shame of damage unexpectedly inflicted, found itself in a new era of strange war, of unpredictability and fear, I felt oddly prepared. New York was a ghost town, people were afraid of it, it was sick and wounded and dangerous. When I went down to where I used to work, to Ground Zero at night, I looked up in the sky and thought I could feel the other ghosts close at hand. What might they tell us if we could hear them?

I see my Normal friends pushing themselves to the limit—cramming activity into every waking moment, getting worked up over petty disputes, nurturing grudges, teetering on the edge of exhaustion, but not tumbling over it, as I did. Prolonged illness, especially when punctuated by periods of panicked, extreme debility, upend your goals and world view. You live very much in the present, as Buddhists and yoga teachers advise. But when I tell my friends to slow down and count their blessings, I see them thinking: *What do you know? You're just a ghost.*

Years ago, my uncle died suddenly. He was the most worried, driven, uptight, manic person I have ever met. Shortly after his death, my sister had a dream in which he came to her. At the time she was going through a rough patch—work problems, boyfriend problems, money problems, family problems. When my uncle came to her as a ghost, he said one thing: *"Don't Worry."* This from the most worried man in the world.

I have a recurring dream where I struggle to explain myself to my former best friend. In the dream, my friend ignores me, doesn't even seem to see that I am there. As I speak, I grow breathless from the effort to enlighten, and to warn.

At times I feel that I, too, have moved on into the next world; at least in part, at least in spirit. We ghosts are the advance party, leading the way to a place others are just starting to sense is even there.

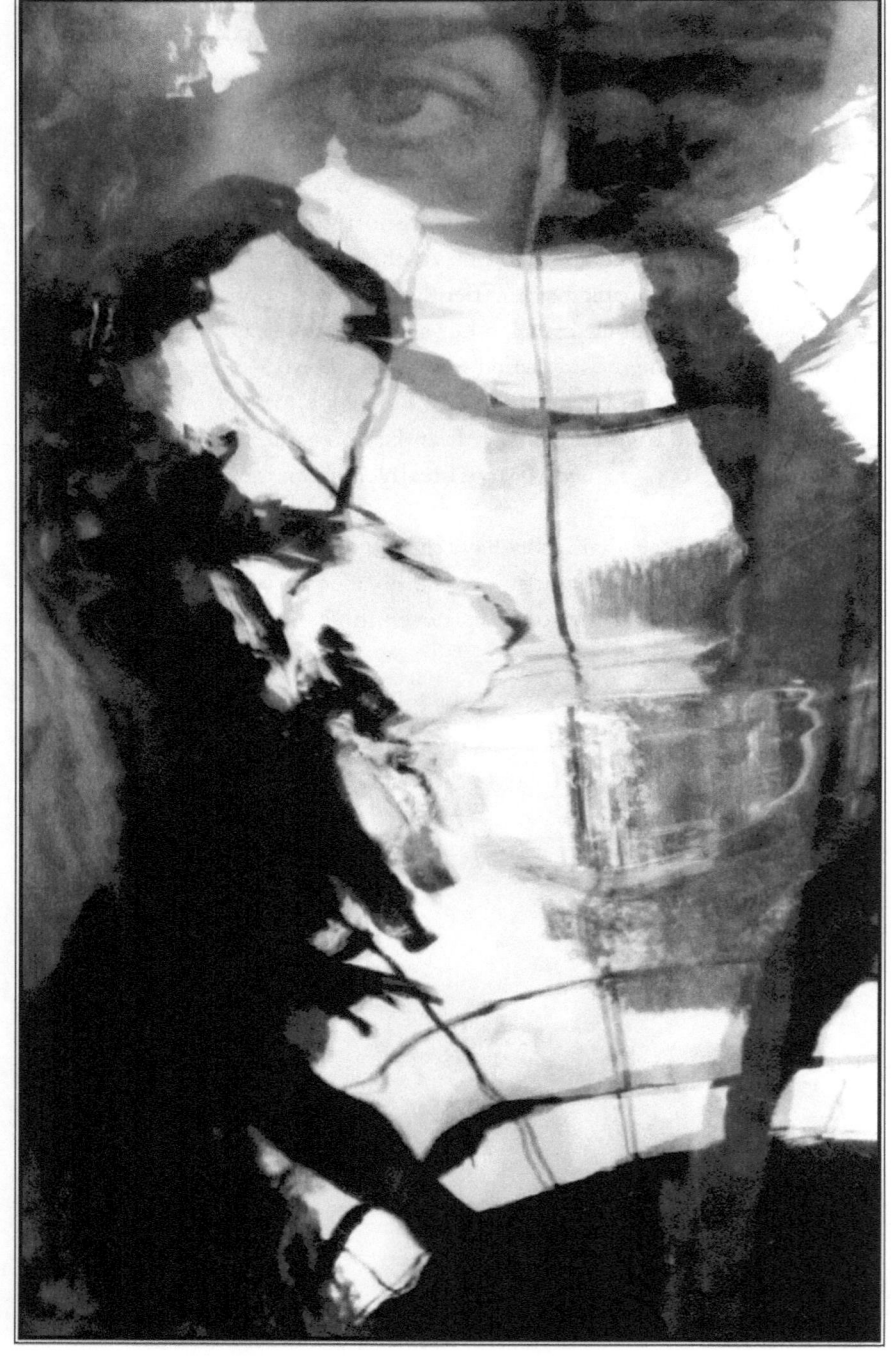

ANDREA ROSENHAFT

SHARP EDGES

I have awakened early in the morning as usual and it is still dark. The time until I get out of bed is spent examining my body. I run my hands from my face downwards in the same order I do every day. First, my jawbones to make sure they are still sharp.

My collarbones and ribs are next: they are still prominent. My hipbones jut out like small peaks and the valleys that surround them are exaggerated because they are practically collapsed. My stomach remains concave. My knees protrude like small mountains from my legs. The tendons behind my ankles stick out like branches from a dead tree. I am not satisfied with this morning's exploration; I think there is room for improvement.

I wait several hours before I can weigh myself. The later I wait, the more time my body has to burn calories and the less I will weigh. I have invested in a waist-high balance scale. It was expensive but worth it as it gives me the most accurate weight next to a doctor's scale. I take off my pajamas, underwear and socks. I play with the slide, trying to inch it down to the lowest possible number while the bubble still remains in the middle. It's down a quarter of a pound. Not enough. I'll have to take some laxatives today to empty myself and get the weight down some more.

That ritual completed, I can now have breakfast. Pajamas back on plus a sweater now that I am no longer under covers—I am always cold. I pad to the refrigerator. Inside are cartons of eggs, bottles of lite syrup and the one luxury I allow myself—sugar free French Vanilla Coffee Mate. I put up the water in order to make two hard boiled eggs and then put up a separate pot of water to boil for the instant coffee. When the coffee is ready I put in Sweet & Low and I measure one tablespoon of Coffee Mate into it, which has fifteen calories. I bought one of those sets of measuring spoons that dangle from a ring because I can't trust the measurements of spoons from a regular set of flatware.

When the eggs are ready, I peel them and throw out the yolks, making sure the whites are absolutely clean and pure. Egg whites are pure protein and only fifteen calories each. Thirty calories for the two egg whites and fifteen calories for my treat of Coffee Mate. My total for breakfast is forty-five calories. Dinner is the same as breakfast and if I get unbearably hungry during the day and succumb to the wicked weakness, I'll allow myself two egg whites and coffee as a snack.

Lunch will be a low-fat waffle at sixty calories and a tablespoon of lite syrup. According to the bottle of syrup, a serving is a quarter-cup at one-hundred calories. I figured out there are four and one-half tablespoons to a quarter-cup so each tablespoon is approximately twenty calories. I don't usually like to approximate but it is only off by two-tenths of a calorie. My drink is a diet Snapple iced tea.

My three meals and one snack total two hundred and fifteen calories. The only addition to that is the extra Coffee Mate as I drink a great deal of coffee during the day because it fills me up when I am hungry.

It is November of 2006 and I am forty-six years old. I have just begun to restrict calories in what will be my fifth episode of anorexia. I am living in White Plains, NY, a suburb about twenty miles north of New York City. I grew up in Queens but came up here for psychiatric treatment in 1990 and stayed because this is where my therapists were, and one of the most prestigious psychiatric hospitals in the country is here as well.

When I became ill, I left behind a network of good friends whom I had mostly met playing softball in various advertising leagues. Softball was a huge outlet for me and I missed it terribly when I became too sick to play. When I moved up to White Plains, I had nobody, no relationships and I never heard from my softball friends again. It felt as if they had dropped off the face of the earth and it is a feeling which persists in hurting me until this day.

I was still living in Queens and working in Manhattan when the anorexia began. My career in consumer promotion (which is a branch of marketing having to do with financial incentives such as couponing) had just taken off after starting in the advertising industry as a secretary five years prior. I had begun seeing a therapist for a mild depression and after several years of working with her, my depression became severe enough to warrant medication and she referred me to a psychiatrist. He was an elderly man with a white beard, a caricature of what a psychiatrist should look like. He prescribed Dexedrine for me. Dexedrine is not an antidepressant; it is a form of speed. It completely suppressed my appetite and I dropped forty-three pounds in six months, going from one hundred thirty-five pounds to ninety-two pounds on a five foot, six inch frame. I was emaciated, a walking skeleton. When I put my legs together, I could fit my fist between my thighs.

It was not Nina, my therapist who hospitalized me, but my mother who saw I was dying and dragged me off for treatment. I stayed in the hospital for six months, gaining back thirty-eight pounds.

I now feel that both Nina, and the psychiatrist who prescribed the Dexedrine for me were incompetent. I have moments where nineteen years later, I want to leave an anonymous message on Nina's answering machine. "You incompetent bitch. You ruined my life." She won't remember who I am but it will make me feel better. I've already found her on Peoplefinders. com and called the number to make sure it was her. I recognized her voice immediately but hung up without leaving a message.

Management at my job was understanding. They held my position for me and welcomed me back when I was well. A year later, in the summer of 1989, I was again down to one-hundred pounds and found myself back in the hospital for four months. One episode of anorexia had progressed into an ongoing illness which has spanned the last nineteen years. This time I received the news that I had lost my job for good and I quickly spiraled down into a deep depression. I would attempt suicide a year later and would not return to work until 1996.

The word 'anorexia' actually means "lack of appetite for food," while the term 'anorexia nervosa' is defined as "an eating disorder characterized by aversion to food and obsession with weight loss, and manifested in self-induced starvation and excessive exercise." At two hundred and fifteen calories a day plus the luxury of some extra cups of coffee I always feel ravenous and deprived. My stomach growls, for which I am constantly making excuses. There is a ferocious creature living inside me, nipping at my caverns with jagged teeth, tearing huge holes in my stomach, which I cannot or will not fill.

My psychiatrist, Dr. L., has told me she has conferred with my nutritionist and they have decided that I must be hospitalized. I have lost twenty-two pounds in not quite three months and at this point even though my weight is not that low at one-hundred and eighteen pounds at a height of five feet, six inches, my eating must be normalized. I am also abusing laxatives, which are causing medical complications like low potassium and that is dangerous. They have decided that I cannot get better on my own. Previously, Dr. L. and I had a contract that I would be hospitalized only when I got down to one-hundred and ten pounds and now she is reneging. I am furious.

I angrily e-mail my nutritionist. "Dr. L. gave me the news this morning. As you can imagine, I'm not happy. What happened? I thought you were going to give me at least another week to get my calories up. Now I feel like I have no motivation to eat. I've been on the phone all day with hospitals and one of them got back to me after taking my information and told me that I didn't meet their criteria for an eating disorder. I guess I still have some weight to lose. Oh, and I spent last night in the ER again with chest pains. Seven f——g hours and they couldn't find anything. All the eating disorder units I talked to have one to two week waiting lists."

She answers, "Dr. L. and I decided that we were just putting off the inevitable. I think hospitalization is going to be needed but I wanted to leave it up to your medical doctor. I think you need more help than I can provide on an outpatient basis and you definitely would need to be seeing someone when I leave on maternity leave in a month or less. I don't feel comfortable treating someone who is as sick as you are right now because I do not have the hours to give you—re: seeing you two to three times per week. I would hope that Dr. L. can make some of these calls for you and find a proper program. We can discuss further but I truly believe you need much more help than you are currently receiving. This may mean seeing a different nutritionist who can give you the hours of care you need. One time per week is not enough treatment for someone in your condition. I truly recommend for you inpatient treatment at this time. I think it is the most efficient in terms of time and money and keeping you alive and well."

When I was in high school in the late 1970's, I was a normal weight for my height but used to envy the really thin girls. That naturally thin body and casual attitude towards food seemed out of reach for me. When I first heard about anorexia, little was known about it, but I wished then that I could just catch it for a short time and lose fifteen pounds. It sounded so convenient. I would lose my appetite for several months and I would emerge, undamaged, with a newly thin body. All the other girls would be jealous of me.

Now I tell adolescent girls whose eating disorders are still in the emergent stages that they don't want to end up like me. The eating disorder has been a major factor in ruining my life. I've been hospitalized five times on eating disorder units in psychiatric hospitals. I've sought out institutions in New Jersey, New York and Maryland, roaming from state to state, searching for the perfect treatment, the ultimate cure. For my most recent hospitalization in January of 2007 I wanted to go to The Renfrew Center in Philadelphia, PA, which is supposed to be one of the best in the country, but my insurance denied me coverage.

In the winter of 2007, following Dr. L.'s and my nutritionist's declaration, I find myself in the hospital yet again. I'm a prisoner with no free choice or free will. They monitor every move we make. The staff locks the doors to our rooms during the day and we must stay in the common room for fear we might purge or exercise. At the end of every meal we must take our tray up to the staff person in charge who checks it for what we ate and what we left on our plate. They check in the containers and under the napkins and the plates for hidden food. Six times a day, they call "commodes" and we line up at the door to the bathroom. We use what look like upside down plastic hats with measuring cups marked inside which fit underneath the seat of the toilet and catch our urine and bowel movements, which much be measured and checked. Every aspect of commodes is supervised to make sure we are not purging into the toilet. We get weighed in hospital gowns at six every morning and our showers are also supervised to ensure we are not exercising while we are cleansing ourselves.

We have some therapy groups and meetings with our psychiatrists and therapists, but mostly we just sit around and talk with each other. The locked unit is a mix of adolescents and adults and there are fifteen girls and women to two teenage boys.

Time passes slowly and most of the patients read, do crossword puzzles, or write in their journals. Weekends are even worse because there is nothing to break up the day. I watch the rest of the patients on unit receive a steady stream of visitors; this hospitalization I have none. Hospitalization is a familiar situation for my family and friends—my brother and sister-in-law, my cousins, and various friends, and I tell myself that they are busy and assume I am alright and comfortable because I've been here so many times. The truth is that I miss them and my heart aches for them to come and comfort me. The monotony is overwhelming and I find myself getting caught up in a whirlwind of nothingness. My mind goes off on tangents and I obsess about life on the outside, what I have left behind. It's not current events or fine arts but more mundane things like the plight of the homeless and of stray animals. I can't decide: would I rather be free and like them or locked up like me?

I begin to secretly examine my body, furtively feeling my bones and comparing myself to the others on the unit. My distorted body image screams out to me. I hear voices reverberating inside my head. "You are fat. You are disgusting. You are gross. You are a pig." These are just some of the words the voices are saying. I ask for and receive a raise in my antipsychotic medication.

Towards the end of my stay I write in my journal: "I'm eating way too much. My stomach hurts so much from dinner, as usual. I've gained four and one-half pounds in nine days. I hate myself. I'm the fattest one here. I don't belong here and I never did. I'm going to lose the weight as soon as I leave here. I don't care what it takes and I don't care what anyone says. F-—them all."

All anorexics have their own relationship with Ed. Ed is their lover, their mentor, their abuser, and their controller. The letters E and D stand for Eating Disorder. My relationship with Ed can be compared to one of a victim and her perpetrator. I love him, yet I am fearful of him. He controls my every move. I long to break free, but am terrified there will be nothing there to take his place if I should succeed. Ed lives and I am dying.

There are a relatively new documentary and companion book of the same title, *Thin*, by the photographer Lauren Greenfield that have recently been released. The documentary follows the lives of four young women as they go through treatment at The Renfrew Center, the specialized residential treatment program for eating disorders to which I had hoped to be admitted. The book highlights them, but also profiles other women at Renfrew with their words and often shocking photographs of them in the midst of their eating disorder. That film and book became my Bibles. I would run my fingers over the emaciated bodies in the photographs and think how much I would like to look like them. I would read their stories and get angry with them when they expressed their furor at being forced into treatment. One girl was being fed through a tube inserted in her stomach because she would not eat enough calories to keep her alive. Another girl had weighed fifty-two pounds and was in a wheelchair when she entered Renfrew. What I do not hear is that they are killing themselves.

One night before I went into the hospital, I started to have crushing pains in my chest. In all my years of having anorexia, this was something I had never experienced before. I was afraid I was having a heart attack and if I lay down and went to sleep, I wouldn't wake up. Foolishly, I drove myself to the emergency room. I was taken right away and they did an EKG and other tests. I lay there tired and bored. The woman next to me was flailing about, screaming for Jesus and the staff was trying to hold her down in order to give her something to calm her. It was very noisy and chaotic and I was restless. After four hours I had had enough and snuck out with the IV still in my hand. When I got home after midnight I received a phone call from the ER.

"You have to come back. You left with the IV in your hand and we have to take it out and your potassium was low and we have to give you medication."

I told them, "It's after midnight. I am not coming back. I already took the IV out myself and I will follow up with my internist tomorrow about the potassium."

"Then we have to send the paramedics over to make sure the needle is out cleanly."

"You've got to be kidding." I said. "I guess I don't have a choice."

They sent the paramedics to my door. They took one look at my hand. "Nice job" they said, and left.

The next morning I called my internist to tell her about the low potassium. She said that I had to go back to the ER and get the proper medication. She was not prepared to take care of it in her office. So off I went. I also called Dr. L. to tell her of the previous day's incidents. When I was at the ER she left a message on my answering machine.

"I gave it some more thought," she said. "I will only be able to see you tomorrow if you bring in a note that proves your potassium is normalized. It is an extremely dangerous, potentially lethal complication of anorexia and it might have been that's why you had the chest pain. You might have had some arrhythmia for all I know."

There is a constant battle going on inside my mind that is being played out with the anorexia. I want to live and I want to die. I am slowly but surely killing myself by starving my body of the nutrients that it needs to survive, yet I take myself to the emergency room because I am afraid I will die of a heart attack. This is an exhausting experience because it is constant and it is physically as well as emotionally tiring. I long to take a break from it but it never leaves the deep, dark caverns of my brain, sharing the space with my food obsessions and rituals. I feel progressively more worn down and unbearably, utterly hopeless.

Currently, seven million American girls and women are diagnosed with eating disorders. Anorexia kills more of its sufferers than any other mental illness, either through suicide or through medical complications. The long-term mortality rate from anorexia is over ten percent. Dr. Katherine Halmi, one of the pioneering and internationally recognized eating disorder experts, states, "Currently, only a quarter of patients with anorexia nervosa fully recover and half have partial improvement but another twenty-five percent remain chronically ill. There is also a forty percent rate of relapse."

I guess I am one of those twenty-five percent who remain chronically ill.

It has seemed at times that I have been able to get the eating disorder under control and stay out of the hospital for several years, but it always comes back. Anorexia is not just an issue with eating and weight. It is a symptom of a deeper emotional problem. It was originally assumed that recovery could be seen in terms of progress that has only a surface quality like pounds. Now we know that is not true. The underlying symptoms need to be explored in therapy and true recovery may take years.

Whenever I was discharged from the hospital prior to this most recent stay, my mother would take me out to dinner or cook for me every night so that I could get used to eating again. In a sense, I returned to my childhood where I felt taken care of. It was only after we were both sure I could eat normally on my own that I would go back to my apartment and eat meals alone. Now it is apparent that eating with her only served as a Band-Aid to the restricting behavior (restricting is eating disorder terminology for drastically cutting calories). I did it to please her: I did it so she wouldn't be angry with me. She passed away in 2002, and as soon as I got out of the hospital this time, I relapsed back down to about four hundred calories a day. It is only because I am working privately with a nutritionist and her almighty scale that I am able to maintain my weight. Although she would like to see me gain back some of the pounds I have lost, I steadfastly refuse to do so.

I have been in therapy for over twenty years and now we are discussing what may have triggered this last episode of anorexia which began in November of 2006. On the surface it was me hitting a weight of one-hundred and forty pounds which I could not handle because it made me feel out of control and intolerably fat. Being able to control my intake so severely, makes me feel in control when the rest of my world seems increasingly chaotic; however as I have learned it is merely an illusion of control. I have rituals around eating: I cut my food into tiny pieces; I find it extremely difficult to eat in public. I can't enjoy food; I limit going out with family and friends because I can't eat the food as it prepared in restaurants.

Restricting my intake makes me feel clean and pure. I won't be satisfied until I can exist solely on water. I hang on to this illusion of feeling light, free and unencumbered, which I imagine stems from a fear of being dirty and is connected to a fear of intimacy on many levels. The fear of intimacy reinforces the positive feeling I have about losing my period. It is the primary symbol of womanhood and of our ability to reproduce though I am past the age of childbearing. One reason I don't want to gain any weight back is because I don't want my period to suddenly reappear. I would need to increase my level of hormones and my body fat for my periods to begin again and I'm not willing to do that. I'm not willing to become a woman again. I am satisfied being childlike.

Sometimes I feel as though my life has been measured by my accumulation of jewelry. I wear a chai around my neck, the Jewish symbol for life because I think it magically provides me with the conviction to live. Additional pieces of jewelry that define the progression of my life are my collection of rings. I have kept initial rings and birthstone rings from my childhood. I have gifts given to me for various milestones throughout my life like graduations and significant birthdays. Depending on my weight at times, certain rings fit and certain ones do not.

I have a favorite. It is a thin gold band with three small diamonds set upon it. The diamonds were taken from various pieces of my mother's jewelry after she passed away. When I wear it, I always have a piece of her with me. I have had to take it off because my finger has gotten too small and I am afraid it will slip off without me knowing. It is the first time I have had to remove it since she died. I often rub my thumb against the base of my middle finger and feel lost when the ring is not there. I fight with myself over whether I want to be able to put it back on. I want to wear it again because I need to have my mother with me in my fight against this disease. If I have it on, it means I am too fat; there is too much of me. The battle is too much for me. As I fall asleep at the end of the day, I rub my protruding hipbones and the base of my middle finger and cry out for my mother.

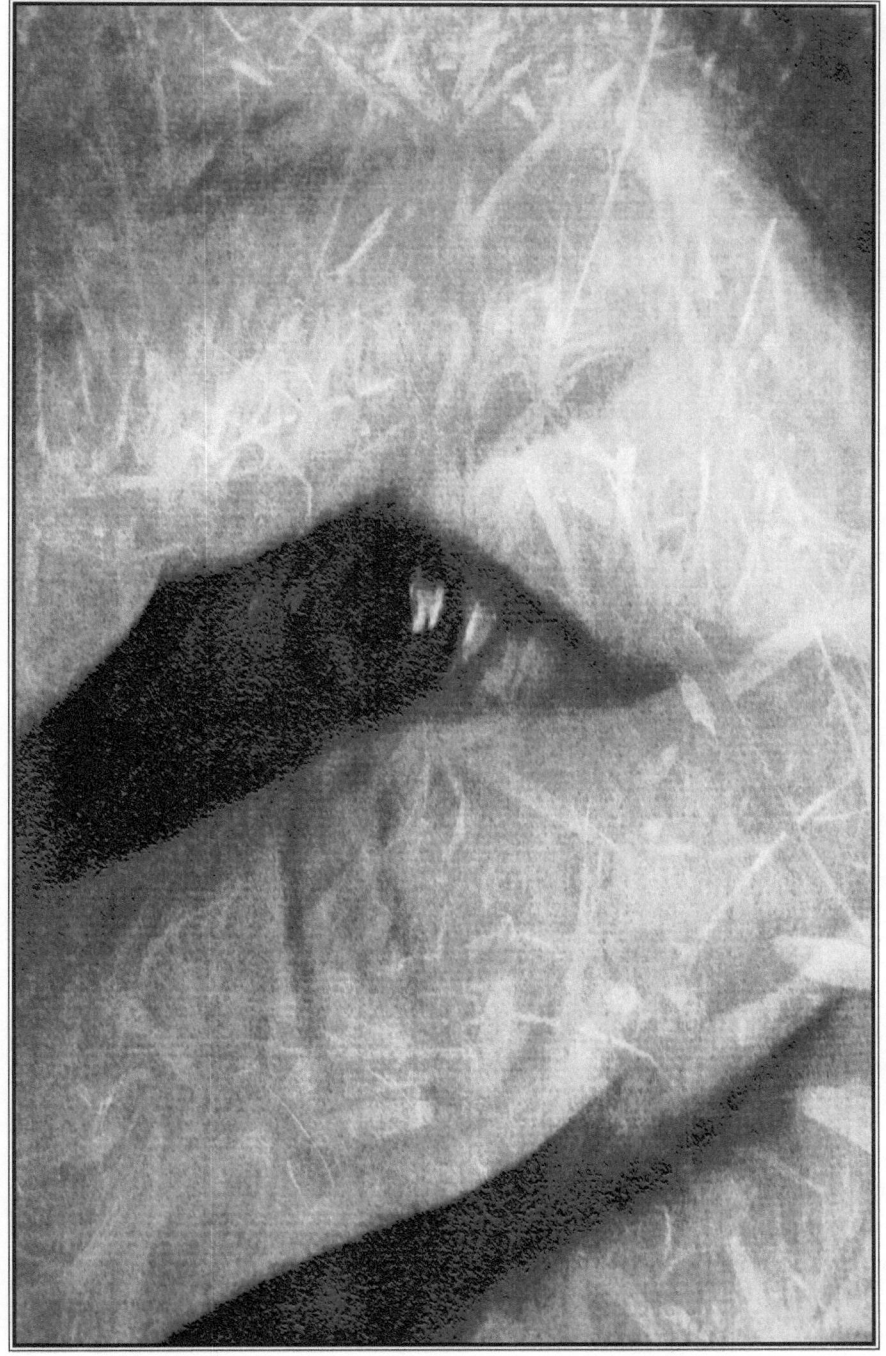

HEATHER TOSTESON

SKIN DEEP

1

The child is alive, flying like an angel
straight into God's face. The surf breaks
against her father's knees, foams
over the crotch of his white swim trunks.
Beneath the brim of his black hat, his eyes
are louvered, intent on the drops of water falling
singular as pearls from his daughter's feet.
One doesn't know, the way her legs bow,
if he intends to dash her to the ground
or bear her, as she is now, aloft and seraphic,
all the way to land.

I return to the image obsessively,
the luxurious graininess and flare,
as if there were something here
I can only learn by looking. Truth can be
skin deep. Which doesn't mean we can reach it.
It retreats with every word.
The father hoists the daughter aloft.
Her back arches, legs spread, in an ecstasy
of trust. The stasis is what I return for,
the water streaming in a neat cascade
from her slick skin back to its origin.

2

In the woods outside my window, the birches
flare in the first light. Here and there
I see their bark has split with the cold,
the incisions unbelievably neat, as if someone had boldly
sliced them with a scalpel, cuts deep enough
to expose, if they were flesh like us, the pleural intima.
As I pass, my hand reaches automatically
to close the fissures. What if I left well enough alone?

I return to the picture obsessively,
the photographer's equipoise, the ecstatic abandon
of the child, the father's almost professorial concentration.
I hear a man's voice saying, the detachment is almost clinical,
travesty is in the eye of the beholder.
(I am, am I, the eye of the beholder?)
Every time I look away from the book on my desk
I see the birches and I don't know what to believe.
I never did.

3

The girl's sex is sealed. Even with her legs spread
all you see is a shadow, narrow as a tendril.
The father's prick dangles limp and pale
over the waistband of the white trunks.
The horizon is a flare of light.
The decade is the fifties. You can choose the year.
The girl hears the surf as if it were
inside her head, cacophonous and sure
as the light, her father's hold on her.

For a day now, I have tried to stay exactly where I am
in relation to the picture. I know what I see
but I don't dwell on it. I focus, like the photographer,
on the naked girl, the way her feet arch toward the sea,
the undulations of her mons and diaphragm,
her obvious innocence. Truth can be skin deep.
Why need we speak of it?

4

Amid the few remaining artifacts of my mother's life,
I find slides of children's birthday parties and Halloween parades,
and, shuffled haphazardly among them, images of syphilis,
gonorrhea, leprosy, slide cultures of sporotvechosis
glowing like the moon. When I find an image of my own thigh
and right arm photographed with a purely clinical interest
against a family dishcloth, I feel relieved.

The truth, you see, can be skin deep. It can scar film
permanently with color. I try to preserve the same
relation to the image on the slide I have to the woman
I see, waking, in the mirror. Could I have spoken clearer
if I posted myself over with words?
The one that occurs to me now as I sit at my desk
and stare back at the black and white photograph
that has mesmerized me for days
would never have occurred to me then.
It doesn't belong to a girl of ten.

5
I hold the slides of my own thigh up against the window glass
so I can see my blemished childish skin against the birches.
I look at the loose dick dandling, an abandoned book,
a stranger's photograph, and somewhere inside I hear
my own voice, fully grown, daemonically clear.
You know this couldn't have happened by chance—
And at the same time I admire how high
he holds her above himself as if she need never know
where she came from, where she's going.

The truth, and herein lies its terror,
is that no one dies of violation. It requires,
for its full power, desire and trust and consciousness.
Everything, that is, we need to live.

HANNAH THOMASSEN

PHONE CALL FROM MY SCHIZOPHRENIC SON

*For EARTH which is an intelligence hath a voice
and a propensity to speak in all her parts.*
                                    Christopher Smart

I dreamed Dad was hugging me, he said.
It was so great, Mom. There were tears
in the back of my face.

I met a lady, he said. She wants to be best friends.
But I'm gonna ask her some questions.
I don't want no suicidals. She was wearing Levi Strauss.
But I need friends who are qualified. No suicides.

I smoke too much, he said.
This board and care sucks. No one worries about my health.

Resperol, he said. Trazodone, Cogentin, Geodon.
They took away my Ambien.

Oh, I said, nodding my head.
Love, we said; we said goodbye.

Outside, from the sky, rain fell
upon the ground where juncos fed.
It could have been the sun and mourning doves.
It was Joe. It was dark-eyed juncos in the rain.

JAMES H. COFFMAN

MAIN EVENT

"She's schizophrenic,"
Said Dr. Hart,
Like someone satisfied
Because he'd figured it out.

"Not my daughter,"
I said to myself.
"She's just got tendencies,
"That's all," I said.

I went home mad,
Swinging my denial
Like a club
To protect her.

But Lady Truth proved gentle,
Sitting by my side
For all the nights I needed
'Til I was ready—

After soaking up
All the hurt I could—
For the main event—
A no-holds-barred
Twenty year talk
With God.

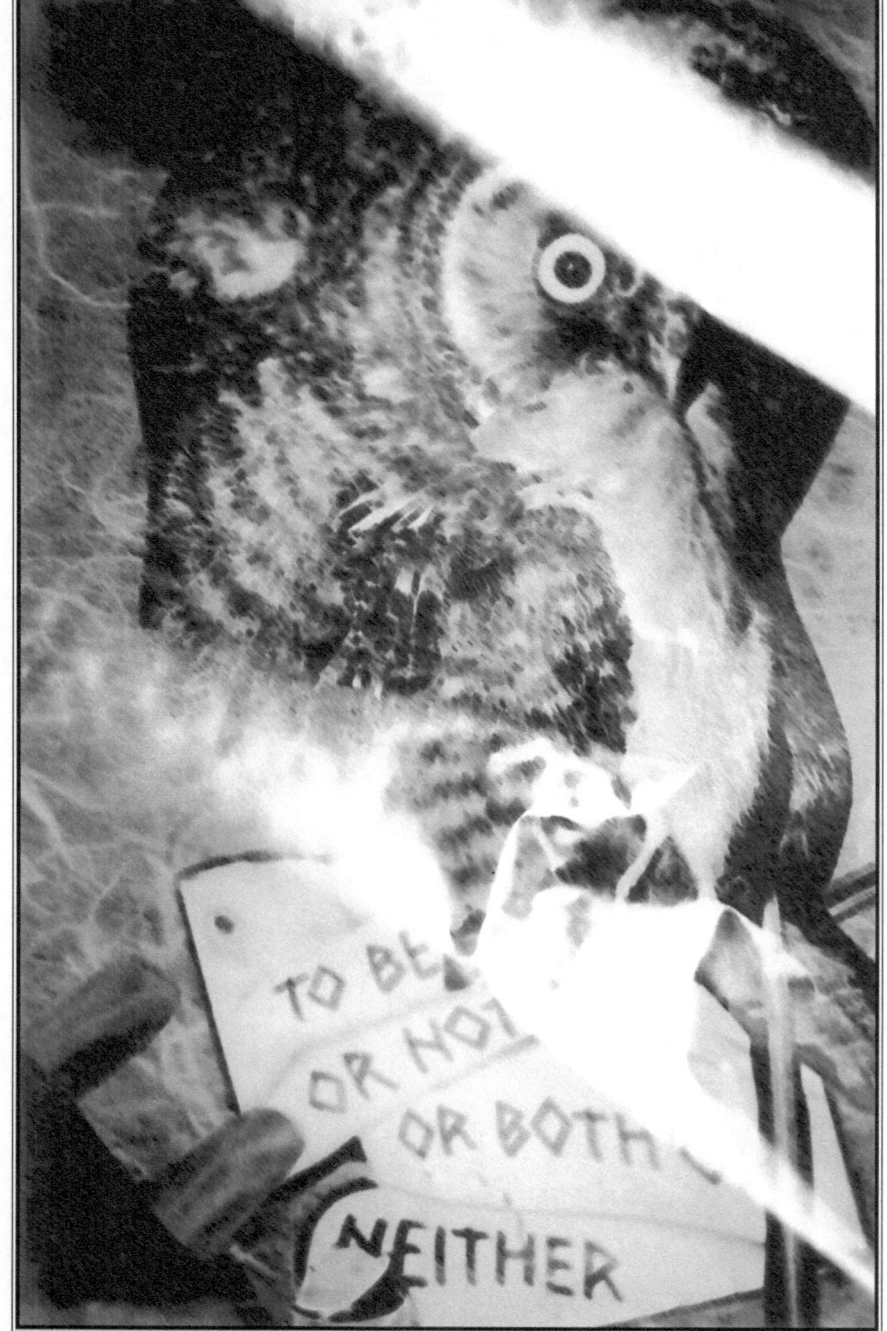

AELENA THOMPSON

ANOTHER ATTEMPT

last wednesday
i attempted failure again—
why can't i die?
i hate this damn place.

dear god,
i've prayed to you to kill me
and you don't
and when i finally do it myself
you prevent my death.

i don't understand.
my life is hell and empty—
why let me live?
why let me go through this pain.

you tell me that it'll be okay
but when i need you the most
you leave.
i'm alone,
confused—
i don't know what to do.

i took 26 pills
(that's all i had left)
equaling 13,000 milligrams
(it should of been plenty enough).
it did nothing
but make me dizzy and vomit.

(why did you keep
the poison from killing me?)
i wanted to go to sleep
and never wake up again…
but i woke the next morning. . .

i fucking hate you.

YOU SEE…

i'm nothing but a faggot,
a failure to society—
a bum on the streets
   a whore to so many
   a quick fuck down the drain.

i am a friend to abuse
   he treats me expectedly.
he bloodies my nose
   and puts my teeth
   through my lip—
him and i are well…
   he loves me forever.

i am a plague to my family,
   food for their mouths.
they take me close
   and cut me down
   with words.

i'm a crazy bastard
and i sleep on the floor
with the germs—
speak of my own name
and talk in the dark.

i am a poet
without a name,
without words,
and now without
thought...

      because today
      i'm a criminal
      quoted by law,

      and a hazard
      to public,

      so they talk
      for me.

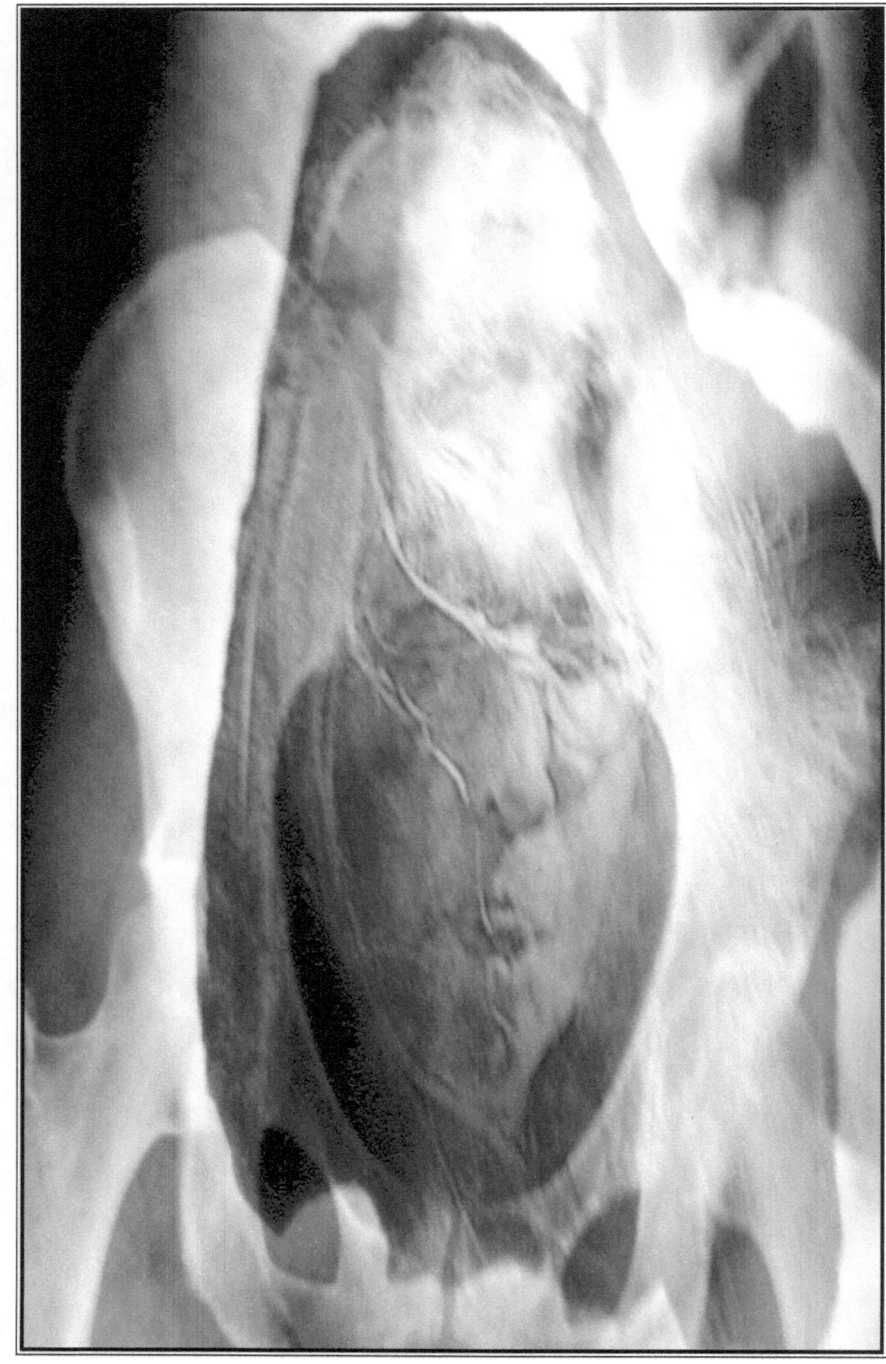

ROSS WEST

CRAZY DIAMOND SHINE

No one in this vast vicinity was and is so firmly grounded in as many various and colorful realities . . . with an intensity best gleamed in her technisparkle eyes and the hue of her lips as she uttered a profound and ancient rune . . . dance your dance, Hatoon.
                    —Posted on Hatoon's Web memorial

Come on you target for faraway laughter,
Come on you stranger, you legend, you martyr, and shine!

Come on you raver, you seer of visions,
Come on you painter, you piper, you prisoner, and shine!
                    —Pink Floyd,
                    Shine on You Crazy Diamond (I-V)

    A 67-year-old woman—homeless, psychotic—ended an improbable, decades-long run as the "campus crazy lady" not long ago when she pedaled her bicycle into onrushing traffic on a boulevard bounding the University of Oregon in Eugene. Unlike so many of society's outcasts who fall like sparrows in the forest, unnoticed, unremembered, unmourned, news of Hatoon's passing rippled across campus only minutes after her death. Within hours an impromptu memorial had sprung up on the sidewalk bench outside the university bookstore where she had been living, her huge pile of grab-bag possessions covered by a blue plastic tarp providing a little protection from the persistent Oregon rains. Votive candles flickered on the bench, smoke coiled from incense. Flowers appeared, lots of flowers—at first impulsively plucked from nearby beds, but soon joined by small and then increasingly elaborate bouquets, culminating in an arrangement suitable for an event of any magnitude of celebration, solemnity, or holiness. Scattered among the flowers and candles were chocolate hearts, lipstick tubes, seashells, lollipops, notes, placards, photos. The bench took on the anguished beauty of other spontaneous outpourings of emotion we've seen over the years—those that followed the deaths of John Lennon, Lady Diana, children gunned down in a schoolyard.

No one knew her and everyone knew her. If not by name, by sight. If not through personal contact, through the opportunity she gave each of us to thank our lucky stars—there but for the grace of God go I. In the days after her death it seemed everyone had seen her, talked with her, or, portentously, thought about her, in the hours and minutes just before the 1 p.m. accident. A typical account:

> *I saw Hatoon at around noon on the day she died. I was riding my bike through campus to a class with only a few minutes to spare. She was crossing 13th [Avenue] . . . and I gently swerved so I wouldn't disturb her path. Usually, I wouldn't think much of it, but yesterday I distinctly remember wondering how she was doing and if she was comfortable at night in the cold weather we've had lately. I'd never really taken a moment to think about her in that context, which made it all that more difficult to hear about her death.*
>
> —from one of Hatoon's Web memorials
> (as are the quotations below)

I too have a memory of her from that fateful day. I often eat Tuesday lunches with my wife and a friend at a cafe on the same block as Hatoon's bivouac. We arrive early to beat the lunch rush. Strolling back toward our offices at around 12:20 we passed the bookstore, Hatoon's mountain of possessions and, sure enough, Hatoon herself, gnomish, fussing with the very bicycle on which only minutes later she would take her final ride.

Having worked at the university for twelve years, I can think of no single person whose death would send so powerful a shockwave across campus. And the reverberations carried much further than that. The school newspaper covered the story, of course, but so too did the state's second largest newspaper, the Eugene *Register-Guard,* with a front-page story. An MBA student posted to the Web this audacious statement: "Her loss will truly be felt around the world." The comment seemed ludicrous hyperbole, but other postings confirmed the prediction. A contributor from Minnesota wrote, "By Wednesday morning, I received news of Hatoon's death 32 times

(17 phone calls & 15 emails)." A graduate student in London posted an online farewell.

We know only the sketchiest of details about her life—and these have only become generally know in any organized form *after* her death. She was born in California on April 30, 1937. Of Armenian ancestry with the family name of Adkins, her parents christened their baby girl Victoria. At some point she shed her identity with Victoria and adopted the name Hatoon, which she would explain means "Mother of all people." She produced a son and a daughter and relocated to Oregon. When the children were still quite small, she'd take them with her to Max's Tavern, a campus-area pub.

She wore lipstick, liberally, usually the commercially available variety, but often she'd find an especially agreeable shade among the vibrant red and hot pink marking pens and highlighters in the bookstore's art supply section. Even on the hottest summer days she'd wear two, three, or sometimes four sets of mismatched, free-box clothes, her layers of sweaters bulging out at her bosom where she stowed her money along with her most valued and secret possessions. She had an income in the form of a monthly government check. When it arrived, she'd sometimes splurge at the local ice cream shop and order five cones one after the other. Friends would help her deal with social services paperwork and other unavoidable intrusions of the straight world. They also chipped in to buy her a pass for the campus recreation center. She liked to lift weights.

Though she had access to the rec center and its locker room showers, she often took care of hygiene in the public restrooms of the university's library and bookstore. A library employee described in a poem the difficulty that paranoia imposed in even the most basic acts:

> . . . *she appears at my desk to report*
> *the latest intrusion on her privacy*
> *in the upstairs bathroom stall*
> *where she cannot urinate, cannot move*
> *her bowels with the camera on her,*
> *everyone watching. Nancy, she pleads,*
> *can't you do something about this?*

Another of her symptoms, graphomania, a disorder of creativity run amok, led her to write, W-r-i-t-e, WRITE, pages and pages of notes, things to remember, screeds, rants, pleas for the safety of the world's children. She felt she was able to hear important communications from . . . well, from someplace or something or somebody. But IMPORTANT!!! So she committed to paper her messages of warning and danger and doom. She needed to get the information to those with the power to help, to guide, to save. So she wrote, pages, thousands of pages, filled with words, then ripped from notebooks, stuffed in mailboxes, squirreled away in her many secret places, blown across campus on the wind.

Perhaps the strangest and most public moment of Hatoon's very strange and public life occurred in 1991 when gonzo journalist Hunter S. Thompson visited Eugene on one of his famously debauched lecture tours. An hour or so late for the talk, Thompson had last been seen drinking in a nearby bar. Local celeb, pop-culture deity, and longtime Thompson *compadre* Ken Kesey tried to calm the increasingly impatient crowd. At long last, an obviously loaded Thompson shuffled and swerved to the front of the ballroom and mumbled his way through a few disjointed opening remarks, gesturing vaguely now and again with a hand bandaged at the wrist, the result of god only knows what intoxicated mishap. Things got more coherent as the audience began to fire questions his way, and more interesting still as they pelted the stage with offerings of various substances that would have been at home in a mobile police narcotics lab.

In the midst of all this goofy Sturm und Drang Hatoon approached the speaker's platform wearing, along with the usual colorful garb, her kidney-protecting leather weightlifter's belt. She had something so important to convey, a matter of life and death, the water, the water in the drinking fountains. On campus, it's poison. POISON!

If anyone felt comfortable center stage in the theater of the weird it was Thompson. Perhaps he delighted in the unpredictability of the moment, its grotesque entertainment value, its high frisson potential; in any case, he gave her the spotlight and let her dance. When it was time for her solo to conclude and their *pas de deux* to begin, he signaled the moment by extending his hand. Maybe the good doctor, despite his carefully forged steely persona, knew a thing or two about the soft frailties of the human condition and the medicines, some as subtle as touch, that can calm a pained and agitated mind.

But she refused to shake. She stared at his hand and the wrist bandage that held it stiff, as if it were an alien being, telepathically diagnosing his tendonitis, wanting no part of it. She grew more excited, trying ever harder to say what needed to be said, about the threat, the POISONED WATER, but—the words—so difficult to keep straight—everything all at once coming out. Finally, in exasperation, she blurted, "If you could point a laser beam at my brain, you might be able to understand."

Had she been talking to most anyone else on the planet this would have been pretty much the end of the show. Where can you go from there? *Somebody call security.* But not so with Thompson; a wry smile crossed his face. The king-hell gun nut reached into a pocket and, with the finesse of the most masterful of magicians, produced the kind of high-tech sighting mechanism that mounts on a pistol. He fired up its tiny laser and aimed the thing, centering the red dot square on her forehead. Even in laser light her thoughts remained unilluminated, incommunicable. Outmatched and overwhelmed—a bower sprite fluttering before great thundering Bacchus—she fled.

Twenty thousand students attend the University of Oregon, plus thousands more faculty and staff. At busy times the place has something of the swarming anonymity of the anthill. Amid the thronging mass few stand out enough to make a mental impression—the seven-footer from the basketball team, say. But somehow the small, hunched-over woman with a babushka scarf wrapped around her head also got noticed—all the time, by everyone. Maybe what set her apart was her manic energy, the day-glo lipstick, or her seeming omnipresence: muttering outside the 7-11, scurrying up the steps of the administration building, pedaling her bicycle down the street with a fixed if not frenzied intensity. Hatoon's tenure on campus— longer than that of any dean—certainly added to her celebrity. But whatever the cause, she had an abundance of her own kind of star power.

And as is often the case with stars, the absence of hard knowledge fired the imaginations of those around her.

I heard she was married to a professor who had jumped out a window of PLC [an eight-story campus office building].

I heard that she was once a professor. That her husband was once a

professor and that they had taken experimental drugs for research,
causing permanent damage.

Like a leading lady on Broadway who never acts in film, Hatoon played
the campus, not the surrounding city. Her character served as the perfect foil
for the university—the rational, material world of evidence and argument,
of footnotes and double blind experiments. She offered a fleeting glimpse
of the ineffable, a torn corner in what we take to be the fabric of reality, an
impish laugh mocking the folly of our mundane lives. Her observations and
insights were not laboratory reproducible, not conducted with feet firmly on
the ground. Hers was neither a sober analysis nor a consensus assessment,
but, for those of us stuck in the ways of being and habits of mind suitable
for and permissible within the sometimes rather narrow halls of academe,
she was a cracked doorway through which, perhaps, we could safely peek into
another world.

A memorial service took place the weekend following her death.
Speakers paid tribute, told stories, reminisced, grew misty-eyed. College
girls who were not yet born when Hatoon was already deep into her own
jangled street existence sobbed uncontrollably. A woman whose bicycle shop
was one of the many stops on Hatoon's daily rounds of local businesses,
restaurants, and university offices, recounted how she and Hatoon had many
long conversations, and that after many years Hatoon "began to make perfect
sense." But even more, the shopkeeper went on, addressing the dead woman
as if she were hovering over her own memorial service, "so many times you
put my own life in perspective."

These words brought to mind Chauncey Gardner, the halfwit
savant in Jerzy Kosinski's *Being There* (played brilliantly by Peter Sellers in
the film version of the book). A groundskeeper who never leaves the estate
he tends, Chauncey mimics the behaviors and speech patterns he has seen
on television, his only contact with the outside world. When circumstances
force him off the estate, he talks in platitudes about the only subject he
knows anything about, gardening. The people he encounters—including the
President of the United States—interpret his earthy but inane words as sage
profundities; they project onto him exactly what they want to see, hear in his
simpleminded utterances exactly what they want to hear. The observers with
the brightest and subtlest minds find in Chauncey the deepest and weightiest
insights. With Hatoon's innumerable faces, moods, and obsessions, she gave

everyone who came in contact with her ample material from which to make of her what was needed:

> *Hatoon always made me feel so beautiful. Often times when I would walk past her, she would compliment me on my hair or a dress I was wearing that day. Her simple praises lifted my spirits.*

> *I remember when I was pregnant with my daughter. Hatoon was delighted when she found out. One day she told me that my unborn child had a wonderful, shining aura and was "an embryo of God." I took this seriously and I was very moved by it.*

> *I often heard little "gems of wisdom" buried in the flow of her stream-of-consciousness monologue. One gem I've never forgotten is "Anger is so aging."*

In her mirror, we at the university prettied up our own faces.

One retired UO professor, quoted in the campus newspaper's first-day coverage of Hatoon's death, reported having been friends with her for 30 years. By the time the story made the city's newspaper two days later his friendship with her had somehow grown to 35-plus years. Maybe he'd recalculated the math . . . or the myth—the clear waters of his memory transubstantiating into wine.

Easily overlooked with someone such as Hatoon, who could be seen going about her business more or less successfully on the street each day, is that she was, without doubt, quite mad. She said she was married to Clark Gable. Said she had borne the love child of the head of university security. She would commonly unleash

> *. . . a disjointed rant about government tracking devices or special patterns of light that only she could see and interpret . . .*

> *. . . she spoke often to herself and sometimes got in fights with the voices she heard. To me she seemed clearly schizophrenic, but to her the voices she heard were the results of "illegal hacking into my brain through my birth certificate."*

One bookstore employee remembered vividly how Hatoon would request change be given to her in dollar bills that bore the U.S. Treasury's L-12 marking

> *because they are printed in California and that would make it sunny instead of rainy in Eugene. Nor will I forget . . . the way she sought to save the children of the world by buying Jr. Mints and apple juice.*

The motif to which she returned most persistently was children, working out the theme in nearly endless variation: conspiracies to harm, her great love for, insights into, monsters seeking to destroy, what we must do to save, and on and on. Her compulsive riffing on the subject raises the question of why this particular obsession?

In contradistinction to all the murmuring voices mourning, missing, and memorializing Hatoon, a Web posting by a detractor suggests an uncomfortable answer. Perhaps most disturbing, this lone, painfully shrill voice is from someone who at least purports to have been a longtime eyewitness.

> *In the early seventies, when I was about 12 years old, I was best friends with Hatoon's son. Hatoon was cruel, inattentive, subject to screaming fits, and endless threats to her son, and myself. I knew her son until I was 15, and he was, at 14, washing dishes at the Rose & Thistle [a local fish and chips restaurant]. She did not provide her son with food, clothes, love. Until recently, I did not know that Hatoon even had a daughter. She certainly wasn't present when I knew Hatoon and her son.*

Reading the essentially anonymous posting—signed only "Bob, Eugene"—it is impossible to assess its veracity. Is Bob an objective observer or a vindictive nut job? (Casting at least a bit of doubt on his comment is a letter, written by what remains of Hatoon's close relatives and read at the memorial service, which concludes, "We loved her. We will miss her . . . In Loving Memory, Her Family.") Bob's tirade broadens into a more general critique as it concludes:

> *Blah. . .! This whole scene is like watching a Catholic Priest being praised, when I know what he has done to my friend. Suffice it to say, that this cumulative sympathy crap is just another shallow ploy, so*

*common to Americans, to be thought of as spiritually deep, etc., when
. . . they will have forgotten about it by the time American Idol is
on again.*

Whatever the truth of Bob's assertions, he remains the outlier, his venom the anomaly. Much closer to the heart of what many felt about Hatoon is a memory posted by a woman working as an acupuncturist in Portland. She recalls a gray November morning when she and her boyfriend were strolling around the deserted campus—the staff and students all off celebrating the Thanksgiving holiday. A soft rain fell and there were not many leaves on the trees. The couple happened upon Hatoon, camped out in front of the library next to her heap of stuff covered over with her blue plastic tarp. The conversation started as many did with Hatoon: first a hello, then, if she is happened to be in the right mood, if she caught the right vibe from you that day, she'd start in. This day things clicked. Soon it was this and that, Thanksgiving and the rain, how the government had put a microchip transmitter in her brain . . . the usual.

A cold wind was blowing and for the couple the thought of Hatoon sitting alone in a drizzle on this of all days just didn't feel right, so they invited her to their home for Thanksgiving dinner.

Late in the afternoon, the rich smells of the feast filled the cozy student apartment. Hatoon sat on the living room sofa in all her glory, smiling warmly and greeting the other guests as they arrived, shed their overcoats and scarves, carried salads and casseroles and bottles of wine to the kitchen. By happenstance, or dint of whatever celestial influence blessed her life, Hatoon had fallen in with students—innocent enough, open enough, free enough not to be put off by her odd dress, unusual manners or disordered thinking. From this group there were no harsh words, as she would sometimes encounter on the street, no sly looks of disapproval darting around the room. As afternoon turned to evening the table was set, the wine flowed, everyone enjoyed Hatoon's sharp sense of humor and got a kick out of her loopy conspiracy theories.

The party's host remembers how her guest's

*spirit shined through that night, which is so poignant in my mind to
this day. The gift in the rain she passed to me was of spirit . . . and
being thankful for what you have. To this day every Thanksgiving I say
a blessing to Hatoon, a quiet spirit that embodies kindness. . .*

And now Hatoon is gone, extinguished, disintegrated, like some star at the farthest reaches of the galaxy, consumed in a final shattering catastrophe. Memories of her persist in many forms: in poems and Web memorials and archived newspaper accounts, in the minds of those who felt blessed to have touched the hem of her frayed garment, in Bob's bitterness and bile. On the site where her blue tarp once protected her heap of material possessions, friends from the bookstore and beyond erected a permanent memorial to Hatoon. Anyone walking down the sidewalk or resting at the site's bench can reflect on the words, etched in granite, selected to enshrine and rekindle her memory for those who knew her, and to give to those who never did at least a glimmer of her technisparkle shine.

BE GRATEFUL FOR EVERY MOMENT OF YOUR LIFE
LOOK WITH FASCINATION AT EVERYTHING
DECIDE TO BE HAPPY
COMPLIMENT OTHERS
BE KIND
BE YOURSELF FULLY AND COMPLETELY EVEN UNTO DEATH

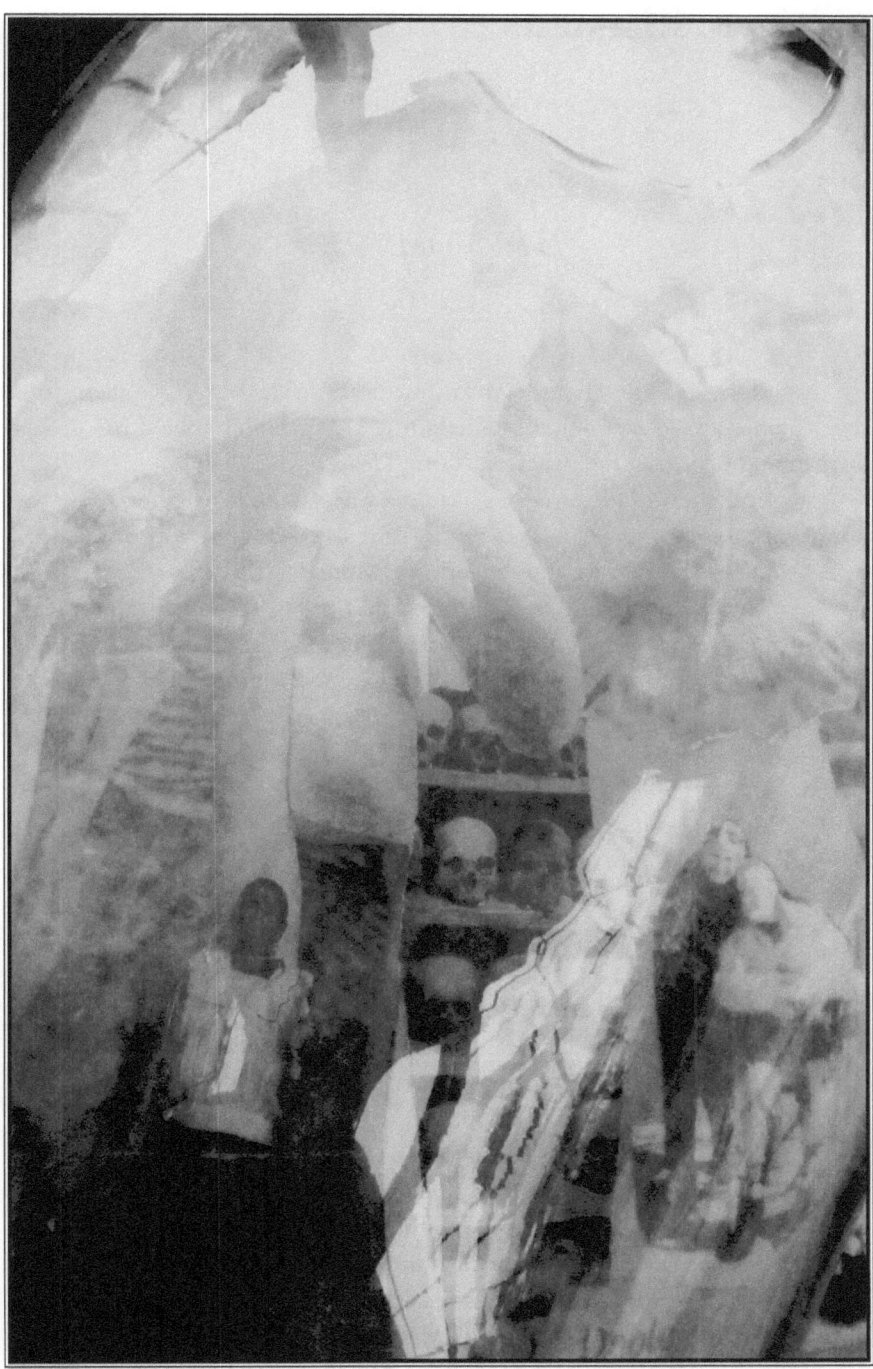

LAURA R. SOMMERS

THE MOMSTER

Mom had the ability to turn into a monster. When we were four, seven, nine, and eleven—my brothers, my sister, and I—we'd run to the kitchen and beg, "Do the monster, Mom. Please!"

And she would shake her head no. She was fixing dinner, there was homework to do, it was almost bedtime—the usual reasons why not.

"You never do what we want!" we whined.

And we went and amused ourselves, trying to jump up and leave fingerprints on the ceiling, doing headstands in front of the picture window, chasing the cat around the pool table. Then we would remember and go beg again.

But she did nothing. And then… Her neck twitched. And her head jerked.

She shook it off and kept stirring the chili or beef stew or spaghetti as if nothing had happened. But we noticed.

"Mom!"

Her head jerked.

Then her legs sagged just a bit. Her shoulders drooped. And still she tried to shake it off. But then her left arm bent and drew up toward her shoulder. The hand flopped loose, a disabled claw. Then her head tilted to the left and stuck. And the good hand stopped stirring.

Now the chase would begin.

She took a labored step toward us. The right foot first, the left leg dragging behind, the way her own father, who had polio, had walked with his cane. She was the staggering zombie, the lumbering Frankenstein, and we were the able-bodied people you yell at in the movies, "Idiots! Run!"

We shoved each other and squealed and ran away. Then we ran back. Ran away. Ran back. *Squealed.* Ran away. Ran back. *Squealed.*

The monster dragged herself down the hall after us. Her fleeing offspring scattered, sometimes falling on the linoleum at her feet and scrambling away, crab-like.

And then her tongue lolled, and she started to drool, and an ungodly sound issued from her throat. *"Unnnnhhh..."*

Our squeals became screams.

"Ewww! She's drooling!" This from my older brother.

"Don't let the monster touch you!" My older sister.

"Get away! Get away!" Me.

We herded ourselves into a bedroom and huddled on the bed. The monster lurched in, her garbled sounds a steady moan, her limp left hand pawing the air. Whoever was in front would get the worst of it, so we pushed my little brother toward her. She raised that claw and dragged it tepidly, lamely, over his back, his arm, the top of his head. She smiled a lopsided smile and laughed, a hoarse imitation of the sound humans make.

"Hunh. Hunh."

All this monster ever wanted was a hug. But she wouldn't get it from us. We yelled at the monster to go away, kicked our feet at it, threw pillows.

Then my sister, who always wore out first, grabbed my mother by the arm. "Mo-ommm! Stop it!"

We begged her to be herself again.

"Please stop."

"Go back to the kitchen! We're hungry!"

"Mom, you're scaring me." My younger brother, the baby.

Slowly, her spine straightened, her arm dropped, and her head, with one last spasm, righted itself. Just when we thought she had it under control, she slurped up one last bit of drool. We ran away, squealing again, begging for an encore. But she looked at us funny, seeming to have no memory of what had just happened. Then she reminded us it was time for dinner or homework or bed.

Forty-some years later, the Momster is no longer with us. She died of cancer decades ago, leaving us on our own to ponder what it all might mean.

For my part, the Momster taught me about fear—that it has the awful power to make you act despicably.

I also believe there was another lesson she was trying to teach us: that deeply hidden inside our loved ones are the things we never talk about, and that those, perhaps, are the things we should be begging to confront.

When we finally succeed in bringing out the monster, we run away, squealing, certain that this is the worst that could ever happen to us.

Then, deciding we haven't had enough, we run right back for more.

CLAUDETTE MORK SIGG

THAT TOO

Cracks in sidewalks and playing hopscotch. And much, much later, it was license plates. If his initial was in the combination of letters driven past her, he was thinking of her—and not of the other woman. It was a particularly good sign if her own initials and his were combined together on the car's blue and gold plate—with no indication of that woman anywhere in the formula. Driving along city streets, she scrutinized each passing car, occasionally exceeding the speed limit in her search for the right combination of letters that insured her future with him. On several occasions, she nearly wrecked herself but pulled away from the near collision in time.

Her mother had counted daisy petals. The child she had been handed the crying woman the last daisy she could find in the lawn, but her father left, moved to the City, leaving wife and two children behind. Then the autumn darkness overwhelmed the garden, and a dreadful weeping had descended on her mother.

The last time she saw him—the man she loved so desperately—his look of boredom, his coldness, his words leaving her no room to move *had* moved her after all. All she remembered years later was crying and driving across the Golden Gate Bridge in blustering rain into sun-streaked skies on the other side. And thinking, why not?

She didn't do it, that leap into a wind-tossed sea—but she thought about it—and then went on living for no discernible reason, except that too was what her mother had done.

LORI ANDERSON MOSEMAN

BEAUTY SECRET

Blunt is beautiful that's my mother's trick.
Her last letter to me begins:
"Finally got this picture reprinted!
I am my usual beautiful self.
Hair-do doesn't help the face!
Have you ever been checked for a goiter?"

There's nothing wrong with her face
save her dad smashing it in with a 2-by-4.
She never told me this. Her brother did
the day we buried his father. So, this
is what she's been saying her whole life?

My grandfather's mother jumped out
a 2nd story window to flee an abusive step-mom.
My grandfather's sister was "murdered"
by her husband. Police said it was suicide.
Honesty is beautiful? Such a legacy.

"Marc Lepine." Anne-Marie Edward's mother
asked that we never say the gunman's name.
Ambrose Lepine helped Louis Riel lead
an armed fight for Metis rights. No relation?

Metis fleeing Canada founded my Montana
birthtown. Marc Lepine was an abused child.
These are not related. There is no relation.

Ralph Tortorici, U of A gunman, sought help
for his mental illness before taking hostages.
His family sought help. They were denied.
Ralph Tortorici killed himself in prison.

Beauty says not of the above are related.
Beauty says all of the above are related.
We are all related. That is the secret.

Louis Riel was hung for hanging a man: execution in the name of liberation (in the name of new nation (in the name of the oppressed)) so hard to redress.

DENISE MILLER

UNFINISHED GHOST STORY

Rose put her sister down.
   She thought,
She buried her.
But really, she lost her
In the truth of family lore.

But she was sure she had placed her
porcelain side up on that table
so they could
swab her clean.

She felt her own skin smooth
and set into a smile as they scraped
stone from her sister's caramel colored skin,
or plucked windshield glass from where her eyes
had been. No. Really. She checked

her mind to make sure she could lean
Ruth far back in the place
of acceptable mourning so that when she
told Ruth's story, it would be truth.

   Yes, Rose put her sister down
and thought she buried her. She thought that
when she closed her eyes thicked over with
cataract and too much seeing that she could
see the story begin and end like this:

Ruth had followed him again.
She was behind them now.

Holding the car that had been theirs
these last ten years close to the
woman's he was driving as the seconds split
a seam into the first time she had seen the back
of him. It was in the movie theater.
His outline was smooth, pecan
shaped and just imperfect enough
to make her want to know him.
And now she knew him. Knew him long and
deep enough to know that right now
his left hand smoothed the steering wheel
and his right reached under the hem of the
dress of the woman who sat beside him.
He had done that to her too, once.
Before she married him. She also didn't need
to see the slick of his tongue lick the curve
of his bottom lip then hang there until the
hunger of the woman next to him
Got the better of her so that she wanted to
take it in to her own mouth. Ruth knew too
without knowing, that they were headed
south and then east to that bend
just before the reservoir where she was sure
he would pull over, remove her stockings,
then his trousers and whisper in her ear, *Ruth*
baby, you ... But, it wasn't her beside him.
She was behind them. So she shifted, then
crossed the line that lawed them
in their places and cruised her car beside.
He looked at her, and the stark white
of his teeth as he smiled
didn't blind her because SHE couldn't turn
her face to see it. In fact, when stark
white changed to gray stone, she
didn't slow because she didn't know.
She was already gone.

And that's why Rose couldn't find her.
Because she had put her down
long before steel met stone. She had put
Ruth down among the helpless

after the first time her laughter was clogged
by his fist, and he drained the wife
from her. Rose lost her, because she believed
Ruth was hers to lose. She believed
It was life that killed her,

not Ruth's own right foot's persistent pushing
through pedal to stone that helped
Ruth run away from home.
Rose put her sister down.

     She thought,
She buried her.
But really, she lost her. And anyway,
she wasn't looking. She was A black woman busy
cooking forty years for a man who would die

and leave her quilting.

THE THING I IMPROVISE

i want to spin around you
spiral and spill like an eric dolphy
serenade played on flute your skin
the grid of treble clef my lips the
mouthpiece but underneath this
is the thing i improvise this love i
was supposed to learn how to live
from a nuclear family in a house with
a fence and a dog i was supposed
to be able to log the way to make
you smile after a difficult day right
above the way to prepare a perfect
meal in minutes so that while we're
in this love we both will want to stay
but in my world nuclear came after
family the house was a trailer and women
blended bruises into love but this thing
this we i want to hold in the soul of
me like a whole note in the throat
of a saxophone then spit it into
sixteenth notes fretting from
freddie hubbard to fusion in the
confusion of a heartbeat i used to beat
my past on the coners of a djembe drum
while the band played on and now i play
out my father's fury i beat out my
child story on the soft of your
soul but i want to begin here begin
now to improvise myself out of
whiskey and bad blood into
safety and sandalwood i want to
transpose terror into tenderness meld
memory into nothingness and be
always right here in the cleft
of your throat.

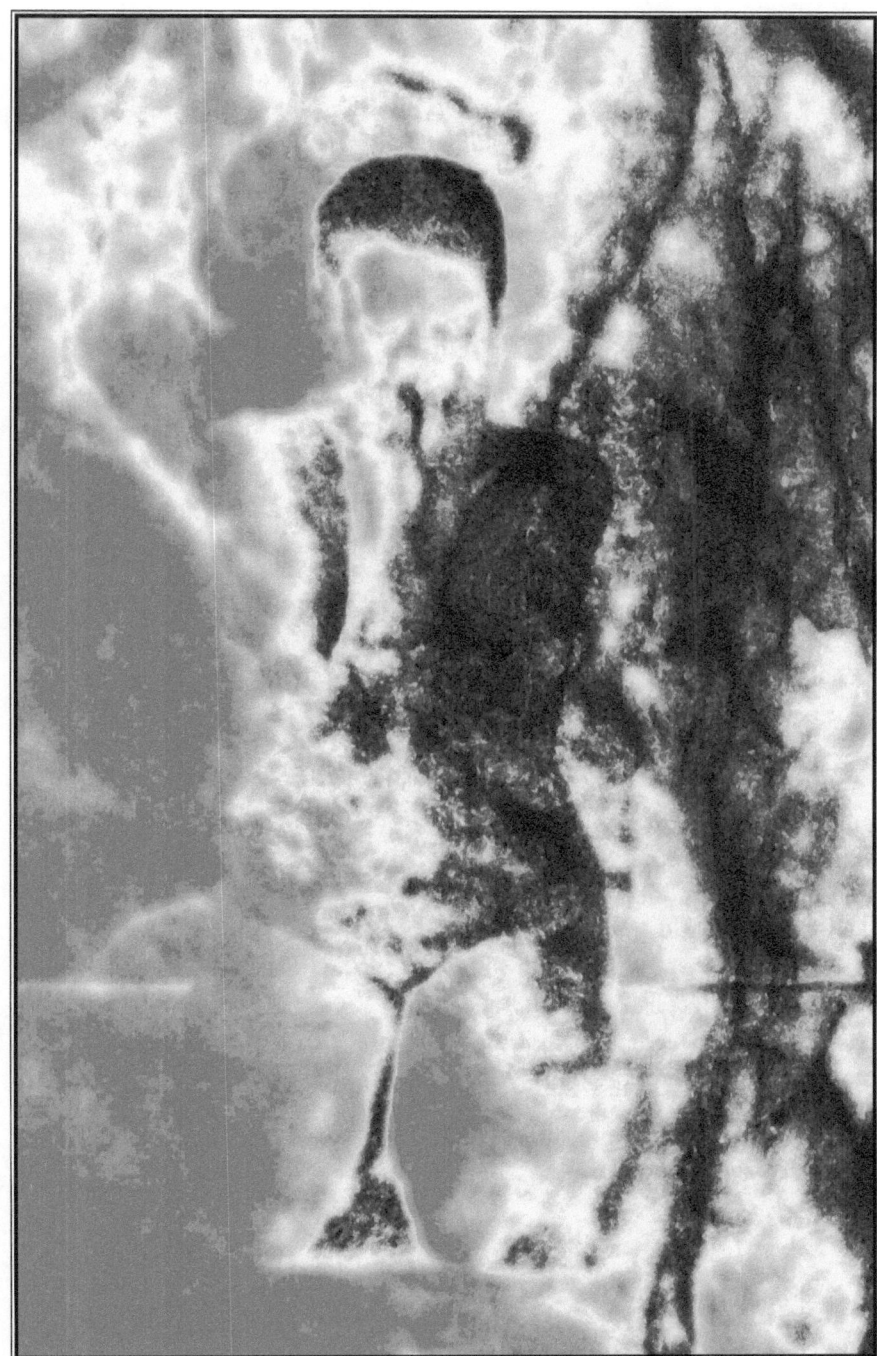

ADELE STEINER

QUICK KISSES

You never see them when
they snap from rubber bands,
sideswipe your forehead, and
crackle through strands of hair.

Pinching a cheek, like your aunt
did when you were young
might remind you how much
it hurt to be so shy.

Some of them can still bring
a chill to the back of
your neck before they have
a chance to dry while

others flatten your nose
or ricochet off your
chin before you notice
the marks they leave behind.

Still, the ones that slam your
lips against your teeth and
bloody the sheets are the ones
you know were really there.

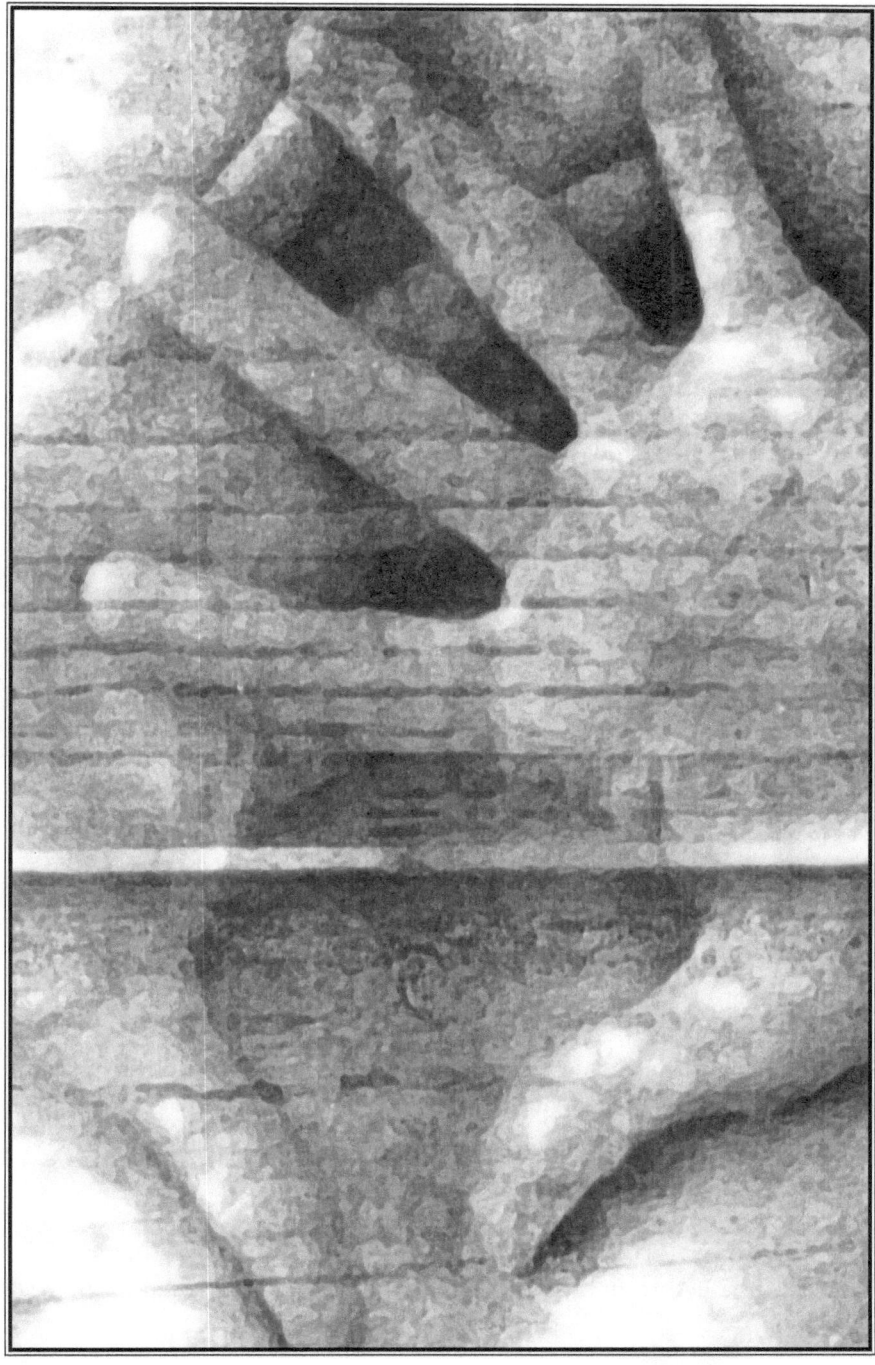

ELIZABETH DI GRAZIA

FAMILY REUNION

At first I thought it was a gift from the cats. Inching slowly towards the hutch, past the Queen Victoria chair, my head jutted forward drawing my body. The uneven piles. . . were they. . .could they be. . .the snaky entrails of a bunny. . .a chipmunk . . .parts of a bird? I kept alert for a reflexive twitch from a dying animal. Kneeling, my chest and face tugged tightening my upper torso; neck muscles bulged and pulsated. With nose scrunched, I willed myself to study the mess. A putrid smell rose up.

It was shit. Three uneven lumps of shit.

The family reunion was coming to an end, the sound of doors slamming and "GET IN THE CAR!" clawed the air. I was left shaking my head studying shit.

Three hours earlier relatives swarmed the three-season porch, dropping sport bags, shedding clothes, and yanking swim diapers over chubby short legs. The hive made a beeline, past the baked beans, past the vegetable tray, the fruit bowl, the sandwiches, and our sister, Patricia's, birthday cake, for the backyard swimming pool. Standing in the breezeway, I waved to my brother Michael. Across the lawn he rushed, a bull in charge of his pasture (though it is was my home), his stubby physique hoofing towards me. I held my ground, met his linebacker lunge with a quick hard squeeze. "How are you? How was the drive from Oregon?"

"Hellish. Van broke down over the Dakota's. We had to take an extra day to make it. I bet you could hear us a few blocks away. Damn muffler fell off and I had to find a junkyard. Shit. I thought I had tied it up good enough."

Stepping backwards, I scanned the parked vehicles. "Why do you have cardboard taped on your windows?"

"For my three boys to watch the VCR and sleep." Michael's wife skittered past the porch not saying a word. "Hey, I'm leaking oil but it's alright, I'm on the street." Michael palmed a turkey sandwich skewing the tray and the hill of prepared sandwiches. "Hey, let me see your kids."

I turned to look out the porch window; I had a view of Jody placing bits of watermelon on Antonio and Crystel's highchair. "There, over there, by Jody, under the tree." Antonio was bouncing up and down, saying, "Duck, duck, duck."

We had celebrated Antonio's one-year birthday the week before. Already he was teeter-totter walking, using dancing hands above his head for balance. Crystel, six weeks younger, turtled behind her brother, following him around the house and yard mimicking, "uck, uck, uck." A few days ago, we had taken the children for a walk when Antonio pointed wildly to the sky and Jody explained that the big noisy birds were ducks. "Duck," became their favorite word and they used it for anything that flew but it didn't stop there. We could hear, "Duck, duck, duck," over the baby monitor when they woke up in the morning.

Michael slapped me on the back, rubbed his jaw with his other hand. "Big sister. Tell me how motherhood is. You don't believe in all that loving kindness bullshit do you? Hell, I belt my ten year old every six months or so. They need it. Got to have it. Toe the line." He patted his stomach. "I have to get after my wife sometimes. She's harder on the kids than me. . .I've got to stop her. . .she loses control." I doubled over slightly, though I should have been ready for his words. If my family thinks it; they say it; they do it. There is no warming up a conversation. No idle chitchat. Unexpected behavior and profanity is the norm. Thirty years ago, prior to AA and therapy, I was this way also. School authorities could not imagine what I might do my last week of high school, thus they suspended me from all school activities including classes. They had to protect the other students.

I examined Michael for a sign that he was kidding, wanting to see a sparkle in his eyes. "Don't you remember when Mom slashed your hand with a knife?" I centered the sandwich platter on the long narrow table. How could I not know that Michael hit his kids? True, I hadn't seen him in seven years and we didn't talk much, still, he had been my favorite brother. Shaking my head and feeling nauseated, I stacked the toppled sandwiches. Barely above a whisper, I said, "I don't think it has to be that way."

Before the adoption process was even final, Jody and I had discussed how we wanted to raise our children. We agreed that we didn't want to use spanking or hitting as a means of discipline and had started earmarking pages in several books: *Discipline without Shouting or Spanking, Positive Discipline For Preschoolers, Love and Logic Magic for Early Childhood*, and *How To Talk So Kids Will Listen & Listen So Kids Will Talk*.

"You just wait. You'll find out soon enough. Hey, It's time for the pool!" he shouted.

The weather was perfect for swimming: sunny, 86 degrees, no breeze. I shivered. Did I make a mistake inviting relation into my home? My sister Margaret had called on the phone a couple of days ago. "It's Patricia's birthday on Saturday. Everyone is in town for the big reunion. Let's invite everyone to your house." I hesitated. It had taken me years to believe that I didn't have to have the sibling get-togethers because I had a swimming pool. The rule in the home we grew up in was that you couldn't have anything that you weren't willing to share. I had to challenge the part of me that felt that I should make a key available to any family who wanted to enter my house. There was also a part of me that felt guilty for owning a home with a swimming pool. I could hear the voices of my relation: How dare I? What made me so special that I could live differently from how I was raised? Didn't I know that we were lower class? I gnawed away at these beliefs until the sibling get-togethers were only once a year. "Come on, Beth. It'll be fun. We'll all be here. It's for your brothers and sisters." When Margaret said those words they wiggled into a deep want in my heart—to be liked—especially by those people that I had lived with for eighteen years.

In our family of fourteen, I was the keeper of birthdays. When he was a teenager, my brother Mark, told me not to tell our mother that it was his birthday. "Are you sure?" I asked. All day on his birthday I was afraid. When it was too late for my mother to recover from her mental lapse he told her. "Stupid, why didn't you say something?" she admonished the two of us.

I tried to protect my sibling's hearts by reminding our mother that a birthday was coming up. Her not remembering my birthday would have been proof that I wasn't liked. I didn't want to know that for sure.

Younger siblings, Johnny, Patricia, and Margaret, called me mom. I waited for my mother to shout, *She's not your mother! I'm your mother! Don't call her mom!* But she never did and I didn't correct my brother and sisters. It didn't bother me to be called mom. That was my place. That was my role. That made me special, important and liked. I left home when Johnny was five years old. As I was driving down the gravel road, he flung the front door open, hollering as he ran, "Mom, Mom." I stopped the car. We hugged. I didn't want to leave him. What would become of him being left to his mother? But it was my life or his.

Living on a farm, my brothers—the seven that surrounded me in age—were my playmates. Hay elevator tongue projected through barn window spit bales and forts—the smooth green supports of the elevator we knew as a child knows their mother. Intimate with her underbelly, the V our home, we explored her parallel beams, leaping from joint to joint. Straddling the length of the pole girders, we pullied up her breasts hand over hand, hanging by her neck till dropping to the ground. The elevator measured our growth from year to year, counting chin-ups and appraising the grip of our bare feet on her skin, as we climbed an artery or rested on her main vein.

Instead of softball, kickball or football we divided into teams, used rows of corn as our playing field. After being tagged in the corn row, imprisoned on the hay wagon, a teammate attempted to free you. In winter, rows of corn shape-shifted to a dark barn and fifty milk cows that we crawled over and under, the calf pen the prison.

Instead of sledding down a hill, we would as easily slide down the roof of our pole shed or tie up the sleds to a tractor and snake up the road.

Before I reported the sexual abuse in our family there was a one for all and all for one feeling amongst us siblings. It was we against you. As damaging as the sexual abuse was, there was a sense of belonging to a group. The lifeline to my family disintegrated when I told. I was nineteen years old. "You're the one who left us," my sister Margaret said. "You can come back anytime you want." From time to time, I tried to reconnect with my family but I never felt again like I fit or belonged. I learned to live with a mixture of sadness, anger, and bitterness that I imagine some mothers have whose children have been taken away from them and they have lost visitation rights though the children continue to reside down the street. This isn't the same feeling as having a baby and giving the infant up for adoption, I've done that too, it's a different feeling, and in a sense harder, because I didn't hold any notion that I'd see the baby that I gave up for adoption. But what about the siblings that were still alive, that I grew up with, that I mothered?

Shaking my head, I walked over to the crabapple tree where Jody and the children were. Our eyes met. I hugged her and kissed each child's head. What was it that I wanted to belong to? Yesterday I had cried when I was told that our sister Catherine disciplined her three children by having them go to their bedroom, pull down their pants, and wait while she got the belt. It's the will of God she said in explanation.

"Hey get off that diving board. I'm first," Michael yelled to his ten-year-old son. "Didn't you know that I'm the champion? Just ask your Aunt. Isn't that right Beth? No one else can do a gainer."

The hot afternoon sun bounced off the water.

"Let's see, big shot," our brother Paul retorted, pulling off his tee shirt. Wincing, he stretched his arm behind his back.

Michael stepped up on the diving board, staggered, balanced, and marched to the end of the board. Squinting he looked into the water, than stepped back two paces.

The murmuring of voices fizzled around the pool and the scent of popcorn settled in the air. Pine trees, usually noisy with sparrows, weren't rustling. Standing on the white of the diving board, Michael's pale body looked even paler. He scratched his red hair and his spindly legs shook with the movement. After rubbing his belly, Michael took a few quick forward steps, bounced, and completed a full somersault backwards. If I hadn't seen it, I wouldn't have believed it. I couldn't do a gainer myself, not that I hadn't tried. How was it that my brother could do something that I couldn't?

Michael's son stepped onto the diving board. "Jesus, did you see him do that?" Michael said, climbing up the ladder, water spilling off his body. He was oblivious to the fact that all of us were still in awe that we just watched him do a gainer. "I didn't even know my kid could swim. Hey, great flip, kid!"

"Beth, I'm going in the house for a moment. Will you keep an eye on Antonio and Crystel?" said Jody. She supported me in having my relation over, helping me make the food, setting out chairs, and welcoming my siblings. She knew me well enough to know that I was on guard, and videotaping the gathering in my head. We'd sit down later and talk about the conversations we had and what our impressions were. I'd replay the movie, pausing at certain moments.

Antonio rocked on his tippy toes to the gardening hose, fingered the dripping water. Next to him, Crystel splashed in the hard plastic kiddy pool. Patricia sidestepped to where I was holding sentry over the children. I uncrossed my arms, returning her hug. "Thanks for having us all, Beth. It's a great day and the kids are loving it."

The companionable moment was broken with a shout from Michael's wife. "I'll kick your ass if you don't get out of the pool right now!" Her three boys, stepping blocks of blonde, were hanging on the rope that divided the little end from the big end.

Quickly, I glanced at Antonio and Crystel, but they didn't seem to take notice of the commotion. I thought, what are my kids hearing, what are they seeing, what am I subjecting them to? My mother's ghost was whispering in my ear, "You're a good daughter holding this get-together, you're a good sister." When my mother was alive, her mother, brother, and sisters came first in her life. Not her spouse. Not her children.

Antonio dropped the garden hose, started walking for the pool. "Oh, boy. There goes Antonio," I said. "Patricia will you watch Crystel!" I grabbed Antonio before he reached the pool steps. "Come on, bud. I've got you. Do you want to swim? Let's go in." Squirming, Antonio propelled his arms, and kicked his feet in the air. I set him in the water, still holding his torso and he became a speedboat.

"Here Beth, let me have him," Michael said.

My eyes widened. Moments ago, I watched Michael feeding my sister's baby, spooning too quickly, scraping his chin, and forcing the squash back into his mouth. I glanced at my son. His dark eyes were big and round trusting me. His small compact body tightened and he pulled himself into my waist when Michael reached for him.

"No," I said.

"Come on. Let me have him." Michael grabbed for Antonio. I backed away, drawing him into my chest.

"No."

"Come on."

"No." I took another step back. "He's my son."

"Look. You've made him suspicious of me."

"Well, maybe he should be."

Picking up the clumps of shit, one by one with wads of toilet paper, and carrying them to the bathroom, I projected three years into the future when there would be another reunion. Could I remember my sour stomach, my clenched teeth, and my closed throat? Could I remember how uncomfortable I was with my siblings, how I could not relax in their presence, how I did not enjoy being with them?

Let there be no mistake the shit said, you need to stop expecting your relatives to be any different from what they are. You can't control what comes into your house, into your family if you invite your relation in. Let there be no mistake the shit said, you will be left to clean up.

I tried to find out who the owner of the shit was. I imagined many things but didn't think any of my brothers were that mentally ill. After talking with a sister, I settled on the shit being from a daughter of a brother who was not yet toilet trained.

My unspoken hope for this reunion was that Antonio and Crystel would bring my siblings and I together, that the children would be the magnet that would bind us once again. Our commonality would be parenting. Instead, the reunion provided the question, who did I consider most important—my family of origin or my chosen family?

REBECCA PAYNE

WEEK OF THE HYACINTHS BLOOMING

Anne is lying in there dying, and this should be about her, but it is about him. It always is, even in these, her final days, it is always him. He's the one she wanted, the one she bore even after the doctor warned her against more children, the son to carry on the name, and he was trouble from birth. He was the loud kid, the bully, the needy one.

He is fifty-seven this week and to everyone else he is still the bully, but her eyes always light up when he comes close. She was the only one who didn't desert him when his temper drove away friends and family, myself included. Through the years he has taken good care of her, planting hyacinths and taking her to doctor's appointments. Now she is on her deathbed and he is crying.

I am here to relieve my son. My son is his son, and the boy is only eighteen, too young to see his grandmother die, too young to do the hard things like hold her on the toilet while her insides turn to putty, but he is a good kid and he is here. His father, in the Sergeant Rock style he learned in Vietnam, will have no less from him, no matter how hard it is.

When I protest, for the kid's sake, he takes me into the bedroom and closes the door and with those blue eyes narrowed down to marbles and red veins standing out on his face he says, "That boy don't know nothing. You shoulda seen what boys his age saw in the 'Nam, they lived whole lifetimes in one night, and all this kid has to do is help his ninety fuckin' year old grandma onto the toilet and you say that is too much? Leave that boy alone and let him grow some balls!"

So I back off and the boy is caught in the middle, his wide eyes bespeaking his innocence. He doesn't want to grow up like this, but such is his karma. Caught in the trap of his parentage, he sits up nights and listens to her moan and flail her arms.

I don't belong here. I divorced out of this family when the boy was still a toddler, glad of it, glad to be gone, but divorce doesn't really do as promised, you are still married to the family you despise; the kids bring you back. I always vowed to spit on her grave after that hard time, when she and he tried to take the children from me. They made a fearsome team with his nerviness and her single-minded belief in him. I was young and naive, like a rabbit caught in a trap. I watched as they held tight to my kids, and so I was held forever in their grip.

Now I put her on the toilet, and she grabs my neck with her feeble arms and tells me she loves me. This takes me off guard. These are words I never expected to hear from her. I say, "That means a lot to me, Anne," but I cannot say 'I love you'. I guess when you are dying you need to say a lot of "I love you's" but I am still not prepared for it.

And then when grief overwhelms even him, he holds my hand. In the gravity of the situation, I let him, though I do not particularly want him to. I even hug him when he breaks down and sobs, his mother moaning in the background, and I cross off that vow to spit on her grave, and somehow I figure the score is even now.

The boy has grown up nicely, so has his sister. Dancing around their dad's fits of anger has deepened them. They have seen more and learned more than they have a right to know at their ages, but I am proud of them for that. If they were shallow kids, I would not like them half as much, still I cry at night for the heaviness that tugs down the corners of their lips.

His eyes harden again when his sisters edge into the house. Even these confident women look at him in fear. They are here only to honor their mother, but he lies in wait for them, he mocks and ambushes their helpfulness. He calls them "the girls." He needs rest, but he prowls around the house all night on watch. He just can't sleep and leave them in charge.

He is still in Vietnam, he is still Sarge, he still can't bear to see his troops die. All over again he feels their anguish. Throughout his life he has tried to make those dying soldiers get up again and walk. Maybe if he raised "the boy" to be strong enough, or stayed awake and helped his mother die well enough, then maybe one of those lost soldiers would pull his intestines back inside and stand up and say, "I'm all right, Sarge. You can sleep now, and I'll take over."

But they never get up. In his mind he bends over for the thousandth time and looks in the glazed eyes of one mangled soldier. For the thousandth time, he tells the kid that he's dying and watches him start to cry and tries to pull last words out of him, anything to send back home in the duty letter, and the boy soldier dies crying, again tonight, and he still has to stay awake and keep his sisters at bay while his mother dies.

On the next to last night she takes off her wedding band and gives it to our daughter, and the little girl sobs with the taking of it, the symbol of her grandparents' union. She knows the gravity of this, and we all cry, he and the boy and my daughter and the sisters and even me. Later, brushing off the need for sleep, he reads poetry into his mother's ear, and then gets out the old home movies of himself and his sisters in happy times, and he gives her the best death she could possibly have.

Despite our troubles over the years, I worry about what happens when she is gone, and the sisters have retreated to their far cities, the house is sold, and sweet old Aunt Jean no longer comes to town. When her last breath fades, this family will dissolve like a bubble in the spring breeze, and my kids will lose this connection. The kids still need her to hold their world together. Is this why death is so painful? Because of our neediness? We lose not only the person, but her place, her relationships, her web, and in this case I am not ready to lose that yet. I want her to live for this selfish reason.

And what will become of him? I've worried about this moment ever since I left him and realized how much he depended on his mother, how she calmed him and fed him and took some of the burden off me. He is needy like a child and could not accept losing me, and tried to win the kids to get me back. She paid for his lawyers and stopped answering my phone calls. I never understood how they could treat me like that. I had shown her the bruises too, where his hands had wrapped around my neck. I told her I had to get away, but she did not see. She only had eyes for her son.

She too fought her Vietnam, and forever tried to get her boy back his innocence, just as he forever tries to scoop those exploded body parts back into place. She prayed the rosary every day he was gone, blaming herself for having let him go. And when he came back full of rage, she carried the shame. All these years later, they still danced their twisted dance while trying to exorcise their guilt. I was just a convenient target.

The day she died, I told her I loved her too, and I guess I meant it. In any case, I needed to say it. I am tired of fighting invisible armies and scared of sending this bitterness through more generations. I told her I loved her in front of "the girls," even though they don't like me so close to their mother.

Later the oldest one told me she was glad I was there. All I could think to say was "We're all just people, y'know. We don't get to pick our life, whatever comes our way, we just take it and do the best we can."

It is ironic that the hyacinths are in full flower as she lays dying. In Greek mythology, Hyacinthus was an innocent youth killed by Apollo's wayward arrow. An accident. Collateral damage. To show his remorse, Apollo had a sweet smelling flower spring from the blood of this beautiful boy. Oh, the ancient gods had such a poetic way of making amends.

In the flower are Hyacinthus and Apollo intertwined. Guilt over lost innocence. Is this the way it has been through all time? We are all Hyacinthus. Shot by unexpected arrows as we make our way through life. We are Apollo, too. We shoot arrows in the due process of our days that take the innocence from those we love.

Here this week we each try to give up a bit of our guilt, we cry for our lost innocence. Anne strews "I love you's" around, he lets loose with unaccustomed tears, and I try to make sense of past injustices. Only mortal people dealing with mortal problems. Hyacinths will not spring from our tears. Nevertheless, this is the drama of our lives. These are the flowers we create.

CAROL V. DAVIS

FEAR

A friend was murdered in an
underground lot of a college campus.
Her hair blond and thick as summer.
I thought women like her would always
be protected. Now she appears
around sharp corners, walking in a
straight and easy way. Sometimes
I am startled, other times, not at all.

What is the exact moment when such
a woman becomes another body to be
identified? She, who minutes before
clutched her brown purse close to
her weed-like body, who called home
to have the oven lit.

*

It begins slowly, imperceptibly.
Click of cricket half an octave
up and scratchy. The cry of mourning
dove transforms to the chant of Kaddish.
I shield my eyes
from the fool of mockingbird,
wake to footsteps only imagined.

Who is to say where the line is drawn?
I am afraid to tell when a spider
the size of an outstretched hand
emerges from the chrome showerhead,
don't question where it came from or why.
I lean in to the wild grasses,

convinced they will divulge their stories.
Each dandelion moon becomes the face
of a child, this one with dark curls,
that one with mirror gray eyes.

FEAR II

My foreign student
calls to say she is afraid

of spiders and what
should she do?

I start to think about fear.
But what I mean to say

is that the face is
on both sides of the window.

And that is why you
must draw the shades.

When I lived
on top of a mountain

the only face
was the white mask

of the unblinking owl
or a smudge on the sill

left as a calling card
by a reclusive cougar.

It is too early to predict
what will happen next.

The dark drops its burden
all night long, deepening

as it empties its buckets
of stars, leaving the expanse

of black on the other side
of the window.

WENDY BROWN

RAGE

Dear Elie Wiesel,
It is easy to see why God saved you,
but why me?
I used to think it was His wrath lashing out
upon my body, my girl's woman-body
used in a war of seduction
paid for at last one night
a finger on the trigger and face to face
with demon lust
lust that was blood as in murder
lust that was blood as in sex.

The night before I wore white lace
bared shoulders like a song
perfume light as summer air
but this night I flashed and shimmered
in blue stretch tight
provocative as stolen kisses
dissolving in smoke.
Alone unto my own fantasy I ignored
the beast prowling in shadow
ready to claim his prey.

My body penetrated and ravished
wiped clean of all pleasure
or innocence ever known.

Begging on my knees
in sweet opposition to all recklessness before
all seductive dances
all drunken stupors
collapsed upon a pyre.

A mask concealed what once had been a human boy
capable of forgiveness
capable of letting go.
I returned with hell frozen and sealed
across my body
a wound never to be revealed or shown.

But still I ask why?
Why sear me, why save me
why rescue me from death's grip?
What have I done
these years out from the gun
now that the healing has begun?
Each day I awake
to the knowledge of this:
it hurts but I live
it never ends but I am free.

If I had known you, Elie,
I would have opened my blouse
to show you my heart
pulsating in remembrance.
Because you and six million
ignited a passion for truth
Because someone drank my tears
and held me safe

these words are left here upon the page
to witness my rage, my despair,
my joy, my gratitude.

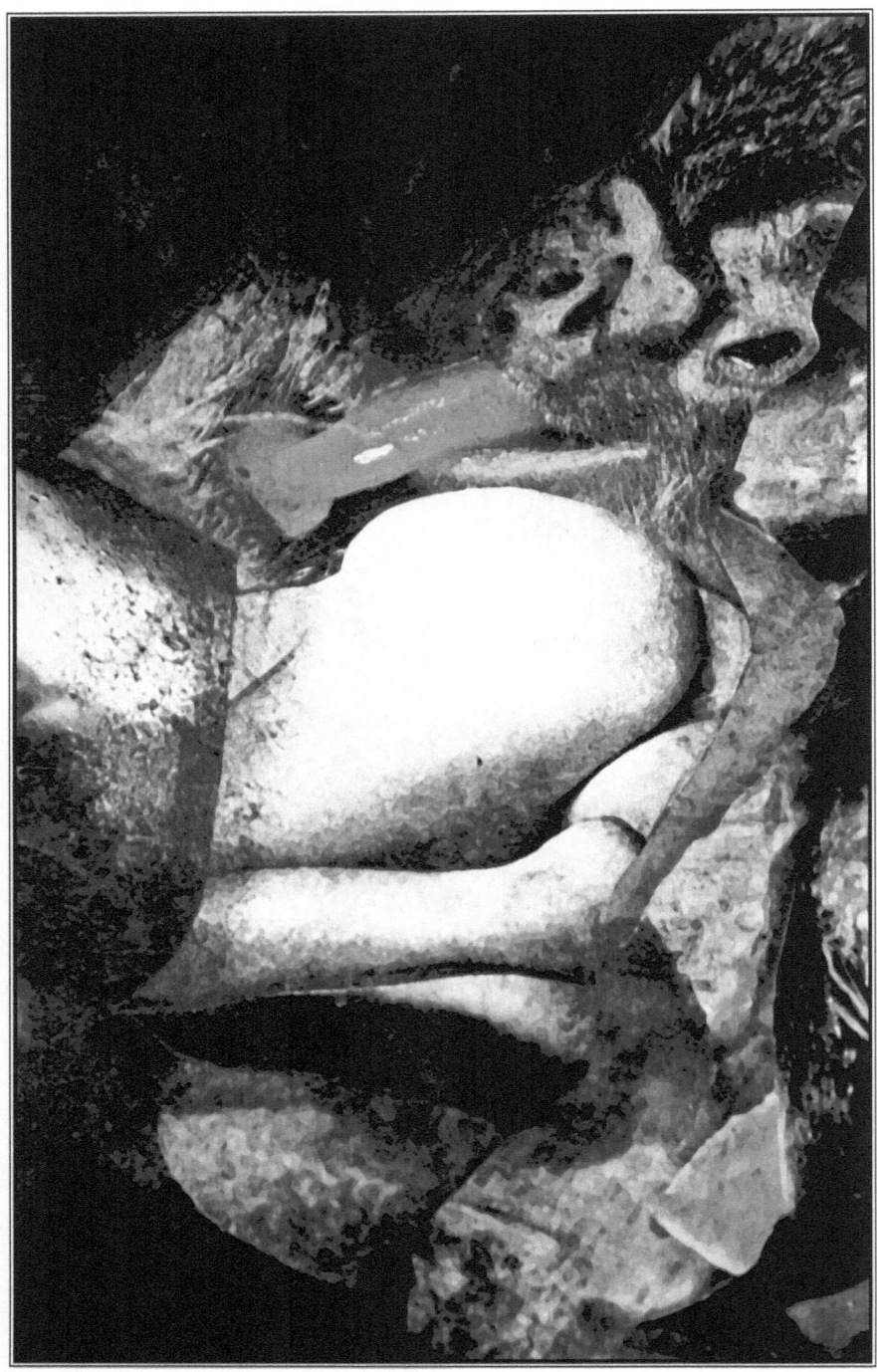

MARCI GREER JAFFER

THE WALL

There is only one wall that separates us. I can hear his every move as if we are in the same room. Three loud taps on a table and I know that he's packing his cigarettes. There is the clanking of silverware, the banging of drawers, the soothing rush of water shooting from the shower head. I'm amazed at how intimate these noises are.

The time is 3am and his engineer boots are heavy on the wood floor. His footsteps are followed by the click-clack of a woman's heals. Her giggle is raspy and loud and then there is silence. I hold onto Starr, cradling her little body, trying so hard not to squeeze her too tightly. Lately it's as though I want to crush her until there is no risk of the world getting near her. Clenching my jaw, desperate for sleep I count in my head...one-one thousand, two-one thousand...why the hell is he always bringing women home? What void is he filling?

The clapping sound of two bodies slapping against each other, and then the familiar sound of strangers engaging in a meaningless one-night stand seeps through the wall. Their moans seem to push through my skin until I can do nothing but hold my breath crushing Starr into my arms even tighter. Starr's arm shoots up and then drops gently onto her pillow. Hovering over her, I can't help but to take in the loveliness of her eyelids. They are so milky and petal-soft with thin pink veins swimming all over them. I stuff my nose into her neck, its scent bakery-sweet, its feel, soft and warm and new— skin that hasn't yet been touched by dirt, by filth, by life.

The woman is crying out, her screams like calls of agony into the musty Lower East side building we all sleep in. My neighbor grunts and then once again there is silence. Starr turns onto her stomach and throws her bunny-pajama'd leg over my hip. She hasn't been able to sleep alone in months. I gave her the bedroom and painted pale pink little pigs all over the walls, and even bought her a canopy princess bed, but she'd rather sleep with me on the pull-out sofa in the living room. Will we live here when she is old enough to suspect the meanings of these moans and grunts?

The click-clack of the woman's heals and then the slamming of my neighbor's door jolts Starr awake. "Mommy," she screeches. The desperation in her voice makes me want to engulf her in my arms, push her through my skin and into my body, hiding her behind my heart so that no one can touch her, but instead I reassure her. "I'm right here, sweetie," I gently pull her down and her body relaxes in my arms. Body limpness creeps through me and then there is the comfort of my shallow breathing.

It's getting darker earlier now. The sky is gray and orange with the anticipation of dusk. Starr is my partner, this is how it is. Nothing has changed really. She walks down the two flights with me, her hand on my wrist, and together we swing the black garbage bag into the bin in the basement. The tiny colored bangles Starr's babysitter brought back with her from India jingle on Starr's wrist making her giggle. I scoop her up and set her on my hip for the upward hike. She has taken to wearing long gypsy skirts and bandannas in her hair, like me. A little me—I pray not. She is only three.

On the way up we bump into my neighbor. He is holding a full garbage bag that smells of ashtrays and beer. He is shirtless, his inked chest like a piece of art, his ribs, breaking through his skin. He pulls the bag up for a better grip and pale blue veins swell on his forearms from its weight.

"Hello," he says smiling endearingly at Starr and she immediately buries her face in my neck.

"Hi," I nod. He smiles at me through eyes that are hazel and glassy. The sound of him grunting last night comes back to me, forcing me to hold my breath as we pass by each other.

As I pack Starr's bag she cooks me a toy pancake on her kitchen stove. She hands it to me on a little green plastic plate and I pretend to gobble it up. "Mmm… delicious."

"Do you want another one, mommy?"

"I'd love another,"

Just as I throw in Starr's favorite panties into her overnight bag, the buzzer sounds.

"Daddy?" Starr asks.

"Yes, it's Daddy." She is always unsure how to feel in this moment. Her discomfort is revealed through the nervous smile on her face. She wants to see him, but not alone, not without me. She has already seen the darkness in him, his hands on me like weapons, right in front of her.

"You wait for me mommy, right?"

"Of course." I reassure her. "I'll be waiting for you to come home. I promise." I kiss her all over her face wishing I could swallow her, make her invisible to him.

As always he is standing in the doorway in his crisp suit looking like a knight from Wall Street. Before he greets Starr he gets so close to me I can see the vein pulsing in his forehead, smell his warm breath that is potent with the remnants of red wine.

"I will take her away from you if I find out you're sleeping with someone." Another empty threat with no relevance, but its harshness somehow manages to shift the balance in our space causing Starr to cry. She wraps her arms around my leg.

"Please," I whisper. "Not in front of her." I still cower when he is near. After all of this, I still shrink inside myself. He reprimands me with his stare and then bends down to be eye-level with Starr, suddenly morphing into honey. "Oh sweetie, why are you crying? You love to see Daddy."

My neighbor peaks his head out, a cigarette dangling from the corner of his mouth, drum sticks in his right hand. He looks at my ex who is too immersed in winning back Starr's affections to notice him, and then at me, his hazel eyes still glassy.

"You okay?" he mouths. I nod and he goes back into his apartment. This gesture leaves me stunned.

My apartment is dark except for music video reflections that flicker all over the white walls, and the light blue glow of my laptop. Roland Barthe's, *Discourse on Love* is on my lap. It's a tattered copy, a devoured book. I've read it over and over, forever fascinated by its concept of immersing oneself in one's lover so deeply as to lose one's soul, one's direction. How destructive it all is—this love thing.

My cell phone keeps ringing. My friends continue to invite me to parties and dinners, proposing men they think I'd adore, men they claim are kind. Uninterested, I do not answer any of these calls, and instead pick up a framed picture of Starr. In it she is wearing a ballet tutu and cowboy boots and her pale hair is matted and wild. She is holding a magic wand in the air. A magic wand—she is my magic wand. Alone, and crying, hugging Starr's framed picture into my chest, I'm suddenly distracted by the slamming of my neighbor's door. It's 11pm. He's going out. It slams again and his engineer boots are heavier on his floor than usual. He's back.

How is it that I'm standing here, my ear now against his wall like some stalker? Is this how women like me spend Friday nights? And yet, I am more interested in my neighbor than anything out my window on Ludlow Street where the noise of drunken bar-hounds and laughter should consume me or at least distract me. He is whispering into his phone, but his words reach me mumbled and incoherent. There is the heavy scratch of a match and then he is sucking in his cigarette.

Quickly, I grab the garbage bag that is barely full, knot it and walk out into the hall. Pale light and cigarette smoke seep out from under his door. Quietly, I open my door again, put the garbage bag back into my apartment feeling crazy, and then pull my hair into a tight knot. Looking down I realize that I'm barefoot, my long black skirt dragging on the floor. My tank top is see-through. I knock anyway.

"Hi."

"Hey." His lips are fuller than I remembered.

"I just wanted to thank you. You know, for this afternoon?"

"Yeah, no problem. Ex, huh?

"Yeah. He's a prick." I smile as if this is funny and suddenly feel stupid for smiling.

"Most exes are."

What the hell am I doing?

"Umm…" He's just staring down at me in his Ramone's t-shirt.

"Okay, well that's it. Sorry to bother you." I turn to walk away.

"No, no, I'm just hanging out. Want a glass of wine or something."

"Sure, okay."

His apartment smells of cigarettes and oranges.

"Sit," he says, walking into the kitchen. Plopping down onto the sofa, I look around. There is a mattress on the floor in one corner of the room and a wooden dresser caddy-cornered in the other side of the room. His coffee table is scattered with clean ashtrays and music magazines.

He hands me a glass of red wine and sits on the sofa leaning into the corner opposite me. "Cigarette?" he holds out a box to me.

"Sure," I grab one even though I quit six years ago.

He leans into me with the lighter and I hold up my hand as if I'm in the wind.

"Are you a musician?" Of course he is. What am I doing here, I suddenly wonder? He is older than I thought. Maybe thirty-five or maybe his skin is rough from the sort of life guys like him live.

"Yeah, sort of. I used to be. Now I work for a label."

I'm not even music savvy enough to ask him what label. The wine is numbing my body and the cigarette has made me dizzy.

"Do you like it? Working for a label instead of the musician thing?"

"It's okay."

"I guess we're always wishing for something else," I blurt out, knowing I sound ridiculous.

"You have a beautiful daughter. That's pretty much the ultimate, isn't it? I mean what more could you want?"

"Yeah. She is the ultimate, isn't she?" I feel myself smiling at nothing in particular, thinking of my Starr and then my gaze turns back him.

He holds me with his eyes, sad eyes, forever glassy, and it's not a look that's unfamiliar, but it's a look I remember only from my past. We both somehow know that there's nowhere else for this conversation to go. It's pointless because there is something desperate happening between us. It's tense and electric and strange. When he grabs my hand I let him guide me over to his mattress and roughly throw me down on it because this is not about love or depth or meaning, it's about something more and it's about nothing at all.

In the dull lights I kiss his tattoos, tattoos that have no significance for me. He may never tell me what they are to him, and somehow that's comforting, knowing I'll never know him. In the soft light I notice his scars that are red and crooked and raised, and run up both his inner arms. I kiss them, suck on them, breath all over them because I understand the soothing effect affection can have on one's scars.

He pulls on me and kneads me and holds me and throws me, and I can do nothing, but abandon myself to this man who I will never love—I will never love this man and that is such a relief.

My apartment is just as I left it. I crawl into my pull-out sofa bed, breathing in the smell that Starr has left on the pillows and in the blankets. My body is still numb and buzzing. Sentiments of deep satisfaction don't come often lately, but right now they spill through me. Drifting, I feel the warmth of Starr in my arms even though she is not there, and swallow the strange taste of my neighbor that still lingers. Is this feeling of safety fleeting? My body grows limp, wondering.

VICTORIA ELIZABETH

APRIL 19TH

all day long my barely seeing hardly hearing aunt sits with her house robe
on eyes sunk deeply her only child a daughter died in 1992 she can't
understand why i must leave her my own daughter will be home soon as
i go aunt eula sits at the window waiting home early enough to glance
out worried because jennifer is late the neighbor who rarely speaks to me
knocks oh she has a dead cat in her yard she is afraid to touch it i go in her
backyard first time ever she somehow begins to tell me about three years
ago when she saw that man she'll never forget his face jump over my back
fence caucasian man with his sandy hair in a ponytail and gloves on his
hands but she didn't want to get involved she'd know him if she saw him
to this day i can't tell her how a year ago when her daughter's young baby
died i wanted to say how sorry i was just didn't know how too late now
she feels you (i think that's me) must be braver than her to pick up a carcass
without caring in such a way my gloved hands hold a plastic sack to bag
the dead a box to put bagged dead cat in i was brave when the bomb went
off in the frankfurt american shopping center i flip my five year old to the
ground throw myself on top of her she hasn't forgotten earthquakes scare
her too i was brave when the corpses in bags came in from beirut (lebanon)
watching bodies be sewn together for burial morticians eating pizza their
smeared in guts unwashed gloved hands i was more afraid walking the
grounds of dachau the air still ashen with filaments of jews murdered
there the earth still screaming souls don't rest incinerators still exist
grand memorial inscribed in many languages the words *Never Again* militia
skinheads a bomb in oklahoma the children we awake living

PRIVACY

"Pull your pants down to your thighs,
lay down on the glass slab, breathe
but lie perfectly still—it
won't hurt; the machine will weave
around—shoot front, back, both sides."
Like fresh kill marked for butcher
I lie, pelvis lined and drawn.
Eyes closed, I become the picture
of a Jane Doe cadaver:
an alert cadaver, still
breathing, hands entwined on chest,
feet bound, privates exposed. I lie, still,
absorb Marie Curie's lamb
of sacrifice. Her dying
from radium becomes my life
through radiation. There, lying,
daily, it enters me: front,
back, left side, right side.
Pubic hairs frizz and fall
from my naked groin, glide
off the glass altar. I rise
remembering their first curls
when I changed clothes in private,
hiding them from the other girls.

THE RESPONSIBILITY OF SECRETS

I am a magnet for secrets,
via a childhood cultivated art
of not telling, never revealing:
Daddy isn't drunk, just happy.
Bruises are from the playground.
Mom's had another clumsy streak.
We must preserve Father's career,
collect the money, pay the bills.
Here's a gift, now shut-up, shut-up.
For a poetry workshop task
I fish out some poet's secret;
I'm given freedom to write, to break
that sacred trust—tell all, tell all.
Her father raped her when she was twelve.
Anonymous writing bombarded
with fisted 'e's and not one 'i'.
Each time I read it and look around
at faces tinselled in candlelight,
no eyes reveal the custodian
of all the secrets: shut-up, shut-up.

HEATHER TOSTESON

FAITH

1
I wake at the window
my hands thrumming at my chest
like trapped birds.
Immediately, you are awake
and your voice guides me back.
The Hotel Richelieu. New Orleans.
This is the moment. This is the moment.
You know me. You are making distinctions.

Hours earlier, in the dark, I rocked over you
like a bark moored on a quiet sea.
Mouth to sex. Mouth to sex.
This is the ultimate act
of redemption. Your voice
in the dark calls me back
from the moment when all trust
was broken. *Jesuschristjesuschristjesuschrist.*

These are not my own words I'm speaking.
But I do know this: the Holy Spirit
is a fierce and living thing that visits
without warning. A child mourns
with a wild, wordless thrumming.
A woman understands that more is coming.
Hotel Richelieu. New Orleans.

Three o'clock in the morning.
My skin burns from the battering
of those wings. We are not talking
about dreams. Everything is exactly
what it seems. I am not alone.

I will never be so lost you can't
find me, and, when you do, take me,
shaking, in. I trust the voice that guides me
back to you, back to me.
Where is my good book hiding?

2
Where is my good book hiding?
Where is God's love biding?
Not on the bookshelf.
Not on the landing where I stand frozen
in the Devil's stare. He smiles
and I know what it is to be known
and completely alone.

Every night I could hear him stalking,
my heartbeats marking his footsteps on the stairs.
Faster. Faster. This is how a little girl dreams
of redemption. She takes flight from the white cliffs of Dover
but there he is, on the far side of the ocean,
waiting, his hands outstretched.
One touch and her bones will blacken.
She is so tired of flying, the way her arms
have to flail at the air to keep her
just out of touch. This is how a little girl
saves herself. She throws herself to the wind.

She never dreams, she never dreams of speaking.
She will be, she will be, she will be, good.
It is only now, when I would love and be loved
by you, that I grow perfectly calm
inside the palms of a man.
But deep inside me I believe God
will bash my head in if I speak even once
of steadfast love. This must have been what he threatened,
after, when I couldn't control my breath.

That's what he must have said, so tall, so dark,
so far from where I'd fallen. His voice must have been so cold
and so hard it held, like God's, the power
of life and death. My forehead sought the inhuman
comfort of stones, and I knew the horror
of a hand I can't wash clean,
of vision severed from all feeling,
of pretending to a unity, hand wrist arm,
that only the world could see.
And hell, it's here now, in my breathing.
How long does it take for a child to die to herself
and come alive again inside a grown woman?
I know to claim my love for you
in all its richness there is no escaping
what I sought, and fought, in all its forms
so fiercely fiercely fiercely
as only a child who knew love,
before ruin, can.

3
Sense is invidious.
A veil comes down.
This is the end of language
but not of sound.

Two little girls are in my head.
One is alive and one is dead.
Her breath doesn't trouble the forest floor.
She is no more.
The other rolls her head on a stone.
Alone. Alone. Alone. Alone.

Terror has no words.

4
How can I tell a good man
from a bad one?
The smell. The smell.
The swell. The swell.
This never happened.

If we can't cherish the origin
of terror, it becomes invincible
as water, seeps through everything
we make to contain it.
Names like good and bad,
love and hate, alive and dead.
It absorbs everything and we
at last are one electrical storm.
Wild mother. Wild child.
Sound allies an infants monotonous sorrow
the keening of a violated girl of seven,
and the love a woman of forty-six makes
in a sea of undreamed tenderness.

I want to bash God's head in.
I don't ever want to forgive him.
Sin is a meaningless word
for a stranger in the woods
to a girl whose head comes no higher
than his belt buckle.
How can I tell what is real
what is horror. Terror seeps
into my thoughts like adrenalin
into my muscles and gut.
I love you so much.

5

There is an explosion in my head.
One is alive. The other is dead.
What have they done to my eyes?
I am alive. I am alive.
Terrible man.
I am. I am.
Clean my hand. Clean my hand.
My forehead stings.
Rings with sting.
Sound makes it all happen again.
The devil climbs the stairs
from night to morning.
Where is my good book hiding?

The cactus have spines.
The spines fly.
I am alive. I am alive.
My skin is broken. Open.
This never happened.
We lie through our teeth.
And the devil speaks
with a forked tongue,
half old, half young,
half cold, half dumb.

6
A veil descends.
This is the end of language
but not of sound.
Forest. Floor. Forest. Floor.
There is no mystery here.
What, once, happened to me
is clear in the breathing,
the ghastly clarity of the keening.
Mystery. Meaning. Mystery. Meaning.
Our parents tear our hearts
and lock us out of sight.
But a stranger hides God from us.
A stranger drives his sex
deep into my mind.
An act repeated, here and there,
by lovers over the years.

And then there is this one
whose sex I take willingly
into my mouth and I think
I can be fed by his hesitant flesh
and then it all comes out,
the ruin and confusion.
Who, we wonder, as she keens
so clearly in the dark, knows enough
to comfort her.

She is lying very still
waiting for hell.
Robin Redbreast
is her headrest.

7
What's happening?
I cannot see.

What do you hear?
She isn't there.

What do you feel?
This isn't real.

Why are you crying?
I'm lying. I'm lying.

Chicken Little didn't give a fiddle
for the truth.

But you?
There are two of us.

One you can trust.
One you mustn't.

Which one is that?
Can you wash my hand off?

Which one?
The right one. The right one.

Gasping in the shower
for the truth that will never come
clear to me, never come clean.

8
Terror has no words.
Crazy rhyme locks me in time.
Language is my life line.

She is lying very still
waiting for hell.
Robin Redbreast
is her headrest.

Never let him in your head
or you'll be dead.
You'll be dead.

Language is my lifeline.
It means I have to leave her there
to die. Terror has no words,
no cure. So I remember nothing.

Blood is red.
The girl is dead.
She never bled.
She never said
what happened.

Where was my good book hiding?
Jesuschristjesuschristjesuschrist.
O deary deary me, cried the woman at the stile.
This is none of I. *This is none of I.*

9
Mother of the universe—
I curse. I curse.
But he curses faster, quieter, first.
Jesuschristjesuschristjesuschrist.

Mother of the universe
you have great powers
of creation and destruction.
And I am your child.
I am your child.

A stranger comes upon a little girl
in the woods and rapes her.
This is just a fact.
There is no taking it back.

And forty years later a man comes to a woman
after thousands and thousands and thousands of days
of isolation and wakes her.
This too is true.

What mystery reverberates between
these two realities. My quiet house stirs
with invisible currents and my prayer wavers
like a single flame, flickering, steadying,
flickering again: *Mother of destruction,
help me love.*

10

What we learn together in the dark,
my wrists beating at each other,
my body beginning to buck, to buckle,
is that I fought it off.
Knowing this, today, so many years away,
breaks my heart. This is a good thing
because I begin to have feeling for her.

Straight sense, this wordless record, etched
into my mind, my muscles, is what makes my soul
grow cold and still with a weight
so immense I can't describe it.
It is the ultimate burden, almost beyond
my capacity, heartmindbodysoul, to bear.
It is the weight of total helplessness.
It is the weight of faith.

A stranger came upon a little girl in the wood
and raped her using the name
of God in vain. I find it so hard
to take in that by that terrible inversion
a seed was laid that could, in time,
save me. He named what I had lost.
For God is everything that moment was not.
I find it now in the quiet with which you watch
my body reclaim its innocence.

It only knows how to seek comfort from the cold
floor. But when I remember this seizure
of memory, now I will always remember
how at the same time I could feel your body,
so quiet and so trusted, a hand's breadth away
if only I could reach for it, if only I could say.
What we heard in all this breathing,
all this tumult and terror

was my soul reattaching to my body
so that I can become, heartmindbodysoul, a home again,
a place where love can thrive.

11
Mouth to sex. Mouth to sex.
This is the ultimate act of redemption.
Death teaches us nothing.
I touch your skin with the insides of my wrists.
This is the ultimate act of redemption.
Death teaches us nothing.

Your sex touches the roof of my mouth,
some exact pressure my whole organism
associates with primal nurture,
and, everything in me alive and unresisting,
I recover the trust of a small child
and it folds, effortlessly, into unspeakable
pleasure, that we can, here and now, give,
man and woman, back and forth, back
and forth. But where was I in my head when I said
it didn't matter who once stripped
all hope from me. The face, in time,
might become clear but it was
irrelevant. And then I heard,
like a knife ringing crystal, these words:
Daddy's girl. Time stopped, reversed.
A girl rolls her head on a stone.
Alone. Alone. Alone. Alone.
Her breath burbles like blood
through her fingers. Everything in her is alive
and unresisting. Who was I fooling?
This is the ultimate act of redemption.
This clanging in my head. The words I never said.
So, so, so many breaths until we're dead.

12
If you let him in your head,
you'll be dead.
You'll be dead.

Horrible thought.
Horrible thought.
Daddy's girl.
Horrible thought.
Pearl without—
Horrible thought.
World without—
Horrible thought.
Frightened, frightened,
the cataclysm of air—
beware, beware.
No. No. Oh no. No.
Pearl without—
No. No. Oh no. No.
World without—
No. No. Oh no. No.
Terror without—
Nonononononono. No. No.
I want to die.
Horrible thought.
I want to die.
Horrible thought.
I want to die.
Horrible thought.
Horrible thought.
Horrible thought.

But I am, and I am alive.
And when this cataclysm of memory is done,
I will sit quietly with you watching
the moon rise above the oaks

and think of every one of us in this world holding
such an enormous universe of feeling.
Then I will ask you back into my bed
and will open my robe and disclose
this body that can hold such inconceivable pain
and still desire and be desired by you.

13
It matters who the agent
of pain is. Faces matter. Names.
Words reclaimed. That is the only way
to make it human. Violation can't be
a theology. But we marry
past and present in one body.
No. No. Oh no. No.
It is so hard to distinguish
what is going on between us.
No. No. Oh no. No.
Here is the difference. These breaths
go on and on and on and on and on.
They don't build to anything.
No. No. Oh no. No.
Nonononono. No. No.
I would put a stop to them,
if I could, now.

But if I do I lose the words,
so few, so small, so soft, all
a little girl could know to call
herself back from the dead—
Nononono. Oh no oh no oh no. No.—
back from that final, fatal inversion,
I want to die.

Healing is taking in the dreadful sense
she made of it so very very long ago
as if it were new knowledge, mutable.

Jesuschristjesuschristjesuschrist.
This is what he said.
I don't believe he left any record in my head
of his face, his name. He was a stranger
who came upon me in the woods when I was seven.
I was carrying my new book of nursery rhymes.
I loved it very much. Its heft made me feel almost adult.
It was my birthday present.
So all this must have taken place in the fall.
A foreign country. I had just learned to read.
By Christmas Eve, on the landing, I would be able
to make that fatal metathesis: Santa is Satan.
But I would pretend for years and years and years
to believe in all the terms the world calls good.
Santa is good. God is good. Love is good.
Trust is good. Touch is good. Touch is trust.
I love you so much.
I would imitate and hate myself, mercilessly,
for my fear. I never heard, *terror has no words,*
my fear for what it was: my soul's call to wholeness.
To do so I would have to return to that moment
when language, trust, touch, self, all dissolved
into one fiery cataclysm of breath.
No. No. Oh no. No.
Horrible thought. Horrible thought. Horrible thought.
Don't let him in your head or you'll be dead.

It is not inconceivable that he was,
Jesuschristjesuschristjesuschrist,
as his words implied, a man of God.
Horrible thought. Horrible thought. Horrible thought.

14

When I first saw you, your hands folded
above your waist, just like a priest,
I couldn't take my eyes from them.
I stood there, speaking glibly,
mesmerized by the unspeakable thought:
I want to be inside them.
All of me wanted, wants, to be inside them
and to call them good. What haunts me now
is that to reclaim my soul
I must know once she was whole
and some one man tore
mind from skin, beginning from end,
sight from feeling, word from breath
and left her, breath burbling like blood
through her fingers, to make her private peace
with the unspeakable.

Out of such rifts artists are born.
But we are talking now about steadfast human love
between a man and a woman and I don't know how
that applies, can possibly apply to me—
if being a child of God means
being a daughter of destruction.

Where were you when I needed you?
The touch of my father was all I knew then
of God or men. Our world has made them one,
God, the father, men, just as he did
muttering as he came inside my head
Jesuschristjesuschristjesuschrist.
It is not inconceivable that he was
a man of God. There was, for me, a moment
of trust before terror. That is what is so unspeakable.
I don't know where that trust came from—his demeanor or me.

Blood does not go cold in a single second.
Could I, truly, have escaped that moment
of confusion if I had been able to know,
immediately, the difference between good
and evil. *Blood does not go cold in a single second.*
It is that shift, trust to terror, that is unbearable to recall.
It exists, beyond words, in my mind and in my muscles.
It came upon me once again when you said,
I would have liked to have known you as a little girl,
and I answered without thinking, *She didn't suffer.*
But when you held me, my arms turned to ice.
This is what it means to be fully alive and unresisting.

Blood does not go cold in a single second
Would it have been worse to have nothing
to lose? Little girls do not choose
to have worlds of meaning explode
inside their heads. But I, who am not a child,
who never said, who never bled, whose breath spills
like water through my laced hands, now, whose agent
am I, really? If I spoke, *no, oh no, oh no oh no*, now,
would you, really, hear me?

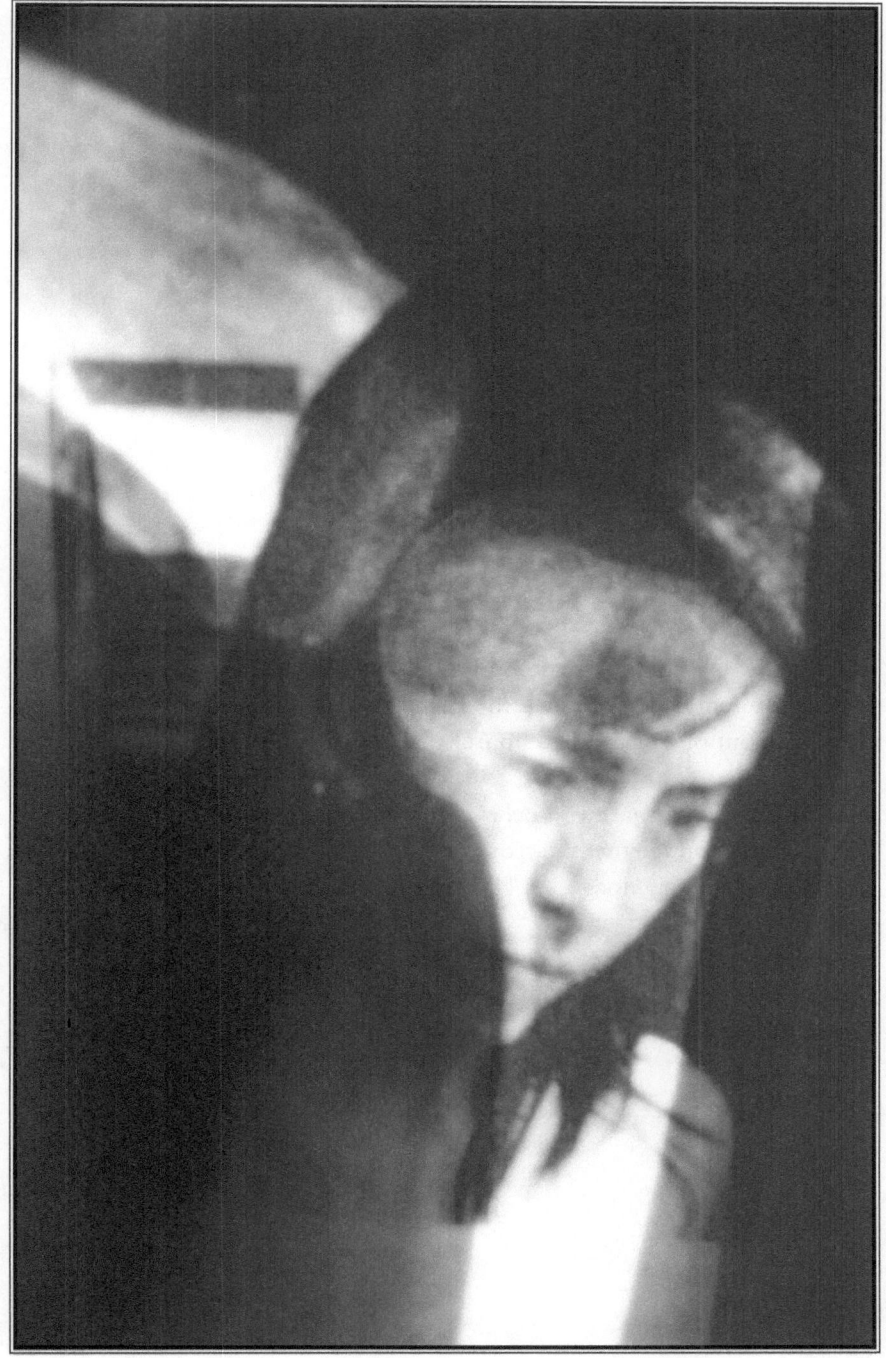

MARY C. O'MALLEY

THE BOY IN THE WATER

My eyes bear down on the image of him, face up,
sinking, caught in a webbed tangle of lotus roots.
Straddling the earth, I reach down and pull. And

with one hand, raise your body. With the other, I
raise the morning sun. Once again I save you from
your liquid fascination, once again I save a discordant

world from night. I have failed to keep them safe. The
sun refuses to rise to a wayward earth entrapped
by humans. In my womb he must have been damaged

or was it the fall off the playground slide. You alone
are my different child. You hear the language of brilliant
stars, walk out of our thorned house spellbound; enchanted

by their light. They make you believe their promise of
flight. I think you see them mirrored in the pond, reach down
to grab their floating image. At 4:00 am I jerk awake,

terrorized by your absence. I always know where he is
I follow his footprints down to the neighbor's pond. There
I perform my twin edged duties of saving son and earth.

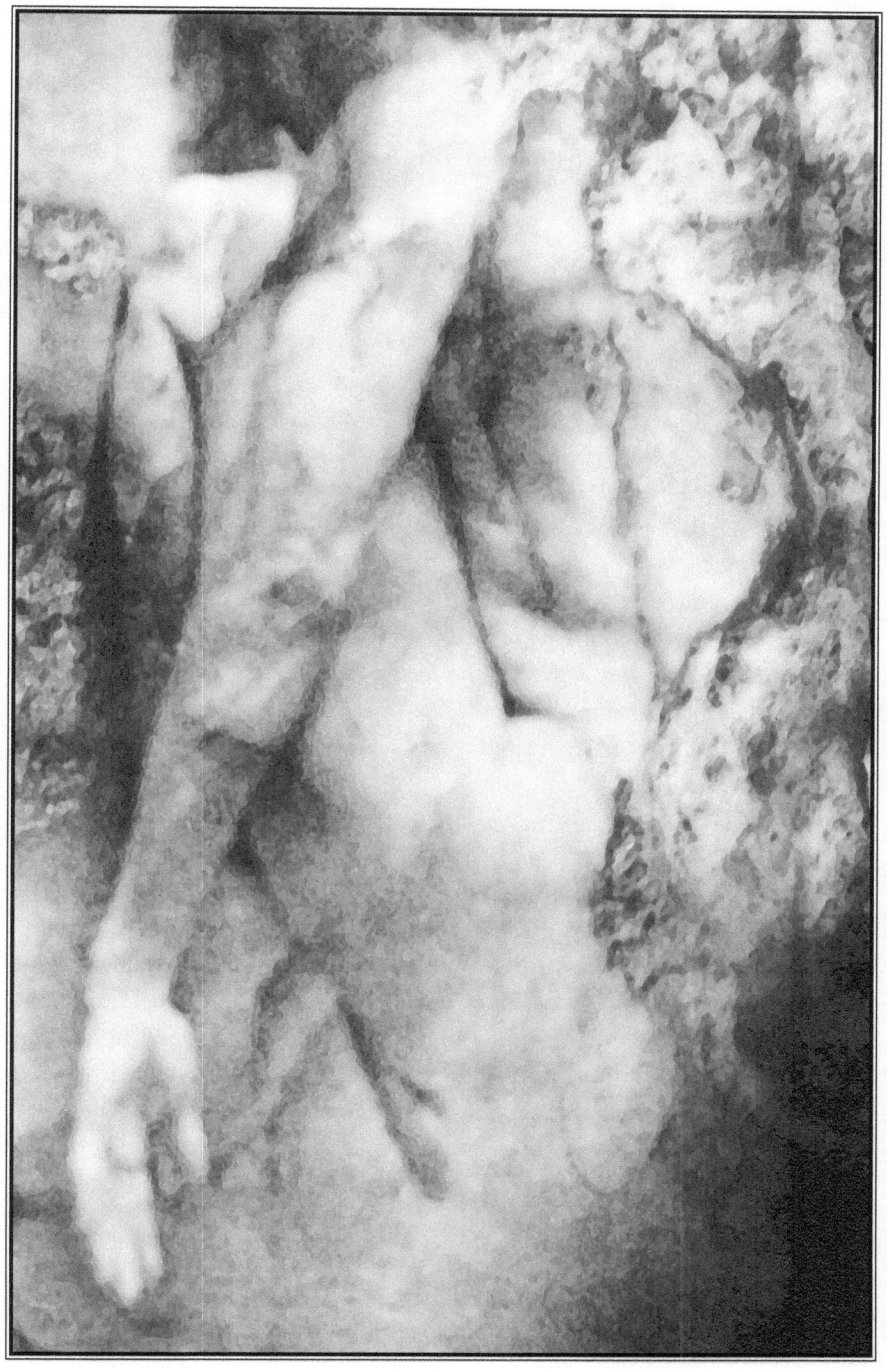

JOEL B. PECKHAM, JR.

RUINS

Friday in Amman is the Sabbath day, so very little is open or active—other than the prayers coming over the loudspeakers and the numerous mosques, whose spires reach up all around us. Five times a day, every day the call to prayer floats over the rooftops from dozens of loudspeakers, each slightly ahead or behind the other and echoing off the sides of buildings and through the valleys, so it sounds like a crowd of angels calling you home toward some kind of reckoning.

On these days I take the boys for walks through some back-lots and up the hillside roads behind our apartment. We live in Jebel-Amman, literally Mountain Amman, on the side of one of the many steep hills that form the city's landscape. And even after a month of living in this churning city, I can't shake the feeling that I could uproot, tumble down into the valley and be lost in the vacant lots and low-lying troughs in the land dotted and shining with rubble.

I can still feel the pressure of the umbrella stroller in my palms though its hard to believe, staring at him from the light of the hallway, that this boy, curled into sleep on his mother's old bed was once that child. His hair once long and curled as any young girl's, is now cropped tight and matted against his forehead with August sweat. Susie would hate it. She loved his hair. Cyrus was nearly four before he had his first "big boy cut." and though Darius is only a year older than his brother was on the day of the accident, he seems almost larger than Cyrus now. And what have I become?

Now?

Then?

Here. In his grandparent's house, surrounded on all sides by the howling August storm, those distinctions slither in and out of time and place like something venomous in the underbrush.

"Hate and love" my mother-in-law said, staring at me in the living room, waiting for some reaction. And for once she did get one, her words cracking the re-enforced concrete calm that I adapt when the subject of Susan's journals arises. "Hate and love. Love and hate. I've never heard anything like it."

The word "hate" is not one I allow myself. Especially when referring to Susan. She is gone, and to hate the dead, to love the dead—it all seems somehow obscene. She is a part of me, like Cyrus; that is all. I don't try to untangle any further. What I felt for Susan was what I understood love to be. "How could she be so unhappy and us not know? And suicidal. She mentions suicide three times." I catch my breath as if to speak. To say, she wasn't the only one. To mention the times when I would wander out on to the railroad tracks in Michigan or stand on the edge of route 31 and think, one step and it is over. But love does not allow for easy exits. Even when everyone you love is gone. The wires pull hard at the chest. And you hang there suspended like a sideshow freak at the fair. Held upward by hooks in the skin, dangling. I say nothing. I nod. I promised Susan I would never read those journals. That I would burn them. I can remember the conversation, sitting in the house in Georgia. I didn't like morbid talk, but even in the first weeks of our marriage, Susan would speak of her death and what I should do should she die before me. "If you want you can keep them for Cyrus and Darius, but only them." I failed in this too. Her parents got to the house before I could, while I laid half buried in a morphine stupor in Mass General; and they took everything from the home that held a memory of her. And those twenty bound journals must have seemed some great treasure trove. And for a moment, it must have seemed they were holding their daughter. But of course they weren't. In the end what they found was paper and cardboard and ink. And words not meant to be read by anyone. If anything, those journals were a trove for Susan to dig through for poems and essays—to shape and form into something palpable and alive. Once in a while she would read a passage out loud if it was funny or sounded like the beginning of something she could turn to art. But I would keep my promise—both to her and to myself. I've lived enough pain in these past years to last anyone a lifetime. And now my in-laws must suffer as I suffer—the anger and guilt of every cross thought, every dark whim. And perhaps the upsweeping joy—finding a mention of love, a happy memory of childhood—only to lead to deeper troughs. They ride those winds—with the blind anger they have for the man who hurt their daughter, loved her, made love to her, nearly drove her to suicide, then had the gall to outlive her. So the most my mother-in-law will get is the blood coming up and flooding my neck and face—a change in breathing. Perhaps some sweat. And of course, hours of sleep lost.

On the Sabbath day I took my sons on walks through the city.

By then I had started keeping my own journal. In it I would set down observations, anecdotes. The title read like pages out of Thoreau's *Walden*—*On Labor, On Difference, Translation, Rubble:*

Amman's rubble is different. Or perhaps indifferent. There is no sediment, very little garbage, almost no twisted steelwork or piping. Just tons of crushed and piled limestone with tufted grass and scrub trees growing up through it. And there is no great effort being made at reconstruction—as if the broken, brittle lots are exactly what was planned for. Where construction progresses, it progresses slowly, at night, so the buildings and bridges seem to grow of their own accord rather than piece together mechanically. On a bright day, the jagged edges of stone light up and the heaps are as bright as any of the new buildings that surround them. Were these once houses, bridges, walls? Without the human story left behind in broken machines and furniture, even the occasional personal item as small as a bent spoon, its hard to tell.

As a boy, I would take long walks though a field behind my house, leading past the water tanks and fish-ponds to the distant tree-line. There, just beyond the forest's edge was a square ten-foot, stone foundation halfway filled with dirt and pine-needles. On humid summer days I would go there and dig in the cool black loam for artifacts—some sign of what the building had been and who had lived there. I never found anything left by human hands beneath the forest floor. But the wind booming across the field and threading into the trees brought other treasures, caught in the depression as if in a lobster trap: a bright red ball, bags blown from the nearby grocery mart, a dollar bill, and once the bones of a small bird, thin as lace and bleached with wind.

"What we want to be sure of," my father-in-law says, his face becoming solemn, stern, darkening, "is Susie's legacy. She worked very hard, you know, to just let it slip away." I have just told them about Rachael. And I'm a more than a little stunned. My father-in-law has hardly paused before moving on to other matters. I am always amazed at the emotional speed of our conversations. Love, Hate, Suicide, Rachael, Legacy. I hadn't been keeping it from them, but I hadn't told them either. Of course they knew. But how much? How much did Susie know? There is a longer story that they've only guessed at. I don't tell them how many years I had spent sleeping in a different room because I couldn't stand to love someone and not be allowed to touch her. Or the bizarre push and pull of affection and bitterness. "Why are you still with me?" I once asked Susan.

"History has to mean something," she responded, her beautiful, tragic face in her hands. The structure that was our marriage had collapsed on top of us, but there was no clear exit. No way out of the rubble, it seemed. I don't mention the long, hot walks with Rachael. The stolen whispers and cigarettes under the awnings of the creaking antebellum houses of Milledgeville. The late-night calls from pay-phones at gas-stations—just to have someone to talk to when things got desperate. When I felt shut in a deep box buried in the ground and looked for any light. The terrible panic of falling in love with the wrong person—or realizing I was with the wrong person all along, ten years into a marriage. The strange mix of anger and hope I felt as Rachael began to confide more and more of her terror, her own desperation. Even if I were to explain it all I couldn't begin. It came. It was beyond me. And it scared me to death. A month into therapy, my therapist looked at me hard and said, "Tell me about Rachael" when I thought I had been talking only of her each day every day.

"No, you talk about your marriage, Susan, Cyrus sometimes but not often." "Avoidance," she said. We still have a lot of work to do. And I knew she was right. But Rachael was still with her abuser—a man who still called me to ask for advice about writing, about love. And I had to pretend I didn't know who he was or what he did. I had to pretend I liked him because Rachael begged me to. Because he wanted to "throw his arms around me and make me promise to be his friend forever," when he disgusted me more than anyone I'd ever known by then. Avoidance. I'm still doing it. But how?

Where to start? Rachael made the world shatter and come together again in new combinations just by walking across a road before me and almost tipping over with the awkward grace of a failed and faltering prima ballerina—at once exquisite and vulnerable. She still compares herself to Susan, but I don't; I never did. What I loved in Rachael were the contradictions: the innocent pout, the arched eye-brow, the easy tears and the sharp retort. But these are abstractions. Is it enough to say that Rachael was the first person I've ever really collapsed in front of? Just collapsed like someone pulled the last pillar of support from a condemned building. Or maybe it only takes one pillar to fall, to take the weight of all those accumulated moments—all that history, a baby being born blue and silent, then screaming all at once, the first shared poem, a photograph of two skiers on a mountaintop in France, the cramped storage space beneath an apartment in Lincoln, Nebraska. And the pillars falling, myself, Susan. Rachael, how gentle your hands were when you touched my shoulder, how gentle you were with the pieces of man who must have seemed to you so very like a ruin. When you asked me, why don't you just leave? And all I could think of all I could think of all I could think of was the ocean I used to stand by in Eastham, Massachusetts as a boy, the ocean and the sand-cliffs behind and the houses peeking over, destined to fall as the sand eroded beneath them and the light coming at me on the water, angry and roaring like a train. Avoidance. Delicate shoulders, slim, graceful neck, the line of a chin. How badly I wanted to feel that again for Susan; but couldn't; how quickly there was only Rachael and that shattering light, and the splash of a thousand pillars falling and the—

How far could it have gone, I often wonder, had we not left for Jordan on Fulbrights? For a long time, lying in bed in one hospital then another, I wondered if my love for Rachael had been the push that set the tragedy in motion. Where does it start? We dig and dig for cause—the origins of things. But I know that beginnings, like endings, stretch off in both directions forever and we are destined to live our lives and deaths in-media-res with all the lack of purpose and confusion that entails.

I could answer my father in law this way—explaining that I have begun the process of sifting through Susie's work, trying to pick up the threads of her projects. But so many of them evade me. We did not speak much in the last months and had different friends. Lived different lives in separate rooms—two caged birds, her the peacock searching for a garden and me, a flightless heron, a hawk, some gull, a bird of garbage, winged and wounded. To this day, men and women—strangers to me—will call at night, weeping, confessing their spiritual love for Susan and it is like a visitation from another dimension. They have and have had no existence for me. So I have done what I can, pieced together a manuscript and sent it to her publisher, gone through the boxes and tried to make sense of projects half-completed. And every word is a sting. Every line a twist of the knife.

The only artifacts are those blown around the city in the desert sand and wind-storms that come once or twice a month, sending garbage bags, sheets and clothes off the lines—anything not spiked, roped or nailed to earth—into the air to be snagged in the rubble for the play and scavenging of stray cats. The urge to join them in their dig among the detritus is powerful. But I don't believe it would yield any discoveries. It's as if before each building was leveled, the levelers had picked it clean of all human record.

Even in a journal entry I could not be completely honest. Even when the audience is the self—one can fear its rejection, its revulsion. And I had grown disgusted with myself. For years I couldn't even look in the mirror without wanted to spit at my reflection. Sometimes I did. I've learned through therapy how hard it is to revisit the past honestly or see the present fully even when, especially when, the only real judge is looking back at you over a bathroom sink. So much lay beneath the lines. It was mere travelogue. And the traveler was moving from one place to another without real contact, accumulating none of the stains of intimacy, floating really, like a plastic bag hopping over stones, parked cars, waiting for a tree branch to catch it for a while. Those words seem so unreal now—so detached and elegant. Of course, it was all fresh paint over rotten planks.

In a telephone conversation, a close friend suggested that this rubble could serve as a fit metaphor for the soul. A poetic idea. But I think it more likely represents the soul's ruins, how hard it is to dig past them. An old man's face, like that of the taxi-driver Ali with his military fatigues and smoldering cigar, is equally ruined—sun-scarred and pocked with insult—both physical and emotional. Perhaps suggested in those lines there is, some great regret or anger, a distant lover, a lost child, a stolen home, shame and humiliations personal and cultural. But the truth is hidden from us beneath this human rubble.

Only a man obsessed with love could imagine a lover for Ali. And of course, I knew it was fantasy. Projection. I was thinking of Rachael, who stopped my heart merely by almost falling over while crossing a street. And the truth was not hidden. It was frightening. What if I left Susan? What if she finally left me? What then? Did Rachael feel this way for me? Or was she merely an imagined beam of light in the rubble? The mind searching desperately for hope. And what of the children, where are they in these notes to the self? How desperately, I would like to read a description of Cyrus now that he is gone. Where are you, my beautiful boy? Pushed from behind by the hands of a man who isn't really there.

"I love you more than anybody," Darius shouts from the back of the car as I weave through the traffic of Hartford Connecticut. He has spent two weeks with Susan's parents and he is still glowing with re-union. Tonight he will cry for his Bibi. Tomorrow he will ask if we can call his mother and brother. And when I say no, they are in heaven, he'll pretend he didn't ask, giving an awkward smile and turning his attention back to his coloring book. "Darius, you don't have to love me more than everybody. You can love us all different."

"But I love you best."

"But you don't have to, you know. For Bibi you can have Bibi-Love. For me, Daddy-Love. For Rachael, Rachael-Love. And mommy-love. And Cyrus-love." He starts to giggle, and I point at our golden retriever, Jack-Jack in the passenger seat. "Even Doggy-love." Now he is laughing really hard, squirming in his car-seat, shouting "Doggy-love. Jack-Jack-love!". "It's the same for me. I love Rachael, and I love you, and I love Jack-Jack. But I don't love any of you in the same way."

"Do you love Rachael more than Mommy?"

Mommy.

Sitting on the colorful carpets of our sitting room in our massive cold apartment in Amman, brochures spread around her, Susan, cell-phone in one hand, personal organizer in another, was a picture of the determined traveler: bright, efficient, and ready to go. We were making our first excursion beyond the borders of the city to Jerash and she glowed with the prospect of adventure. To be honest, I wasn't that enthusiastic. I was excited to see the Roman ruins but the expedition seemed touristy. I imagined myself walking behind a smiling, head-bobbing guide, eager to show me everything I wanted to see and tell me everything I wanted to know, catering to my every wish and charging me for every second of it. I've never liked tour-guides—in any country. No matter how well they treat you, you know the experience is false. That human being is reduced to his function, which is to please and you are reduced to commerce. You stop being Joel or Susan or Cyrus and become ten dollars, francs, pounds or dinars.

Still it was an easy sell; the brochures written in Arabic, French, German, and English with bright photographs of columns marching into pale blue sky were more than I could resist. I've always believed that ruins have a special pull to the American, for whom an old city was founded 200, not 2000, years ago. Where there are no ancient castles in the midst of its cities, no temples from long abandoned religions—where what is ancient in our land is only beginning to be excavated in the western prairies and deserts, and our sense of self is based more on faith and system than by tradition. Separated from the ancient civilizations not only by time but oceans, the possibility of actually traveling to an ancient city is as remote to most of us as a trip to Mars, and just as alluring.

More than that, there was something personal. If ever I had been lost in my life, I was lost then, and no-matter how hard I tried to focus on the moment, I could not look at this beautiful talented woman without thinking of all that I had lost, was losing each day. And to look at Susan was to fall in love with her. She had an undeniable beauty, not only of body—with her long black hair, dark almond-shaped eyes and teardrop chin—but of spirit. Susie emanated. I've never been sure what exactly. But she emanated. Her presence literally seemed to push out the air around her. And this presence was compelling and isolating. It pulled people to her, but kept them from ever really getting to understand her deeply. The previous night we had had one of those brutal arguments that you know will follow you for the rest of your marriage. We were hired to teach American Literature and Creative Writing. But of course, at the University of Amman there were only a few course offerings in those areas and most were taught by senior faculty. And Susie wanted them. The truth was, she didn't want to teach at all. She wanted to write. And her experiences talking to the Palestinian refugees had galvanized her. She wanted to write of them, for them. And she wasn't going to spend her time preparing lessons on 17th Century British Literature. At first I acquiesced. Susie had a way of making her position sound not only like the most reasonable one, but the only one. "It would be easier for you, Joel; you are a scholar after all. You can learn anything, teach anything. You're brilliant." She was good at appealing to my vanity. But I knew I was being manipulated.

"Susie, look this isn't fair; you must see that." Then her expression darkened as it always did when she felt accused of a breach in ethics or morals. "Don't talk to me about fair." And then, "I gave up my life for you. You wouldn't even be here if it weren't for me." There was little I could say. As usual, a minor disagreement had exploded into something far beyond its scope. She was right. Whatever my accomplishments as a scholar and a teacher, it was her work as an Iranian-American poet and National Poetry Series winner that made us attractive to the Fulbright people. But it was the statement, "I gave up my life for you," words that had become a sad refrain over the previous years, that lingered. I know that Susie believed this. Her marriage to me was what locked her to the United States. It was what lost her Swiss citizenship; it was what kept her from visiting Iran; it was a sacrifice I could never repay, and one which placed our relationship in such disharmony and imbalance that nothing in our marriage existed without its permeating vapor. And then I did something that still makes me shudder. I closed my eyes to her beautiful mouth and chin and pleading hands, "You cruel, cold, bitch."

And the door slammed shut.

Perhaps that night, Susan wrote in her journal that she would leave me. I wouldn't blame her. Perhaps she wrote down her hatred for me. At my worst moments, I still believe I deserved it. Susie was never cold—when she finally retreated from me, it was not from a lack of passion but I think, too much. We used each other up and quickly. The way a fire makes quick work of old wooden buildings in a market square. We were both exhausted. Literally burned and hollowed out by it all. By the massive *effort* it all took. But there we were, caged together by hatred and love and children, and that huge weight that had built up on top of us of harsh words, and poetry, and all that stretching to meet halfway when the distance between us had always been oceanic—as broad and churning as history itself. And history meant something, after all.

Though not very clean, the bus ride to Jarash is quick (45 minutes total) and comfortable. The busses are small, like oversized versions of the torpedo-tube VW van my father used to own and drive all over the country—though Dad's bus didn't have burgundy, tassled drapes hanging from the windows, or an old woman fingering torquise prayer beads while draped in a hajab of black and gold cotton. The outlying hills of Amman offer a stark contrast to the bustling, industrial streets of the city, with its towering deluxe hotels and extensive markets. Out in the pastures and orchards life is lived closer to the land. The squat, limestone houses do not so much nestle into the hillsides as cling to them as if they could, any moment, be picked up by the wind and blown away. And this seems deliberate. Few trees rise above seven feet and most are bent toward the earth as if in prayer. The ones that venture upward are thin, conical firs that resemble a too-skinny girl's arms thrust into clear quick, water, awkward and graceful at the same moment. Towns dot the landscape and seem to blend into the farmland. Here a young girl in a blue fleece pull-over leans against the dusty wall of a gas-station, a mural of Rambo over her head; here two boys chase each other, playing some form of violent tag beneath and around a gigantic diesel tank, suspended in the air by chains tied to metal girders; here a girl in a pink pull-over skips down a hillside and throws her arms around a mountain goat. On the side of the highway, a shepherd guides a flock of 30 dusty, but obedient sheep toward better grazing on some distant plateau.

The hills themselves are rolling and golden brown, speckled with white limestone boulders and green grass, or fruit trees. Occasionally, in the deepest valleys, a small lake shines. I find myself comparing the landscape to the red dirt of Georgia, or Virginia. And just before reaching the city, passing through the highways cut most deeply through the mountains, the dynamite blasted limestone passages remind me of similar roads torn through the hills of Vermont and Massachusetts. We carry our worlds with us wherever we go.

But we don't necessarily reveal them. With my blond hair, blue-eyes, and blue jeans, I was as obviously American as a can of Coca-Cola or the Nike swoosh. As a result, I was a magnet for the searching eyes and broken English of those Jordanians as curious about my country as I was about theirs. And at that time, I so desperately wanted to blend in somewhere, somehow. A part of me was always afraid—not of being targeted as an American but as a hypocrite. And if a pair of dark eyes looked too deeply, I always wondered, "Can they tell? Can they see who I am?" I had thrown a pearl to the sea, after all, and I knew it and felt the regret of it, but at the same time I couldn't stop thinking of Rachael. She grew up on a farm I thought, staring at the small farms blurring into the landscape as the bus picked up speed suicidally down the mountainsides—what kind of farm? And I thought of the essay she read about pig-busses—converted yellow school busses filled with pigs—rolling through the cornfields of Michigan. I stared hard out the glass, away from Susan, away from any potential searching eyes.

There was little need. Susie was with Darius in another aisle. And on the bus, I was left alone. In my pocket of silence, staring out the window with Cyrus propped against my shoulder, drifting in and out of sleep, I seemed of little interest to any of my fellow travelers—another passenger among passengers. To people splitting their lives between city and suburb on their way to work, or to visit a loved one, a lone tourist, whatever his appearance or nationality seemed of no consequence.

But everything was of consequence to me—the foreigner, tourist, scholar, father, husband. Everything new and old at once. Everything charged with the shock of similarity—some moment, some tree or valley, some expression called up from childhood. Everything charged with the shock of difference and distance, with how far away I was, how uncertain the ground beneath me. And how weak the rattling roof above. Each breath seemed to take concentration. And when I wasn't floating above the land beneath my feet or totally walled off from the world around me, I was so raw from feeling that at times I imagined I'd been flayed alive. That I walked through wind and rain and sandstorm without any skin at all. There were times when I could barely look at my children—especially Cyrus, with his wisp of a body, ghostlike skin and eyes so dark they seemed all pupil, as if he were always staring wide-eyed into darkness. He knows, I'd think. I still do sometimes. What must it have been like for him—caught between adults traveling at high speed in opposite directions with him in the middle—each of us overcompensating like crazy. Smothering him with overtight embraces. "You're squishing me," he cried one night as I sang him to sleep. And he laughed, then asked. "Daddy, are you going to sleep in another house?" "Are you leaving us?"

By the time the columns of Jarash (Garazia to the Romans) loomed on the horizon, I was already worn out.

Thankfully we were spared the necessity of a tour guide when we met a computer science teacher in a local high school named Ahkmed, a Palestinian who took us under his wing, first marching us to the best place to get humus and kabob and then guiding us through the ancient ruins. Later, over coffee at our apartment during a break from Arabic lessons, Ahkmed told us that it was God who noticed us on the bus, God who made him see that we needed help, and God, in the guise of my mother-in-law, who made us see that he would be a good teacher.

My mother-in-law of course, loved this. And immediately loved Ahkmed. As did we all. And though she was constantly comparing Jordan to her native Iran—at Jordan's disadvantage—she loved Jordan, too. It was not her home, but it was her element. She spoke no Arabic, but she could communicate with these people, mixing English, French, Farsi, and hand-signals dramatically to make a point, learning words and laughing off misunderstanding. And with Ahkmed there was recognition. They understood each other. None of us were suspicious of him. And we had no reason to be. He was a beautiful and spiritual man. One of the few true men of God I have met in my life. My mother-in-law convinced him not only to guide us around Jerash that day, but to teach us Arabic three nights a week. I've forgotten almost all of it now. But I remember him, the thin brown coat that seemed to be rotting around him, the constant five-o'clock shadow, the tar blackened fingertips, the way he would lean over my shoulder, breathing in my ear as I strained with effort, then leap up, celebrate when I would get a word or concept right. *He study. He study. Al hamdel Allah. Al hamdel Allah.*

Thanks God, Ahkmed said. And God may have been at work. I don't know. If we hadn't met Ahkmed that day, Susie and Cyrus would most certainly still be alive right now. We would not have been in his friend's van traveling to Aqaba on the Sabbath day; we wouldn't have placed our lives first in his hands, then the sleepy-eyed driver's, then God's on an unlit desert highway. We wouldn't have hit that sand-truck. Ahkmed would be alive too. I wouldn't be a single father writing forlorn essays in a two-bedroom apartment on the side of a mountain in New Hampshire. And I wouldn't be with Rachael now. *Al hamdel Allah. Al hamdel Allah.* How the ironies accumulate. How my life has become this convoluted mix of suffering and hope. My father-in-law says he doesn't know if he believes in God anymore.

For a long time he would sit on the couch in his family room, not sleeping, trying to figure out a way that someone was responsible for it all as the news droned on behind him. As the world refused to stop even a moment in its revolutions. It was a "hit" he said once, that Ahkmed was really a terrorist and Susie, as a writer of controversial poetry, was a target of the Iranian government or some branch of Al Quaida or the Israeli Secret Service. The banality of accidents is more than he can take. Accidents are meaningless, pointless, and brutally real. What was that sand-truck *doing* across the road at that moment on that day? (Laying sand). And who was this driver, this man with the droopy eyes who my mother-in-law now swears was on opium? (just a friend of Ahkmed's, picking up presents in Aqaba for his wife and kids). And Akhmed. How well did we really know this Ahkmed anyway? (He taught computers in a Palestinian neighborhood for a school that had only two computers for 200 students).

My mother-in-law is mostly silent on the matter of God. She writes poetry now—tells Darius she is writing a book for him. Like me, trying to understand it all, make something of it all. Not so much accept it, but make events spin and turn and change to what she would make them. An epic story with heroes and villains. And I find the poems beautiful. Tragic in what they try to do, in what they represent as much as what they are. There is recognition. I understand these people. Even if we don't communicate as well as we'd like, even when the simplest disagreement erupts into the ugliest of arguments. There was a time when I was always looking into the essence of things. Years ago a poet friend of mine returned a manuscript with just a few words scrawled on it: "Joel, I worry about you; you are always almost desperately searching out the meaning of things. But not everything is meaningful. Most things just are." I took it as an unintentional compliment. I am not glib. I am not clever, I thought; I am passionate—intense. And I still believe in essences, in the soul. But I guess I have become less determined to understand them, more willing to accept that some knowledge is not mine to have. I believe in God more than ever. But I don't know why.

Avoidance?

Perhaps I believe because I have to. Because I survived. And there must be a reason. But to believe that would be to believe that there was purpose too in a young boy flying through shattered glass at seventy miles an hour on a cold night in a desert. "I can't believe in a God who would let this happen," my father-in-law says, and I feel myself thinking, "Neither could I."

And yet I do believe. I so desperately believe.

Now my mother-in-law sits across me, and I honestly don't know what she feels as I tell her that Rachael and I are together. That we love each other. That we are happy. I want to say, "you don't understand. The building had collapsed, you see. There was no light. I was buried in it and I was going to just lie there. But something said, Get Up! Get Up! And there was a hand and there was light. Rachael came to me. To me and Darius."

Heroes and villains. Poetry.

Al hamdel Allah. Al hamdel Allah .

Under Ahkmed's more certain gaze, following behind in the path of his relaxed gate and the vapor trail of his always burning cigarette, we moved through the gates of the ancient city. I'd not expected the ruins to be so complete or large. Two gigantic theatres were nearly perfectly intact and I was able to climb to the top, boys in tow, and sit in the cheap seats, imagining what entertainment went on down below. The Oval plaza was also intact and one could still see the grooves worn in the roads by chariots and carts. The two temples to Artemis were in worse shape, nearly flattened both by earthquakes and by the desecration visited upon them by Christians in later centuries. It was exhilarating to stand and sit in places that were once the center of commerce, trade and art for centuries, to look down the columned thoroughfares and wonder how busy they once were. But it was also overwhelming. Leaning on a wall in what was once the inner chamber of the temple of Artemis, I couldn't help but wonder what men and women labored and hoped and prayed here, what rituals they performed to give contour and meaning to their lives. Again I was struck with an almost desperate longing, trying to re-populate the city, filling the lonely market square with men and women like those I'd seen in the suq on the other side of the highway, shouting laughing, and struggling, a certain desperation behind each barter, each lowering of price. A woman with blackened hands sews a pair of shoes, another pulls the hand of a small child as it screams and laughs, two men shout over the price of perfume, or the hind-end of a lamb. What scents of spices and burning fuel made the air shimmer? What colors and clothes did they wear? Did they love and hate each other? Were their desperations like mine? And if they could stare across history to meet my gaze would there be a recognition; and would that recognition comfort or horrify? Would I still avert my eyes?

From my vantage point on the ruined temple mount I could see Susie and Ahkmed in the distance. Ahkmed was standing thirty feet above the ground on the ledge of a stone tower and was waving Susie over. Bending at the waist, open hand turned up, as if asking for a waltz. She hugged her arms around her, shook her head and laughed, that bright, sharp, wind-chime laughter. I cannot honestly recreate what I felt just then.

Avoidance.

Jealousy.

Love.

Fear.

Exhilaration.

Regret.

Longing.

My mother-in-law remembers this moment, too. And offers it up as evidence of some sinister intent on the part of Ahkmed. But I don't think she believes it. Because when you meet a good man in this world, you know it. And Ahkmed was simply and beautifully good. And if he was reckless then, he was reckless like a man who has discovered the reality of God and finds in that belief no answers, just some powerful creative presence that may or may not be just or kind. Whose ways are foreign to us and whose powers beyond our understanding. And so he dances on the ruins, thankful for his little life, his little death.

And I wonder, did they love or hate their Emperor, that lonely foreigner in whose name the taxes were levied and temples built. And when Hadrian at last made his one visit and viewed the great arch constructed in his honor, did he feel as if he knew these people, did he care to? Or did this city blur and blend as cities must to an Emperor, something to hold in his worldly hand and toss in the air like a ball.

That arch, finished just before his arrival, was to stand as the new gate to the city. But the gate was never finished. And still, it stands a lonely sentry to the city in the distance. After thousands of years as one of the hubs of commerce in the Middle East, the trade routes changed and very gradually, Garazia became depopulated, fell into ruin and was covered in sand where it remained preserved in obscurity until a German traveler recognized the ruins. Eighty years later, archeologists are still uncovering the remnants of this ancient and mysterious world.

We spent many hours walking through Garazia before hiring a van to take us back (the next bus was a good 30 minutes off and the children were exhausted by then). Driving back I nodded off to sleep as our new teacher began his lessons, reciting the names of towns and cities. One of them, where I had seen the two boys playing beneath the fuel-tank, was originally a Palestinian Refugee camp. Now its squat houses spread out for miles, the land swelling with their descendents. I was struck, as usual, by the enormity of what I still don't know about this country, about the world. Ahkmed smiled, guiding me through it as best as he could, taking me home to other journeys, other, more lonely excavations.

Such is the work of the archeologist of the city and the city's soul. Where we are always pulled along as much by mystery as beauty. And rubble is merely a name for traces left by human hands and loss and time.

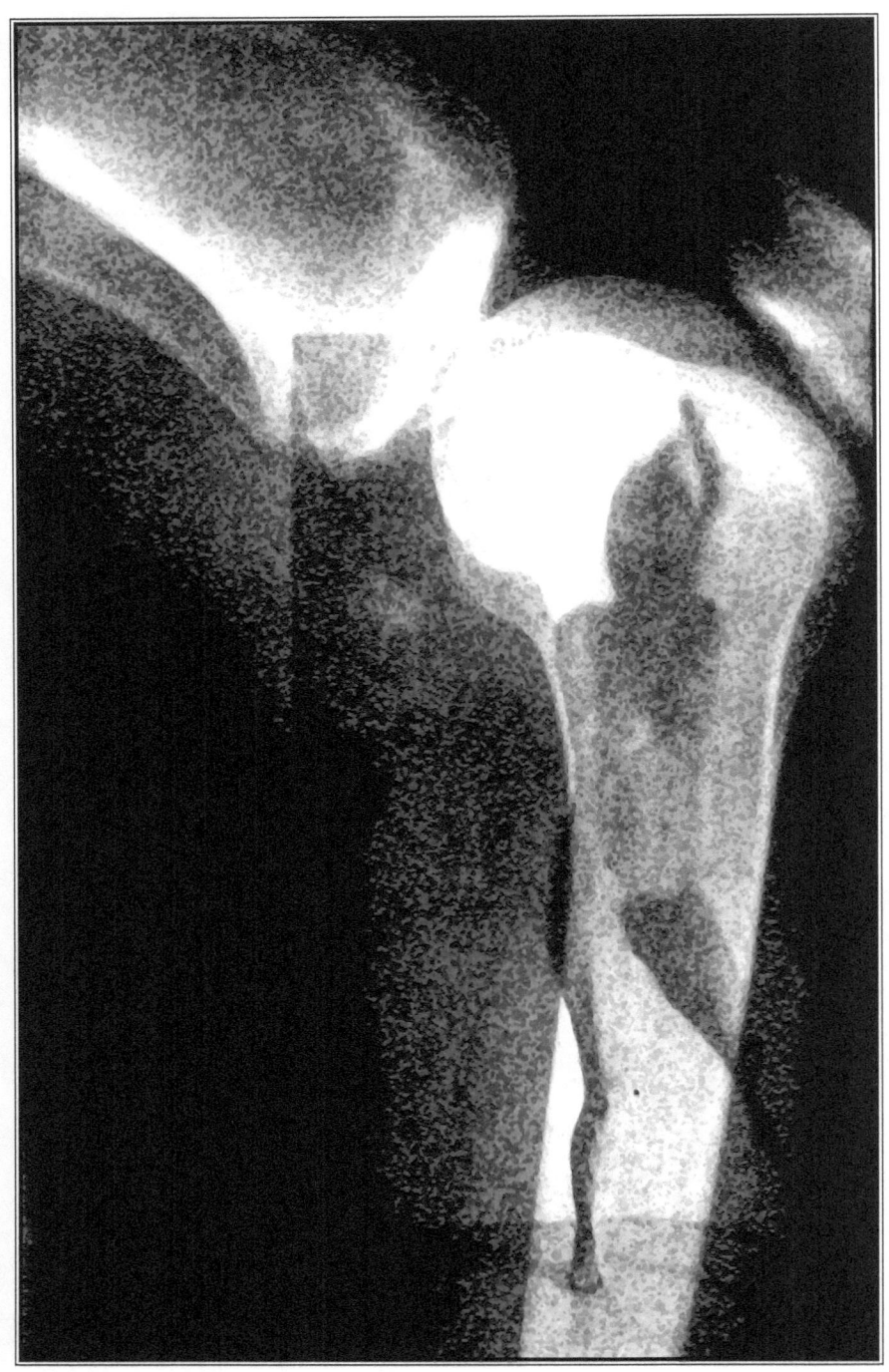

KATHLEEN M. HEIDEMAN

THE TRANSFIGURATION BOX

—it's a mean little tin
filled with claws and hairballs
and everything else I ever tried to lose:
blood-stained snippings of a straw broom,

four too-memorable wine corks,
and that dog's back molar crumbling into death
—a worthless nugget of domesticated calcium, really,
but it resembled the way I held on tight.

Even architectural drawings, those violet plans
for a bridge we never built between us. And the perch-bones
I threw away so many times but found, always, floating
like a warning in the toilet bowl or reclined luxuriously

on the butter; and those roaches I couldn't kill,
so I sealed them into drops of molten amber,
fossils that hardened as the sap cooled.
Husks of dead sin grown permanent as a gemstone,

and secret potentials: an egg under glass,
framed by yellowed lace and penny nails
and resting in its nest of short hairs. Intimacy.
An avocado pit painted golden; saintly camouflage,

a round flame to warm the heart. And a locked drawer
with three tallow candles given to me by an elderly plumber
who promised, as his fingers found mine,
"They light up the dark places, honey, and they burn for so
long. . ."

To get at the candles, though,
I'd need a little key. Perhaps that tarnished one
that hangs from its brass string
singing "Remember me—? Remember me—?"

A LIGHT LIKE FIREFLIES

Forgive her, but she needed a light like fireflies,
those martyred bulbs
burning themselves out in captivity
— she believed in something back then, black-olives for pupils,
reading books by bug-lamp, her skin spark-green
from that jar of heat lightning blinking beside her pillow.

A childhood illuminated by insects:
forgive her, but she believed luminosity would hover
like a winged butler, forever at her shoulder.
She wasn't ready to lose faith, thumbprints on her forehead:
the holy soot of naiveté, loneliness, several
cities that could have used a few fireflies.

In war, she smeared herself black to remain invisible.
Shadows said which prayers to hum and how many times each.
Cassocks absolved her sins. Timeclocks doled out rewards.
In the dark, she nodded, she waited. Dull decades went by,
nothingness & moonlessness. Then a curtain was pulled
and she went blind—! friends were reading aloud

"Sister, how unearthly!"—see that glow worm
undulating through leaves, how on its forehead
there burned a light like a green star— ?
and she did see it! Yes! The sun was burning
wormholes in the deep white snow outside their window,
the words, the brilliance overwhelmed her, she confused the
    floor

with heaven and fell back against the wall —
it was pure poetry, pure Spirit, the same jig her father danced.
when she was younger, when his screwdriver
touched a wire in the transformer box and six cheap inches
of screwdriver puddled onto his work-boots, mercurial;
Forgive her. It always happens like this.

High-voltage fireflies flash—then everything goes black,
as in Caravaggio's painting of Paul on his back in the ditch.
In that moment, we are undone, knocked to the ground,
the everyday world suddenly dark and upside down
and only the crushing potential of our faithful horse,
that filly named "Doubt," fully illuminated.

After Caravaggio, "The Conversion of Saint Paul," 1601.

AFTERWORD

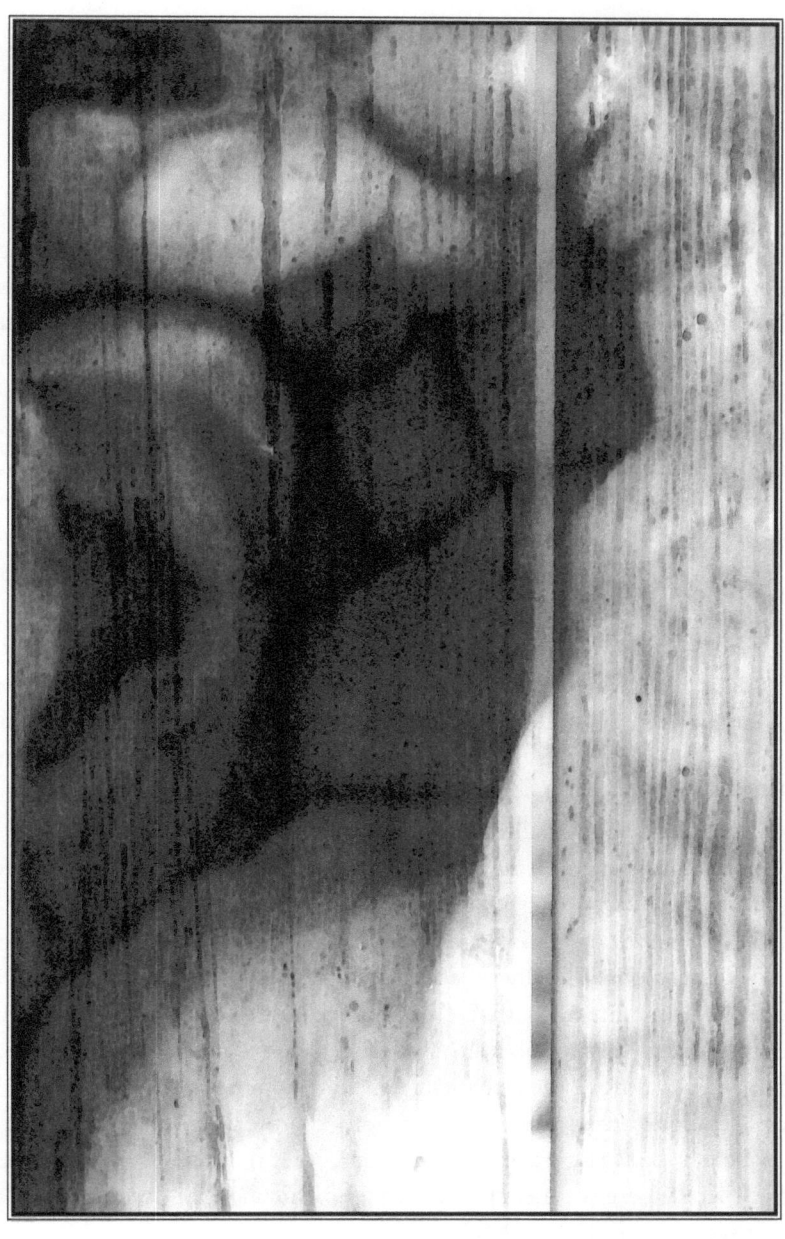

HEATHER TOSTESON

WRITING OURSELVES BACK INTO THE FLOW OF LIFE

Experiences of serious or chronic disease are traumatizing—meaning they exceed our capacity to absorb, integrate, make faithful meaning of life itself, *our* life, for some period of time. So, these experiences of illness also include, whether defined so or not, the distinctive experience of trauma, which is the shattering of our personal narrative. In both experiences of illness or trauma, people hunger for known and trusted ways of being in themselves and with others without any assurance that they can return to them—indeed a conviction that the world they knew, and the ways they knew of being in it—are forever lost to them.

None of us believe at the most basic physical level that life should include death. Our mortality shocks us repeatedly. Our physical vulnerability—to disease and assault—does the same. Deep down we just don't get it. It wakes us at night, our mouths dry and tasting of metal. Raw fear. Suddenly the light has gone out of everything. There is no echo, no shadow, no shiver of purpose to our world. We rebel. We cry out in protest. We use narrative for its most basic purpose—to draw us back into the flow of life, the human continuum. This happened! It really happened! And then this. And then this. We begin, almost without noticing it, to enter into the familiar, consoling, faithful rhythms of story.

Narrative writing is of particular use when we are trying to absorb certain dimensions of illness and trauma because it both bounds our experience and unites it with the experiences of others. If we write those narratives down, we do so because we are fed by the idea of lasting words—their meaningful flow, their shapeliness, their common nature. If we write, we can read ourselves, as we have read other authors, back into the flow of life. We can rebel against the deep inhuman quiet that has come to surround us, this place where we believe deeper than believing that no one knows the trouble we have seen. Absolutely no one at all. We begin to write ourselves back by becoming our own first reader. Or perhaps we hear ourselves clearly at last only after our words have been absorbed by many other eyes and ears. We may be the very last to hear what we are really saying. But hearing is where it's at. For that we need to return. Written words allow us to do so.

Catharsis is one of the first benefits of creative writing. We write to know what happened to us, to bring feeling and sensation back together, to let those little strands of thought that the body is spinning—metaphors, symbolic certainties, old wives'/New Age tales of complicity with our disease—to untangle, furl out in a strong wind. *Why?,* that wind howls even when we whisper. *Why me? Why this? Why now?*

When we put our words down on paper, something happens to our experience of our experience. We realign with time even if our inner narrative feels chaotic, shifting, shattered. We create a point of return—the one where our pen first touched the page. A still point from which we can, once again, begin to move our world.

My comments here concern two dimensions of narrative writing that are helpful in integrating traumatic experience for anyone—professional writer or not. The first is the containment afforded by words put down on a page, separated from us, made concrete, manipulable. Other. The second is the role of craft in moving us beyond discharge to a deeper, more complex, mysterious and fluid understanding of our experience that allows us to accept it in all its uniqueness and also see it as part of the more general human condition. Both. Simultaneously.

CONTAINING WALLS

Illness and trauma bring into question the nature of life, the fragility of our physiology and psychology, our identity, the definition of our social value, causality, death. All the small stuff.

One of our first uses of writing is to *fix* the experience. Pin it down. We do this by putting the words outside ourselves—on the page. Something that can be read. Something that can be put aside. Bounded. Ordered. We try to make sure we have the particulars in place. Even if we don't dare see what they are adding up to. What really happened to us? Exactly? How many days were we in that bed? How many stitches close that incision in my belly? What color are the eyes of my elderly father who no longer knows me? What thought flashed through my mind just before that fist found my cheek?

Each genre is especially helpful with some part of our first effort to define our category-shattering experience. Poetry helps us, as Garcia Lorca says, become a professor of the five senses. Something especially important when we are reclaiming the body. Meaning can shiver around us, implicit but enfolded in perception, scent, sound, weight, texture. Until we can recall fully, safely, no interpretation is reliable. Simply by being as present as possible we are doing the essential groundwork needed for all that follows, sensory impression by sensory impression.

In addition, poetry helps us express that feeling of eternal present, a single moment of sensation, insight, that expands infinitely—a very distinctive dimension of traumatic experience. Time stops dead for us at these times. However the act of trying to describe these moments, to find the accurate image or metaphor, however surprising, apt but illogical, also invites us into relation with new, possibly more life-giving categories. For to describe these sensory impressions, we relate them to other sensations, other experiences. And these associations open up a whole metaphorical world for us; they both ground us and begin to shed light forward and back. (Think of Darlene Montonaro's description: "But today my heart/is straight backed, little nuns/lined one after the other/across the EKG sheet,/heads bowed,/ penitent.") By simile and metaphor, we bring to consciousness the sense and nonsense our body is continuously spinning through us. We begin to use that thread. The very idea of death as a feral cat we are trying to bag opens up a new way of understanding the concept and the vividness of our response to it.

Memoir helps us weave the experience back into time and, more importantly, back into our own identity, our self-narrative. "I would take it all if I could have my old husband back," Joan Potter writes. But we can't. We can have the one we are seeing as if for the first time. We can have the new response that flows, if we can only know it, from everything that came before. We can review the steps—internal and external—that have brought us to this new mountain top, chemo ward, or sweet gesture. Step by step. Old self and new self become, once again, a continuum. We can begin to talk to others again out of a sense of inner coherence and narrative integrity. From where we are now, not who we were then. Memoirs, like essays, are about thinking our way into intellectual coherence again, firmly embedded in our biographical context. *Then* and *because* are equally potent terms.

Cinda Thompson captures this combination in the close of her memoir:

> The child in Room 210 awakening from the velvet dark of a coma, not-so-simply, and rather too suddenly, simply came "of age". However, at this point in her life, she had no words to express or describe the sudden deep river she felt sweeping through her. The might-be-meanings of my "diagnosis" seemed beyond me. Indeed, I began to toy with the concept of "meaning" altogether. Meanwhile, the whisper of elevator doors opening and closing to shafts of light, shafts of dark gave me a rhythm for "recovery," and one day I bolted from my bed to run through them. To be carried down to the outside world. The world as I'd known it, now on some other level.

Short stories, even when they are lightly disguised memoir or autobiography, can bring us more fully back into social focus. They link us with the continuity of story itself—which assumes abrupt breaks in our understanding of life are catalysts, the engine of narrative. Stories assume that life happens, to all of us, story-teller and reader. Whether we like it or not. And that it requires response. And that those responses differ, blessedly, from person to person, point of view to point of view. And that through the telling, event by event, a new creation comes into being, point of view by point of view, that isn't any one of those individual stories but something larger, stronger, more liberating and meaningful when they are all brought together. Story, as story, helps bring our own experience, however devastating, into relation to what we feel is life-like, essentially human, communicable. Cradled in time. Then and then and then a story goes, and we are securely within the envelope of circumstance. We feel solaced by the essential shapeliness of existence that story presumes, the sweet promise of meaning, as people have been since the beginning of once-upon-a-time.

Sara Lippman in her memoir, "The Dying Tradition", which has some of the expansiveness of story, captures this sense of continuum:

> The ICU waiting room smells of apple juice and French fries; it is filled with married couples and families. They pace the linoleum and sink into chairs, they bury faces into necks, they blow noses, they have begun the long slow process of grieving. Children kick over towers of blocks. A woman sobs into her cell phone. All of them have been robbed, their loved ones stricken abruptly by accident or prematurely by disease. I stare up at the television monitor. The picture quality is poor but through the static I can still make out the soap opera I knew well in my childhood. My grandmother is ninety-four years old. she has seen me fall in love; she has seen me get married. I am the luckiest girl in the world.

FLOW

Our first use of writing is often to create a containing wall for experience—by what we choose to write about and the genre we choose. But creative writing can also expand our sense of the shifting meanings of experience, make it safe to see more, feel more, and, sometimes, know less. The structure of literary forms can make it safe to liberate new meanings, to bear the larger implications of these life transforming experiences that we have not voluntarily chosen. Writing can return voluntariness to us by moving us from involuntary reaction—discharge—to craft, where experience is not just contained but seen as in some way neutral, the *stuff* of life. Stuff that can be, unbelievably, graciously, shaped and shared as a gift of redeeming beauty.

Writing that remains only discharge, whose purpose is solely to reattach us to the very real, up close, and personal isn't taking full advantage of what writing can offer us. My assumption is that the more whole, rounded, and multivalent our experience *of* our experience is—the more we know it as irrevocably intimate and unique and simultaneously common, the more it enlarges our compassion for ourselves *and* for those around us. Focusing on the craft of writing can help bring us to this second stage of integration.

Intentionally shifting genre can help us expand our experience. What happens when we break out of a well-practiced story—either tragic or comic—and let the sensory details cast their own symbolic shadows, ones that we may not even recognize? What happens when we take a story that is concealed memoir and make it explicit memoir—change "he" or "she" to "I"? How do we know ourselves differently? What direct conversations in the real world are we now more open to? What connections are we invited to clarify? What literary conventions have we, perhaps, been misappropriating? Have we affected a neutrality toward our 'character' that we cannot afford toward ourselves? Have we sentimentally inflated the importance of the experience? Have we, worse, denied ourselves and those around us compassion?

What happens, on the other hand, when we open a memoir couched as story to the expectations of story—deepen that saving fiction and think about it in terms of narrative structure, the introduction of other characters and points of view? Know it as part of the continuum of human stories, not just our own self-narrative? Does our sense of identity falter or feel strengthened by the three-dimensionality we introduce by meeting the expectations of story for multiplicity of perspective and meaning? What happens when we imagine a completely different person experiencing what we just have? What if we see ourselves and our experience and our meaning-making through the eyes, ears, and hearts of our children or spouses or a stranger on the street?

What genre we choose to write in has a powerful effect on how we understand and bring our experience into relation to ourselves and to others. We don't have to restrict ourselves. The same experience can be explored through poetry, memoir, essay, story. We learn something different each time. We can choose, through choosing a genre and respecting its expectations, different dimensions of our experience to explore—sensations, thinking, sense of identity, social embeddedness.

The social context in which we write and share our writing has a powerful effect on how we understand our experience as well. We don't have to restrict ourselves here either.

Often when we are trying to understand physical illness, we need to shut everyone else out—to give voice to an experience that is essentially mute, which does not yet know language. What *is* the word for this dark solace whose boundary is constantly expanding, collapsing? What *is* the word for the sweetness at the center of the most unbearable pressure? We need to hear this new language first ourselves before we can share it with anyone else because the essential ruptures are between our own mind, own imagination, own body. We can become our own first reader, at our own pace, and share with others only as we feel this new experience has been integrated in us. Knowing that there is something in us large enough to hold our own experience is sometimes the greatest hearing of all.

Other times, however, especially in cases of abuse and rape, the division of mind and body is socially created. Done to us by someone with a distinct name, a distinctive face. Essentially similar. Essentially different. In such circumstances, the question is finding the right words—*your* right words. Not the words you were originally given, words that tied you to the frames of belief, the affective relationships that justified this behavior—or the words that rejected those beliefs and relationships completely. Many of the writers in *Terror & Transformation* are looking for the language that moves them faithfully beyond the language of perpetrator and survivor. In such circumstances, sometimes the writing needs to develop in a more fluid, immediate dance with other writer/readers who share the same need to explore, not just contain, the experience. People who honor your need to be accurate to your own experience, however ambiguous and ambivalent it is. Who can hold you in good faith as you explore the difficult dimensions of your own truth—today and tomorrow. A truth that changes as you do.

Writing groups or writing partnerships can, in our process, hold us in good faith at difficult times, provide the containing wall, the absorbing ear, while we find our first true sound and loose it, whether or not it forms into speech. They can walk with us through that first discharge to something that is shaped, communicable, beautiful. Knowing that there is a real live, present community that can hold your new, internally authenticated, difficult, ambiguous story can help you to bring that story to voice. Here the distinction between these two steps of containment and flow, catharsis and craft, are important. Craft should and can be used to increase the ambiguity and complexity and exactness of our experience. It is not enough just that life happened to us but that we responded to it in full, with all our distinctive gifts and our most common humanity. A wonderful writing teacher of mine, Jack Matthews, expressed this as the distinction between articulation (coming to language) and communication (coming into communion with others).

For writing about illness and trauma to be healing we need to end up honoring both how unique our experience is *and* how it unites us, in all its uniqueness, with what is most deeply human in others. If it doesn't reunite us with others—and with the constantly changing flow of meaning—it doesn't help us become larger, more resilient. For writing to do its healing we need to consciously embrace these essentially faithful assumptions of narrative: our experiences have meaning; that meaning can be shared; and we can, individually and together, bear to know what we know, return to it, learn again from what we have recorded as if it came from the mind and mouth of someone else. We can read ourselves back into the flow of life. We can be read back into the flow of life by others, as they can do the same for us. This is a more fluid, spacious form of containing. Craft helps us separate each expression of an experience, each coming to understanding, from our self identity so we can continue to change, our understanding of our experience can continue to change, the context in which that experience is held can continue to change. Life can continue to flow in and through us, provoking, assuaging, changing, changing, changing but never letting go.

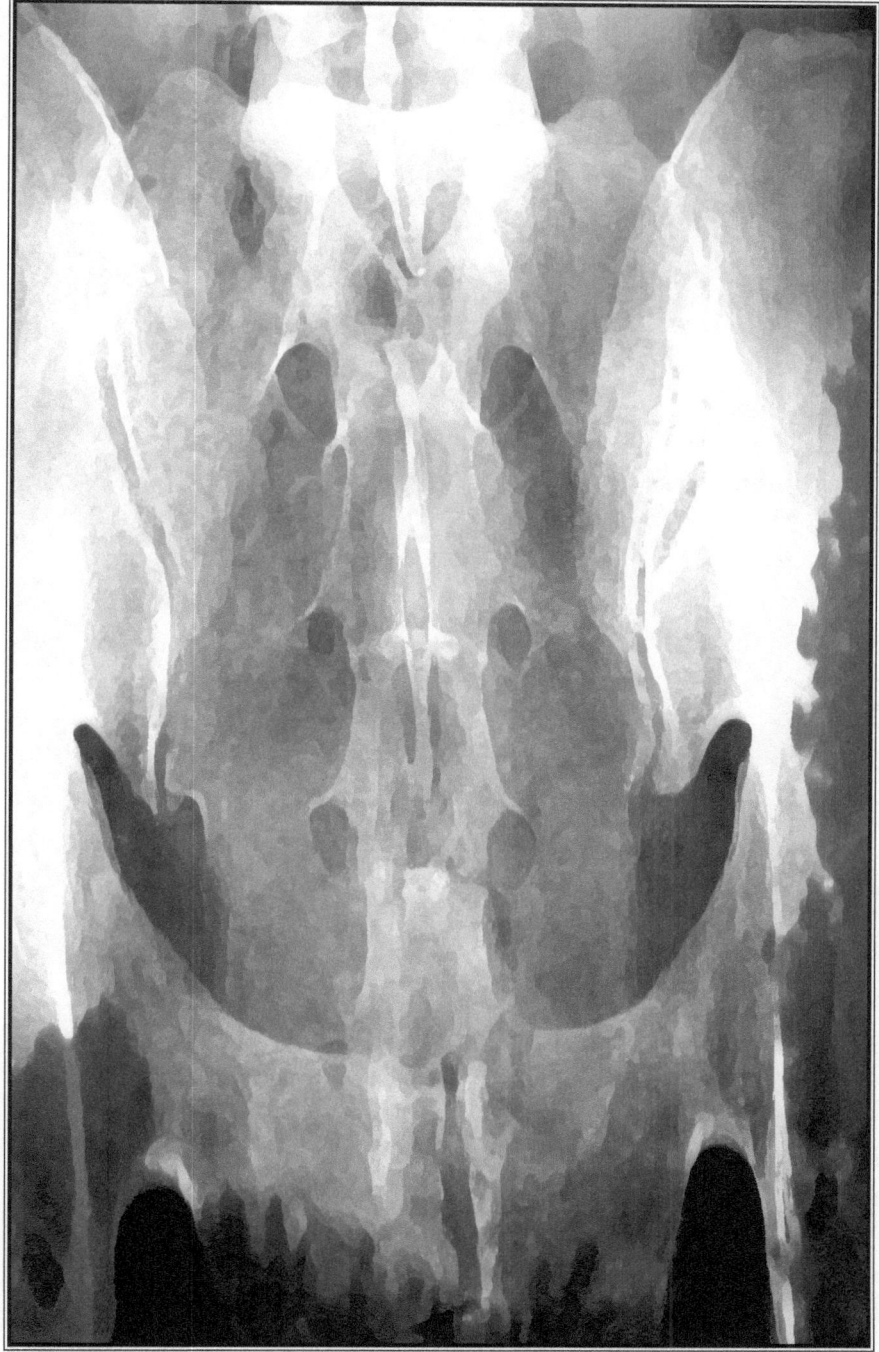

AUTHORS

Mark Barkawitz has earned local and national awards for his fiction, poetry, essay, and screenwriting. His work has appeared in newspapers, magazines, literary anthologies, 'zines, and on numerous websites. He wrote the screenplay for the feature film, *Turn of the Blade*, has taught creative writing at community college level, and coaches a championship track team of student/athletes. He lives with his wife, two teenage children, and breeds golden retrievers in Pasadena, CA.

Wendy Brown is a performance poet who has performed nationally and in Mexico in cafes, bookstores, galleries, and private homes, solo and in collaborations. She has published poetry and creative non-fiction in a variety of prestigious magazines. She is the creator of Writing Circles for Healing, a writing support group to write through loss, grief, and life-altering experiences. Her novel *MoonSense*, a spiritual parable, is forthcoming in spring 2008 at www.writingcirclesforhealing.com.

Cathryn Cofell has been published frequently in such places as *Prairie Schooner, NY Quarterly, MARGIE* and *Cream City Review*. She is the recipient of two Pushcart Prize nominations and the WI Academy's Outstanding Poem designation for two consecutive years, among other awards. Her fourth chapbook, *Sweet Curdle*, was released in 2006 by Marsh River Editions, with a fifth forthcoming from Parallel Press.

James H. Coffman is a retired Disciples of Christ minister, having served congregations in Kansas, Indiana, and Missouri for forty years. He is a freelance writer and is active with the Missouri Writer's Guild and the Columbia Chapter of the MWG. His poetry has appeared in several regional publications. He is now working on two books of poetry, slated for publication in 2008.

Mary V. Davidson is a Professor of English at the University of Wisconsin-LaCrosse. Her teaching specialties include British Literature, Contemporary American Poetry, Afro-Caribbean history, Literature of the American West, and G/L/B/T literature. Her pedagogical passion involves using poetry to unlock the hearts of all her students as well as her own. She did raise four children "once upon a time". B.A. Northwestern University; M.A. Bradley University; Ph. D. University of Colorado.

Marion Deutsche Cohen's latest two poetry books (of eighteen) are *Crossing the Equal Sign* (Plain View Press, TX), about the experience of mathematics, and *Surviving the Alphabet* (Huge Pathetic Force, PA). She teaches math at Arcadia University and is the author of *Dirty Details: The Days and Nights of a Well Spouse* (Temple University Press) and of another "well spouse book", *Cruel and Unusual*, available as a free download at www.marioncohen.com.

Pamela Z. Daum is a writer and photographer who currently lives in Hudson, OH. Her work has appeared in *Gray's Sporting Journal, ADR, Insights, Taj Mahal Review*, and *Ascent Magazine*.

Carol V. Davis is the author of two chapbooks, *Letters From Prague* and *The Violin Teacher,* and a bilingual collection, *It's Time to Talk About. . .* She was a Fulbright scholar in Russia in 1996-97 & 2005. Her poetry has been read on NPR radio and on Radio Russia. She received the 2007 T.S. Eliot Prize for *Into the Arms of Pushkin: Poems of St. Petersburg.* She teaches at Santa Monica College, California.

Lucille Lang Day has published a children's book and seven poetry collections and chapbooks, most recently *The Book of Answers* and *God of the Jellyfish.* Her work has appeared widely in magazines and anthologies. She received her M.F.A. in creative writing at SF State University, and her Ph.D. in science/mathematics education at UC Berkeley. She is the founder/director of Scarlet Tanager Books, and director of the Hall of Health, a museum in Berkeley.

Elizabeth di Grazia has published short work in a number of periodicals, including *The Phoenix, Rockhurst Review, Beginnings, Penniless Press, Hackwriters, Minnesota Parent, Adagio Verse Quarterly, The Mom Writer's Literary Magazine,* and four essays with *Edge Life*. She has two completed memoirs: *House of Fire* and *Mama Jody, Mama Beth, A Family Takes Root*. Elizabeth earned her MFA in writing from Hamline University. She can be reached at edigrazia@msn.com

Victoria Elizabeth is a three-time cancer survivor, an Army veteran, a teacher, and an usher for the San Diego Padres. Her poems have appeared in *Main Channel Voices, Troubadour, Standing On The Ceiling, Unbearable Uncertainty, Exquisite Reaction, Verve, Urban Spaghetti, The Externalist,* and *The Mid-America Poetry Review.*

Kimberly K. Farrar is a writer and teacher currently living in Astoria, New York. She holds a B.A. in Creative Writing from the University of Arizona where she studied with Jon Anderson, Steve Orlen, Richard Shelton, and Edward Abbey. She also has an M.A. in TESOL from Hunter College and teaches English as a Second Language. Her work has been published in *Long Shot, Mudfish, Lullwater Review, The Ledge,* and other literary journals.

Susi Gregg Fowler lives and writes in her hometown, Juneau, Alaska. She has had prose and poetry published in *The Christian Science Monitor* and is the author of eight children's books (published by Greenwillow Books and Scholastic Books), including the Christopher Award-winning *I'll See You When The Moon Is Full*. Susi and her artist husband Jim have two daughters and two grandchildren.

Christina Gombar, before becoming a full-time writer by default, worked at everything from scrubbing toilets to writing annual reports for Fortune 50 financial firms. Publishing credits include *Working Woman, The London Review, Scholastic* and *The Providence Journal;* her prize-winning work is internationally anthologized. A book, *Great Women Writers, 1900-1950,* was published by Facts On File. She recently completed her first novel. "Ghost Life" derives from a memoir-in-progress, "Breathing Under Water."

Kathleen M. Heideman is a recent fellow in the NSF's Antarctic Artists & Writers Program (observing scientists in various disciplines conducting research in field camps). Previous residencies include Eastern Frontier Society, Voyageurs National Park, Devils Tower National Monument, Apostle Islands National Lakeshore, and Anderson Center for Interdisciplinary Studies. Her poetry has received support from the Bush Foundation, Jerome Foundation, Loft-McKnight and the Minnesota State Arts Board. She suffers from wanderlust.

Susan Hodara is a writer who works as a freelance journalist and editor, and who has been writing memoir for more than 15 years. Her articles have been published in the *New York Times, Communication Arts, salon.com*, and more. Her short memoir pieces appear in several anthologies. She and her husband live in Westchester County, NY, and are the parents of two college-age daughters.

John Holbrook hails from Missoula, Montana, where he lives with his wife Juidth and their two increasingly idiosyncratic and perspicacious cats, "Bobbert" and "Frogger." Thirty eight years of marriage have taught John and Judith a good deal about the seriousness of human relationships, of forgiveness and trust, of the need for daily nurturing through expressions of humor, warmth and affection. John's work has appeared in nearly 100 literary publications and anthologies.

Marci G. Jaffer resides in New York City with her almost-five year-old daughter, Dylan and their dog, Edgar. Marci teaches high school English. She wrote poetry and prose for a multimedia production produced at Latea Theater in New York City. She received an M.F.A. in Creative Writing, an M.A. in English and a B.A. in English. She is presently working on a novel.

Mary-Lane Kamberg, Olathe, Kansas, has published poetry in seven anthologies, as well as *Kansas City Voices, Kansas City Star, Mid-America Poetry Review, The Midwest Quarterly*, and other journals. She wrote "Artist's Eye" for a friend, who later read it at her mother's memorial service. Mary-Lane co-leads the Kansas City Writers Group, and serves on the board of directors of the Kansas Authors Club and the Missouri Writers' Guild.

Robert C. Knox is a freelance writer, a correspondent for *The Boston Globe* newspaper, and a fiction writer. His short stories, poems and book reviews have appeared in numerous publications and he was named a Finalist in the Massachusetts Artist Grant Program. A story about his father ("Lost") appeared in *The Rambler Magazine* and another ("The Man Who Would Be Me") was recently published on the online magazine *uglycousin.com*.

Dr. Phyllis Langton, PhD, RN, is Professor Emerita, George Washington University, Washington DC. Her specialty fields include: Health and Illness, Health Policy, and Management of Large Organizations. Widow, and grandmother to Claire and Lorna Ramage, Executive Secretary of the DC/MD/VA Chapter of the ALS Association for three years. Her essay, "Mission Accomplished", is an excerpt from her memoir in progress, *The Last Flight Out*. She lives in McLean, Virginia.

Jane Levin is a retired psychologist, volunteer community worker and eight year survivor of ovarian cancer. Her poems have recently appeared in *Dust & Fire 2007, Coping with Cancer, Subterraneans: A Journal of Lesbian and Gay Writing*, and *Cosmopsis*. Awards include a 2006 Intermedia Arts/Jerome Foundation Writer-to-Writer Poetry Mentorship, finalist for the 2007 Loft Mentor Series and a 2007-2008 Howard B. Brin Jewish Arts Endowment grant. She welcomes your comments at jkiwi@gmail.com.

Sara Lippmann holds a BA from Brown and an MFA from The New School. Her articles and book reviews have been published in *GQ, Details, PublishersWeekly.com* among others. Her fiction and interviews have appeared in the *Beacon Street Review, LIT and Carve*. She lives in Brooklyn with her husband and son.

Denise Miller is a Kalamazoo college instructor, writer and visual artist currently writing a manuscript focusing on the commonalities among the ways African-Americans resisted enslavement and the ways abused partners and children resist enslavement created by domestic violence. She received a B.F.A. from Bowling Green State University in Creative Writing in 1992 and an M.A. from Central Michigan University in 1995. She lives in Kalamazoo, MI with her partner.

Darlene Montonaro was born and raised in Cleveland, Ohio. Her professional career has been dedicated to work in the non-profit sector, especially in arts and arts management, including serving for over twelve years as the Executive Director of Cleveland's largest independent literary organization, The Poets' & Writers' League of Greater Cleveland. Her poetry has appeared in a variety of literary magazines including *Calyx, Slipstream, Visions International, Earth's Daughters,* and *Poetry Motel.*

Lori Anderson Moseman curates the High Watermark Salo[o]n, a performance/chapbook series she created after Federal Disaster #1649, a Delaware River flood. Her books are *Walking the Dead* (Heaven Bone), *Cultivating Excess* (The Eighth Mountain Press) and *Persona* (Swank Books). Her Doctorate of Arts in Writing is from the University at Albany, and her MFA in Poetry is from the University of Iowa. She has been an educator for decades.

Susan R. Norton's poetry has been published in over seventy literary journals, magazines, anthologies, newspapers, greeting cards, two art exhibits, a cruise brochure, a tear off calendar and even fortune cookies. Her work has appeared in such publications as: *The Southern Poetry Review, Writer's World Magazine, Silver Quill, The Knews* and read on National Public Radio. She has received 10 awards in writing.

Mary C. O'Malley has both a MSW and MFA. She is the mother of five children including two sets of twins. Her poems have been published online and in print. Puddinghouse Publications has chosen her new chapbook for publication this year. She lives with her family in Cleveland, Ohio.

Michael Onofrey grew up in Los Angeles, but now lives in Japan, where he teaches English as a Second Language. His stories have appeared in the *Bryant Literary Review, Cold-Drill, Green Hills Literary Lantern, The MacGuffin,* and *The William and Mary Review,* as well as in other literary journals and magazines in the United States and Japan. One of his stories was nominated for the Pushcart Prize.

Rebecca Payne has written political and social commentaries for the *Lansing State Journal* and other periodicals. Living in East Lansing, Michigan, she works as a mail carrier and adores her children, Joe, Molly and Nina; and her husband, David. The gentle grace of her Quaker friends has helped her remain calm through the hard years. She hopes her words bring a measure of clarity to the human condition.

Dr. Joel B. Peckham, Jr., is an Assistant Professor of American Literature at The University of Cincinnati, Clermont College. His essays on grief and recovery have appeared in *Brevity, The North American Review*, and *River Teeth*. He has also published two books of poetry: *nightwalking* and *The Heat of What Comes* (Pecan Grove). Currently he lives with his son Darius in Batavia, Ohio.

Joan Potter's nonfiction writing has been published in numerous magazines and newspapers. Her essays appear in the anthologies *Rooted in Rock* and *Living North Country* and in the online journal Perigee. She is the author of three books and has edited several others. She teaches memoir writing at the Hudson Valley Writers' Center in Sleepy Hollow, New York, and lives in Mount Kisco, New York.

Patricia Smith Ranzoni turned to writing after the onset of disabling Paroxysmal Generalized Dystonia at 43. Now 67, her work has appeared in education and mental health journals including the ERIC data base. Her poetry (three collections), documenting the outback Maine from which she comes, has been published across the country and abroad; drawn from by U ME departments of English and history; and acquired by archives of class, disability and women's studies.

Andrea Rosenhaft is a social worker who is on hiatus in order to focus on writing. She has suffered from anorexia and depression for the last twenty years and continues to struggle with it in her life. In the fall of 2008 she plans to enter a Masters of Fine Arts in Writing program and when she graduates, is going to start therapeutic writing programs for populations in need.

Terry Sanville lives in San Luis Obispo, California with his artist-poet wife, Marguerite Costigan (his in-house editor), and two cats (his in-house critics). As an emerging author, Terry writes full time. Since 2005, his short stories have been accepted by more than 50 literary and popular journals, magazines, and anthologies. He is also an accomplished jazz and blues guitarist.

Marian Kaplun Shapiro practices as a psychologist and poet in Lexington, Massachusetts. She is the author of a professional book, *Second Childhood* (Norton, 1988), and a poetry book, *Players In The Dream, Dreamers In The Play* (Plain View Press, 2007). Her poems have also appeared in over 100 journals and anthologies, and have won seventeen first prizes and many other prizes. Two chapbooks are currently in press: *Your Third Wish*, (Finishing Line); and *The End Of The World, Announced On Wednesday* (Pudding House).

Claudette Mork Sigg, a former English teacher as well as director of a dance company, has had work appearing in *Natural Bridge, The Atlanta Review, The Journal of the American Medical Association, Colere, Pinyon*, and *Into the Teeth of the Wind*, as well as in the anthologies, *Sierra Songs & Descents, Rough Places Plain: Poems of the Mountains*, and Chapman and Strasser's recently published *75 Poems on Retirement*.

Laura R. Sommers has made her mother proud by publishing features, poems, essays, and articles in major publications. Her career also includes more than 25 years as a creative writer in advertising and design. But her latest passion is writing women's historical fiction. Currently, she is working on her second novel, *Plein Air*. Ms. Sommers graduated from the University of Rochester with a B.A. in English. She lives in Granville, Ohio.

Merry Speece has published two chapbooks of poetry and been a recipient of a state arts commission fellowship in prose. Her *Sisters Grimke Book of Days*, which one reviewer called a prose poem, was published in 2003 by Oasis Books (England). She has lived most of her life in rural Ohio.

Adele Steiner is a poet, writer, and teacher. She received her B.A. and M.F.A. in English Literature and Creative Writing at the University of Maryland. A poet-in-the-schools in Maryland and an instructor with The Writer's Center in Bethesda, her work has been published in *The Maryland Poetry Review, Gargoyle, So To Speak, Wordwrights, Smartish Pace, IInnisfree, Scribble, The Lucid Stone*, a chap-book, *Refracted Love*, and a book, *Freshwater Pearls*.

Hannah Thomassen finds inspiration as writer in the Pacific Northwest landscape, where she lives a good life with her husband, Julian, three sheep, three donkeys, a dozen chickens and a dog. Themes of illness and healing have permeated her life both as parent and sister of persons suffering from mental illness, and as a nurse and healthcare administrator. Her work has appeared or is forthcoming in *Verseweavers, Big Bridge, Presence, Fishtrap Anthology* and *Windfall*.

Cinda Thompson has been a juvenile diabetic for over forty years, finally discovering the subject to be "life-giving." She has been a contributor to many anthologies, periodicals, and program—*Cries of the Spirit, When I Am An Old Woman I Shall Wear Purple, Grow Old Along With Me* (PBS). Her award-winning work is also interpreted in *Mother of All Living* (Cornell, Crosscurrents). A chapbook, *At the Core*, is available.

Ross West is managing editor of *Oregon Quarterly* magazine and has taught in the University of Oregon School of Journalism and Communication. His work has appeared in *Orion, ICON Thoughtstyle, The Oregonian*, and numerous other publications, books, and anthologies. He earned an M.F.A. in creative writing from the University of Oregon in 1984 and served as associate editor for *Northwest Review* and text editor for the *Atlas of Oregon*.

ACKNOWLEDGEMENTS

Cathryn Cofell's "Anxiety Attack" previously appeared in *Roadkill* (Neville Public Museum).

Marion Deutsche Cohen's "On Reading to Sick People," "March 6, 1998," "One-Woman Show," and "Calling a Spade a Spade" are from the collection *Chronic Progressive*, which can be downloaded for free at www.marioncohen. com.

Lucille Lang Day's "Intensive Care," "MRI Scan," and "The Hot Tub" previously appeared in *Wild One* (Scarlet Tanager Books, 2000).

Victoria Elizabeth's "Privacy" previously appeared in *Recycled Quarterly* (Summer, 2002) and "April 19th" in *City Works* (1999).

Kathleen M. Heideman's "A Light Like Fireflies" appeared in an earlier version as "Conversion" in *Loonfeather* (Bemidji MN, 1995).

Jane Levin's "Complexity" previously appeared in *Subterraneans: A Journal of Lesbian and Gay Writing* (December, 2006).

Joel B. Peckham's "Ruins" previously appeared in *The South Loop Review.*

Patricia Smith Ranzoni's "Husband Cut My Hair" first appeared in Gravity. Both it and "from Another Long, Numbers 26-29 and 43" were previously published in *Settling, Poems by Patricia Ranzoni* (Puckerbrush Press, 2000).

Mary Speece's "Sweet Face of the Khmer Woman" first appeared in *Green Mountains Review* and "Sick" in *Quarter After Eight*.

Photographs by Heather Tosteson.

EDITORS/PUBLISHERS

HEATHER TOSTESON is the author of seven books of fiction, poetry and non-fiction, including most recently the novel *The Philosophical Transactions of Maria van Leeuwenhoek, Antoni's Dochter*. She has worked in health communications with a focus on communication across disciplines, racism, social trust, and how belief systems develop and change. She has an MFA (UNC-Greensboro) and PhD in English and Creative Writing (Ohio University).

CHARLES BROCKETT has a PhD from UNC-Chapel Hill and is a recipient of several Fulbright and National Endowment for the Humanities awards. A retired political science professor, he has written two well-received books on Central America and numerous social science journal articles and book chapters. With Heather Tosteson, he is co-founder of Universal Table and Wising Up Press and co-editor of the Wising Up Anthologies.

See our booklist and calls for submissions for new anthologies
www.universaltable.org
wisingup@universaltable.org